By Lisa Van Allen

The Wishing Thread

The Night Garden

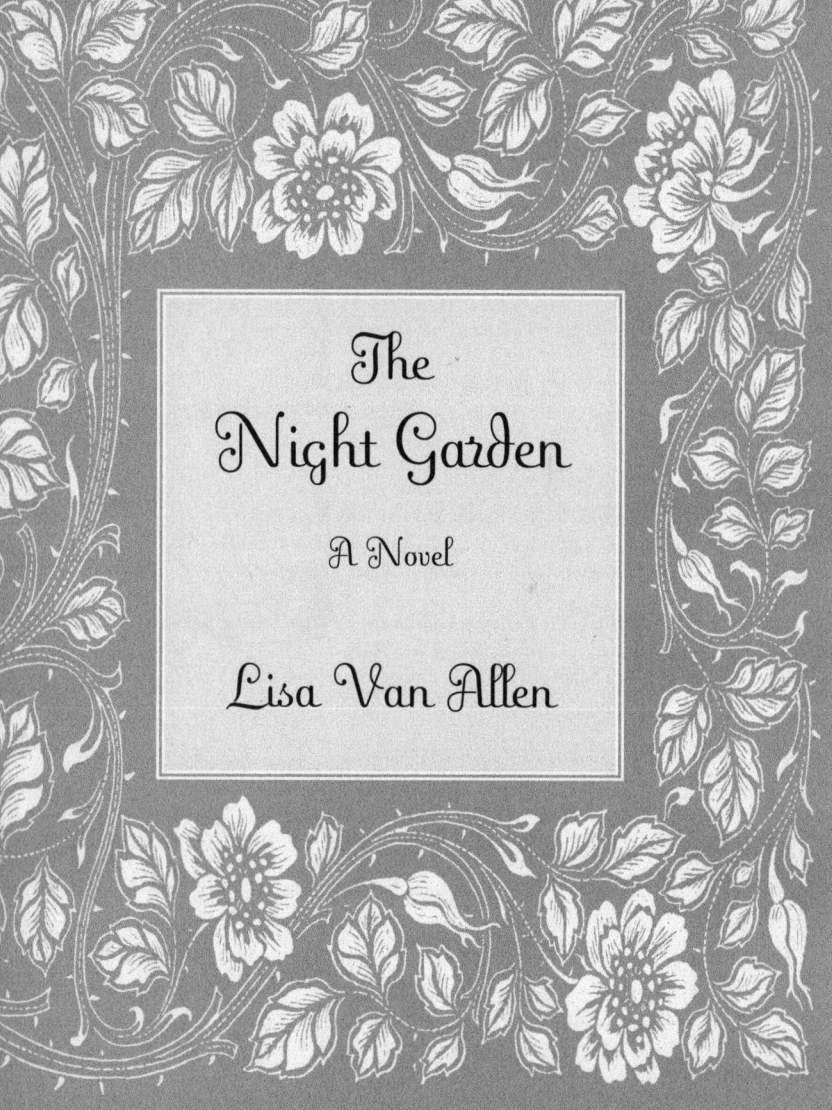

The
Night Garden

A Novel

Lisa Van Allen

Ballantine Books Trade Paperbacks | New York

A Ballantine Books Trade Paperback Original

Copyright © 2014 by Lisa Van Allen
Reading group guide copyright © 2014 by Random House LLC

All rights reserved.

Published in the United States by Ballantine Books,
an imprint of Random House, a division of Random House LLC,
a Penguin Random House Company, New York.

BALLANTINE and the HOUSE colophon are registered trademarks
of Random House LLC.
RANDOM HOUSE READER'S CIRCLE & Design is a registered trademark of
Random House LLC.

ISBN 978-0-345-53783-6
eBook ISBN 978-0-345-53757-7

Printed in the United States of America on acid-free paper

www.randomhousereaderscircle.com

2 4 6 8 9 7 5 3 1

Book design by Virginia Norey

*"And down he hastened into
the Eden of poisonous flowers."*

—from "Rappaccini's Daughter"
by Nathaniel Hawthorne

The Night Garden

Up the Garden Path

loria Wallace Zeiger had been peering through her binoculars for such a long time that when she turned to her husband to speak to him, two red indentations had appeared on the bridge of her nose.

"They're watering. They're *definitely* watering," she said.

Her husband of forty years, Richard Zeiger, did not look away from his television show though it had gone to a commercial. "Can you see sprinklers?"

"No," Gloria said. "But I know they're doing it." She made a noise that was halfway between a sigh and a huff, and then dropped her binoculars on the nylon strap around her neck. Her hair scrolled into two perfect blond commas under her earlobes, and her makeup was unsmudged. "They're probably doing it at night so that nobody sees them. But they *are* doing it. They have to be. Nobody can have a garden like that in the middle of the worst drought in twenty years unless they're watering."

Outside the window, the gentle hills of the northwestern Catskills looked dusty and tired. Rows of corn that should have been ebullient emerald were instead a resigned color between yellow and green. Cats had begun taking dust baths like birds, and birds began lazing on porch stairs like cats, and the black bears that frequently wandered through the hamlet of Green Valley lumbered about shaking their massive heads disapprovingly from side to side. In nearby White Lake—where hundreds of thousands of hippies had once flocked for the Woodstock Music and Art Fair—the usually abundant lake waters had shriveled away from the shores. The paint on the old mom-and-pop bait shops and motels blistered and pruned in the sun. The crossing guard near Rick's Hardware—who first showed up in White Lake for what everyone called "the Concert" and who had manned her post year-round by sheer force of habit ever since—swore that she'd had to hold up her sign and stop traffic because a tumbleweed had rolled across the intersection on a scorching, windless Wednesday at high noon.

And yet, below the Zeigers' picture window in Green Valley, the sunbaked terrain was interrupted, preposterously, by the wild, lush, profligate, effusive green of the Pennyworts' private gardens, blooming ferociously despite the water ration laws.

Although the gardens were not world famous, they were locally famous (*infamous,* Gloria told her friends back home in the city) because a whole acre of the Pennywort farm had been devoted to a dozen or so small, individual garden "rooms" that were joined together by tangled pathways of tall evergreen hedges. The whole thing might have reminded Gloria of the garden maze she'd seen on her honeymoon in France, but that diversion had been mild-mannered, neat, and austere, while the maze on the Pennywort farm looked like it sprang directly from the earth: toothy, rambunctious, and snarled as climbing vines.

Every year, the Pennyworts expanded the maze to be one or two rooms bigger. Flowers grew out of season, and plants that should not have bloomed in western Catskills soil were hardy and flamboyant. Dog violets that were the size of pennies in most yards grew to the size of small dogs. Trumpet vines with their horns of bright orange and yellow were nearly the size of actual trumpets. Gloria had taken a stroll through the gardens only twice: The first time had been more than three years ago, when she'd visited the garden maze as an excuse to meet her new neighbors. She remembered everything, each individual garden that made her eyes go wide and her breath catch in her lungs. She remembered the soft-as-cloud lamb's ear and prickly cones of teasel in the Petting Garden. She remembered the large orange koi fish from the Rock Garden that wagged their golden tails in happy greeting, and the children who reached into the pond to tickle their bellies as if the fish were dogs. She remembered bright walls of bougainvillea standing neighborly beside creeping, spidery Venus flytraps—how such exotic species grew in the Catskills seemed halfway between a miracle and an abomination. And she remembered the bright sentinel sunflowers that lined a long corridor of tall green hedges; if she didn't know better, she might have sworn they followed her with their big drooping heads when she passed by.

But mostly what she remembered was the thing she wanted most to forget: the Remembering Garden. The maze, some people said, could bring on a kind of mental or emotional clarity—if a person was open to it. The things a woman didn't understand about herself might become clearer; the difficult choice a man had to make would not become less difficult—but he might feel more confident about making it after a visit to the garden.

Gloria had dismissed the rumors and ducked into the Remembering Garden. The little green room of tall hedges was classical and poetic: elegant ivory columns, a pretty marble fountain of a woman pouring water, and words chiseled simply in a stone architrave: SIT A WHILE AND REMEMBER WHAT'S FORGOT. The plump honeybees were buzzing, the fountain was singing, and the garden was gently landscaped with champagne-colored roses, cascading green ivy, and hummocks of forget-me-nots. Gloria thought of nothing special. People passed by. Thoughts of an old friend that she had not spoken to in a long time popped into her head; she could only assume this was the power of suggestion. Later, after she'd spent a sleepless night wrestling with fitful dreams that were full of apologies she had no intention of making to her long-lost friend, she blamed the Pennyworts for the annoying crookedness of the bumper of her car, which had happened as a direct result of both the Remembering Garden and the guardrail that had kept her from going into a rocky Catskill ravine when she'd fallen asleep at the wheel. This was not magic, mind you; it was simply a thing that happened because it's never a good idea to sit and ponder the past too long.

Although most people in the vicinity of Green Valley did not like to say much about the Pennyworts and got an odd look on their faces whenever Gloria tried to tease out a little harmless gossip, no one denied that the family was a bit different, if not strange. At the very center of the Pennyworts' garden maze was a squared-off area, no more than the size of a one-car garage, surrounded on all sides by heavy stone walls and accessible only by a locked, opaque wooden gate. Dented metal signs were posted every six feet on the wall at varying heights and in multiple languages: *Mantener fuera. Hålla ut. Keep out.*

All of the little plots in the Pennyworts' garden maze looked healthier than they should under the tinder-dry circumstances, but it was this walled-in center garden that was blooming most voraciously in the summer drought. Gloria could see down into it from her vantage point on a hill that overlooked Green Valley, and the garden's reds, yellows, pinks, whites, oranges, and purples seemed to be frothing out over the tops of the stone walls in certain places and spilling effulgently over the sides like a sloshing, heady beer. Once, on a neighborly trip to see if the Pennyworts could make use of her old dehumidifier before she threw it out, Gloria had asked why no one was allowed in the walled garden at the heart of the maze—no one except for

Olivia Pennywort, who apparently made her ingress and egress as she pleased. But the answer Gloria got was so noncommittal and vague that within an hour of hearing it she could no longer even recall what it was.

Now, it annoyed her that the Pennyworts were not only watering their gardens illegally, but they seemed to be squandering community resources on a garden that nobody from the public was even allowed to see.

"Maybe there's a loophole," Richard Zeiger said from his armchair, his remaining hairs shivering in the blow of the air conditioner. "Maybe they're allowed to water because they're a commercial enterprise."

"They're not a commercial enterprise," Gloria said. "Or at least, they're not *supposed* to be. They don't charge anything for people to get in."

She didn't need to raise her binoculars to see that two women, clasping hands and wearing gauzy, matching skirts, had stopped by the Pennywort farm to tour the gardens and divert themselves a little from the doldrums of a rainless summer, as people were known to do.

"I'm calling," Gloria said.

Her husband was quiet.

"I am."

He looked at her, his formidable eyebrows raised.

"If they were watering their peas and carrots or something, I wouldn't care. But the fact that *they* get to water their enormous maze of a garden just to keep it pretty, while *my* two hanging baskets of phlox have just about turned into ashes—it just isn't fair."

Her husband was quiet still.

"It's our civic duty," Gloria said. "Don't you think it's our civic duty to report somebody who's abusing the water supply? The very *limited* water supply?"

She held the phone up listening to the dial tone with exasperation. She and Richard had retired up to Green Valley three winters ago. The landscape had been the very picture of peace: deer tracks in snow, bare trees and pale sky, just a sliver of smoke coming from the chimney of some distant, hidden house. They'd had no idea what summertime in the valley would be: Cars lined up and down the road as people stopped to buy vegetables or walk the "magic" maze, homeless people sleeping in a falling-down barn, immigrants from obscure Central American countries milling about in hopes of work, the noise of tractors and yelling men, the stink of manure hanging like a putrid-sweet cloud on muggy days, the horrid flies that descended on the valley like a biblical plague and just as suddenly were gone—there was no peace and quiet whatsoever from thaw to frost. Gloria had come to Green Valley seeking an Eden—her reward for many long years of sitting in a windowless city cubicle. Instead, she had found a dry, noisy, dusty, backwoods, stinky, fly-infested hell. She couldn't fight against the weather or flies, but there were things to be done about bad neighbors.

Her knuckles turned white from her grip on the phone.

"Okay, okay," Richard said from his armchair. "You don't have to convince me. If you're going to call the police, call the police. I don't want anything to do with it."

"Watch me," Gloria said. "I am."

At the police station, the officer who heard the phone ring looked at the caller ID and rolled his eyes. Thanks to Gloria Zeiger, they'd already sent guys out to Green Valley twice this month, and it was only mid-July. The first time, they'd sent a car because Gloria had reported "strange purple smoke" coming from the property, but it was gone when they arrived. The second time, Gloria had ratted out her neighbors because one of the various squatters who lived in the Pennyworts' old barn was doing her calisthenics routine. Topless. Again.

Now Gloria was complaining about the gardens being watered, but nobody wanted to investigate. To visit the Pennywort farm was to be reminded of everything in the world that was beautiful, and bountiful, and luxurious, and endlessly good. And this was a terrible thing for a man to be reminded of, because it made his heart black with despair. Trips out to the Pennywort farm always followed the same emotional trajectory: the melancholy resolve of the drive into the valley, then the inevitable springing up of hope to see the garden maze with its promise of youth and rampant possibility, and then the absolute certainty that life could change, *would* change, that the thing a person most wanted and deserved was right around the corner, right *there,* just a moment away—and then, the lonely, empty drive back home.

The problem, as most men of a certain age in Green Valley knew, was Olivia Pennywort. If a man could be guaranteed that he did not have to set eyes on her when he paid a visit to the farm, he might have felt less wary of his assignment. But old Arthur Pennywort was pretty much off his nut—living in a dilapidated shack in the woods like some kind of wild animal— and his twenty-nine-year-old daughter, Olivia, had been running the show since she'd dropped out of high school. These days, Olivia lived in the top of a tower that had once been a silo, and if any man could have coaxed her to let him in by climbing her hair like a ladder or slaying a dragon with a sword, he would have gladly done it. At all hours of the day, she could be seen working the farm that her family had owned since before she was born. Sometimes, bicyclists and Sunday drivers slowed down if they caught sight of her hoeing weeds or loading produce onto a truck. Sometimes people who came to visit the garden maze wandered away from it to watch her scrape paint off an old fence or chase away Green Valley's horde of wild, obnoxious goats. In spite of the fact that Olivia tromped about in work boots and overalls, in spite of the fact that her apricot-red hair was always semi-undisciplined in a messy bun, in spite of the dirt under her nails, the dark freckles on her sun-brown skin, the metallic smell of soil or even fertilizer that wafted about her, she was, without a doubt, the most beautiful woman in all of Green Valley, and perhaps beyond. She was young, and vigorous, and magnetic, and her hazel eyes were the luscious brown-gold-green of the Swamp Garden, which despite its lowly name was a high fantasy of dark pools of water, rich green lily pads, floating flowers, and sprays of blue-tinted vines that twined up the bark of delicate mandrakes.

Part of Olivia's particular allure was how mysterious she seemed, how kindhearted yet distant, how nurturing but withholding, how resistant to summary of any kind. Over the years, many men and a few women had rallied to win her affection. Bids were placed on bar tables, teenagers goaded one another into dares, rookie cops volunteered to go out to her place to try their hand. Some of the older guys on the force, who never ceased being amused by the yearnings and strivings of younger bucks, had to hold their tongues to keep from dishing out warnings: *That girl isn't just your everyday heartbreaker; she's full-on dangerous. Watch out.* Hopeful swains returned from the Pennywort farm with nothing but heartache and a grudging, sorrowful respect for their opponent; those who did dare to make a pass at her never did it again.

Olivia Pennywort was like a beautiful but dangerous plant kept safely under glass, a thing to be admired only from afar. And though few people in Green Valley knew it, she had not come to be so standoffish for her own good, but for the good of everyone around her. Her natural inclination was to be affectionate, trusting, and warm. It had taken many years of careful practice for her to learn how to rein in her enthusiasm about making new friends, to act as if her personality fell in the precise center between friendly and aloof. There was no choice: Much as she loved her neighbors, she had to stay slightly away.

To the cops who were regularly sent to check up on her, she was friendly, conversational, and patient—but she never let herself do anything that might be construed as flirting. To the children who came to her garden maze, she was generous and amusing, always offering them her homemade lemon drop candies or saying "catch!" and tossing them fresh strawberries until they'd caught one in their hands—and yet, she was always careful to stay a few feet away. To the tribe of transient women who slept in the Pennywort barn and took care of the gardens, Olivia strived to be a sympathetic leader, a good listener, and a patient caregiver—but because none of the women ever stayed on the farm very long, she was saved from the moral conundrum of becoming anyone's actual friend. It was only with her father, the one person who knew what she was and loved her anyway, that she could truly be herself.

Her summer days were as busy as days could be from sunup to sundown: Her farm crew needed constant direction and adjustment as they worked her fields; the boarders who lived in her barn and tended to her garden maze needed reassurance and TLC; her father needed regular monitoring and supervision to keep him from being an accidental danger to himself; and her garden—her private garden that housed her most personal and important plants—needed constant pruning and trimming; otherwise it would roil like bubbles blown in a glass of milk. She did not, and would never have, the things a normal woman could have: intimate friends who knew and accepted her innermost secrets, a husband to warm her on long winter nights, or children who would lift their arms to her and say *Up! Up!*

But still, she was alive—and that was something. She had the work—the wonderfully exhausting and meaningful work—of running her farm. She lived in a paradise of such extravagant enchantments that the world had not seen such a place since Adam and Eve, and she alone heard its secrets whispered in her ear. The Pennywort farm with its fields and woods and out-buildings and barns and garden maze was like a living, human-sized terrarium: exclusive, self-sustaining, self-contained. What happened on the farm happened *for* the farm, so that in the same way a plant made its own food from sunlight the farm kept itself running by effortlessly drawing toward it and claim-ing the things it needed—including Olivia. The edges of Olivia's universe were delineated by wooden fences or old railroad spikes on the property lines, and even on the worst day of the year the farm was the best place a person could be—the *only* place Olivia could be what she truly was with any degree of happiness about it. Even now, as Olivia noticed a woman run-ning toward her at top speed across a field of acorn squash, the great green gears of the farm were turning, and the things that manifested themselves as "problems" were actually just signs of life going on.

"Hey, Olivia! There you are!"

"Here I am," Olivia said. The woman—a boarder named Lib-bie who had started sleeping in the barn three weeks ago—stopped a few feet before Olivia. And Olivia, without thinking, stepped a few feet back. She had been hoeing weeds down row after row of cucumbers for hours; her arms ached and her lower back was cramped. But this was not unusual—just another sign of midsummer, like cicadas and thunderstorms.

"We caught somebody!" Libbie said, breathing heavily. "Try-ing to steal . . . from the farm stand!"

Olivia frowned. "Really?"

"Yeah. Bram saw it with her own eyes." Libbie put her hands on her hips, her shoulders curved with the effort of breathing. This was the most exciting thing that had happened on the farm in a very long time. "This girl just starts shoving things in her bag—like we wouldn't notice. How do you like that?"

"Not someone we know . . ."

"No. A stranger. From out of town."

"Of course." Olivia squinted toward the distant structure of the roadside farm stand. No one from any of the Bethel hamlets would steal from the Pennywort farm; they knew better. Since the garden maze had first been built in the years following the Concert, speculation about it had been vigorous. People said that a person who picked a flower from the maze would be cursed. They pointed to the birds and the bears and the foxes for corroboration: Not even the hungriest wild animal would pilfer its breakfast from Pennywort land.

But an outsider who didn't know any better—that was a different story.

Olivia squinted at Libbie in the relentless sun. Libbie was in her mid-twenties, and her colorful and slouchy skirts always put Olivia in mind of a woman overplaying the part of a gypsy in a stage show. She'd had a field day with the clothing donations that were sometimes dropped off at the barn by the local churches and synagogues. Libbie had come to the maze trying to decide if she should continue with college or follow her dream to act. When the maze hadn't offered an immediate answer, she did what so many maze-walkers did: She'd decided to stay on. Olivia peered at her face. "Do you . . . are you getting a black eye? Did somebody *hit* you?"

Libbie smiled, beaming proudly. "Don't worry. We caught her and locked her in the pen. She put up a fight, but it was three of us against one of her."

"Wait. You locked a person in the *peacock* pen?"

"The birds aren't using it right now," Libbie said, sheepish. "Plus, we didn't want her to run."

Olivia tried to hide her reaction. "Well, I guess that's . . . functional."

"Do you want me to call the police?" Libbie asked, perhaps a bit too enthusiastically. "Have them come arrest her?"

"Not just yet," Olivia said.

She thanked Libbie for handling the situation as best she knew how. Then she carried her hoe and crossed to the far side of the barn, near the old silo, where the peafowl were set up to roost. She wore clothes typical for her workday: a close-fitting tank top, work boots, and a long cotton skirt that she took a lot of flack for but that struck her as cooler and more accommodating than denim—it was the best balance she'd found between being protected and being comfortable. Her hair, so heavy and long, had been braided and swirled into a loaf that sat smack on the middle of her head. A wet red bandanna around her neck helped her keep cool.

As she approached the peacock's cage she could see a figure sitting on the hay with her back curved against the wire fencing. Her knees were curled into her chest. She wore old white tennis shoes with beaded denim shorts that were so tiny the pockets stuck out under the hem. Her tank top was hot orchid pink and tacked with spangles that threw lasers of fuchsia every which way. Her black hair was held back by a glittery teal band.

"Hello there," Olivia said to the thief. She leaned against the front of the cage but did not open it. The girl did not answer, did not even turn her head. "This kind of gives a whole new meaning to the idea of getting thrown in the pen."

The girl didn't laugh. "Bite me."

"What did you try to steal?"

The girl didn't answer.

"Are you hungry?" Olivia asked.

"I want you to let me go."

"What's your name?"

The girl's face was shaped like a cut diamond, wide temples and narrow chin, and her eyes sparkled like anthracite coal. Her nose was small and flat at the tip, her skin a warm color between taupe and cream. Her hair was long, thick, and black, running straight as a river at midnight.

"Are you going to call the cops?" the girl asked. "Or are you just going to leave me locked in here all day."

"That depends on you," Olivia said. "Look—you don't have to tell me your whole name. Just your first name's good enough. Just so I know what to call you."

Suspicion cut through her gaze. But she said, "I'm Mei."

"Good. And I'm Olivia. I own this farm, so it was me you were stealing from."

The girl made a noise that was a cross between a resigned sigh and a huff of frustration. "I'm sorry, okay? Yes, I was hungry. You've got, like, a ton of food. It's not like it was going to throw you into bankruptcy if I took a tomato."

Olivia leaned the hoe against the peacock pen. Her fruits and vegetables and beans were irresistible, even for the most stubborn of meat-and-potato types. She believed that her produce called to people, that if it had arms it would stretch them out and draw people in the same way that people reached out and picked up an apple or plum, so that it wasn't a customer picking a peach but the other way around. She also had learned that a little human salesmanship didn't hurt, either; they crushed the unsellable onions on the underside of the tables so the scent bloomed beautifully around the stand. They sprinkled fragrant basil leaves among the tomatoes, and offered cubes of watermelon on toothpicks. It was impossible to resist for adults with full bellies; it was more than impossible, Olivia guessed, for hungry kids.

"How old are you?" Olivia asked the girl in the pen. *Mei.*

"Nineteen."

"Do you live around here?"

"No."

"Where you from?"

"Everywhere."

"Are you a runaway?"

"I'm an adult," she said. "Nobody owns me. I didn't run away from anybody."

Olivia pulled a handkerchief from the back pocket of her pants and rubbed her sweaty face. Though she and all the farm's denizens wore loose-fitting cotton and big straw hats to fight the high summer sun, there was no escaping the tyrannical, merciless heat. Humidity congested like water in everyone's lungs; dust became a skin on their skins. She tucked her handkerchief away.

"Listen, Mei. I—" The walkie-talkie clipped to her waistband chirped for attention; Tom was looking for her. She'd told him she would walk the fields with him (again) today to inspect the drought damage and talk over the possibility of putting in an irrigation system—which they normally wouldn't need. Eastern farms had to contend with difficult, rocky soil, but one thing that did work to their advantage was a normally reliable amount of rain. This year, though, the fact that they hadn't put in irrigation was finally catching up to them. She didn't have much more time to give to Mei at the moment, though the girl seemed like she could use a little attention. Olivia told Tom she would be with him in a minute. Then she flipped open the lock of the cage where the girl was penned. "Come on out."

Mei crawled through the door. The girl stood and brushed

off her knees, and in a moment, everything Olivia had been planning abruptly changed.

The girl's belly was swollen before her.

Tom would have to wait.

A runaway was one thing. A pregnant runaway was another.

"Am I free to go?" Mei asked. "Or are you just going to keep staring at me because I'm pregnant."

"Sorry," Olivia said. "Why don't you walk with me for a minute?"

"Why should I?"

"I want to show you something."

"Just tell me what it is," Mei said.

"I can't tell you. I can only show you. And, given your situation, I think you'll want to see this for yourself." Olivia started walking; the girl stayed put. But when Olivia didn't slow down, or gesture for her to come, or even ask *Did you hear what I said?* Mei began to follow on her own just as Olivia guessed she would. (Over the years Olivia had seen many women come and go. The farm—the valley—seemed to open up and draw in, and in the center of the valley was the garden maze, filled with its own enchantments for wanderers, worriers, and women trying to find their way.)

Olivia spoke as they walked, softly, so that Mei had to stay close by her to hear. "The first thing you should know is that you're welcome to stay here, if you want to. No questions asked."

"You mean, like, on the farm?"

"We're not exactly the Hilton, but we're . . . well . . . we're here. See that old barn there, the one that looks like it's about to fall down? There are cots, blankets, outhouses, outdoor showers, a little kitchenette, and all the food you could ever want and then some."

"Seriously?"

"Seriously. I've got eleven women staying with me right now."

"Staying in there. You're not kidding."

"It doesn't look like much. But it's been standing for over eighty years and it hasn't fallen down yet."

"Why?" Mei asked, her voice having lost some of its hard edge.

"Some people come to Green Valley because they're trying to find direction. Or answers. They want to make a decision or a change, and they don't know what to do. For the people who need a little time to themselves and some room to think, there's nothing better than a stay in the barn. We Pennyworts have been doing this since before I was born."

"So how much do you charge a night?" Mei asked as Olivia walked them closer to the garden maze, as slowly as she could stand.

"It's free," Olivia said.

"No way."

"Well, you don't have to pay any money to stay."

Mei narrowed her eyes. "What's the catch? You might as well spill it now."

"You have to work while you're here."

"What exactly do you mean by work? This isn't some sex trafficking place . . . ?"

"God no," Olivia said. "Anyone who stays works on the gardens in return for room and board."

"I'm not sure how much work I could do." Olivia watched Mei's big eyes begin to water. "I just . . . I can't do much of anything right now. I'm pregnant, see?" She gestured awkwardly toward her belly. "And everybody wants me to give up the baby. But I'm not sure if I should."

Now Olivia looked blatantly at her belly; she wasn't past the six-month mark, if Olivia had to guess. "You don't have to do any work you're not comfortable doing. And . . . maybe there's a way I can help you."

Mei wiped her face and blinked rather prettily. "How?"

"Our garden maze has these . . . I don't know . . . properties. If you walk through it alone, and you hold your question or your problem lightly in your mind, you might just get your answer by the time you find your way out."

Mei looked at her incredulously. "Your garden maze is supposed to bring me a magical answer to my . . . my question. That's what you're seriously telling me right now."

"You haven't been in Green Valley very long," Olivia said. "But things are different here. Lots of things."

Mei made a noise between a snort and a laugh. "And what if I don't get an answer?"

"Then you're welcome to stay here until you do."

Mei glanced at the barn as they neared it. "So . . . like, all the women in the barn . . ."

"They're waiting on answers," Olivia said. "When they're ready to go, they'll go."

"*Hmm,*" Mei said. And now, instead of looking at the barn, or the tall hedges that marked the maze, she was looking at Olivia. Olivia didn't flinch; she'd been looked at this way before, with speculation, distrust, and even disbelief. She'd been looked at this way her entire life—by people who called Green Valley home and by strangers passing through. The fact that she allowed outsiders to sleep in her barn didn't help her popularity in town: Some people supported her, some people felt bad for her boarders, and some—like her neighbor Gloria—seemed to hate her guts. Inevitably, the crowd that lived in the barn was ragtag, scattered, sundry, and mismatched. Most of the women were quiet minders-of-their-own-business; a few were occasionally rowdy and had to be escorted from local watering holes by annoyed policemen. Somewhere along the line, people got the idea that the women who stayed on the Pennywort farm were moochers, freeloaders, and delinquents—lazy and unwilling to get real jobs. The town had given the Pennywort tenants a nickname: the Penny Loafers.

But Olivia knew better than the people of Green Valley; she knew the Penny Loafers intimately. They were as close to her as the sisters she didn't have. Green Valley, and all of the Bethel communities, simply had trouble knowing what to make of them: They were women who couldn't be defined by the people they took care of (husbands, daughters) or the people who took care of them (mothers, sisters, aunts). They came from hard lives of every kind and were never the same group of women twice. In another century, they might have had something in common with vestals, or handmaidens to a goddess, or sacred oracles—they dedicated their waking hours to cultivating the Pennyworts' garden maze as they waited to discover what they meant to do with their lives. All summer long, Olivia welcomed them and then watched them go. They were her family, her staff, and the closest thing she had to friends. Then in the fall, when the garden died away and the nights grew too cold to sleep in the barn, she did what she always did: she watched with a heavy heart as they left, not to return until the maze began to bloom again.

Mei's eyes seemed clearer now, cautiously hopeful. "You're not going to, like, try to convert me to join some cult to save my immortal soul, or lock me in a peacock cage again, or turn me in to the cops?"

Olivia laughed. "No. None of those things. But—there are some rules you have to follow."

"Of course there are," Mei said. "Here we go. What are they?"

Olivia cleared her throat, and for the first time since they'd started talking, looked away. "If you decide to stay, two things are off-limits. The first is the garden in the center of the maze, the locked garden behind the high stone walls. Don't go in."

"Why not?"

"Because that's the rule," Olivia said, in the tone of voice that she'd learned from her father when she was young, the tone that said *No conversation allowed.*

"Okay . . . What's the second thing that I'm supposed to steer clear of?"

Olivia steeled herself. "That would be me."

And though she'd warned people off a hundred times, a thousand, she'd never quite been able to fully defend her heart against their reactions. It always cut her, always hurt, to have to build the same kind of wall around herself that she'd built around her garden. But she had no choice. For a very long time, Olivia had been stuck with a particular affliction: an accidental brush against her arm, a bump of summer-bare legs—anything— would inflict uncomfortable skin irritations on the person who touched her. The pain was not immediate, but it was inevitable. Within a few hours of directly touching Olivia's skin, a person would begin to itch. Then he might see the first strawberry- colored smatterings of deep irritation. Soon the itching might turn into welts, and then welts into blisters, and no amount of calamine lotion or long baths in oatmeal could fully erase the angry burn or make it more quickly run its course.

As far as Olivia knew, the secret of her condition had not spread far and wide; the very few people who had reason to suspect it kept the suspicion to themselves with a kind of soured reluctance, an unwillingness to outwardly admit a thing they could not inwardly believe. The best thing to do, Olivia had found, was to warn people to stay away from her right from the beginning. Olivia had hurt people, even when she tried not to.

She'd hurt her father long ago when instinct had compelled her to grab him and stop him from falling into a manure pile (she would have been better off letting him fall). She'd hurt the occasional male who attempted to make love to her with friendly, hands-on offers of an *oh-you're-so-tense* massage, or an eyelash brushed off her face and wished upon. She hurt her boarders even though she did her best to stay away from them; when she heard them complain of how they must have gotten poison ivy somewhere while hoeing weeds, she could only keep silent, her skin prickling with self-awareness and guilt, as she listened. She'd used to hurt children—back in the days before she stopped leaving the Pennywort property—and that was the worst: to feel the thump of a toddler just learning to walk as he crashed into her at the hardware store, and knowing the anguish and confusion the child's mother would feel when the redness began to form on her baby's skin. It was better for all of the Bethel hamlets if she stayed where she was: hidden, safe, minimizing her interactions and minimizing the damage she might do to the town she loved.

Mei was looking at Olivia now with pointed distrust. "I'm supposed to stay away from *you*?"

"I don't like people to touch me," she said, the lie coming off her lips so easily that it almost felt true. "It's important that you don't—not even by accident. Not under any circumstances. No matter what."

"So . . ." Mei tipped her head. "So, say you were drowning . . ."

"No," Olivia said.

"Say you were hanging by your fingertips from the top of a cliff, and I was bending over the edge holding out a hand . . ."

"Not even then."

"But what if—"

"Never," Olivia said sharply, feeling her muscles go rigid with tension. Mei apparently liked to instigate. But she wasn't the first woman to arrive at the barn with a chip on her shoulder and she wouldn't be the last.

"You must not have much of a sex life," Mei said.

"Do you always have to say everything you're thinking out loud?"

"Generally, yes."

They came to the entrance to the garden maze. It was the kind of entryway that teetered between impressive and gaudy, between awe-inspiring and way-too-much. It was in the shape of an enormous yellow flower with glittery purple tendrils corkscrewing away from the center. A crosshatch of deep purple lines drew the eye into the center of the petals, where a tall opening had been cut to allow humans to climb through. The flower was called henbane, a beautiful but deadly plant when ingested. A sensitive person could faint from standing too close to henbane on a hot day. Henbane was also a key ingredient, supposedly, in the potions that made medieval witches fly. Olivia loved henbane: its gorgeous, gaudy bloom, its wicked green tongues of leaves, its centuries of folklore. When faced with the task of replacing the old, crumbling wooden entrance with a new one, she thought henbane was the perfect choice.

Mei eyed the gigantic, not exactly friendly-looking flower with suspicion. "Why aren't you getting me arrested right now?"

"I'd rather help you."

"But *why?*"

Olivia was quiet. One thing she'd learned from having kept herself so isolated was that the less she could say about herself, the better. Once, a woman named Editha had come to the barn, and Olivia had the strangest sense upon meeting her that they were intensely connected. It was the pull of innate understanding and friendship; in five minutes, they'd talked as if they'd been friends for a lifetime. Editha had told Olivia about every detail of her impending divorce—which was not unusual, since the boarders talked about their problems all the time. But Olivia had shared something of herself with Editha too; she'd talked about her mother's death, her father's retreat from the world, the rewarding agony of being so closely tied to the land, and she'd *almost* confessed the truth about her condition, how she'd become the woman she was and what cruel Green Valley magic was behind it.

But one day, she and Editha had been gathering eggs inside the musty shadows of the old coop, and Editha had put an arm around her in happy camaraderie faster than Olivia had been able to dart away in the small space. For one moment Editha had forgotten the "no touching" rule, and Olivia had been too horrified and upset to make an excuse for herself or explain; she told Editha to go shower, immediately, and as far as she knew the woman did. But whether she got her answer from the maze or not, Olivia never knew. The next morning, the other boarders had told Olivia that Editha had gotten a case of poison ivy all down her right side, and she'd left in the night for treatment. Olivia waited, hopeful, but Editha never returned. Whether Editha had left because she'd realized Olivia's secret was unclear, but the result was undeniable: She would not, after all, be Olivia's friend.

It had been an extremely painful summer, and the winter that followed was especially lonely and cold. But it had served as a good reminder that the only way Olivia could safely love the world was from a distance. There was too much danger—to her and to others—when she opened her heart.

Mei was waiting on her for an answer. Olivia said, "My family ended up with a lot of open space in the old barn when my father had the new one built, so when my mother was still alive, she figured she should put it to good use."

"Your mom's dead?"

"Yeah."

"I'm sorry."

"It's okay. I don't really remember her that much. She died when I was four."

"How did she die?"

"She used to forage for wild foods. Berries, leaves, that sort of thing. One of my last memories of her was walking through Chickadee Woods while she pointed out the young pokeweed shoots—which you'd only want to eat if you knew just when to pick them. Otherwise, they turn toxic to humans."

"She died from pokeweed?"

"No. It was a mushroom. We don't know what kind, exactly. I remember she had a bellyache and then a few hours later said she was better. We thought she just had a bug. But the thing about some kinds of mushrooms is that they kill you when you're not looking. By the time we realized what had happened, she was too far gone."

"God," Mei said. "I don't get it. Why didn't she get help right away?"

"That's just the way of the farmers of Green Valley; they don't complain about things." Olivia put a hand on the large henbane blossom that led into the maze. "Anyway, that's why the gardens are so important to me. And why I keep the barn open. I lost my mother early on. But I like to think we're close to each other because of how much we both love the maze."

Mei uncrossed her arms and peered into the opening of the maze. Olivia knew she was thinking the things that all the new Penny Loafers thought, having the internal debate they all had. Should she stay with the lonely, crazy woman who was offering her a sanctuary but who had seriously bizarre rules and apparently a phobia of human touch? Or should she hit the road and burn rubber out of the parking lot and thank her lucky stars she got away?

"I have to get back to work," Olivia said. "If you stay or don't stay, it's not up to me. But take a stroll in the maze before you go. Here's the entrance. But there are any number of exits you can take."

"Isn't a maze supposed to have only one finish line?"

"Not this maze. The good thing about problems is that it seems like there's only one way to get into them, but there's usually lots of ways out."

Mei sighed, and a kind of distance crept into her eyes. Olivia saw suddenly how young she was, and how tired. She wished she could reach out a hand to squeeze it, or even offer a pat on the back. But a gesture like that would hurt more than help.

"I'll leave you to it," Olivia said. "When you're done, stop by the farm stand. Whether you stay with us or go on your way, I'll have the other boarders make up a bag of our best produce for you. And hey—you don't even have to steal it."

"Thanks," Mei said.

"It's no problem. I'm not doing anything my mother wouldn't have done for you if she were still here," Olivia said. "The garden maze should help."

Of course, the Pennywort maze was not the kinder and gentler way of getting at the heart of a tough decision: It could be cruel and blunt, as it did not temper its advice with platitudes or gentle coaxing as a kind listener might. Instead it flung people from their comfort zones like a plane's ejector seat, it severed relationships as with an executioner's sword, it bound lovers to affairs that would be best swept under the carpet, and it mangled people's peace of mind. Some visitors were thrilled by the discovery of an inner truth. But others were angry when the clarity that they'd hoped to find turned out not to be an easy clarity, but instead the kind of clarity that makes a person forsake loved ones, or give up valuables, or throw away their future, or go after a dream without the safety net of common sense or a viable Plan B.

"Go on," Olivia said. "Just keep your question in your mind."

Mei gave her one last uncertain glance. The entrance to the maze was before her, the flower so big it could make a human feel like a bee, the large human-sized hole in the center of the flower beckoning Mei into the maze. For a split second before Olivia could quell the feeling, she was struck with a pang of jealousy. Because for as generous as the maze had always been in helping others make difficult decisions, the maze had never—not once—seemed to convey anything of value to *her.*

She could only suppose the maze's silence toward her was because she had no more need of difficult answers than she'd had need of exits or escape routes: everything she needed was all around her, right here, on the farm. It would be wrong to expect more of her life than what she had.

In the bright blue sky, turkey vultures had gathered over Solomon's Ravine, riding the current of the heat. Olivia listened as the sound of Mei's footsteps softened inside the maze. Then she returned, mindlessly if not contentedly, to the work of the day.

An Olive Branch

amuel Van Winkle, who had lived across the road from the Pennywort farm during his young life, had been unable to prevent himself from entertaining the idea that if he returned to the gardens of his youth, he would find a little bit of his old, youthful energy waiting there to be reclaimed. He would walk into the Pennyworts' garden maze, where he'd played for so many hours as a kid, and be overwhelmed by its infinite botanical stimulations—because wasn't stimulation what gardens were about?—and he would drink in all the wild and profuse colors of snapdragons and phloxes and roses and orchids; he would breathe in the fragrant musk of flowers with its faint underpinnings of fertility and sex; he would listen to the droning of overfed honeybees as they bumbled from bloom to bloom—and then, maybe, if he was really freakishly lucky, he would run his hands over the green walls of the hedges, and he would *feel* them, *actually feel them,* in the normal, miraculous, and mundane way he used to feel things before his accident.

But—as it turned out—he'd been right to keep his ridiculous optimism about miracle cures boxed up and buried. Because even in the Pennyworts' garden, where anything was possible, he found no miracles. He still couldn't feel, not like he used to.

He touched the petals of lady's slipper, pink and pretty when it should have already lost its bloom. He rubbed a soft leaf of a flower he did not recognize against his chin—but there was nothing. No small frictions from infinitely tiny hairs on the underside of a leaf, no raised veins catching his fingertips. His skin might as well have been a leather hide. He let his hand fall.

The Pennywort maze could do many things for a man, but it couldn't cure him of a disease that the doctors said didn't exist. For eighteen months, Sam had been unable to feel the workings of the world around him through his skin: If it was raining gently, he knew it only by the look of drops on his shirt. If a bag was heavy, he could sense the weight of it in the workings of his muscles, but he could not feel the bite of a strap on his skin. And though he'd gone as far as kissing a few women, it had been a long time since he'd felt even the slightest pleasure in human touch—almost two years of walking around in his own skin with the understanding that he was, at the most basic level, hardly more feeling than a dead man.

The doctors had told him that despite the violence of his accident, they couldn't find anything wrong with his brain. His condition, they said, was probably the result of emotional trauma as opposed to physical—*a somatoform disorder,* one young doctor had said, though an older physician had called it *psychosomatic.* That word alone had been enough to keep Sam from sharing his secret with anyone—not that he would have mentioned it anyway. *Psychosomatic,* he said the word to himself sometimes. *It means you're nuts,* his father would have said.

No one in Green Valley knew what had really happened to him before he'd returned. No one would glance twice if he slipped up and let his limp show occasionally, or if he groaned too much when the weather got cold. All over Green Valley men and women bore the injuries of life in farming: gnarled nail beds and missing fingers and toes, arms scarred by machinery and faces turned leathery by the sun. Compared to some of the old-timers, Sam looked perfectly intact. And that was a good thing: He would never be able to tell anyone what had happened, especially not his relatives. The Van Winkles were tall men, lanky and knobby, with scrawny chicken necks during puberty and pronounced Adam's apples later down the line. They were known for having big, amiable personalities no matter the kinds of dark thoughts that were going on inside their skulls. The Van Winkles were born noncomplainers. Heroism was not merely woven into their genetic makeup; it was their makeup. Sam came from a family tree of long, forking lines of doctors and paramedics, firefighters and cops. If a guy was ejected out the windshield of a car and lying in a pile of bones on the roadside, it was a Van Winkle that he wanted to see bending over his body, because no Van Winkle had ever let anyone in Green Valley die. Their talent for rescuing people who could not be rescued and reviving people who could not be revived was legendary—even if more than one branch of the family tree had been snapped off by Van Winkles who hadn't hesitated to throw down their lives to save others.

For many years, Sam had forestalled, skirted, and deflected his filial obligation to Green Valley. He'd wanted to be young and free, to see what there was to see and do what there was to do. But mostly, he'd wanted to get the hell out of Bethel. Like many young men, he'd done his best to demonize the land where he'd grown up—decrying it as a place of backwoods, aging, redneck flower children who were wallowing away their golden years in the deluded and watered-down fantasies of youth. The few times he had returned to his parents' house during his twenties, he was regularly struck down by a terrible indigestion—a sour burn that flared like a match in the back of his throat and only began to fizzle out when his tires were putting Green Valley in his rearview mirror.

After his accident, Sam had lost the will to fight against the current that had swept up so many of the Van Winkles; he didn't have to work too very hard to find a place on the Green Valley police department. If there hadn't been a position open for him, they would have created one. He'd only had to let it be. After zombie-walking his way through training and testing and working out, Sam had officially taken up his post at the police department last week, and the entire force seemed to breathe a sigh of relief that a Van Winkle was once again among them— even though Sam himself felt unsure that he could live up to the Van Winkle reputation. In the week since he'd been back, he'd gone out for shots at Kilcoin's Tavern; he tossed horseshoes (badly) in Matt Weber's backyard and listened to classic rock albums; he chased a raccoon out of Mrs. Alexandrov's garage and then helped her from her rocking chair though he could not feel her hand; and when he got the assignment to check in on the Pennyworts, he told the guys it really was no big deal. No big deal at all.

Now, as he walked among the hedgerows, the maze made him feel as if he were in a pocket of air in which lightning was about to materialize—which was as close as he'd come in eighteen months to feeling anything at all. He paused for a quick moment in the Remembering Garden, which might have been cut out of a Victorian greeting card. And though he could not feel it, he dipped his hand and let the water from the fountain wash over his palm. He said hello to the fat koi in the Rock Garden, and if he didn't know better, they seemed to remember him, coming to the surface and wagging their bodies in greeting. He passed by the Promise Garden and did not dare to look inside for fear of encountering the ghost of his old, smitten, stupid teenage self within it, still standing there, still clueless and hopeful, still utterly ignorant about the many ways life could and would disappoint a man as he went along.

People had told wonderful tales that had filled Sam's head with magic when he was a child. They'd said the maze was magical—that it could help a person better know him- or herself. That each room of the garden had its own particular kind of magical workings, magic that couldn't be explained except to say that all of Green Valley had seemed enchanted since the Concert had come through in 1969. Sam had spent enough time in the garden to believe that strange things could happen there; Olivia's blooming lady's slipper was proof enough for him that Green Valley was special. And he'd seen people go through the garden maze and come out the other side claiming to be *changed*. It was, in part, the idiosyncrasies of the Green Valley that had driven him away. He'd wanted to go where flowers bloomed only when they were supposed to, and wild goats did not look at you as if they understood English when you spoke to them, and nobody had ever heard of the Van Winkles.

But—here he was. Back again.

It wasn't until he was standing at the padlocked wooden door surrounded by rusted warning signs that Olivia Pennywort caught up with him. He heard her footstep before he saw her. He prepared himself, then turned around.

"Can I help you?" she said.

The outdated black radio clipped to his belt went off, and he looked down at it quickly to lower the volume. The frisson of shock he'd felt at seeing her was gone by the time he looked up again. "Olivia."

"Yes?"

She stared at him blankly and he realized: She no longer recognized him.

"Can I help you?" she said again.

She was as beautiful as she'd ever been, or more beautiful, since he remembered her as a flighty, giggling teen—all elbows and teeth and knees—and she had grown into a woman of muscle and curves. She stood with her work boots slightly apart beneath the dusty hem of her yellow skirt. Her white tank top was dirt-smudged, threadbare, and torn at a spot near the bottom. Her hands were on her hips and her wide shoulders were squared as if she were readying for a battle. And yet, in spite of all of this, she was the most breathtaking, staggering, punch-in-the-throat-beautiful sight he'd seen in a long time.

He didn't know what to say. Would it be easier, he wondered, if she *didn't* recognize him—for the moment at least? Should he wait for her to recognize him, just to see how long it took? He cleared his throat. "This is a heck of a garden."

She didn't exactly smile. "Thank you."

"It's very green."

"I have a green thumb," she said.

"Maybe a little too green. We got a report that you're watering. Illegally."

She crossed her brown, bare arms. "Well, I'm not."

"It sure looks like you're watering. There's one green patch in the valley, and it's right here." His voice sounded harsher than he'd meant it to. But he'd expected to find she was at least a *little* glad to see him.

"I only water once a week. I swear. There's a brook that runs through the center of the gardens—I can show you. I borrow a little water from it from time to time. But I'm not doing anything wrong."

"You'll get a fine if you're caught watering illegally."

"Thanks for looking out for me," she said not impolitely. "But if you don't mind, if you're not going to fine me or write me a summons, then I'd like to get back to work."

The shock of her hard words was a wake-up call. At one time, Olivia had been as close to him as one child could be to another, digging together in the gardens, playing hide-and-seek in the cornfields, pushing each other on an old tire swing that always smelled of sweet black rubber and dry rope. Together they had gazed up at the lolling, lazy mountains—the hills with their bluestone teeth cutting between the green trees—and they'd picked out recognizable images from amorphous, leafy shapes: *I see a dragon, I see a ship, I see a horse, a cow!* They waded into the cold mountain quarry and were dazzled by the way the sun sliced into the clear water, lighting it up all golden like rippling leopard spots. They had lived side-by-side lives for what had seemed back then to be a lifetime but had in fact been not very long at all.

And now, she didn't recognize him.

He'd known that returning to Green Valley meant he would have to see her again. There was no way around it; they were neighbors. Eventually their paths would cross. He'd ignored the urge to go looking for her because he hadn't wanted to appear overly eager to connect with her again.

But of course, now that she was standing before him, he realized that he *had* been eager—overly eager—to see her. He'd thought about Olivia as many times over the years as there were stars in the sky. His on-and-off bar buddies had heard stories about her—stories that were always drunken, always mournful and pathetic, always told late at night, when men begin to swap their remembered heartaches under cover of dim lights and bad music. *Are you thinking of your Olivia?* a friend might say. And if Sam hadn't been thinking of her at that moment, he inevitably started to. Though he'd lost Olivia's friendship before he left the valley, he knew she would always be *his Olivia,* because he would always be burdened with the memory of everything she had given him, everything she had taken away—and all of that, the whole big picture of their history together, was his to bear now and forever, so that she was and would always be *his* Olivia, even in absence.

But *this* woman standing in the obscenely decadent throes of the garden maze—with her cold and wary eyes, her crossed arms—this was *not* his Olivia. This was a brick wall, not much different than the high stone wall behind her, dotted with warning signs, topped off by barbed wire, and surrounded by jewel-weed (also called *touch-me-not,* Olivia once told him) blooming at the base. This Olivia was not what he'd expected or known.

She tilted her head. "Are you okay?"

"Oh, I'm . . . Well, I'm . . ."

He hitched up his belt a bit, buying time.

He was suddenly assailed by the oddest, most fraught, most fist-clenching desire. He wanted Olivia to know him, somehow, to *know.* And he wanted her to feel the way he was feeling, standing in the garden maze with her again after all this time.

"Olivia," he said. He started toward her, compelled by the urge to stand a little closer. But she took three juddering steps back, a cloud of yellow dirt rising around her work boots, and he withdrew. "You really don't know me?"

He saw her throat, the long narrow column of it, work as she swallowed. *"Sam?"*

He smiled.

"You're a . . . cop?"

"Wasn't it inevitable?"

"A cop in Green Valley," she said. "I'm surprised."

"Why?"

"You always said you wanted to be a cop here. But then—" She broke off. And unless he imagined it, she'd colored slightly under her tan.

"But then I left," he said.

"You did."

"But I'm back now."

"Yes. And a cop."

He nodded. "Yes."

"Look at you," she said so brightly, so chummy, that he

couldn't help but think she was trying too hard. "You're just like what you said you'd be."

"Right," he said. "Just like."

He squinted at Olivia in the cruel sun. As a child, he'd wanted what his father had. As a young man, he'd rejected that dream. Now he didn't know what he wanted. He had come back to Green Valley, back to the police force, solely because he'd failed at everything else—not because he *wanted* to be here, living alone in the house his parents had deeded to him out of pity, with nothing to show for his time away from the valley but a few books he could fit in a suitcase, his favorite pillow, and skin as impervious to sensation as the neoprene seats of his old Jeep. Olivia was supposed to have been the bright spot in his return to Green Valley—and yet he couldn't get past the awkwardness of being with her again, as if he was just some half-remembered acquaintance, and not the person that she'd once trusted with her most intimate thoughts and dreams.

"Look, could we go somewhere, um, shadier to continue this conversation?" he asked.

"But I told you I'm not watering. You've got to believe me. I don't know what else to say. It's not my fault that Gloria has it out for me. She—"

"Olivia—"

"She decided she doesn't like the boarders living in the barn, and I swear she'll do anything just to get under my skin. She doesn't—"

"Olivia!"

She stopped. And in the silence was forced to meet his eye.

"I don't want to talk about the garden," he said.

"Then . . . what do you want to talk about?"

He rubbed the back of his neck but didn't feel it. "I just wanted to talk with you."

She said nothing; but she looked away with a pained expression on her face.

He'd heard the latest stories about Olivia from the guys at the station: that she was kind and self-sacrificing, that she'd be the first person to send fresh produce to a family in need if she heard of them, that she cared for her screwball father who got screwier by the year, that she could look at a man and make him feel like he was the only man in the world who mattered—but that beneath her outward radiance and kindness she was oddly inaccessible and cold. She lived like a nun, people said. No one could remember the last time she'd been spotted on a date—not that Sam cared if Olivia was seeing every guy in Green Valley. Her love life meant nothing to him—not in any practical sense.

Losing the sensation of his skin had quashed his interest in women like losing his taste buds might have made him turn away food. He was, in many ways, dead to the world. He'd died eighteen months ago on a mountain in the Adirondacks called Moggy Knob. After his Cessna went cartwheeling along the tops of the thick green pines and landed half crushed against a rocky outcropping, he'd managed to hold on for three and a half days, drifting in and out of sleep, in and out of shock, eating handfuls of snow from pine boughs through a broken window, pinned inside the jagged metal teeth of his crushed plane. In the chattery cold of Moggy Knob nights, when the clear, starry sky gave a man all the room he needed to think, he'd realized that he had no idea what he was meant to do with his life, except to know that what he'd done already wasn't it.

Minute by minute, he'd managed to grit his teeth and hold on, hold on, hold on. But the moment his rescuers found him, he could hold on no more. And he'd died. Just like that. He remembered it perfectly: He heard the sound of a helicopter, then voices. He felt strong hands. As his relief at being rescued swelled, the mental scaffolding that had kept him conscious for more than three days suddenly imploded, and he passed gently away.

Later, they told him he'd been clinically dead for almost six straight minutes. Six minutes—gone. And when he came to again in a hospital bed, everyone gathered around him and called him a lucky son of a bitch—as if anything about two broken legs and a wrecked face was lucky. *We've got a saying,* one of the orderlies told him. *A guy's not dead unless he's warm and dead. You, my friend, were definitely not warm.* Apparently, the cold temperatures that had nearly killed him had also saved his brain when his heart finally gave out.

Six minutes you were on the other side, his buddies said with admiration. *What was it like?* Sam half recalled making a joke about asking St. Peter for directions, to get the guys off his back. But what he did not tell them was that even though the doctors had claimed Sam was well on his way to a full recovery, some part of him secretly feared that his real self was still caught in that dark, cold place that he couldn't fully remember or forget. He had not, in fact, revived in the helicopter, as everyone said. Yes, he looked like he was a living, breathing guy. He could eat, sleep, and piss with the rest of them. But he felt *more* certain of the fact that some part of him was still high up on the frozen mountain than he was certain of being alive. His ego, his heart, his soul—whatever word a person could scrounge to talk about fundamental self—had been lost to him like Peter Pan losing his shadow. And it was cruel that the part of him that remained couldn't stop longing for the part of him that was gone.

Now Olivia was looking at him like he was somehow dangerous to her—he couldn't fathom it. She wasn't afraid, but she was wary. He felt like he needed to excuse his request to spend some time with her, as if he'd asked for some outrageously intimate favor instead of just a chat. He said, "I just thought we could, you know, catch up. But if you don't have time, that's fine. It's not a big deal. Just a thought. Spur of the moment. You know. Just for . . . for old times' sake."

"I . . . I only have a few minutes."

"A few minutes is perfect. I only have a few minutes, too."

"I guess we could go look at one of my gardens. I think . . . maybe you'll like it."

"Yes. Let's do it. Lead the way."

They wound the twists and turns of the hedge maze. He passed garden rooms he recognized and rooms he did not. The maze unfurled and kinked and unfurled again before him, green walls running parallel and even, running before him and alongside, and he had to walk quickly to keep up with her. It was so familiar. He'd dreamed of the garden maze a thousand times since he'd been away from Green Valley. In his mind, brick alleyways had transformed themselves into the maze's straight reaches. Politic bronze statues in city parks morphed into memories of the Marble Garden, with its classical nude figures draped in diaphanous stone garments and posed for maximum erotic appreciation. And now he was in the maze again. It had changed over the years; he no longer knew the byways and shortcuts. But the fantastical, fundamental character of it had not changed and did not disappoint him. In the sky, near the edges of the tree line that peeped over the top of the hedges, he thought he spotted the slightest gathering of clouds. *Maybe,* he thought. *Maybe today it will rain.*

"Keep up, slowpoke," Olivia said, laughing a little. "If you lose me, you might never find your way out."

There would be worse things, he thought. He followed her into a room at the edge of the maze that he'd never seen before. The space was perfectly circular, trimmed green hedges tall and straight on all sides, so the effect was like standing inside a vase open to the sky. But the room was empty. No shrubs, no flowers, no benches. Just perfect green grass, even and thick, that carpeted the ground in a flat circle like a pie chart. A hole in the hedges led to the outside, an exit from the maze. But there was nowhere to get out of the sun.

Sam put up a hand to shade his eyes. "This isn't really the kind of thing I had in mind."

"No?"

"I was hoping for something with a little more UV protection."

Olivia grinned. "Well then. I hope you're not claustrophobic."

She walked into the middle of the plain, grassy circle. Then she bent down and plucked up what seemed to be a brass ring. As she pulled, a hidden door groaned open like the cover of a heavy book. Olivia carefully let the door drop until it was flat on the ground, the undersides of old wooden boards exposed now to the sun.

A rectangular stone stairway had been sunk sharply into the middle of the grassy circle. It descended into the ground, its terminus obscured by shadow.

"We usually keep it open all day long," Olivia said, brushing dirt from her hands. "But not when it's this hot." She walked a few steps down into the earth, and it looked like she was walking into a grave. Her smile as she glanced up at him was friendly and yet somehow, it made her more opaque. "Coming?"

He nodded and followed her down the stone stairs.

It took a moment for his eyes to adjust. He was standing in a square, small, low-ceilinged room like a root cellar. It smelled of things wet and sweetly rotting, fallen logs and moss. He guessed the room was made of cinder blocks.

At first he saw nothing. But then, little by little, he noticed the mushrooms. They were scattered like families of river stones along the ground. They billowed like giant eggs in the corners. They climbed the walls. When Sam's eyes had fully softened to the darkness, he saw that the mushrooms emitted the faintest, ethereal phosphorescence, like pinholes of green glowing against a dark canvas. They were everywhere, odd flowers of alien light blooming through the chthonic murk, casting a faint green shadow on darkness itself. He was looking down at the bowels of the earth, but he was seeing stars.

"Do you like it?" Olivia asked softly.

Around him, the spongy darkness seemed to breathe bright electric green and to glow as if it had been filled with embers of green coals. Only Olivia could have had the vision to understand how a cave full of fungus could be so transcendent.

He tried to control his excitement. But he'd always loved mushrooms. Other boys had loved dinosaurs and trains and professional sports: He had loved mushrooms. He loved that they were such alien little things—shy, fast-growing, unique. His amateur interest had managed to stay strong for his first few years out of Green Valley. But eventually, like so many fading passions, his love for mushrooms became little more than a passing interest.

Now he was surrounded by mushrooms, all of them phosphorescent, and he had to control his breathing. He had not remembered how much he loved them, and seeing them again, his old friends, was like encountering his younger, happier self—disorienting and exhilarating at the same time.

"Is that . . . foxfire?" he asked.

"Yes," she said softly.

"And jack-o'-lanterns?"

"You got it."

"When did you get to be such a show-off?" he said, making light of the whole thing because if he didn't, he might begin to gush and emote like a ten-year-old boy.

"I think of it more like stretching my creative muscles."

"This isn't stretching. This is horticultural contortionism. How did you . . . ? How is this possible?" He bent to look more closely and smelled the strong odor of decaying wood. He reached out to touch it, but could not feel its dampness or cold. "How did you do it?"

"It's not me. It's the valley."

"It's a little you." He stood up again and looked at her. "A lot."

"So you do like it?" she asked. It was the first hint of vulnerability he'd heard in her voice.

"It's incredible," he said. Ages ago—a lifetime ago—they had talked about making a garden of mushrooms together, back when they'd been naïve enough to believe that he, and she, and all of Green Valley would never change. In the back of his mind, he thought: Was it overly hedonistic of him to wonder if perhaps she'd made the Mushroom Garden *for* him, that she'd meant for him to see it someday if he ever returned, and that perhaps she'd been thinking about him as the years went by, even when he'd been thinking of her?

Of course, there was no way to ask. Not without admitting he'd thought of her a lot, too—and he wasn't quite prepared to do that with this cold and distant version of *his* Olivia.

"Do you . . . ?" She gestured toward shapes in the dark. "Do you mind if we sit?"

"Feet hurt?"

"Feet, and . . . other things," she admitted. "*Every* thing. The farm's been busy."

"I bet. I wasn't back in the valley for five minutes before I heard people gushing about your strawberries," he said. He saw her cross the shadows; he could track the motion by the way her body blinked out the spotty green glow as she moved. Apparently, some of the mushrooms were not mushrooms at all, but poured stone garden stools that looked like mushrooms. He chose to sit on the seat nearest to her, and he did not fail to notice that she leaned slightly away.

He asked her about the farm: He thought it was a safe topic. She talked about the day a hailstorm had ruined all her lettuces, slicing them to pieces as efficiently as any food processor; about how she'd swept the produce awards last year at the Sullivan County fair, winning in every category she entered. She seemed happiest when she was talking about her vegetables. But she also talked a lot about a man, Tom, and Sam felt an entirely unjustified pang of irritation.

"And who *is* Tom?" he asked.

"Oh right. I hired an AFM. A manager. He's great. He oversees my crew, handles the farmers' markets and the subscribers, soil management, and a whole bunch of other things besides—marketing, making sure we're within regulations, deliveries, everything. He's really good with people, too. Everybody likes him. Frees me up to spend more of my time with the boarders, working in the maze."

"And what about your father?" he asked.

"Good. He's good."

"Just good?"

"Yeah. Just good. The same."

Okay, he thought. *Arthur is off-limits. Fine.* "And what about Roger the snow leopard? And David Bowie?"

Olivia laughed, and Sam felt a small charge of triumph to see a spark of green-tinged light in her eye. After Alice's death, Arthur Pennywort had amassed a number of strange hobbies that Alice never would have allowed. The Professor—who had earned his nickname for his constant indulgence in "experiments"—appreciated the artistry of a predator preserved at the height of predation. The more savage the beast, the better—panthers with long yellow teeth and sharp-hooked claws, wolverines with beady black eyes and twisted snarls. In short, he liked things with built-in biological weaponry.

But if Sam had ever felt afraid of the dead-eyed beasts as a child, it was only in the way that a person fears a ghost story or a nightmare—things not real. He and Olivia were fascinated by the menagerie, with its undercurrent of impotent threats. They named the stealthy snow leopard Roger and the silently screeching owl over the mantel David Bowie. Arthur encouraged them. For Easter, he put pink bunny ears on the bust of Cesare Maximus, the ferocious man-eating brown bear. And for one whole summer, Roger wore neon sunglasses, a plastic lavender lei, and a Hawaiian shirt. The day the elementary school teacher asked the class to bring in favorite stuffed animals was epic in Green Valley lore.

"The taxidermies are still here," she said. "In the farmhouse. But I don't live there anymore. I moved into the silo."

"Why?" he asked.

"I just wanted to."

Sam couldn't see her face to read it. Her eyes picked up the dragon-green glow of the mushrooms, lending a fairy glint to her pupils. She was as beautiful and fearsome as a stone angel, otherworldly and remote. "I'm glad the farm's doing so well."

"Me, too."

"And it's good to hear Arthur's still the same."

"He is."

"But what about you?"

He could tell from the tilt of her head that she was puzzled. "What do you mean?"

"How are you doing?"

She laughed. "You must have dozed off for a while there. I've been talking about myself for ten minutes straight."

"You've been talking about the farm. I'm asking about *you*."

She raised a shoulder, half a shrug.

"What's your life like? Is it what you wanted?"

"Sure," she said. "Why wouldn't it be?"

He wanted to sigh. She was acting obtuse—and he knew it. He adjusted his perch on the concrete mushroom and wondered about Tom, if she was seeing him or if she wanted to. One of her knees was bouncing: Was she impatient? Nervous? A pale scrim of light lay on the surface of her skin, painting green on her bare shoulder like the glow of the sun on a half-dark earth, carving a green shadow beneath her jaw. Sam felt as if a thousand green eyes were scrutinizing him, nightmarish but beautiful in the gloom.

"You didn't bring a lot of stuff with you," Olivia said, glancing at him. "When you moved in, I mean. I thought maybe you were just . . . checking up on the house. I didn't think you'd actually stay."

"I'm not going anywhere," he said.

And for the first time since he'd returned, he'd felt *sure* that he actually was going to stay, that being back in Green Valley was more than a temporary pit stop so he could put his life back together and move on. He felt the luminous green dark expanding within him, filling him up, green seeping in between the cells of his body, pushing them infinitesimally apart. And though the sensation was heady and not exactly pleasant, he welcomed it, courted it in the silence of his mind, because it had been so long since he'd felt anything, and this, this was *something*. Orpheus descending into Hades must have known this feeling, must have known hell by its eerie green mushrooms. Or maybe this wasn't Virgil's version of hell, but Dante's—with Olivia as Beatrice to guide him through the inferno, into the circle of punishment where a man was doomed to love the torture of being simultaneously near to and distant from a woman he wanted quite badly to know, a woman who looked so very touchable but whose smooth skin was completely wasted on him, a woman who was herself as luminous as foxfire and who even now was leaning slightly away. "Olivia—"

"What will you say in your report?" she asked. "You're going to tell them I'm not watering, right?"

He didn't answer immediately. Not because he didn't have an answer, but because he didn't like the question. "I'm not going to give you a hard time. Gloria does enough of that for all of us."

She smiled crookedly in the half dark. "I should get back to work."

"Right now?"

She laughed. "I told you I only had a few minutes. You can stay down here a little longer, if you want to. Just shut the door when you go."

She stood.

"I'll see you again," he said. "Now that we're neighbors."

"Seems like," she said. And that was all.

After she left, he stayed in the dark until it seemed to him the mushrooms had started to fade and so had his weird brain fever. (Olivia as Beatrice—*really*? Maybe the mushrooms gave off something less innocent than phosphorescent light.) He realized, now, that Olivia had not asked after his parents, or if he was married, or if he'd thought of her. She had not asked him anything, nor had she offered him anything of substance.

He got to his feet. There was magic in the maze, people said. Magic that gave inner clarity, that stripped away all the pretensions that a person fabricated around himself. He felt oddly shaky, light-headed, and strange. On Moggy Knob when he'd died, he'd given up on life in the most fundamental and complete way a man could. Then, when he'd found himself in the hospital—still very much living but unable to feel—he'd given up again, choosing Green Valley not because he meant to start anew but because he meant to quit. To return to Bethel, he had simply needed to stop resisting its pull, to give up fighting, and Green Valley simply absorbed him back into it, easily and naturally, like a tree that grows around and eventually engulfs a fence or pipe. In Green Valley, he could allow himself to be puppeted by normalcy, unfeeling and uninspired, and nobody would notice or care.

But then, in the garden maze, there was Olivia. And he realized that there was, to his surprise, something in Green Valley that was still interesting to him. Something that nudged him out of his stupor and made him want to actually *try*. He wanted to know more about her, this new Olivia who seemed both hardened and hesitant. He wanted it like he hadn't wanted anything in a long time. He did not expect that she might ever love him again—if she ever had loved him to begin with. And he wouldn't *want* her to love him—she deserved better. But the idea of getting to know her better, of drawing her out and discovering what it was that she so desperately guarded, *that* was a project that invigorated him. He would stay in Green Valley. He was back for good. He felt more clearheaded than he had in a long time.

He climbed the stairs out of the hidden garden, feeling oddly energized. Then he was outside in the blazing, antagonistic brightness of July, which was July in all its copious Julyness, baking the earth to powder under the sun.

In the Bud

any years ago when she was still alive, Olivia's mother had liked to tell her daughter a story: *Once upon a time, a woman and her husband longed for a child. But the woman grew older, and the man grew older, and they came to believe they would not have a family of their own. Then, one day, the woman happened upon a fairy splashing and frolicking in a valley stream. And in order to keep the woman from giving away the secret of her existence, the fairy agreed to give the woman a daughter in exchange for her silence.*

For many years the woman waited. She waited, until she decided she must have dreamed the whole thing. But then, one beautiful spring morning, she pulled up a clump of yellow dandelions only to discover the tiniest of human babies, curled up within the root ball and sweetly speckled with dark brown dirt. And she knew the fairy had not forgotten her after all.

Sometimes the story changed as it suited Olivia's mother's mood: The man and the woman found the baby in the hollow of a tree, in a fallen robin's nest among the blue eggs, in the closed bud of a peony after all the other flowers had bloomed. But always, the story had the same ending: The man and the woman were the Pennyworts, and the baby was Olivia, and they were very happy and surprised when she arrived.

Olivia had loved the stories—though it had been a moment of great embarrassment when in the third grade she realized that she had not in fact been found floating on a water lily, and that her appearance on the farm had more to do with what the geese and goats did in the springtime than with pixie dust or magical storms. But her mother had always insisted that the stories she'd told Olivia about her birth were the perfect truth, if not the *actual* truth, because they got to the fundamental moral of the story better than facts ever could: Of all the people in Green Valley, Olivia had been born special.

From the beginning, all types of flora had been drawn to her. Houseplants turned away from the sunlight to bend in the direction of her crib. A formerly well-behaved patch of Dutchman's-pipe had climbed up the side of the farmhouse to her nursery, where it plastered itself against the windowpane as if it wanted to reach in. Olivia's mother said she'd noticed all of this, but had decided that there was nothing menacing about the phenomenon, and if the plants wanted to be close to her little human miracle, she couldn't blame them.

Alice's ideas aside, Olivia did believe certain people were born gardeners, and she was one of them. She grew up playing with pill bugs and millipedes and butterflies in the furrows of her family's fields. She'd learned to wield a dibble for seeding before she'd learned to walk on two legs. She cried like the world was ending when her parents tried to bring her indoors even for a quick snack, and the instant they set her down in the weeds and grass she turned sunny once again.

When Olivia was barely four years old, her mother had set her up with a small raised garden behind the farmhouse, and Olivia had sat with her seedlings each morning and talked softly to them as if it were the most normal thing in the world to hold a conversation with a patch of peas. When the people of the Bethel hamlets came to the farm to pick up their produce, they exchanged glances with their eyebrows raised almost off the top of their heads. They stopped one another at christenings and bar mitzvahs to speculate: *What do you make of it?* they said. *Witchcraft? The Devil's curse? Dropped on her head?*

But Olivia herself had no idea that at four years old she'd already caused such a sandal. Her peas grew up their teepee so quickly that a person starting on a glass of fresh lemonade might see them climb a good inch by the time the last drop was gone. Her sunflowers shot up two stories high. For a time, Olivia had assumed that her experience with plants was typical. But as she became aware that the exclamations of garden visitors were not simply the obligatory phrases of adults giving praise, she came to understand that plants behaved differently in her care.

Of course, there were logical explanations—everybody knew Pennywort soil was the best in the valley, that it had been the best ever since the Concert had come to town. But Olivia had seen that when she gave any plant her attention, it flourished abnormally whether it was a tiny seedling or a half-dead peace lily brought from a neighbor as a gift. Her talents had limits; she could not single-handedly defeat drought, and there wasn't much she could do about floods or early frosts. But in general, the Pennywort fields fared better than others in the same area. And her secret garden—that was the most prolific garden of all.

On summer nights after sunset, she could sometimes be seen heading alone into the garden maze, where it was presumed she locked herself behind the gray stone walls for hours at a time. Some people said that once inside she transformed herself into an ugly old black bear—so that when garbage cans were raided and bird feeders were pulled down, old-timers were only half joking when they said it was Olivia Pennywort having her way. Others hypothesized that when she touched the enchanted soil of her garden she turned into a giant calla lily, and so she needed the earth of her garden the way Dracula needed to sleep on native soil. Still others said the Pennyworts weren't doing anything magical or supernatural behind their garden walls—except for growing a highly potent form of wormwood, which the reclusive old dingbat Arthur Pennywort had used to make such a powerful form of absinthe that his brain had turned a toxic, fairy green.

Wormwood and calla lilies aside, what Olivia grew in her garden had the distinction of being just as outrageous, if not *more* outrageous, than what people believed she grew. Her plants were the kind that unfailingly jarred mothers to tug their children's hands and warn them to *stay back, don't touch,* and *get away.* Some species were so rude that even the marauding, yellow-eyed goats of Green Valley—goats known to eat everything from newspaper to electrical cords—tended to avoid them. They were poison ivies and nightshades, stinging nettles and poison hemlocks, laurels and sumacs and doll's eyes. And on certain summer nights, Olivia slept the deep sleep of a child among them, the most dangerous, toxic, and itch-inducing plants of the rudest kind.

She took a heavy key from around her neck, opened the door to her garden, and slipped inside. The sun had set, but there was still some light in the sky, and her plants seemed to rustle in greeting. Olivia felt a change come over her, as it always did when she returned to her garden—a cellular ignition that made her feel both relaxed and energized. Green poison ivy crawled up the stone walls, writhing and twisting strand over strand. Climbing nightshade clung to a moon-shadowed trellis in dozens of brilliant purple droplets. In the soft dusk, her handful of red and orange poppies were as bright as if the sun were shining on their flared petals.

But for as dangerous as the poison garden was to the outside world, Olivia herself was far more dangerous than any one of her deadly plants. Unlike them, *she* had human desires.

She ran her hands along the top of her rhododendron. She could not—not for one moment—allow herself to think she could spend any more time with Sam. Nor could she let herself think that he would want to spend time with her, if he knew what she was. She needed daily exposure to her garden's miasma of various alkaloids in the same way that a normal person needed vitamin D from the sun. She was a freak, a monster—and if she ever forgot it, her garden called to her, claimed her, roped her back in. *Mine,* it seemed to whisper. And most of the time, Olivia whispered back: *Yes, I am.*

Tonight, however, she longed to see her garden set on fire, or plunged into a sinkhole, or hit with an asteroid. Tonight, she wanted something other than what she had.

It was Sam's fault, of course. The questioning. The wondering and wanting. She'd known him again immediately, even before he'd turned around. He was taller than she might have expected him to be. He had a kind of poetic and not unattractive slouch, thin for his frame. His jaw was of average prominence above his big Adam's apple, his eyebrows were not too thick, and his nose was straight and good-sized. His hair, so black it was almost blue, was buzzed close to his head, and it made his robin's-egg eyes stand out in a way that made her think he'd seen things in life that he wished he hadn't. The Sam she'd remembered was frenetic with all the energy of a young boy; the new Sam moved slowly now, as if underwater or carrying some invisible new weight within his bones.

She'd met Sam when she was six and he was eight; he and his parents had moved from a house over in Briscoe to Green Valley. One afternoon Sam had shouted to her from across the road, his toes daring the edge of the pavement: "Hey! Hey you!

Can I come over?" He'd been wearing a shirt with a toadstool on it, *Amanita muscaria,* he told her proudly. And she knew they would be friends.

When they were very young, they'd played the way so many Green Valley children played—wildly, without supervision, their imaginations leading them to build kingdoms and exotic lands in the Catskill hillsides. She'd felt perfectly in sync with him: She was fascinated with the world of plants, and his personal fascination was with fungi. Where they were different, they complemented each other. The hard work of farm life meant that Olivia prized efficiency above perfection, practicality above precision. Sam, on the other hand, would get frustrated and even a little obsessive if the kite they were building together did not meet his exact specifications. Olivia knew when to leave him alone to work out his desire for absolute accuracy and when to give him a nudge toward a more practical approach, saying, *The only thing that matters is that it gets up in the air.*

Growing up, he was part of her family, as fundamental to her life as the fields and trees of the farm. She expected it would be that way forever between them, easy and effortless as breathing air. But then one autumn day when she was fifteen, Sam had wrapped his arms around her waist and picked her up—he was thrilled that they'd just found a dainty white destroying-angel mushroom growing in Chickadee Woods—and the world went spinning in many ways. He twirled her around, she held on to his neck, the trees blurred, the wind gave one great, sweeping gust that kicked up the leaves beneath them, and in that moment, everything changed. He put her down and blushed hotly red. He excused himself abruptly and went home. At night in her bedroom in the farmhouse, she revisited the strangeness of his chest, so firm and flat compared to hers. They were not the same. Not at all.

Two years ago, she'd made the Mushroom Garden in the maze for him. They'd always talked about creating a garden of all mushrooms, but fungi had never been Olivia's specialty. Mushrooms lived in a different scientific kingdom than green and leafy plants, and she had a more difficult time connecting with them. She also suspected that she was not immune to their poisons due to a lack of exposure—though she had not tested the theory. In spite of her arm's-length relationship with fungi, Olivia told herself two years ago that she would make the Mushroom Garden for Sam not because she was still thinking of him, but because she had completely let him go. She did not expect to ever see him again.

But then, there he was. Today. In her maze.

She picked a pretty baneberry and popped it into her mouth, not worrying about how its toxins could stop a person's heart. Her mind was spinning—and for once not even the garden could make it slow down. There was no point in asking questions: Would Sam come see her again? And—what would she do if he did? For his sake, could she act more indifferent toward him than she felt?

She heard a noise near the door of her poison garden and she turned her head. But she didn't panic. Maybe some animal was in the maze with her. A squirrel? A goat?

The knob began to turn.

Definitely not a goat.

She lunged without thinking; the door was opening slowly, but Olivia managed to slam it closed. She held tight to the handle so it couldn't turn. A woman on the other side exclaimed, "Oh!"

Olivia held the handle. "Who's there?"

"Olivia?"

"Who are you?"

"It's me. Mei."

Olivia felt the moment Mei stepped away from the door because the handle went loose in her fingers. Her heart was beating madly, her breath was fast. "What are you looking for, Mei?"

There was a beat of silence. "Oh. Oh my gosh. I'm sorry. Is *this* the garden I'm not supposed to go in?"

"Yes," Olivia said tightly. A line of sweat had broken out on her brow.

"I'm so sorry. I didn't realize."

"It's okay," Olivia said, but she didn't take her hand off the knob. She supposed it wasn't impossible that Mei would absentmindedly open the door of her walled garden, in spite of all the warning signs. She wouldn't be the first woman to wander the maze without really paying attention.

When Mei spoke, her voice was soft. "Actually . . . I'm kind of glad you're here. I'm glad I found you."

"What do you need?"

Even from behind a stone wall and solid wood door, Olivia could hear Mei sigh. "It's just that . . . Well—I've been walking the maze, like you said. Walking and walking and walking. But nothing's *happening*. I'm wondering what I'm doing wrong."

"You mean, you've been walking in the maze all day? You haven't stopped since you got here?"

"Isn't that what you told me to do?"

"Oh Mei. I'm sorry. Just—just hold on." Olivia turned the handle. Normally she might not risk opening the door to the poison garden with another person around. But Mei sounded so forlorn. Olivia eased the garden door open only enough to let herself through, so that not an inch of her plants could be accidentally seen. Mei was sitting on a bench made of fallen and twisted branches. Olivia sat beside her. "I'm sorry the maze didn't give you an answer today. Sometimes it just isn't possible to rush these things."

Mei said nothing for a while. "Did you get your answer?"

"My answer?"

"Isn't that what you were doing in there?"

Olivia glanced at the walls behind them. "Oh. No. I was just . . . relaxing."

"Is that your private garden?"

Olivia nodded.

"Why can't anyone go in?"

"Sometimes a person just needs her own space. To get away."

Mei frowned. "I can understand that."

"Do you need to get away?"

Mei glanced at her. Her eyes were dark and shiny. Her features were small, her skin a creamy olive, her lips a natural plum. All the toughness and bravado she'd shown earlier in the day when she'd been locked in the peacock pen was gone now, making her appear small and fragile and much younger than her age.

"It's okay," Olivia said. "You don't have to tell me unless you want to. I'm here to listen, whenever you need. But the maze . . . you've just got to give it time."

"How much time?"

"I can't say. But you're welcome to stay here as long as you want to, Mei. For however long it takes until you're ready to decide what you want to do."

Mei looked at her feet. "Thanks."

Olivia could feel the garden at her back, calling to her. She did her best to ignore it. "Why don't you go into the barn for the night? Don't worry—the others are very nice. A little rough around the edges sometimes, but they'll set you up with something to eat and a place to sleep. And they won't ask any questions."

Mei stood. She was looking at Olivia now, speculation in her eye. "You actually seem pretty nice."

"Is that not what you expected?"

"I don't know. I guess—I guess I didn't expect you to actually seem nice."

Olivia couldn't hide a small frown. She knew people talked about her. A lot. But she didn't think her character had ever been in question.

Mei rubbed her eyes. "You know what? I'm sorry. I think you're right. I need to stop walking. I need to get off my feet."

"Can you find your way out to the barn?"

"Well, I guess if I could find my way into this mess, I can find my way out of it, too."

Olivia smiled. "I don't think you'll end up waiting for your answer for too long."

"Thanks," Mei said.

When the girl was gone, Olivia let herself back into the poison garden. She had a sense, sometimes, that it had its own awareness of her, an expectation, so that when she opened the door and closed it behind her, the garden seemed to sigh, *Ah! There you are!*

She picked the leaf of a stinging nettle and felt its furry skin against her skin. Normally she could keep her desire for a different kind of life at bay; but the world was conspiring against her tonight. There was Sam, with his hesitant smile and all of his unbearable, unanswerable questions. There was Mei, her difficulty as obvious as her belly, her solution, not. There were all the people of Green Valley, everyone she had to keep away.

In ancient stories, Daphne was turned into a laurel tree to escape Apollo, and Olivia wished sometimes that the gods would do the same thing to her, turn her into a quiet stand of nightshade, or a stalk of meadow deathcamas, or even a toxic pink laurel—and let her live out her days as plants did, simply *being* without questioning, without the unceasing self-flagellation that comes with the human condition, the *why me?* and *why this?* and *what now?*

But, human she was, and so she couldn't shake her human loneliness, or the feeling of her heart being squeezed inside her chest for some reason she didn't want to think about. She took in a deep breath of wet air. The valley was silent; even the night creatures were still. Pink bundles of oleander, gorgeous and bitterly toxic, clustered softly. She was safe here: She had to remind herself of that. No one could see her; no one could touch her; she didn't need a thing but what she had. She checked to be sure that the door was locked. Then she slid out of her clothes, lowered herself into the bower of her belladonna, and dozed contentedly among her poisonous plants.

Touch Wood

When the Woodstock music festival charged like gang-busters to the vicinity of Green Valley in 1969, many things changed, but no individual person had changed more than Arthur Pennywort. All these many years later, there were still folks in Bethel who could talk about the Arthur everyone knew before the Concert and the Arthur everyone knew after. As for the man himself, he'd expected the Concert to be a nuisance; he had not expected it to be the seminal event of his life.

He was thirty-eight when he first caught wind of the grumbles about some music festival that got booted out of one distant town only to set a trajectory for his little corner of the world. Before the Concert, Arthur had been what most people in Green Valley had considered a "lost cause," which was to say he had been a solitary, know-it-all bachelor for so long that it would be impossible for him to be anything but a solitary know-it-all bachelor going on.

But he hadn't set out in life to be that way. When he was a young boy, working the Pennywort lands with his father at his side, he'd forged a vision of himself as a gentleman farmer, the kind of lost-breed, American renaissance man who mixed his own ink for his pens, who had a library full of dog-eared books of the Western canon, who felt deep affection for his quietly brilliant and unfailingly supportive wife, who drank the best wines, who broke new ground regarding natural digestion aids, who wrote lengthy and elegant essays on husbandry, who was invited to speak at lecture halls about his innovations, and who did all these elegant things with cow manure under his nails.

But by the time the Concert came around in his late thirties, his parents were dead and he'd fully given up on his dreams. Nobody cared for gentleman farmers. His produce was acceptable, but not great. His essays didn't get published. The only place he'd ever lectured was the local library, and the only reason he had an audience was that a high school ag teacher had forced students to attend. He was terribly constipated no matter how much bran he suffered through—no miracle discoveries of digestion health for him. And, worst of all, he'd lost his sense of wonder. The brilliant and supportive wife he dreamed of might as well have come out of a magic lamp.

Then, the Concert happened—which was to say, the *people* attending the concert happened. For most of the long history of Green Valley, the land had known more cattle than humans, and at any given moment during the growing season there was more food attached to root systems than was in all the local supermarkets combined. While other Bethel hamlets regularly courted the summer rusticators who came in their station wagons and RVs to soak up the fading glory of the Borscht Belt, Green Valley was merely a rolling collection of sleepy hills that people passed through on their way to somewhere else. Arthur and his neighbors liked it that way.

Like everyone during the summer of '69, Arthur had known what was coming. And he'd known it was going to be trouble. He'd stopped buying Yasgur's milk to demonstrate his disapproval— and sense of betrayal—that one of his own would be willing to violate the sanctity of the land by inviting so many longhairs in to party. He'd never liked hippies, with their goofy, progressive ideas, and their slurred ideologies, and their lyrics that got up in a person's face and tried to tell him how to live. And he'd never liked loud music, either. Or drugs. Or people who couldn't see that peace—the ubiquitous, doe-eyed, goobery kind of peace that everybody was going on about—could only be achieved with force sometimes.

But more than that, he found that everything he'd hated about his life—his parents' deaths from working their bodies as hard as they'd worked their land, his failed dreams of scholarship, his loneliness over the woman who was supposed to have shown up in his life but never had—all of his angry disappointment had found its voice when he became the elected leader of the Green Valley League for Common Sense, which had formed to try to keep the Concert out of the area. It was only when he began organizing petitions and marches, talking to lawyers and giving rousing speeches held in his front yard, that all his book smarts and bitterness gelled and he finally made sense to himself. It wasn't until many years later that he understood it was far more difficult for a man to understand what he stood *for* than what he stood against.

By the time he and his neighbors realized that they would not be able to stop the hippies from descending on their farmland like a plague of locusts, Arthur had solidified his place as one of the most respected men of his generation, and the last of a dying breed. The Van Winkle policemen and firemen and nurses leaned on his porch rails in the evenings to vent their frustrations, and they talked with him as if he had the wisdom of Solomon in his bones.

As the Concert grew close, Arthur prepared. He loaded his shotgun with fine corn kernels—because of course he didn't want to kill anybody, but he wouldn't accept trespassers ruining his beds of lettuce and mucking up his potatoes. He blocked off his driveway with fifty-five-gallon drums and battened down the hatches of his farm stand.

When the kids arrived—he called them *kids* because he felt so very ancient then himself—it was as bad as he'd thought it would be. They sped through Green Valley, music blaring, hanging out the windows of their psychedelic vans and howling like demons. Little groups or individuals in all kinds of bizarre dress and undress would walk their slow, backward walk down the road with their thumbs raised. When the traffic backed up to a standstill, the hoodlums just left their cars in the middle of the road and made an indecent parade of themselves in their moccasins and macramé, their feathers and fringe, singing at the top of their lungs. Once, he'd had to warn a handful of sky-high kids in camo not to eat the flowers on the side of the road—and though they didn't know it, he'd saved them from ingesting deadly poison hemlock. The kids had thanked him as if he'd done no more than point out a pretty flower. For five nights, Arthur kept vigil sitting on the fence beside his fields, his shotgun balanced on his thighs and his fingers itching as the throngs walked by.

Sometimes, in those lonely hours, he struggled with the ache of his own curiosity. The kids seemed so at ease in their bodies, so . . . content. He did not hide his contempt for them as they flowed past his house like a throng of refugees—and yet, instead of calling him names they flashed him peace signs. They walked with their arms around one another, laughing or singing or both. To join them would have been as easy as throwing himself bodily into the current of a river and allowing himself to be swept along. But of course, his buttoned-up personal dignity wouldn't hear of it. He sat on his fence all those long nights, eyeing the revelers, smoldering inside his skin.

After the festival ended, quiet had returned to the valley, but it was an eerie quiet—the kind of scrubbed-clean silence that comes after a violent storm. Arthur expected life to return to normal. But on the third morning after the Concert, a cicada fell from a tree branch and landed on his shoulder with a quick, short tap that made him turn to see if someone was standing behind him.

And someone was. One of his workers alerted him that a person was sleeping in the barn. He was instantly, blazingly angry, so angry that he'd retied one of his shoes so tight it cut off the circulation. But what he found was not the drugged-up draft dodger he'd expected; it was Alice. Sleeping in some roughed-up hay. She looked like a cross between a young street orphan and an angel. Her short dress was like it had been sewn of patched-together handkerchiefs, and it dropped so low in the back that it showed the sweet, catlike curve of her spine. Her hair, teased into an impressive dark corona of an Afro, was clumped with sticks and mud.

She opened her eyes and blinked up at him, languid as a jungle cat. He'd waited for her to say something like *Oh, I'm sorry I know I'm trespassing.* Or *I swear I was just leaving.* But instead, she smiled a little, stretched her arms, and said, *Hey, Daddy-o, you got anything to drink?* And he knew he was a goner.

That evening, she'd asked if she might stay in his barn for a few days, because she'd lost track of the friends who had brought her from California, and she thought his barn was *groovy* and *kind of hip* in a way. Arthur had told the girl he was a scientist, and she believed him. Nobody had ever believed him, because of course there had never been even a kilogram of proof that Arthur had a scientist's brain or training. But Alice had always been a skeptic when it came to proof. She only stayed one more night in the barn. And the rest of her nights, until the day she died, she'd spent with him.

Gradually, Green Valley began to put itself back together after the Concert—people carting truckloads of garbage that littered the roadsides, and birds cautiously considering whether to return to their nests. But Arthur could see that his home would never be the same again. Something had happened. Something was fundamentally changed.

After the Concert, the night was brighter in Green Valley than it was anywhere else in the Catskills, so that a person could read a book by the moon when it was only the barest crescent. The birds in the valley began to sing such intricate and virtuosic songs that scientists with recorders and binoculars started to come from miles around, enraptured by avian talent. The soil, too, changed: The inexhaustible rain that had drenched so many concertgoers and coated them in suits of mud had lent the earth new fertility, and the valley quickly became renowned for its vegetables and fruits.

The Concert had worked its magic on Green Valley, and Alice had worked her magic on him. He began to see the world as more than just a collection of facts; he forgave his parents for so doggedly instilling in him the idea that life was about work, and that work was drudgery, and that happiness was not an acceptable life goal. He resigned from the League for Common Sense, for he no longer saw anything particularly admirable in too much levelheadedness. He fell in love with his life, as if a faded curtain had been drawn back and revealed Green Valley in all its magnificent colors, and the hopes of his boyhood returned.

As for his wife, she'd seemed to be broken in some way when he first met her, but every day on the farm seemed to make her stronger. She called herself a gypsy; Arthur had never been fully sure if this meant she was of gypsy blood or merely gypsy mentality. She mentioned an abusive father who was a descendant of freed slaves and a mother who read palms and talked wearily of suicide at least once a day. She had always wanted a maze garden, and for their first wedding anniversary, Arthur had staked out an acre of land in the front of the farm and said: *For you.* Within a year, the maze had started taking shape. Each day she watered and planted, and each night she worked with an artist's coiled energy to design new garden rooms. Rumors began to circulate that the maze was clarifying, that it helped a person make up her mind, and the garden rooms themselves seemed to harbor their own subtle enchantments. Eventually the work got to be more than Alice could handle on her own. And so, one summer when she found a woman crying in the Supplicant's Garden, she told the woman she could stay in the old barn that Arthur was about to tear down—the barn that she had such fond memories of sleeping in—and for payment, all the woman needed to do was work a little with Alice on the maze. The woman agreed. By the next summer, the barn was teeming with visitors and the maze was a thing people came to see from miles around. The gardens grew wilder and wilder, as if they had intentions of their own.

The Green Valley farm became the Pennyworts' joint project, tucked low in the folds of the hills. Arthur and Alice were building their own world with their own rules and whimsies, a place where they had complete and perfect mastery and did not have to adhere to other people's ideas for their lives. If people had ever scoffed at them or condemned them for their vision, or if they shunned them because his family had been white and Jewish and hers was neither of those things, they were too in love to notice or care. Arthur reapplied himself to working his fields, to pushing himself to create the best growing conditions that he could, and the soil rewarded him bounteously. Many years passed and it seemed they would not be able to have a child, but then, finally, Olivia arrived pink-faced and wriggling on the farm, and their family was complete.

When Arthur thought back to the man he'd been before, he saw a pessimist who'd proclaimed that the Concert would ruin life in Green Valley as he knew it. And he'd turned out to be right. The Concert had obliterated everything he thought he knew about the world in the best way possible. Alice had opened his eyes. She told him: *It's not where you're born that defines you; it's where you're reborn.*

Now, from outside his shack in Solomon's Ravine, Arthur had a sense that Green Valley was changing again, in some way that was unseen and immeasurable and not good. Even the animals of Solomon's Ravine could feel it. His sparrows—which he'd been attempting to train as homing pigeons to prove that all animals had a sixth sense—had stopped singing abruptly, their throats parched by drought. For three days now he'd got a coppery taste on his tongue each time the wind blew from the east. And then there was the goat. It wasn't a pet, exactly, because it had shown up in Solomon's Ravine two years ago and attached itself to Arthur's side, so that Arthur sometimes thought that the goat considered him a pet, not the other way around. But at any rate, the goat could feel it, too—the strangeness. He kept staring at Arthur with an eerie look in his yellow eyes, as if to say, *Are you going to do something about this, or am I?*

He needed to warn Olivia, to point out the signs. All morning he listened for his daughter, since there was nothing else to listen to apart from the chatter of chipmunks and the wheezy gray squirrels in the trees. He knew the moment she'd started to make her way down the fern-spotted slope by the sound of rocks tumbling to the ravine floor.

"Hello?" Olivia called as she walked. "Hello? Where are my two old goats?"

The goat, which had never been given a name, got to its hooves and went bounding toward Olivia. She reached down to pet the wiry white hair between its brown horns. Unlike humans, goats were not allergic to the particular chemical makeup of Olivia's skin, and Arthur sometimes suspected that if the beast would only follow Olivia up the side of the ravine one day, she would be more than happy to spoil him rotten. But, of course, the dumb animal didn't know what was good for it, and it remained at Arthur's side in the ravine's murky gloom.

Arthur got up from the rock where he'd been sitting and pondering the world as it went by. His bones ached with age. "At last!" he cried. "Olivia! Come—look at this!"

He motioned for her to follow. With the goat between them nipping at Olivia's cotton skirt, they walked down to the streambed. One little meandering finger of water hobbled down the center of the rocky bed. "Look," he said.

Olivia bent toward a patch of moss growing on the side of an old tree. It was called British soldier, red-tipped and uniform as its colonial namesake. She stood. "So?"

"So . . ." He shook his hands in front of him. "So? It's on the wrong side of the tree."

She stared at him blankly.

"Something's coming," he told her. "We have to be careful."

Had she been a different woman she might have patted him on the back to reassure him. Instead, she adjusted her bag. "Have you been doing nothing but waiting for me all day?"

"What time is it?"

"Two."

"Then, no."

"Good."

"I couldn't have been waiting for you *all* day, because all day hasn't passed yet."

The goat head-butted her leg and she reached down to scratch it. "I just don't know how you put up with him."

"I don't know, either."

"I was talking to the goat," she said.

Arthur laughed; he was glad to see her smiling.

He followed her as best he could over the blue, shadow-speckled rocks along the streambed and back toward his shack. Solomon's Ravine was a shady swath of bottomland that cut a jagged interruption through the center of the Pennywort property. It was inaccessible to all but the most intrepid of intruders. Arthur's two-room hovel hunkered at the flat, narrow bottom of the ravine, so organic and ramshackle that unless a person passing through happened to know where to look, the structure was virtually invisible to the naked eye, perfectly blended with the tumbled bluestone rocks, poplars, and elms around it. Only the occasional curl of smoke catching in the high green canopy suggested to the people of Green Valley that some fire-making animal lived in the gorge.

Arthur himself had the same kind of natural camouflage as his home—an air of organic dereliction that made him blend in. His natty gray beard caught cockleburs in the summer and frost in the winter, his floppy hat was the mottled white and brown of an old-man-of-the-woods mushroom, and he rarely smelled better than the tiny green carrion flowers that bloomed not far from his shack in early June. His skin had an undeniable greenish tint that only augmented his green eyes; people said he had spent so much time beneath the diffused light of the canopy that his skin had taken on the color, absorbed it, the same way that a person turns brown and spotty if he stays too long in the sun.

Olivia was walking a bit faster than Arthur. He watched as she sat down on one of the large, spotty rocks that marked his front door and pulled her bag onto her lap. The goat was at her feet, waiting for a treat. She retrieved a bruised potato and began to feed him, petting him all the while.

"Olivia," Arthur said, joining her on the rocks when he caught up. "You've got to listen to me."

"I'm listening, Professor."

"No, you're not. You're not listening."

She looked at him with put-on patience as the goat ate a carrot noisily out of her hand. "Dad. I'm listening. I can do two things at once."

"The mushrooms. And the wind? Hear it?"

"I don't hear anything."

"Exactly."

She sighed. "How's your hand?"

He frowned down at it. "The splinters?"

She nodded.

Yesterday when she'd come, she brought latex gloves so she could tweeze a half dozen splinters out of his palm. He'd got them from tripping and falling face-first on a rotting nurse log, but he'd told her they were from running his hand over the side of his shack. "Much better. No problems at all."

"Why don't we see what I brought for you today?"

She handed him the contents of her bag one item at a time: a new book of crossword puzzles; a knob of bread and hunk of cheese in foil; the batteries he needed for his radio; a cylinder of propane; two jars of peanut butter; a box of 12-gauge shotgun shells; and a handful of new pipettes, because he always broke them. Thanks to Olivia, he got along well enough in the ravine: He had a propane stove for cooking, a woodstove for heat, an outhouse, and a bubbling, natural spring. He also had Olivia, his only visitor, supporter, and friend.

"What about the glycerin?" he asked.

"It hasn't come yet."

"Oh, baloney."

"Language, Dad."

He looked at her and she smiled.

"What do you even need glycerin for?"

"What I always need things for."

"Right—right. An experiment. But what kind of experiment?"

"It's for soap. I'm making soap."

"You have soap."

"I'm making new soap. Or, I would be, if I had the glycerin."

"If you moved back into the farmhouse, you would know the moment it arrived," Olivia said.

Arthur raised his hands and dropped them. "Olivia. My love. Daughter. My moving into that old house is the *least* important thing when there's moss growing on the wrong side of a tree."

"We can have the house open for you again in half a day. And you would know the moment something you were waiting for came in the mail."

"And if I moved back in, where would the mice go?"

"I don't know . . . Disneyland?"

He smiled and shook his head.

"Dad, the questions you ask . . . I don't know where you come up with this stuff."

Arthur said nothing. Olivia was a good daughter, the best daughter a father could ask for. She'd been so young when Alice died that Arthur was sure she would grow up to have very little maternal instinct. He knew her memories of Alice were spotty. And yet, even though Olivia's time with her mother had been short, Arthur saw so much of Alice in her—not necessarily in her look, but her nature. Almost as soon as Alice was gone, Olivia had started taking care of him, first in childish ways—like offering her favorite stuffed animal—then later on in more adult ways, like pulling a chair over to the stove so she could reach it to make him a grilled cheese, or always knowing where his slippers were when he'd misplaced them. He'd seen so many fellow farming couples, husbands and wives, die in pairs: first one, then the other within a year—an accident, a heart attack, a freak cold. After Alice died, he was certain that Olivia's existence was what had kept him alive. She was his reason for going on—but she was also the reason he *could* go on. Even now, her visits to the ravine were all that sustained him.

She sat beside him, not speaking. He wondered for the first time since she'd arrived if something was on her mind. With Olivia, it was always difficult to tell.

He cleared his throat. "Anything going on?"

"What do you mean?"

"Out of the ordinary?"

"No. No. Not at all."

"All right," Arthur said.

They talked about the farm, the drought, ideas for new recipes. Then Olivia bent to give the goat a scratch on his white-bearded chin, and she got to her feet. Arthur did the same. "Well," she said. "If you don't need anything else . . ." She knocked twice on the tree trunk beside her. That meant *Love you.* He reached out and did the same. It wasn't a hug or a kiss, but it was something.

She smiled and started her climb out of the cool, dark shade of the ravine and into the bright hot sun. Already Arthur felt lonely without her. Ever since he had moved down into the ravine when she was sixteen years old—when they had realized she was poisonous—Olivia had been his only connection to the world. She had been patient with him, humored him, and tried to make him happy. She'd been his only source of joy since Alice had died. He simply didn't know what he would do without her. Unfortunately, thanks in part to her condition, he would never have to know. Olivia was as tied into the farm as the old Lightning Oak in Stony Field, as tied into the garden maze as any flowering plant, as much a part of the valley as the land itself.

Of course, it was Arthur's fault. The Poison Garden had been his idea. The potential for a garden of poisonous plants had been a small shot of excitement and adrenaline in the melancholy years that had followed Alice's death. He wanted a garden unlike any Green Valley had seen before; he thought a poison garden would be an experiment only a true genius could handle and appreciate. Plus, he'd had the perfect accomplice: Olivia. Her uncanny abilities with plants of all kinds—as well as her complete lack of allergic reactions to plant-based alkaloids— made her a perfect partner. Day in, day out, he sent her to work among the poisonous vines and flowers, not thinking of what the work might be doing to her. And she always went, uncomplaining, unquestioning, because *his* enthusiasm carried her along. When the garden got too big and too dangerous for him, he donned his "bio-protector suit" while Olivia went in barefoot and gloveless. It was only a few weeks after he'd realized what had happened to Olivia that he banished himself to the ravine.

Near the rise of the ravine walls, Olivia paused with her hand on the trunk of a tree. Her forehead was deeply creased. "Oh, I forgot to tell you."

He knew it; he knew there was something. He leaned forward.

"Sam Van Winkle's back in town."

It took a moment to place the name. But when his brain plugged into the proper circuitry that lit up his memory, he saw a milk-faced little boy with a dark buzz cut and a sincere but partially toothless smile.

"He's a cop," Olivia said.

Arthur took in a deep breath through his nostrils. "He's back for you, you know. He came back for you."

"Don't be silly, Dad," she said.

But Arthur knew it was true. He broke out into a cold, prickling sweat. It was an old feeling, full of vinegar and rot. He reminded himself he had no use for it anymore. The fear of losing Olivia was as fresh as it had been when she was sixteen. But he was stronger than his fear now. He would no longer allow it to master him. "Has Sam . . . been by to see you?"

"Yes."

"Because he's back for you."

"No. Because he stopped by on a call. Gloria again."

"What this time?"

"She thinks I'm watering the garden maze."

"Well, you're not," Arthur said. His voice sounded shaky. "You don't need to."

"Dad? Are you okay?"

"Yes, yes. Fine." He waved her off.

"Are you sure? Because—"

"I'm fine," he said. "I just need to sit." He lowered himself to a fallen log. "Perhaps . . . perhaps you could send Sam down here to pay me a visit. Would be nice to see him all grown up. It's been a long time."

"If you want," Olivia said.

"We could have dinner. The three of us. Like old times. What do you think?"

"You can eat whatever you want with him. But I won't be around."

"Why not?"

She was quiet a moment. "It just wouldn't be a good idea."

"Olivia—the boy is going to want to spend time with you. Think of it! You were such good friends. And I always thought that someday he might—"

"Please, Dad. There's no point. Just . . . *stop.*"

Arthur dropped his fist onto his thigh. And all at once, he couldn't help but see the thing he always tried not to see: how very sad his daughter was under all her usual good cheer. How much older she was than her years. How such a lovely face could hide such pain.

When Arthur had first moved down into the ravine, they'd only just begun to understand the full ramifications of her condition. Arthur had felt guilty—guilty for having led her into the garden. He could not look at her without feeling sad, and he could not stand to be happy because *her* unhappiness was his fault. At sixteen, Olivia was more serious, responsible, and poised than all the other children in her class. Girls that age needed mothers, not fathers who no longer had anything to offer. He knew she would be better off without him. And so, down into the ravine he went.

The first year was an adjustment for them both: Arthur learned to do without modern conveniences. Olivia quit high school in the spring so that she could take on the work of running the farm. For years, Arthur had attempted curing her. He'd promised her, every day, he would find a way to undo what had happened. But as time went by, Olivia seemed less and less interested in his failed attempts at finding solutions. She seemed to grow comfortable in her own, toxic skin. Once, he almost felt reprimanded by her: *You don't have to keep trying to fix me, Dad. There's nothing wrong with me. I like my life just fine.*

He wanted to think she'd found a way to be happy in spite of the Poison Garden. And some days, when the fields were growing and the birds were winging about, he could almost believe she was. But then he would catch her at times staring into the middle distance with such a hollow look in her eye that his heart would break. She wasn't happy. No matter how she tried to convince him, or herself, that she was.

Now Sam Van Winkle was back. And maybe he could make Olivia happy again in a way Arthur never could. Arthur was nearly trembling with hope for his daughter—even as he dreaded the idea of losing her attention even in the smallest way. She was his last, meager connection to happiness. Without her, he had nothing, not even a hint of joy, just a tumbledown shack and an ugly goat and the long, slogging hours.

He cleared his throat and pretended he was thinking of something entirely ordinary. "Well," he said. "Don't forget that glycerin when you come back, would you?"

"Sure, Dad," she said.

The Wrong Tree

he days passed. Green Valley continued to wither under the hot sun. Birds panted and dogs lazed and the half-wild horde of goats that roamed the valley could barely muster the energy for the amusement of terrorizing Olivia's chickens. The heat and drought were causing trouble in the fields, too: Although the plants were miserable, not even the Pennywort's enchanted land could stop the aphids from having the party of the century. Olivia and Tom were bent over their watermelons, looking under leaves and inspecting stems for signs of the infestation, bugs that fed off the watermelons by inserting their long piercing mouthparts into the plants' veins and sucking out the sweep sap as through a straw. The formerly vivacious leaves looked tired and unhappy, slumping down.

Olivia swore under her breath. Her watermelons were her best bet for good fruit during the drought. Watermelons were creatures of the desert, the camels of farming. They could thrive when other plants died of thirst. The Pennywort watermelons were among the most prized in all of Bethel: While other farmers were growing the insipid varieties of seedless melons that were so plentiful in big supermarkets around the country, Olivia had decided to buck the seedless craze and stick to the kind of watermelons that the family had been planting since before the Great Depression. She would never stop loving the old, sweet varietals. Part of the fun of eating a watermelon was spitting out the pits. And her melons were usually fleshy, firm, and sweet as honey, thanks to the Pennywort farm's industrious colonies of bees. But today, they seemed exhausted.

Tom stood up and frowned. "It's not good."

She sighed. "Call Robbie. Tell him I want the ladies here no later than tomorrow. We can't wait."

"I don't know if he'll be able to get them here that quick," Tom said.

"We have to," Olivia said. She bent and turned a leaf in the sun, looking at the glistening trails of sticky honeydew that the aphids had excreted. "First it's the aphids, then the black fungus shows up, then the ants. If the ants move in, we're done. We need the ladybugs ASAP to start taking down the aphid population."

"We're going to have a lot of well-fed ladybugs," Tom said.

Olivia wiped her hands on her long blue skirt, which she'd hitched into the belt at her waist, and she squinted under the woven brim of her hat at Tom. Tom had been working with her for eight years; he'd grown up in another of the Bethel hamlets on his own family farm. But he and his parents had different visions for farming: Their approach was chemicals first, Tom's was more organic.

When Tom was focused on the farm, he was serious as a soldier—determined, intelligent, and bold. He was a stocky man, thick-necked and barrel-chested, and his eyes always danced solicitously when he looked at her. His face was wide across and his chin had a dimple in the middle. If someone had told her that Tom hadn't been born but had instead been found in a field after a meteor shower, she wouldn't have been surprised. She'd had a number of applicants on the day that he came looking for work, but Tom had gotten the edge over his competitors for one reason and one reason alone: He'd talked to her plants. While all her candidates, Tom included, demonstrated appropriate knowledge about tomato hornworms and nitrogen enrichment, only Tom had rubbed the waxy, bold leaf of a cornstalk between two fingers and said *Aren't you a pretty thing?* Olivia was instantly smitten. It was also entirely comfortable for her that he was openly gay, living with a partner of ten years, and she knew there would never be a reason to worry that the terms of their professional relationship might change. She could not say that Tom was a *friend* exactly—in the same way that she could not say any single Penny Loafer had ever been a *friend*—but their relationship had been forged on hard work, mutual respect for each other's skill and talent, daily exchanges of ideas, and many hours of picking vegetables or weeding side by side.

"Uh-oh," Tom said. "Don't look now. It's Sergeant Pepper."

Olivia stood upright and there—at the distant end of her field—was a cop.

Tom adjusted the cuff of a long cotton sleeve. "What do you think he wants this time?"

Olivia watched Sam walking toward them, down the furrow as if along a tightrope, stepping carefully. Since he'd turned up in her garden maze last week, he'd been back to visit again and again. And again. It was not enough for him to simply stop by her farm stand and buy what he needed; he always found a reason to seek her out. Some reasons were more credible than others: *I was wondering if you wouldn't mind coming over to look at my mother's roses; she'll kill me if they die. I wanted to ask you which kinds of herbs are more drought resistant if I decide to plant them. I caught this spider in a sandwich bag; look at the size!* Olivia had done what she'd always done when people came to visit her: She was friendly and patient, but not in the least bit encouraging. She responded to comments and questions, but did not make them—though she so often wanted to. It was a necessary evil. If Sam was like any of the other men who took a passing interest in her, he would pursue her for a little while, then move on.

The difference with Sam, though, was that Olivia didn't want him to move on. She liked the surprise of him—how unexpected he was in the middle of an otherwise ordinary day, how wonderfully handsome in his tired, hangdog way. She enjoyed looking up when she was lying on the ground inspecting the undersides of her butterhead lettuce leaves or pulling up heads of cauliflower to hunt for root maggots, to see Sam coming toward her—or, better yet, to see his tall body blocking out the sun behind him as he smiled down.

She'd dreamed of him in the days since he'd returned. She dreamed he could touch her. She'd dreamed that she could touch him. They were in her garden maze, and he ran his warm hands down her arms, circled her wrists with his fingers and let them go, traced the line of her collarbones and settled his thumb into the dip at the base of her neck. He'd wrapped her up in his arms, pressed against her, and she felt warm, safe, sated, and whole. The feeling had been so real, so exquisite, that she'd cried in her sleep for pleasure. But then the dream changed—she saw Sam's hand turn black, charring as if it were burning from the inside out, the flesh withering beneath the skin, the bones disintegrating like wood in a fireplace, the contamination torching its way up his arm to his shoulder, his neck, his chin—and then she woke up.

Of course, it was only natural that she would remember him, the feel of him, so intimately. The body had a memory of its own, and hers had never stopped remembering Sam. Their first kiss had been premeditated, scheduled and planned. They'd seen their friends pairing off and breaking up and pairing off again in bursts of vivid drama, but Sam and Olivia had banded together in their platonic friendship and scorned other kids their age for being silly, shallow, or just plain dumb. *Who needs a boyfriend?* Olivia would say, even as she wondered about what it would be like if Sam offered to be hers. Often, Sam seemed more interested in pursuing the secretive little mushrooms in Chickadee Woods than in pursuing girls—and Olivia made sure he knew she loved that about him. But even if he had wanted a girlfriend, he might have had trouble finding one: He'd been a skinny kid, with features that seemed too large for his face, an unflattering haircut, and worst of all—a widely known interest in fungus. He'd also had allergies—so many allergies that he was regarded as a kind of irritant himself. He was allergic to foods that triggered him to break out in ugly hives and to flowers that made him dissolve into wet sniffles and sneezes. He was also violently allergic to bee stings, which gave him a reputation for being a wimp. Students pointed down their throats to mime gagging at him, and even the teachers would say *Oh Sam* with more annoyance than compassion when he sneezed. Olivia didn't care if the other girls whispered that he was gross. His sensitivities had never once stopped him from climbing a tree, or trekking through the woods, or eating foods from her fields right off stalks and vines. As for Olivia, boys became increasingly interested in her, but it was difficult to muster any feelings of interest toward them. None could hold a candle to Sam.

In a way, Olivia and Sam had paired off, cut out the possibility of seeing other people, even without knowing it. And so, one September evening when Olivia was fifteen, they decided that since it seemed like everyone was so far ahead in the relationship race, it only made sense that they should conduct an experiment of their own. Sam, who'd always had an empirical mind, had taken the lead, telling Olivia to meet him at the tripod rock after dinner, saying they would do it there. And Olivia had been more nervous than she'd ever been before, agonizing. Should she chew a piece of gum beforehand, or would the taste of mint be too obvious? Should she put on perfume, pull back her hair that sometimes caught on her own lips if she was wearing Chapstick and might also catch on Sam's?

In the end, she'd decided to do nothing she wouldn't normally do. She chewed a mint leaf from her mother's old herb garden. She wore her hair long and messy down her back. She didn't let herself change into prettier clothes. She told her father she was leaving—he never asked where she was going or when she planned to be back—and she marched into Chickadee Woods toward the pile of stones they called the tripod. In a shady glen, an enormous boulder balanced on three smaller, nearly uniform ones—dazzling and preposterous in its arrangement. Occasionally, people liked to sneak onto the Pennywort property to visit the tripod: Alien enthusiasts came to see the signpost that they believed had been left by an ancient civilization of visitors from outer space; geologists came because it was an incredible freak show of glacial erratics; new-age types came because they believed it was a sacred worshipping space. To Olivia, it would always be the place where Sam first kissed her.

They'd settled themselves beneath the monolith as if they were hiding under a table in the farmhouse, and they'd attempted a bit of stilted conversation. *We'll just look at it as practicing,* Sam said, *so that we know what we're doing when we do find other people to date.* And then he'd gone on to talk about the benefits of study and practice and *applying yourself* until Olivia could stand the suspense no more and she leaned in. The first moments of their kiss were awkward: His lips felt so foreign against hers. Olivia thought, *This is it? What's the big deal?* But then Sam did something—pulled away, shifted closer to sit beside her instead of across from her—and when he kissed her again the

awkwardness began to fall away in one fluid collapse, unravel-
ing even as Olivia's thoughts began to unravel. He kissed her
again, touched her hair, said, *Try putting your arms around me,*
and little by little, with hands seeking skin, bodies seeking contact, they got better at kissing, and soon, the kiss that had started
out so tepid grew hotter and wilder until it was something
much more, something that made Olivia feel like she was being
pulled into some deep, bottomless abyss from which she never
wanted to return.

They'd spent the rest of the school year sneaking kisses and
caresses when they could. Sometimes, they even talked about it
in front of other kids. *Do you want to practice after school today?*
Sam would say, right in front of everyone. Or Olivia might com-
ment, *Do you want to study later? Really* apply *ourselves?* And no
one would think anything of it, but a wash of heat would crest
over Olivia's whole body, and Sam would grin at her, and she
would know that they had long passed the threshold of *practicing* and were as coordinated, synchronized, and hot together as
any two teenagers could be. It was only by the grace of God
that they'd managed to not have sex; Sam would stop, or she
would, though neither one of them had a precise reason as to
why they should stop except that Sam, who was two years older,
said he would feel guilty if they did it because she was too
young.

Now Olivia wished Sam hadn't been so damn considerate all
those years ago. Her only experience with romance would be
forever limited to the illicit, fumbling, but wonderful interludes
she'd had as a teenager with the boy next door. As the summer
of her sixteenth year slogged on, Sam had been having increasingly sensitive reactions to what seemed to be poison ivy. It was
nothing at first—just a minor itchiness. But by the summer's
end, he seemed to have poison ivy all the time. Olivia—who had

no idea she was the cause of his discomfort—would have to keep herself from touching him while his skin healed. Then, once he was better and she could touch him, the rashes would reappear. It became a kind of miserable cycle. *On your mouth, again?* his mother asked. *What, are you eating it?* Sam began to spend all of his time inside.

While he was trying to figure out what was wrong with him, Olivia was beginning to wonder if there was something wrong with her. She had been trying to ignore the signs because the very idea that she might be dangerous seemed ludicrous. But the evidence of her own toxicity was constricting around her like so many merciless vines.

After she could no longer deny her condition, after she'd tried keeping herself out of the garden for a time, and after she wrestled with the problem of how she was going to tell Sam what was causing his allergic reactions, Sam's parents finally took him to see a doctor. When he came home from the appointment, he let himself into the farmhouse, found Olivia in the kitchen cleaning up after dinner, and told her everything: The doctor said he had a rare kind of sensitivity to urushiol, that he was "exquisitely sensitive," and that the more he was exposed to poison ivy, the worse his reactions might become over time. He did not seem especially concerned by his sensitivity; he seemed only perplexed about where he might be getting poison ivy at all. That, he said, was the main problem. He *had* to figure out where he was being exposed to the allergens; otherwise, he would just get worse and worse. *How bad could it get?* Olivia had asked him. And he'd told her that he had no idea, but that the doctor had shared a story about a patient who couldn't get within a foot of poison ivy without having a reaction. *But everyone's different,* he said.

Olivia had stood quietly at the kitchen sink, washing her father's dishes, listening. She knew then she would not be able to tell Sam the truth about what had happened to her. She needed to keep him away from her—at least until she found a cure. She could not bear the idea that repeated exposure to her might make him worse.

Sam came up to her where she stood at the sink and started to put his arms around her waist. But she elbowed him lightly, told him she wasn't feeling well, and did not kiss him good night at the door. The next day, she'd broken up with him. She hadn't actually expected that she would never find a cure for her condition and never be with him again.

Now she tried to go easy on herself when she spotted Sam in the distance crossing the fields toward her. If her stomach fluttered weirdly and the backs of her knees began to itch every time she saw him, it was only because her teenage self was still lurking somewhere down beneath her pragmatic and level-headed twenty-nine-year-old self.

"I'll tell him to back off," Tom said. "If you want."

She gave a smile she didn't feel. "It's okay."

Sam was with them a moment later; he wore his dark blue uniform, which only seemed to emphasize how long and trim he was. His shoes were shiny and his radio crackled at his side before he turned it down. Even in the middle of the summer, the allergies he'd suffered as a child seemed to have abated. She'd been watching him closely to see if his occasional proximity to her was causing any reactions; so far, she'd seen nothing to indicate that his sensitivity to her had worsened over time.

"Hi, guys," he said.

"What's going on in Mayberry, Officer Fife?" Tom said. "Rescuing cats out of trees?"

Sam stood tall in his uniform. "I need to talk to Olivia. Alone."

"Now?" Olivia said. She felt suddenly self-conscious of the

way her long cotton skirt was hitched in her belt, exposing her work boots and socks and perpetually bruised shins.

"I'm on the clock," Sam said, his face tight. "So, yeah. Now would be good."

"What do you think, Liv?" Tom asked.

"Well, we were just about done here anyway," she said to Tom. "You'll call Robbie about the bugs?"

"You got it," Tom said. "I'll page you in ten, let you know what he says."

She nodded; Tom didn't need to page her. He was just telling her he'd check up on her. The gesture embodied the kind of tacit affection that had marked her relationship with Tom from the beginning, though they'd never spent time together apart from work. She watched as he walked away, and when he was out of earshot, she turned her attention to Sam.

"Are you okay?" Olivia asked. "You seem upset about something."

"Your neighbor's at it again."

Olivia rolled her eyes. "What is it now? Are the peacocks too noisy for her? Did she find one of my barn cats sleeping on her porch swing?"

She waited for Sam to laugh but he didn't. "She was down at social services yesterday. That's what everyone's saying."

"What's that have to do with me?"

"Not you. Your father."

"I don't understand . . ."

Sam told her how Gloria had made her way to the social services offices and began asking questions—off the record, she'd said. *Hypothetically speaking, what would you do if I knew someone who was abusing an elderly parent? I'm not saying I know anybody, but what if I heard this person had her father allegedly living like a dog in a shack in a ravine, without even the basic necessities? What would be the next step?* Of course, the woman who worked behind the front desk, Sam's childhood babysitter, had known immediately that Gloria was talking about old Arthur Pennywort. And she'd called Sam to tell him right away.

"But they can't do anything," Olivia said. "It's not like I'm abusing him. Or neglecting him. I trek down there to see him at least once a day, sometimes more. He's got everything he says he needs. There's nothing more I can do."

"I know that. Everyone in Green Valley knows that."

"Except Gloria. What do you think she's trying to do?"

"Hard to say. She hasn't actually made a move. But it seemed like she was asking about getting him in protective custody."

"You mean, she wants him taken away," Olivia said.

Sam nodded.

"But she can't, right? There's no way she could do that?"

"I don't know. Gloria's made friends where it counts. More every year. She's looking for the spot where you're going to have your greatest vulnerability."

She looked out at the gentle rise of the field. *That's definitely my father,* she thought.

"Or, who knows? It could just be that she thinks she's doing the right thing," Sam said.

Olivia wished there were something she might sit down on other than the ground, for her legs suddenly felt wobbly. "I don't know what I can do to make him come back to the farmhouse. I've tried everything. It's his choice."

"Why is he down there?"

"I guess he just likes it down there."

"Whoa. I'm not judging. If he wants to live in the ravine, then he wants to live in the ravine. But . . . is he . . . *okay?*"

Olivia looked toward the dense woods where the sunny fields stopped and the shadows began. She had not mentioned to Sam that her father wanted the three of them to get together; she wasn't nearly ready for that. She didn't like to talk about her father. She didn't talk about him with anyone. Not even Sam. His reasons for moving down into the ravine had never been entirely clear to her.

"Dad's fine where he is," she said. "He's been there for ages, getting by. I just don't understand why Gloria's doing this. I think I'm a pretty good neighbor. I mean, I try to be. I know that living next to the farm can be kind of—kind of—"

"Like living next to a farm," Sam put in.

"Yes. But still—it's not like I'm going out of my way to antagonize her."

"Is there anything she wants from you?"

Olivia thought a moment. "She wants my boarders out of the barn."

"That makes sense."

"Most of the time things are fine," Olivia said. "But then once in a while, there's a, oh, a minor problem. Like last month, when one of the boarders took a nap on her porch swing. That's wrong—I know it. But I can't evict all the boarders because of one or two bad apples. And they're not *bad*. Not really. They're just . . . lost. People don't come to stay with me because they're perfectly happy. They come because they're stuck in the middle of something tough. And it's not always easy to make good decisions when you're in that mind frame."

"You're good to them, Olivia," Sam said. "I bet your mom would have been proud."

"Thanks," she said. "That's . . . I . . . It means a lot."

A moment passed. She glanced at Sam to see him looking firmly back. Men had been coming to the farm, heaping praise on Olivia for years—lauding the beauty of her tomatoes and her rarely brushed hair—but not one compliment had made her chest feel as warm as if the sun itself were shining from inside her. Though he hadn't moved and she hadn't moved, she felt as if she was being drawn toward him, that the afternoon around them was shrinking down so that the only point to exist was the patch of earth where he stood and she stood and a small watermelon grew between them. She thought maybe Sam was feeling it, too—until he stepped back and cleared his throat rather abruptly. "So Gloria wants your boarders out. Where does she expect them to go?"

"Oh. Right. Well, she wants them in the new homeless shelter. She keeps stuffing these fliers about it in my mailbox for the grand opening. I'm pretty sure the reason Gloria and her White Lake Ladies Club had it built was because they want my boarders out of the barn. They don't understand that these women aren't here because they have nowhere else to go. They're here because they don't want to be anywhere else. At least, not until the maze gives them their answers." She shook her head, wishing Gloria was with them right now so they could clear things up once and for all. "I won't let her take the Penny Loafers away from me. I won't. They're too important. They're—"

She stopped. She'd almost said, *They're the only friends I have.*

Her father had moved into Solomon's Ravine early in the winter when she was sixteen. The days at school were bleak and lonely. The nights alone in the farmhouse were filled with noises that they'd never been filled with before, sinister and lowering noises that made her heart race with fear. When she trekked down into the ravine to see her father, he no longer smiled; instead, a look came over his face that was so despairing she couldn't help but feel it echo within her. It was the longest, coldest, saddest winter of her life.

When the Penny Loafers finally began to trickle in with the spring rains, Olivia felt a relief like nothing she'd ever known. She crawled into an empty cot at the end of a row and faced the wall so no one could make her doubt her right to live among them. But as days passed, not one woman reprimanded her for skipping her showers, or for not doing homework, or for throwing rocks at the window of the farmhouse kitchen until it broke. Olivia hadn't been surprised, exactly, when the boarders began looking to her for direction about the garden maze. It was their faith in her that gave her the confidence to quit school and take over managing the farm.

She remembered her last day of high school in vicious detail—mostly because there was nothing special about it. She hadn't told any of her former friends she was leaving; only a few teachers knew, and she avoided looking at them because she didn't want to see the pity in their eyes. Her former friends did what they always did: They mocked her openly because she'd pulled away from them without explanation. She passed Sam in the hallway—he didn't look at her—and she wished she could curl up in a hidden hallway and cry. By the time the bell rang and school let out, Olivia was filled with a sense of enormous relief that she would never have to return to high school again.

The Penny Loafers had gathered her in, opened their hearts, and made a place for her in their improvised and jerry-built home each and every summer as she grew into adulthood. They didn't question her rules about not wanting to be touched; they simply treated her as one of them, a woman as lost as they were, in a way. In the cold and brittle chill of the winters, when the barn was empty and the fields were frozen and the possibility of summer seemed as remote as the possibility of flying to Mars, the Penny Loafers' return was Olivia's sustaining hope. She would never have close friends, never know a husband's touch, never have children of her own. Her father would eventually pass away. But as long as Olivia had the Penny Loafers to care for, as long as she could offer them something they couldn't find anywhere else, she knew she could bear the loneliness of her condition for the rest of her days. Otherwise . . . she could not think of the *otherwise*.

Sam was studying her; she could feel it. She began to look

down, but he reached to tip up the brim of her wide, round hat so that he could see her face.

"Olivia," he said. "Whatever I can do to help you with your father, with the boarders, I'll do it. You must know that."

"I . . . I don't know how to thank you."

He held her eye, not speaking, and she knew—then—how he might want to be thanked. She broke away first, looked out to the long fields, and balled her fists at her sides.

"Okay," Sam said.

"Okay?"

"Don't worry. I'm going."

"Going? Why so fast? No enormous spiders to show me? No questions about what the shapes of the clouds might mean?"

When he spoke, his voice was unusually flat. "I just wanted to tell you about Gloria. That's all."

Some of Olivia's happiness at seeing him began to ease out of her. Although he had come to the farm many times in the past few days with an eagerness to talk, it appeared that her façade of indifference was finally starting to wear down his determination. He just looked at her, with a hint of sadness in his eye that caused disproportionate pain to bloom in her own heart.

She tried to smile.

"Well, I'll let you get back to it," he said. He started to walk away. Her whole body felt heavy with disappointment. He'd been so unfailingly kind to her. He looked out for her. And yet, how awful she'd made herself act toward him. His walk seemed heavier than normal as he headed away.

"Wait, Sam!" she heard herself say. He stopped. The words had come out fast, and once they had left her mouth, she wished she could take them back. She really had nothing else to say to him; she simply didn't like to see him leave looking so sad. "I'm sorry if I seem . . . if I . . . you know . . . I just want to say, it's good to know someone's looking out for me. It's . . . it's a nice change."

He did not fully face her. "I'm not going to give up, Ollie."

A shiver rustled along her spine. *Ollie*. What he'd always called her. "What do you mean, give up?"

"I'm not going to just disappear. I live here now, so I don't care if it takes twenty years for you to warm up to me again. I'm not going anywhere."

"I'm not *not* warm to you," she said softly. Some part of her was feeling quite warm, warmer each day she saw him crossing her fields. She looked at his narrow face, his skin that was less pale than it had been a few days ago. "I just don't understand . . ."

"What?"

"I don't understand what you want. From me, I mean."

"What I want?" He frowned, tense with frustration. "What I want is to have at least one neighbor in Green Valley that I actually like. And Gloria's not exactly the leading candidate."

"You want us to be friends?"

"Yes," he said.

"Oh. Well—okay," she said. Her relief felt like a rush of cool wind. He only wanted friendship, nothing more. The declaration should have made her happy; instead, she felt the slightest chill of disappointment—which she intended to ignore. "I'd like to be friends."

"You would?"

"Sure," she said lightly. "I didn't know we *weren't* friends already."

He smiled, but there was something to it that wasn't exactly pleased or earnest. She wondered if he knew she didn't quite believe her own words. Like him, she too thought it would be nice to have a neighbor again—someone who could sit on the porch with her in the evenings and talk lazily about the day past, someone who might come over during the long, lonely winter for the occasional game of cards. But were the risks of befriending Sam greater than the rewards—for both of them?

"See you around," he said. He turned and walked his slow, serious walk back toward the road. And when her walkie-talkie chirped she was glad to hear Tom's voice, calling her back to the steady, dependable work of the farm.

The Forest for the Trees

I t was just before sundown when she went in search of her father. She did not bother heading into the geological gutter that was Solomon's Ravine because she knew he would not be there. She'd come to know his habits like she knew her own. On an evening like this, when the air felt a little lighter on a person's skin than it had in ages, he was more likely to be found at Hemlock Pond than in the ravine. Certain summer days were made for fishing, and this was one.

"Hey!" Olivia called out toward the lake as she strode through knee-high grass. Her father, who was struggling to push the rowboat off the rocks and into the glassy pink water of the lake, looked over his shoulder with the quickness of a wild animal. He relaxed when he saw it was her.

"Olivia. How nice. You're just in time!"

Hemlock Pond had been dammed in the early 1900s by some enterprising Pennywort. It was the family's private fishing hole. The moldering ruins of a small bungalow stood near the water's edge, its only inhabitants a family of mischievous raccoons.

She hurried past a cluster of wild rhododendrons toward her father; the keel of the rowboat was half in the water. "Allow me," she said. He climbed in, groaning a little as he pulled one leg into the boat using his two hands. Olivia took off her boots and left them at the water's edge; then she gave the boat a strong push and hopped in. A blue heron stood at the lake with its head bowed as if in prayer.

Her father had long relied on Olivia to bring him his food, his coffee beans, and his vitamins, but he had never stopped taking pride in catching his own fish. Pike, bass, perch, and sunnies—as well as a fair number of frogs—were plentiful in the pristine waters. Though Arthur's move out of the farmhouse all those years ago had curtailed many of Olivia's favorite father-daughter activities—like pancake breakfasts and hours spent paging through field guides and seed catalogues—they had never stopped fishing together. It was a thing they had done when Alice was alive; it was a thing they did now.

"Good day today?" Arthur asked in the way he always did.

"Yeah. Good," Olivia replied in the way she always did. "Where we headed?"

Arthur scanned the perimeter of the quiet, low lake. "Round about those aspens at the far edge."

She pulled the oars gently, in no hurry, absorbing the peace of the evening while it was still there to be absorbed. There were choppier waters ahead. She and Arthur had not had many serious talks apart from discussions of the farm. In conversation they regularly avoided anything that might call up any kind of deep emotion. They did not acknowledge Olivia's long life stretching out before her, forever void of romance, children, or lasting friendship; and they certainly did not talk about what had happened with the poison garden—what was the point? What was done was done, and what was coming they could not control. Instead, they chatted as any two strangers would chat. They talked about their most basic of basic needs, always off-handedly. Moments of mild discord sometimes came when Olivia said Arthur needed a doctor, and Arthur was insistent that he could self-diagnose and heal. In the end they'd learned to compromise: No doctor would trek into the bowels of Solomon's Ravine, but Arthur's old friend Jacob, a retired veterinarian, agreed to do it—and according to Arthur, what was a human but an animal anyway?

There had been times, Olivia thought, when her father had meant to have some heart-to-heart with her. He would get a cloudy look in his eye and say *I need to talk to you.* She would wait patiently while he struggled to find the right words, muddling through convoluted logics and non sequiturs that would eventually sidle right up close to the thing he wanted to say— but then, inevitably, fail to reach it. He would remind her of a misstep or mistake that he or she had made, utterly trivial compared to the dramatic warm-up, and Olivia would know he'd dodged his true topic yet again. He usually ended on a note that went along the lines of "Well, I suppose we're okay then." At which point she would assure him, "Dad. We'll always be okay."

But now, they truly did need to have a difficult conversation. And Olivia found she had little useful knowledge of how she might seriously and directly approach the subject of his leaving Solomon's Ravine. He knew it was on her mind; she alluded to it often enough, nudging him via offhanded remarks and short asides to consider it. But the time for consideration was over. This was serious, and needed a full, serious conversation. The few times she had tried to have a heart-to-heart with him— about Alice, about his unending grief—he looked afraid he might shoot him and she'd felt so guilty afterward that she regretted putting him through it.

She rowed in silence, glad for the friendly song of the peepers in the trees around them, while her father went about arranging his bait box and pole.

"Dad," she said.

He blinked toward her; the rough gray-white of his beard

made the color of his eyes stand out with shocking greenness, like moss against a fresh snow. He seemed, for the moment, happy. It had been some time since they'd fished together and she hated to ruin the moment. But the great hidden gears of Gloria's machinations were turning, and something had to be done.

"There was one thing I needed to talk to you about," she told him.

He was slow to answer. He put on his glasses then baited his hook, his eyes crossing as he focused on the work. "Go ahead."

"You know the neighbor, Gloria."

"Gloria?" He stuck his tongue out of his mouth sideways; his eyebrows were raised as he focused on his task. "Gloria . . . Gloria . . ."

He wasn't paying attention. "The neighbor, Dad. *Gloria.*"

The worm popped on the hook. "Ah yes. Gloria. The one on the ridge."

She hesitated. "You know Gloria's been after me to kick the Penny Loafers out of the barn."

"Bah," he said. Olivia held her breath as he cast, and breathed easier when no bit of fabric or flesh was inadvertently hooked. "That barn's as sturdy as it's ever been. Hasn't lost so much as a roof tile in ten years."

"How would you know that, if you haven't been up to see it?"

"Oh—well. An educated guess."

She let off on the oars. "It looks a lot different since you were last up there."

"I'm sure it does."

"You should see the maze. We've been working on a new garden of all yellow flowers. I swear it's shaping up to be as bright as the sun."

Arthur glanced at her as if to say, *I know what you're up to.* He adjusted the tension on his line. "So what's this Gloria person doing?"

"She's snooping."

He scoffed. "For what?"

"Information on you."

"Well, that's not very polite."

"We think there's a possibility she's considering asking social services to, um, intervene."

"Who is we? You and Tom?"

"Me and Sam," Olivia said.

"Really? Well then . . ."

Well then what? she wanted to ask him. But instead she said, "You're missing the point here. She's got a problem with you living in the ravine."

"It's my right to live here."

Olivia dug the oars in hard. "Yes, it's your right. But I'm the one who's going to get in trouble for it. She could say I'm neglecting you. Or abusing you. She could say that you're unable to take care of yourself, and that I'm incompetent as a guardian."

"Guardian? You're not my guardian; you're my daughter." He shook his head, frowning. "I spend more time taking care of myself than any man my age. Look at me: I'm out here *fishing* for my own dinner, for God's sake. I don't have a guardian."

"Okay, Dad," she said softly. "Just calm down. I just . . . I'm afraid you'll be taken away if we don't do something about your living situation."

The end of his fishing pole bobbed. "What's this, *taken away*? To have me *taken away*? Do you mean to jail? Because I can't be put in jail, Alice. I never broke a law in my life."

"Olivia. *Dad,* I'm Olivia."

"Of course you're Olivia. That's what I said."

She sighed and rested her arms for a moment. She didn't believe her father was crazy—even if the evidence mounted more each day to suggest otherwise. But he was getting older. And while he wasn't losing his mind, he did seem to momentarily misplace it now and again. His life of solitude didn't do much to help his clarity of thinking. Olivia knew this from her own experience: The long cold winters did things to her, body and mind, wrecking her with bouts of miserable and interminable loneliness, when the minutes crystallized into hours as the temperature dropped. As the days grew shorter and harder, she caught herself talking to people who weren't there, or to herself, or to her houseplants. She waited in desperation for the mailman, who—truth be told—always seemed a little afraid of her. She lived for the work that needed to be done over the winter: of breaking the scrim of ice on the chicken's water before she fed them, of organizing the seeds in her greenhouses, of chopping wood, of shoveling snow and ice, of anything that might ease the ache of being so completely and utterly alone. By March, when the Penny Loafers began to return, she had trouble finding the words she was looking for, trouble following the thread of a conversation for very long. Little by little as the valley turned green once again, she felt her spirit rejuvenated, her hope renewed.

Arthur, however, spent *every* season alone, spoke to no one but her, and never had the opportunity for the mental restoration that company brings.

He was not looking at her, and so she spoke in as confident a voice as she could. "Gloria hasn't done anything yet. I mean, she hasn't officially logged a tip with social services or anything, so right now we're still okay. They can keep doing what they've always done—you know, ignore it. But if Gloria does put in a report, it's definitely going to look like I'm neglecting you. And they might not be able to look the other way."

"Neglecting you?"

"No. Not you. Me." She knew her father was plenty sharp. But he didn't always *listen*. His mind wandered into territories that demanded all of his attention, and when he realized it was his turn to speak, he sometimes tried to hook back into the conversation by repeating the last words she said. This was nothing new: He'd been doing it for as long as she could remember. When he was young, it had been a quirk. Now that he was old, it seemed to be more sinister. "Are you listening?"

"Of course I'm listening. You're the most devoted of daughters. The most devoted in the world!"

"But . . ." Olivia felt her throat tighten. "But from the outside I doubt it looks that way."

"Then just . . . well, just—" He fumbled for words. A fish nibbled the line but he didn't seem to notice. "Invite the woman to come down and pay me a visit. Invite the pope for all I care. They'll all see that I'm really quite comfortable. And then they can all go home and leave me alone."

"It's not as easy as that."

"Of course it is."

"First of all, *she* wouldn't be the one coming down to the ravine."

"Then have Satan send her minions—it's all the same to me."

"You don't understand," she said, trying to keep the frustration out of her voice. "I'm talking about social services. You think they'll see a happy old guy who's doing just fine. The way you live—bathing in a creek, cooking on a camp stove, wearing clothes that are a step away from rags—all of it will just strengthen her argument."

"No it won't."

"Dad, it will."

"It's a man's choice to live the way he wants to."

"Yes, but they'll think you're, uh, not in control of your mental powers."

"I am!"

"Yes, but—"

"I'm perfectly lucid. Hear that? I can use the word *lucid*. If this Gloria person can't see that, well then, I'll . . ."

"You'll what, Dad?"

"I'll go live somewhere else. Somewhere she can't find me."

"Or you can move back into the farmhouse. Which would be better for everyone," she said. Olivia bit down on the inside of her cheek. Did her father not know that he sounded like a child? Couldn't he *hear* himself?

It seemed to her that Arthur had given up on living shortly after she'd become poisonous. Alice's death had drained some of the life from him, and he might have gone on for the rest of his days in that state of half-miserable automation, marking time. But then, Olivia had confessed that she was poisonous, and sent him over the edge. Within a few weeks of learning what she had become, he had holed himself up in the ravine. Though her logical mind knew that it would be unjust to think that he'd left the farmhouse because he'd become repulsed by her, she'd been unable to stop the thought from occasionally creeping across her mind. Instead, she'd forced herself to cling to the more likely idea: that he felt responsible for what had happened to her, since it had been his fascination with poison plants that had exposed her to their toxins. It hadn't been disgust that sent him packing; it was guilt. She tried to always keep her focus squarely on that idea, because if her focus strayed, it strayed into dark and miserable places, possibilities in which her father could not stand the sight of her and so moved away.

Occasionally—rarely—an old feeling set in, and she knew it to be anger. She'd forgiven her father for his unintentional crushing of her heart, for forcing her to grow up so fast, for putting her in charge of the farm when she hadn't really wanted it yet. But once in a while, she suspected herself of being mad at him. And when that happened—when she woke up from a restless sleep with her jaw aching from some dream she could hardly remember—she reminded herself: In spite of everything that had happened, she'd actually done just fine. She'd learned hard but important lessons of depravation and loss. And those lessons had served her well as she'd got older because she'd learned how to be alone, how to expect very little, and how to keep from relying on others for any sense of her own happiness. In a way, all of her early difficulties meant she would be able to bear her loneliness—with grace, if not with a modicum of contentment.

She saw that her knuckles had turned white where she held the oars, and she loosened her grip. "*Why* won't you move back to the farm? Back with me? Would it really be so bad?"

He began to reel in his line, but said nothing.

There was so much more she wanted to say: *I know Mom's death was hard for you. I know you dealt with it as best you could. And I know you wish we'd never made that poison garden.* She wanted to tell him that it was all okay now, that enough time had passed, and that all their old sorrows were behind them, if only he could stop holding on to them so tightly and allow himself to move on. Olivia could take care of everything for him; all he needed to do was let her.

When she spoke, she kept her voice soft. "There aren't any choices here, Dad. If you don't move back into the farmhouse, Gloria really could take you away from me." She felt her eyes begin to sting, tears forming. "I don't want you to *ever* be taken away from me. I . . . I still need you. I know I'm not supposed to—I'm too old for that—but I do. I need you. If something ever happened to you, Dad, I don't know what I'd do."

She wiped at her face. Arthur was looking at her now, his

gaze steady and green. She wished she knew what he was think-ing. Slowly, she watched the bright, intelligent focus in his eyes become dull as the lake in January.

"I don't want to be difficult."

"Then help me. If you're not going to move back to the farm with me, at least tell me why you won't. Maybe I can make it better."

"Olivia," he said, his voice creaky. "I'm sorry. For everything. I want you to be happy."

She felt her brow wrinkle in confusion. Sometimes it was hard to follow her father's logic. "But . . . I am happy. I *am*."

"What about Sam?"

Olivia stilled. "What about him?"

"That's what I asked."

Olivia sighed.

"What's the problem? Has he expressed interest in you?"

"It's complicated."

"Of course it's complicated. Happiness is complicated. All the poets and whatnot spend their lives going on and on about how sadness and misery are the most complicated emotions— but they would be better off trying to figure out what it means to be happy. You—Olivia—you're young. You've got to take happiness when you can get it. Believe an old man."

Olivia looked out to the edge of the water. The surface was shimmering pink, blue, purple, and gray. She wasn't precisely sure what her father was trying to say, but she knew it had to do with Sam. Occasionally over the years, Arthur would ask, *Any new friends coming around the farm these days?* Olivia suspected that he was fishing to find out if she was seeing anyone. It was as close to a personal question as he'd ever asked. Of course, the question was ridiculous. Her father seemed to think that the fact that she was as dangerous as poison ivy was not enough to put the right man off.

As he fiddled with his fishing line, it occurred to her that her clever father had managed to steer the conversation away from the problem at hand: his tenancy in Solomon's Ravine. That, perhaps, was the point of bringing up Sam's name. Nothing more. She decided not to let him get away with it. She said, "The question here isn't about me. It's about you moving back into the farmhouse before they can come take you away."

"Let me think about it," he said.

"Please think quickly. There might not be much time."

He sighed. At the water's edge, the heron lifted its wings and rose into the air. "You better row us in, Olivia. Fish aren't biting. And the sun's starting to go down."

With a heavy heart, she began the slow, tedious rowing that would bring them back to the shore. Waterstriders made circular ripples on the pinkish water. Arthur spooled the line.

"Listen," she said. "I don't want you to worry about this, okay?" She was wavering now, and she knew it. She was on the brink of giving him an out. But there was nothing she could do to stop herself. She didn't like to see that distant look on her father's face, that wall of resolve that shut her out. It made her afraid.

Her father was the only person in the world who knew her. He was, in some ways, her closest friend. Her only friend. She could not afford to lose his affection. "Either way, whatever you decide to do, if you move into the farmhouse or stay here, everything's going to be fine. Gloria's not coming anywhere near you. I won't let her."

"You're like me," he said. "Stubborn. But one thing you get from your mother."

"What's that?"

"You've always been so good about taking care of others, Olivia. But not so good at taking care of yourself."

"I take care of myself better than anyone else could," she

said—and then, she wished she hadn't, because she saw her father remembering that he had left her alone, and he seemed sad.

He knocked on the wooden boat. "I'm simply saying, you've got to give that young man a chance. Will you think about it? Will you at least try?"

She didn't answer. She thought: *What a pair we are, having two conversations at once and trying to tell the other what to do.* When they reached the shore, she did not try to help him to his feet or out of the boat because she knew he wouldn't want her to. She busied herself with putting her boots back on, tying them slowly, her head bent in case he caught a glimpse of errant wetness in her eyes.

A New Leaf

rom the bedroom window of his parents' house, which was now his house, Sam could see the Pennywort farmstead. He'd spent many an hour looking out at it when he was a boy. He knew the way the snow tended to gather most heavily on the west gable, and the way steam on one particular window meant that someone was taking a shower. He and Olivia had invented a code involving lights turned on and off, and some nights he would watch her window for an hour, writing down letters that corresponded with her flashing bedroom light, hanging on every timed blink, only to decipher her message as: *Seeyoutomorrowsam.*

So much had changed. The Pennywort house had been inhabited since it was built sometime in the 1840s. But it was all boarded up now, the windows covered with plywood and roof tiles having slid to the overgrown lawn. It was hard not to be depressed about the ramshackle old place because it was as if so many of Sam's happiest childhood memories had been barricaded inside, sealed as if in a decaying mausoleum to a lost time, or his *life that might have been.* Back in the old days, he'd believed he would grow up to be the kind of man that his father was, and his grandfather, and his uncle, and all the Van Winkle men he knew. He'd heard the stories about how John Van Winkle had rescued triplets from a flooded car, how Alphie "Junior" Van Winkle had saved a friend's beloved hound dog with mouth-to-nose resuscitation, how even his toddling baby cousin had saved his parents' lives when he escaped from his crib and tugged on their covers in the middle of the night to tell them the house smelled of smoke. He'd been prepared to fully embrace his own fate as a hero, with a pride of ownership that could never be bought in a store. And he'd also been prepared for women to fall in love with him in the way they loved all the Van Winkle heroes, so that even the old women and the married women and the little girls preened a little under the light of a Van Winkle smile.

But then, he'd had his heart broken. By Olivia. And Green Valley might as well have been Blue Valley for how awful he felt within it. He might have stayed away forever if it hadn't been for the accident. But now he was back—back because he lost the fight to stay away. The guys down at the station were waiting for him to do something amazing—wrestle a copperhead away from a baby, or return an injured fawn to its mom. But what they didn't know—what only Sam knew—was that the Van Winkle gift had skipped him. He'd never saved anyone from anything. As a guy who had been dead for six full minutes, he hadn't even been able to save himself.

When calls went out for emergencies—the *real* kind that involved accidental ingestion of poison or heart attacks that dropped people in their tracks—Sam made himself scarce. He was a Van Winkle in name only, and he didn't know how long he'd be able to keep the guys from realizing that. He could only keep his head down, and give people believable answers when they asked where he'd been when they needed him, and get through the hours.

Today, his day off, he was spending his afternoon at home

cleaning up some odds and ends with the ex-landlord in Vermont who had refused to return his security deposit. He had been sitting on his bed checking his email when the smell of strawberries eased into his room. He didn't notice at first. He'd thought only: *I could go for some strawberries.* But as the scent became more defined so did his longing. After a time, the desire for strawberries was so intense that it made his eyes blur, and his hands tremble on his computer, and any logical and serious thought he might have had was edged out by the more pressing need to sink his teeth into the smell that filled his nose. This was entirely strange: Since the accident, he'd had next to no cravings for anything. He could taste his food, but not being able to sense its temperature or texture had flattened the urge to eat.

And so to want a thing as badly as he wanted strawberries was a shock to his system. He wanted them in a way that was rapacious, desperate—greedy and almost violent. He kicked open the front screen door and took a deep, forceful breath of summer air, trying to get the smell out of his head. But it only got worse, because he *saw* what he wanted, down the road about five hundred feet, *strawberries,* red and gleaming and unmistakable, piled on the Pennywort farm stand.

If he hadn't been wearing flip-flops, he would have walked barefoot. The farm stand bore up a sloped, corrugated roof on four-by-four posts; its chicken-wire shutters were hooked open, its evergreen paint had peeled. Bright flaring poppies and orange lilies leaned in white five-gallon buckets marked for sale. His tongue was burning by the time he picked up a carton of strawberries, so plump, so promising. He was dying for them, and he felt glad of it, because if he was dying for something it meant he was not dead. He put one in his mouth and it was everything he'd hoped it would be: a burst of sweet-tart juice, all the tastes of summer running down his throat. He thanked

God that even though he couldn't feel the fruit with his skin, he could still taste it. He hadn't lost that. And yet, even after he had a strawberry on his tongue, his craving was not pacified.

He left the stand and went in search of Olivia—this time, he had no prefabricated excuse for seeking her out. He wanted to talk to her—really talk—in a way that went beyond pleasantries. He wanted to get things out in the open, all the silly, residual insecurities left over from those many years ago, so that they could attempt having a friendship as adults. The farm was a big place: She could be anywhere. He went to the chicken coop, the herb garden, and the barn before one of the boarders took pity and told him she was near the apiaries. The smell of strawberries was everywhere, not just coming from the carton he held, but *everywhere.* It floated to him like ribbons of scent on a breeze that wasn't actually there. He wondered if he was having a stroke. His brain was playing tricks on him, memories that he'd kept a tight lid on suddenly breaching their banks.

From the day they'd first played together when he was in the second grade, all the way up until he'd been a senior in high school, they'd been inseparable. Sam had a small family and no siblings. But he and Olivia had grown up together, side by side, and he never felt that he'd lacked for companionship of any sort in his childhood. His parents were not farmers; they'd purchased the little plot where their house stood when he was eight, and Sam had embraced everything that was fun about living next to a good-sized farm. Arthur Pennywort had taught them to fly kites and make barometers out of live leeches. The Penny Loafers kept an eye on them and taught them how to love the flowers in the garden maze.

He and Olivia had slain imaginary dragons, survived imaginary shipwrecks on deserted islands, and become world-famous scientists who had found a cure for an alien disease. Alice had already been dead when he'd moved to the valley, so he'd never known her, but he and Olivia grappled with the finality of her death as best they could, with "memorial services" held on flat, glacier-polished rocks and with games of "let's pretend I'm dying and you have to save me" until finally, together, they managed to understand what exactly the adults were talking about when they said *come to terms*.

But all of their childhood closeness had begun to disappear the year Sam turned eighteen, shortly before Arthur Pennywort had confined himself to Solomon's Ravine. Now that Sam was reconsidering the prospect of being friends with Olivia again, it surprised him to realize that he'd had no female friends since he'd left Green Valley. It wasn't that he'd set out to eschew friendships with women—he liked women. He'd dated, of course. He'd been good at dating. But friendships with women had never materialized.

Sometimes, he thought Olivia had ruined him. He'd been so very close to her: She'd been everything to him. He couldn't remember which of the two of them had suggested that they'd first start making out—had it been her? As a guy who hadn't got much (any) action until that point, he'd been unspeakably glad and embarrassingly grateful. Who better to make out with than the only girl he knew who didn't judge him, who didn't put pressure on him to be romantic—whatever that meant—and whom he'd known and trusted like he'd known and trusted himself? Then, as time passed, he realized that Olivia was more than just a friend with benefits: She was what he wanted. He loved her, sincerely, and thought he would always have her to love.

That's why it had been such a shock when, in the beginning of his senior year, she shot him down. Their make-out sessions had tapered off and then vanished entirely because he'd had such prolonged and disgusting reactions to poison ivy that summer. He lived for the promise of feeling better, when he could once again take her hand and lead her into the woods and touch all the soft, smooth skin under her clothes.

But then one day—the day he'd returned from a doctor's appointment—she'd acted cool to him. He'd thought it odd but decided that she simply must have had a bad day. The next morning, with his rashes once again beginning to clear, he'd asked her to meet him at the old janitor's shed near the tennis courts after school for a "study session." The school day dragged on, he could hardly think, he was full of expectation and excitement to once again be close to her, to touch her the way she liked and to know that she still loved him. But when she met him beneath the dripping eaves, she had no warmth for him, not even the smallest smile. She told him that she didn't want to be his girlfriend anymore, that she'd never really meant to be, that she'd thought they were making out just as an experiment, and that she'd never meant for Sam to think they were supposed to be a serious couple. Then, just like that, she'd walked out into the rain.

The shock left him standing there, bereft and stupid, with no idea what had happened or what do to. Olivia had never been moody or dramatic compared to other girls; he knew her explanation had to be full of lies. But what was the real reason for her dismissal? Had he done something to offend her? Had she fallen for someone else? No matter how he tried, the only explanation he could come up with was that she'd been disgusted by him, all his blotchy skin and hives, and she wanted someone she could touch without worrying about triggering his itches. Almost as quickly as his sadness had swelled, it was replaced by anger and resentment. Standing beside the shed, he put his hand out beneath the leaking gutter, and the marker between his childhood and his adulthood was the cold slip of rain running between his fingers and splashing on the ground.

As the school year went on, he could not get himself out from under the misery of losing her. He hadn't realized that when the poets from his English class talked about the pain of love, they'd meant *real* pain, sometimes like the very tip of a knife pricking his heart, sometimes like a thousand books had been piled on his chest and made it too much trouble to breathe. When he heard the rumors that Arthur Pennywort had abandoned her and moved into Solomon's Ravine, he forced himself to go to her. Some small, dark part of him half hoped she was suffering—just a little—because maybe then she would need him the way he still needed her. He planned to offer her his friendship—only that and nothing more—even if he secretly hoped that she would begin to want him again now that his poison ivy problems seemed to be gone. He planned to ask if she was okay, to ask why Arthur had moved out, and to tell her he would do anything to help. But when he got to the farmhouse and started in on his meticulously planned speech, she'd only looked at him, a little sad, and told him she wanted to be left alone. Months later when she quit high school without even a word to him about it, he understood that whatever they'd had—or almost had—was really and truly over. Three weeks after his graduation, he put Green Valley behind him and didn't look back.

Now he spotted Olivia in the distance near the bee yard, where five boxy whitewashed hives stood on a gentle, grassy rise. And when he thought back on all the drama and pain of their breakup, it struck him as a little silly and melodramatic. The real dramas of life didn't happen in high school hallways. They happened in hospitals, in ambulances, and on mountaintops where the cold could feel so intimate and death came like an old friend.

Olivia was examining the frame of honeycomb, and even

from a distance Sam could see that it was undulating with the dark bodies of bees. Though he wasn't quite as sensitive to poison ivy as he'd been that one summer, he was still allergic to bee stings, and so he hung back from the hives. The veil Olivia wore fell over her face from the brim of a large straw hat, the netting wrapped winsomely around her neck. She wore denim overalls that were so blocky and worn they only made her look more fresh and feminine. The smell of strawberries was stronger than ever; Sam bit one from the carton he carried, but still—the craving did not go away.

She waved to him slowly, as if underwater, not to startle the bees. Everyone in Green Valley knew the Pennywort bees; they were recognizable by sight because of the faintly copper-green glint in their eyes. The farmers who worked the valley held that the Pennywort bees were good luck; they were as big as hailstones, dumb creatures that occasionally knocked themselves out on windowpanes and bird feeders, and they were exceedingly friendly to people who were friendly toward them.

But for as goofy as the Pennywort bees were, everybody knew that their stings were the most painful kind of stings a person could get—more painful than the stings of the paper wasps that made enormous gray nests under the eaves of the abandoned summer motels, more painful than the sting of the yellow jacket and hornet combined. Sam had never been stung by a Pennywort bee, but he knew enough to be wary of them. Pennywort bee stings turned children's arms swollen and black, and killed curious spring black bear cubs, and landed more than one angry, swatting drunkard in the emergency room. If the bees were docile, it was only because they were coaxed into docility by Olivia's particular, drugging magic, which apparently had as great an effect on bees as it did men. She was beautiful, more now than before. Sam could only stare.

As she walked toward him, she unwrapped the veil around her neck and tossed it up and over her stiff-brimmed hat. She stopped a few feet away and put her hands on her hips, looking at Sam. He felt the faintest illumination like the light that comes through the crack of a slowly opening door.

"Hi, Sam," Olivia said. Did he imagine that she was happy to see him, but was trying not to seem that way? "Any new intel on Gloria?"

"No," he said. He looked down at his clothes—his shorts and T-shirt. "I'm not working today. Just—stopped by for some strawberries."

"It's . . . good to see you," she said.

He smiled and something within him warmed.

She cleared her throat. "How are the berries?"

"Perfect."

"Perfect! Wow. High praise."

"It's been a long time since I've had strawberries like this," he said. "I forgot they were so good. I mean—I remembered they were good, but the memories can't compare to the real thing."

She tipped her head and looked at him, and he felt the tremulous hope that something had changed between them, that she was willing to let him in at least a little. He couldn't imagine what made her keep acting so cool toward him. It was hard to believe that she would still hold a grudge against him for high school. But just in case, he wanted to make sure they got their old childish shenanigans out in the open so they could move on.

"So, how are the bees doing?" he asked.

"The summer's been so dry," she said, almost a little shy. "The honey yield isn't looking good for this year."

"Do you still sell it?"

"No. I'll keep it for the winter. I use it in my tea and whatnot.

And like I said, it might be a small yield this year. They're really suffering."

"Can you move them to the garden? To be closer to the flowers?"

"I could," she said. "But it's a weird thing about bees. If I moved the hive far away, they wouldn't have a problem finding their way back home. But if I move it across the yard, I'll lose some of my field bees because they'll keep trying to return here, to the original location."

A honeybee circled and Sam held his breath.

"Oh, shoot. I forgot you're allergic." Olivia glanced back at the hives and worried her lip between her teeth. He knew what she was thinking: She was considering making an excuse to go on her way.

"You could take a *quick* break," he said.

He saw the rise of her chest, the pause of a held breath. She was still looking out to the fields and not at him.

"Come on," he said. "What's it going to hurt?"

She glanced at him—a quick flash of the most beautiful copper brown he'd ever seen. "Okay. But I really can't stay long."

"Not long. Come on."

He led her away from the beehives, to the edge of the field where thick trees held their browning branches high, and Solomon's Ravine began its steep plunge into the rocky depths. Olivia took off her hat, then sat down with her back against a tree trunk. Sam joined her, lowering himself stiffly to the ground. His joints hurt, and each flare of pain felt so exceptionally cruel—because even though he couldn't have felt the softness of Olivia's, he *could* feel the kinds of pains that happen deep in the body—the ache of wrecked tendons, tired bones. The doctors had said he would recover, and technically he had. But what the doctors hadn't told him was that "recovery" wasn't the same thing as going back to the way he'd been before, when his body had been so good to him, though he hadn't known enough to appreciate it at the time.

"I used to be better at this," he joked as he tried to adjust his legs on the lumpy, acorn-spotted grass. "My bones aren't so good at sitting on the ground anymore."

"You'll get used to it again."

"Strawberry?" He extended his arm as far as it would go in her direction, the carton in his hand. She looked at it for a moment like Eve might have looked at the apple from the snake.

But at last she said, "Why not?" She leaned toward him, and the breeze picked up ever so slightly. She took a bite and closed her eyes.

"Are you wearing perfume?"

"No."

"Are you sure?"

She laughed.

"Right," he said. "Right."

She was not looking at him, and that bothered him. She had the kind of nervous alertness he'd only ever seen in red foxes and white-tailed deer; it was an edgy awareness that straddled the line between suspicion and fear.

"We should talk," he said.

"What's on your mind?"

"An apology, actually."

She slanted her eyes at him. "For what?" she asked. But then he saw her chest flush red between the straps of her thin green tank top, and he knew she remembered.

On the night before he planned to leave Green Valley for good, under the purple-blue shine of moonlight, Sam had gone to the maze. He wound his way through the crawling, slinking shadows, down the maze's kinks and turns, over footbridges, under tunnels of hanging flowers, past moon-gilt ponds. He wanted the maze to give him answers. As much as he'd burned to leave Green Valley—with its irritating quirks and familial expectations and memories of heartbreak and failure at every turn—he was also reluctant to leave it. He'd arranged to stay the summer with a cousin in New York City before he went away to college. And he wanted the maze to tell him whether he was doing the right thing.

He walked the corridors slowly in the dark, feeling the weight of the whole world on his shoulders and wondering if he would ever *not* feel that way again. He'd been through the maze countless times, and he knew every curve and bend, but that night, it had seemed as if the maze was changing around him even as he was walking through it, and he quickly lost his way. Nothing seemed familiar, and what did seem familiar was positioned in an unfamiliar place.

When he came to the walled-off garden in the center of the maze, he was surprised to discover that the door was just slightly open. The door was never open. Olivia and her father had built the garden without Sam's help; in fact, he'd been told to stay far away. And he'd never once thought to question what was inside the garden walls. But now the open door was a temptation he couldn't resist, and he dared, inch by inch, to look through it.

He wasn't alone.

Inside the garden, to his intense shock, was Olivia. In the middle of the night. She was standing beside a pink shrub with her nose to one of the flowers. She might have been whispering, or talking, or at the very least, smiling. She looked as slick as a water creature in the moonlight, smooth, silvery-blue, and languid. He realized this was because she was naked.

It was only much later that the rational observations and questions took hold: What was she doing in the maze in the middle of the night? And why was she doing it with no clothes on? But in that moment, Sam was not thinking of things like meanings and repercussions. His overwrought and blood-starved teenage brain wasn't thinking much at all. He forgot his grievances with Olivia. He forgot his plans. He thought: *Of course I won't leave Green Valley.* Gently, he said her name.

Olivia gasped, turned her head. She stuttered over the word *Sam.* And then the invectives began. She walked straight up to him, not bothering to cover the smoothness of her belly, the slight bounce of her breasts, and she whispered loudly, *Don't come in here. Get away.* She was so forceful he felt as if *he'd* been the one who had been caught off guard, and not the other way around. He was stunned into silence.

Go! She'd said. *Please, get back!*

He'd walked backward heel over heel until he tripped, knocking his tailbone on the hard dirt and scraping his palms. She'd slammed the door in his face. The next morning, his father drove him to the city and he didn't see Olivia again.

Now she looked at him. The shade of a leafy tree dappled the weedy grass around them. Her gold-tan skin gleamed with sweat. Her hair, the color of a mild sunset, peachy and red, was gathered back into a tight, single braid that had been pinned up off the back of her neck.

"I didn't mean to surprise you that night," he said. "I didn't expect you to be there."

"I know."

"I've always kind of wondered what you were doing in there, in the middle of the night like that," he said, as lightly as he could.

"Oh, nothing really. It wasn't anything mysterious. I went into the garden when I couldn't sleep. Sometimes I still do."

"Naked?"

She laughed. "It just makes me feel more . . . I don't know . . . uninhibited."

"I imagine you'd have to be kind of uninhibited to start with."

"Not if you don't expect to bump into anybody," she said.

He smiled, and she smiled, too, for a moment before she looked away. He could not get a read on her. Sometimes she seemed so sincerely glad for his company. Sometimes a little crease would form like lightning between her eyebrows, and he suspected she was going to bolt. He wondered what she would do now. She fiddled with her bee hat, turning it like a steering wheel inch by little inch. In the distance Sam heard the drone of a gas engine.

"So," she said. "What have you been doing since you left Green Valley?"

"Flying," he said. "Small planes. Mostly cargo."

"Whereabouts?"

"The Northeast. I flew over your farm once."

"You did?"

"You wouldn't believe what it looked like from above." He described for her the long fields, the swath of Chickadee Woods and Solomon's Ravine, and the maze—a tangle of gnarled brambles from above. He saw her relax, just a little, as he spoke. She asked him what had brought him back to Green Valley, and he'd told her only that he'd felt it was time to take up the family banner and join the police force. His parents had moved to Florida two years ago, leaving the house empty in hopes that he might return to claim it. At some point, he figured he might as well.

He did not mention the accident; he didn't want her to know how broken down he was, how rain made his bones ache, how his skin might as well have been a thick canvas, how he was the only Van Winkle who apparently didn't have the hero gene. He kept the conversation light, asking about her farm and maze and boarders. Anything that would prevent her from having to talk about herself. People said she had stopped leaving the farm; he couldn't imagine why. As children, they'd played many games that involved exploring—pretending Soldier's Hill was Everest, or that Stony Field was the Serengeti. He knew her heart would always be firmly rooted in Green Valley, but he thought she might have traveled at least a little, even if she didn't leave the east coast. But here she was—nine years having not stepped off the Pennywort farm. He couldn't ask her about it, not yet. She would shut him down.

And so he resolved to be patient as he talked about one inconsequential thing after another, until the set of her shoulders had softened, the stiffness of her spine had mellowed ever so slightly, and the line that flickered between her brows had ceased making appearances. Only when she got up and said *I've really got to get going* did he decide to take a risk.

"Come over later and let me make you dinner," he said, his voice light.

"Oh, Sam—I—"

He hauled himself to his feet. "I've got these rosebushes my mother planted that I just can't get to bloom. The woman calls once a day—and do you think she wants to know about her son? Nope. It's the rosebushes. She wants to know about her roses. I could really use your help."

Her eyes had been bright, open, friendly—like what he remembered. But now a darkness so complete and opaque fell over her face, it was as if someone had dropped a heavy curtain between them. She set her hat on her head and pulled it down. "I can't."

"It's okay. I get it."

"You do?"

"You're afraid of my cooking. But I haven't poisoned anyone yet . . ."

Her lips nearly curved into a smile. "I'm not afraid of being poisoned."

"Then what?"

"I have . . . things to do."

"What things?" he asked in a tone that was almost sweet. "Anything I can help with?"

"No. Nothing like that."

"Olivia . . . Tell me the truth," he said softly. "Is it that you don't want to have dinner with me? Or just that you don't leave the property anymore?"

Her eyes went wide.

"Whatever the truth is, I can handle it. But I'd like to know."

She looked away from him. "Sam, things in my life are complicated. I can't even begin to explain. And even if I could . . . Well . . . No—no, I couldn't. I *can't*."

"Hey," he said. He'd upset her. He reached out. He meant to squeeze her arm—in his mind he intended the gesture to be brotherly and comforting. It wasn't as if he could feel her anyway. But everything happened so fast he couldn't take it all in.

He touched the curve of her upper arm just beneath her shoulder, ran his palm down.

"Sam! No!" She jerked away from him. "Oh no. Oh no, Sam. Why would you do that?"

He looked down into his open hand, his tingling, open hand. He'd *felt* her. Hadn't he? Her skin was smooth and warm, her muscle firm beneath. He needed to touch her again—to be sure he hadn't imagined it. The craving for strawberries had vanished; it was her he wanted now. He looked up to find her breathing hard, one hand covering the spot on her arm that he'd touched. "What's wrong?"

"You . . . you shouldn't have done that."

"But I did. Olivia, you're going pale. You should sit down."

A tendon shifted in her neck. "Don't worry about me. You've got to worry about yourself."

He took a step toward her. He wanted a reason to put his hands on her again—to brush her hair behind her ear, or draw her to him to steady her. But when he reached out—he wasn't even sure what he meant to do—she moved away.

"Don't," she said.

He let his hand fall to his side. "Why don't you want me to touch you?"

"I didn't say that."

"Then, what is it?"

"You have to stay back."

He put a few steps between them, though the last thing he wanted to do was stay away. He wanted to pull her hat from her head, touch his fingertips to her lips and see if he'd imagined the feeling of electricity passing between them, that lively, crackling shock. He wanted to run his hands along her collarbones until the straps of her overalls fell. He was sure she wanted him to do it as well; her chest and neck had flushed. And yet, she seemed afraid. "I'm missing something here. What's going on?"

"I don't even know how to begin telling you," she said. Her eyes glinted with emotion, possibly even with tears. "Please. Just—listen to me. There's not a lot of time. Go home, right away, and wash your hands."

"I don't understand . . ."

"I know you don't," she said, her voice taut with frustration. "But I'm asking you to just trust me, okay? Please. Go home, right now, and wash your hands with the harshest soap you've got. Then douse them in vinegar. Okay? You promise?"

Real worry gripped him. "Do you . . . are you sick?"

"No. Not exactly. But . . . there's no time for that now. You have to go."

"Okay, okay," he said. He started walking away from her sideways, step by step, though it seemed she wanted him to run. His skin still felt the live charge of contact; he curled his hand into a fist. "I'm going. But I'll be back. For an explanation."

"Fine!" she called after him. "Just—go!"

He turned, trotting lightly toward the road, his head filled with the clanging of his thoughts. He couldn't explain one thing about Olivia's odd behavior; but he knew this—he'd felt her. He was sure of it. He'd touched her and he'd felt her. He let his trot turn into a jog, and his jog turn into a sprint, and then the ground was flying beneath him, and he wondered about how he could feel so happy when Olivia had seemed so afraid.

Consider the Lilies

fter Sam had touched her, Olivia had started walking. She'd walked under the heat of a blazing afternoon sun until she was damp with sweat, until she couldn't think. She'd walked across the features of the land that had been named long ago: Stony Field, the Trough, Chickadee Wood, and on up the steep, rocky climb of Soldier's Hill, past humble woodland blooms of motherwort, yarrow, and enchanter's nightshade, until she could see all the acres of her farm lying low in the belly of the valley before her, and the closed-up farmhouse sitting in the lee of the mountain by the road, and the Van Winkles' faded blue colonial across the street, and on the hill above it, Gloria's Tudoresque mansion. This high up, at some distance from the world below her, the breeze was refreshing on her overheated skin.

One of the side effects of having been so seldom touched during her lifetime was that when she was touched, her reaction was far bigger and more unwieldy than a normal person's might have been. So few people had touched her in her adult lifetime that any innocent brush, bump, or graze could send her entire day into a dizzy tailspin of both guilt and exultation.

Because she could not touch other people, she'd long taken comfort in everything tactile. She did not walk through high grasses without skimming her hands over the tops, or pass lamb's ear without bending to rub its fuzzy leaves between her forefinger and thumb. Food was not merely sustenance. It transported her, lifted her out of her body. She loved all food so much that she sometimes liked to eat alone so she could fully focus her senses on the tastes that lit up her mouth. During the winter, she inevitably put on ten pounds, spending her days experimenting with whatever foods were on hand. By the end of May, the hard work of running her farm and maze reduced her back to her usual size again.

Her sense of touch, too, was blazingly accurate, hypersensitized in the extreme. She supposed this was a side effect of being so untouchable; she felt *everything*. When she guessed the temperature she was never off by more than a single degree. When the cicadas rattled in the trees during high summer, she felt the soft breath of wind fanning from many distant wings. She never ironed her sheets—not only because she didn't have much use for fastidiousness, but because she liked the sensation of the bends and creases in the fabric running over her skin. She'd even embraced pain, to an extent. Once, in the bleak of winter, she'd held her hand so long over a candle that it blistered—but it had felt like heaven to rush outside and bury her burning skin in the snow. For all her untouchability, she was intensely keyed into, focused on, and obsessed with physical sensations of every kind.

So while she could have beaten herself up over her unnecessarily intense reaction to Sam's touch, she decided instead to go easy. To breathe deep. To focus on the red hawk that was lazily riding a thermal over Soldier's Hill, to think only about the burn of her legs from her climb. She would *not* think too hard about how she was still trembling, even now, in a deep and nonspecific way. Nor would she think about how when the snow began to fall and she inevitably began dreaming about the heat of summer, she would remember the feeling of Sam's skin on hers, the slight stickiness and salt between them, the pressure of his fingers, such a small moment, blown out of proportion by denial and memory.

The people of Green Valley and the Penny Loafers believed Olivia was strong because she was evenhanded and independent, because she didn't blather and prattle and make idle chatter, because she wasn't frivolous or wasteful but tried to be generous to those in need. *I wish I was more like* you, one of the Penny Loafers had said as she was leaving to return to her husband. *You don't need anybody.*

But only Olivia knew that none of the superficial claddings of her personality could make up for the hard truth: that deep down, she was afraid to be alone. She was so constantly in danger of self-pity or loneliness or despair over her lot in life that she needed to hold herself in a perfect posture of unshakable strength. She compensated for her desires by setting hard rules for herself: She would not regret, she would not be greedy for a life she would never have, she would not tolerate fear of being alone.

But the way Sam had smiled at her as she'd walked toward him from the beehives, smiled as if she were a bride behind her veil and he a groom ready to attend, gave her an unexpected and unsought glimpse into a kind of happiness that she would never normally have allowed herself to acknowledge. And the touch of his hand had literally made her tremble with a thing that felt, she had to admit, like her every hope and fear had been ignited into a wild burn.

She had thought, for a moment today when the sun had been so golden on her fields, that perhaps, just maybe, she might just find a real friend in Sam. She enjoyed his company, his conversation, and she felt a deep sense of curiosity to know more about him. Was he still so cerebral, as he'd been when they were children? Always analytical and impatient? Did he still strive for perfection and get irritated when it was out of reach—or did his new slouch, his tired eyes, and his banged-up shoes indicate that he no longer cared about looking neat and tidy? And if so, why the change?

She looked down at her watch and was surprised to see it was so late in the day. She'd thought they'd been talking for fifteen minutes; it had actually been an hour, which was an excessively long break for her to take. While she'd sat with him under the tree, she'd been unable to withstand the great swell of hope and optimism that his aggressive friendliness made her feel. *Maybe,* she'd thought, *this will work. Maybe I'll have a friend.*

But then, he'd touched her. The feeling of his hand on her skin was still a distinct impression, like ice that holds the shape of a leaf long after the leaf has crumbled away. And two things changed: First, she knew she still wanted him in that same old way, on a level that was elemental and animal and chemical and utterly miserable and thrilling and miserable again. Second, in a matter of hours, depending on how quickly his skin reacted to her, he would know her for what she was. And in all likelihood, he would run away.

She stayed on the top of the hill, looking down on the valley, until she was breathing evenly again. Soon the sun would sink, the bats would begin to wake, the moon would appear over the edge of the horizon. She had just enough light to make her way down to Solomon's Ravine to quickly check in with her father and return to her silo. By the time she climbed down the mountain and into the ravine, she was feeling no better—though she should have been.

"Dad." She found Arthur bent over a beat-up silver pot set on the rock he referred to as his kitchen. The goat bleated at her loudly, dancing on its hooves, as she approached.

"Olivia! Care to join me for a bite?"

She said she would. She wanted to be distracted; her mind

was a whirlwind that she needed to slow down. She sat on a cut tree stump while Arthur went to fetch a second bowl and the goat nuzzled against her. The dish Arthur had made was nothing fancy: just blanched peppers and corn, tossed with black beans, cilantro, garlic, and oil. It was cool food for a hot day, and she was glad. They ate together in silence for a time, which was not unusual. The goat settled onto the ground. Arthur did not bring up moving out of the ravine, and neither did she. All the while, the imprint of Sam's hand burned on her skin, and the urge to tell her father about what had happened was enormous. Arthur was the only person who knew of her condition—for the moment. But there was a chance that by morning, Sam would understand as well. And that terrified her.

When they were finished she cleared her throat and said, "Sam was here today."

"Of course he was," Arthur said, and he smiled his crooked smile behind his beard. "And did you send him away or did you let him enjoy your company for a while?"

"He . . . he grabbed my arm."

Arthur's gaze shot up. "He hurt you?"

"No. He would never. But I might have hurt him."

"Ah. I see." Arthur's gaze returned to his bowl.

"He was so extremely allergic to everything," Olivia said. "I'm sure he's going to have a reaction. Everyone does—but, Sam especially."

"So you'll have to tell him. Is that what you're worried about?"

She nodded.

"My love, you are what you are. Sam will understand."

Olivia shook her head, but said nothing. Perhaps Sam might understand. Perhaps he wouldn't mind or care. He would tolerate her, be polite to her, treat her no differently. But she didn't want him *knowing*. She liked it better when she could be distant and perfect, as opposed to intimate and imperfect. She didn't want him to look at her and feel sorry for her, or feel afraid of her, or think *What a shame.*

But there was no way around it now.

"Think of this," her father said. "Once he knows, he'll know. And then you won't have to worry about him finding out anymore."

"Thanks, Dad," she said. She knew he was right. And she should have felt some relief. But she'd liked being able to look into Sam's eyes and know that when he was looking back, what he was seeing was not a monster, not a freak, just a woman.

She felt her father looking at her, trying to puzzle out the things she couldn't say. At last, he stood up. The goat too got to his hooves, ready to follow. She thought he would say good night, but instead he said, "Just a minute."

She watched the brief argument between them as Arthur told the goat to stay put and the goat resolutely followed him inside the shack. When they emerged Arthur was holding a pink bottle of sunscreen she'd given him the year before. His face was somber as he put it in her hand. The goat sniffed to investigate, looking for food, but she tugged the bottle away.

"What's this?" she asked.

"I've been working on it. It's for you."

"Sunscreen?"

"Oh no. That's just the bottle I had on hand. This is something much more special. I've been working on it since Sam got back."

Olivia twisted the lid and brought the bottle to her nose. It smelled bitter and metallic beneath a heavy dose of menthol. Her father was always making one concoction or another—his own brand of animal scent for hunting, his own ointment to keep the winter cold off his cheeks, his own form of antacid tablets. She peered down into the bottle's neck but could not see what was inside. "Well, don't keep me in suspense any longer. What is it?"

"It's a protective serum, made with a linseed oil base. It forms a barrier between one person's skin and another. Or at least, it's supposed to."

"Wait. Say that again."

"It forms a barrier, Olivia. A nearly imperceptible one. Between your skin and someone else's. In theory. But I haven't tried an actual test."

"I thought you stopped doing this years ago. Trying to . . . to find a solution, I mean."

Arthur glanced up sheepishly. "Do you not want it?"

Olivia looked at the bottle. All of Arthur's cures and experiments had failed in the past; she could not imagine this one would be any different. But still, the fact that he'd continued working on her behalf when she'd thought he'd given up touched her deeply. "I don't know what to say."

Arthur shrugged. "It might not work. We don't know precisely how your condition has come about, if one kind of allergen or another is more prevalent in your skin, or if it's a cocktail of allergens, or what. I did what I could to cover our bases. But there's no telling."

"Still," she said. Her heart was beginning to pound. The implication of the serum working was enormous—if it worked. Her breath came fast.

Maybe she could hug her father.

Maybe she could kiss someone hello.

Maybe she could high-five a child.

And . . . Sam . . .

"Oh now," Arthur said. "No cause for waterworks."

"Sorry," she said. She composed herself quickly while her father busied himself with picking up dirty pots and bowls, the goat puttering behind him. He'd never quite known what to do with himself when Olivia accidentally displayed a bit too much emotion. She took quiet breaths and gathered her wits. She ran a thumb over the plastic bottle. Even if it could work, who might she ask to try it with her? Her father was no longer a suitable test subject because he was old and didn't heal the way he used to; even if he'd volunteered to let her try it with him, she would have refused. He needed his strength.

But surely her father didn't mean for her to try it with Sam? He was far too sensitive to take that kind of risk. Plus, there was every chance that Sam would avoid her, and rightly so, from here on. Probably he would take a conciliatory approach: He would not mention his irritated skin, would continue to flash a neighborly wave now and again, would stop to talk with her politely about the weather, would perhaps throw her newspaper on the porch if he saw it in the road. But he would never touch her again.

She felt a familiar tightness in her chest, and she ignored it. "I've got to get going," she said, more because she was afraid of betraying the oceans of her feelings than because she had work to do. She tested the weight of the bottle in her hand; it felt about half full.

"Well, thanks for this."

"It's nothing," Arthur said. "Nothing at all."

She patted the goat and then headed up the hard slant of the ravine, thinking she might go into her poison garden for a while. She felt shaky and off, unfamiliar to herself in some way. When she first truly understood the life that had been put before her, she'd mourned for a year that began with her twentieth birthday, indulging in self-pity of every kind. She gained weight, she grew mean-spirited, she sulked. Then, on a winter day when the snow fell and she realized she had not spoken to any other human being besides her father in three days, she understood that her despair had been nothing but a prolonged temper tantrum, a protest like throwing herself at the feet of the Almighty if there was one and saying *Make it stop!*

Lilies of the field did not threaten to uproot themselves if they didn't like where they were planted. On the slopes of the mountains, saplings struggled to grow in the shallowest puddles of soil that collected on bald rocks. Along the side of the valley's single road, chicory and yellow trefoil had learned to thrive in waste spaces, where passing cars blew exhaust against them all day long. Like Olivia, they had no say over where their seeds took hold: When they could not change their surroundings, they themselves had to change.

And so, Olivia realized that she would never be able to change her desire for a normal future, but she could change her expectations. She would farm; she would continue her mother's work in the maze and she would hold her work as sacred to Green Valley; she would keep her father company in his old age; she would create a world that sustained the Penny Loafers, who were colorful if inconsistent company. This would be all the satisfaction she would allow herself to expect, and it would be enough.

But with the bottle in her hand as she reached the top of the ravine, she saw that all her many years of telling herself *it's all okay* were now in jeopardy. Denial was a fragile and reedy thing, possible to keep in place as long as there were no strong winds, no distractions, no temptations.

What would she do if the serum worked?

What would she do if it *didn't*?

From outside of her central garden, she could smell the fertile odor of her plants, notes of sweet green hanging in the air, calling to her like old friends, welcoming, affirming, telling her she was okay, she was perfect, she should never change. She took the key from around her neck and went inside.

Garden-Variety Magic

Sam saw the first fireflies speckling the shadows in the bottom of the valley and knew that tonight would be a firefly night. It was as if the creatures came to gather from all the far corners of the earth; their yellow-green glow dappled the shadows of bushes, made halos of treetops, and trailed through the air like a glowing vapor. Arthur used to say that he could make a wish if he caught one of the bugs, which wasn't a difficult task when the weather shifted and brought the lightning bugs in: All he had to do was reach out a hand and close it, like catching rain. Some nights, Olivia and Sam would run around gently corralling as many bugs as they could, filling glass jars with fireflies and then free-ing them all at once, so a brilliant column of light would erupt into the night, bathing their upturned faces in gold. Sometimes they would lie on their backs and let their eyes go unfocused until Sam lost the difference between the fireflies and the stars.

Tonight was a firefly night. And as Sam settled on a bench in the maze to wait for Olivia, the air was a dark ocean of electric-ity, simultaneously peaceful and charged. He'd come back to Green Valley thinking he would never again be surprised, that life was mostly a dull thing, and that what surprises did come were more likely to be misfortunes than windfalls. And yet, the town had done nothing but surprise him since his return.

When Sam had opened his eyes in the morning, his right hand had been itchy. Just a little. And it made him think of his mother. *That's good luck,* she would say. *An itchy palm means something good's coming your way.* He was certain the superstition was right, because in the hours before he went to bed last night, he'd wondered—*Am I actually feeling the sheets and the lamp switch, or is it my imagination?*

By morning, he was certain: He could feel—everything—again.

The joy was overwhelming. He'd been living under a cloud for a year and a half, and suddenly the sun was out. He'd wanted to run to Olivia to tell her: *Look what you did!* He was certain that, somehow, contacting her skin had boosted his sense of touch like a defibrillator jolts the heart of a dying man. Getting ready for work was a carnival of the senses, absolute decadence. The water in the shower was wet. *Wet!* The shaving cream was cool and silky. The bath towel was scratchy—he'd had no idea they were so cheap, and he couldn't have been more thrilled because the texture of stiff terry on his cheek was heaven.

In his daydreams as he dressed for the day, he imagined the silver-haired doctor at the hospital—the one who had insisted Sam's condition was all in his head—telling him that the only thing to change had been his state of mind. But he was certain that Olivia's touch had changed him, or at least, her touch had flipped the switch that turned his nerve endings back on. His cells were waking up again, snapping back to life one by one like kernels of popcorn. He knew it by the dewiness of the morning air, the feel of the sun on his face, and the itching on his palm.

He'd bought doughnuts for everyone at the station—it didn't matter that it was cliché—and he gave the ancient and angry secretary Dorothea the shock of her life when he kissed her good morning on her papery cheek. In spite of the mild itch of his hand, he could not stop himself from wondering: Had he been brought back to Green Valley for a reason? The whole of his twenties—spent in bars and motels, spent with women he didn't love and friends who hadn't really understood him—had been an utter waste of a perfectly good life. Then the accident had wrecked him, and he'd lost all sense of desire, all feeling, all purpose.

But now, he *wanted* again. He was interested and excited and curious and greedy and eager to see what might happen next. And he had plans. Because when Olivia had touched him, he realized: Part of what he wanted was *her.* He'd barely given a thought to anything remotely sexual for almost two years— there was no point—but now he felt as if desire had been building up in his system all along and was suddenly battering him from the inside out.

Olivia was conflicted about him, reticent and withholding—he could acknowledge that. But he'd never been patient. He felt oddly giddy, intoxicated, as he cruised Green Valley. He allowed speeding cars to go by unimpeded; he didn't yell at the kids who threw rocks at the decaying drive-in movie theater; he almost hit a disorderly shopping cart at the grocery store. His fantasies were wild distractions that raced well ahead of his rational brain and blazed into ridiculous territories—he saw himself making love to Olivia on a blanket in Stony Field, he saw Olivia laughing as she unpacked her boxes to move into his house, he saw a crackling winter fire and an evening spent contemplating the name of their first child.

The morning sun, the heat of the steering wheel, the gentle giants of the green hills, the songs on the radio—everything seemed to be saying: *Yes! Sam! You're meant to be here! This is all for you!* If each of his prior struggles or miseries was like a puzzle piece that ultimately created this exact picture of his life, he would not change a single struggle or misery or mistake he'd made—except for one. Things were turning around. This feeling of his mood being a hot air balloon and carrying him through the day, this, at last, was the definition of the word *sublime*.

But by lunchtime—a Coca-Cola and an egg sandwich from the convenience store/pharmacy/bait shop/deli—the itching of his palm had stopped being ignorable. The webs at the base of his thumb became an angry hornet's nest of red skin. The creases on the undersides of his knuckles were like miniature whip lines, and the bumps at the bases of his fingers swelled. He itched, and itched, and itched, and the misery of it would not go away.

The afternoon also descended into the mundane: His colleagues teased him about holding the record for the longest stretch a Van Winkle had ever gone without saving somebody's life; Mrs. Oradell had yet another raccoon in her garage; Dorothea, who had seemed so sunny when he'd kissed her cheek in the morning, suddenly turned mean as the north wind and refused to give him a new notepad upon request. The swell of his good energy and optimism eroded as the minute hand swept the wondrous morning under the rug of an average day.

Some of the guys saw him itching—or forcibly trying not to itch—and asked if he'd gotten himself into poison ivy. Some saw him itching, slid their eyes away from him, and asked nothing at all.

All afternoon long he repeated a silent mantra: Olivia had nothing to do with the itching. She wasn't his irritant. She was his cure.

But as the day went on, he found himself stopping once again at the convenience store/pharmacy/bait shop/deli—this time for Benadryl and calamine lotion. And soon the horrible, awful, heartbreaking truth of what he didn't want to suspect became impossible to ignore.

Olivia had tried to warn him.

The one woman in almost two years he'd been able to feel—and he was allergic to her.

Despair wasn't the word.

Now, under the diffused glow of fireflies, he looked up from the bench in the garden maze to see Olivia crossing toward her central garden. He'd known she would come, here, where she always retreated when she wanted to get away. The fireflies had concentrated around her, so he could see that she was wearing a pale cotton dress that made her look as sweet and cool as an ice cream cone. Her hair had been loosely pinned off her neck, tendrils hanging artlessly around her face, and a large white flower was tucked behind one ear.

"Olivia," he said softly.

She was startled but she didn't cry out. She only pressed a hand to her chest for a moment. "Sam," she said. The fireflies rippled a little on the vibration of the word.

He suddenly felt the heaviest pain in his heart that he'd known since he'd died on Moggy Knob, a despair made to feel even darker by juxtaposition with the wild joy of the morning. His flirtation with optimism had been the practical joke of a cruel universe. The return of desire wasn't a reward; it was a punishment.

"Is it just *me*?" he asked. His voice was hoarse; he hadn't realized how long he'd been sitting alone in the garden. He held up his bandaged hand. "Am I the only one this happens to?"

"It's not just you," she said. "It's anyone I touch. I . . . I hurt them."

He got to his feet and immediately he noticed a change in Olivia's posture, that animal wariness he'd glimpsed before but hadn't been able to place. He saw now that she was always on guard, keeping herself away, watching for sudden moves. No wonder she worked so hard to hold him at arm's length—physically, but emotionally, too. She was afraid.

"How did this happen?" he asked.

"I promised you an explanation," she said. "But . . . I don't know how to tell you. I've never told anyone."

"But you'll tell me?" he said.

"Don't I have to?"

"No. You don't have to tell me anything you don't want to."

She looked at him for a long moment. Then she gestured to him, and he followed her through the maze. The fireflies circled and clustered curiously around them, lighting the quiet pathways and twinkling like drunken stars. He smelled every earthy and floral scent, felt the air as if each molecule had noticeable weight, but the sensations no longer thrilled him as they had this morning. As she walked before him, he stared at the base of her narrow neck, the smooth expanse of skin between the straps of her dress and the arcs of her shoulder blades, and it was the most simultaneously beautiful and excruciating sight he'd ever seen. He was intensely gratified when she took a wrong turn. Even in the dark he could tell she was blushing with embarrassment. She excused herself and they continued down the hollows and meanders, beneath a long, firefly-lit tunnel of tumescent purple flowers, until she stopped.

"Here we are," she said at last. She gestured for him to go first into the room of the garden maze.

The garden was laid out in a circle. Lunettes and stars had been pruned into the tops of the hedges. And the flowers, softly white under the moon, seemed to glow, actually glow, as if lit from within by their own secret light. The Mushroom Garden had been impressive. But this, this was astonishing. Each white petal of each white flower echoed the light of the moon behind the gauze of threadbare clouds. A heavy perfume of flowers hung in the air, which itself seemed to be a living thing, a breathing thing, full of the songs of night animals and the glow of fireflies. Olivia had created a garden for lovers, a place for stolen kisses, extravagant promises, caresses as intense and heady as the garden itself. Sam reached out, touched the edge of a petal that felt shockingly like flesh. Much as he loved the romance of the garden, it also made him sad: so many implied fantasies that he knew he would never own.

"What do you call this place?" he asked.

She looked at him over her shoulder. "The Night Garden."

"It's beautiful," he said.

She sat down on a white marble bench and he joined her, too aware of her proximity. She smelled of flowers and coconut oil. He wished he could lie down with her, explore all the possibilities that had been promised by the return of sensation in his skin, lose himself in the overwhelming textures and scents of the Night Garden, of her. But he only sat beside her and stared.

"Can I see your hand?" she asked him.

He told her it was better if she didn't.

"I'm really sorry," she said.

"How could something like this happen?"

"I don't know—not specifically. I only have theories."

"Tell me."

She leaned back with her palms against the bench to look out to the garden, where fireflies clustered low among the leaves of the moon-pale flowers. "It was the garden," she said. And then she explained. Sam could remember one afternoon that Arthur had spent telling stories about poisonous plants, how jimsonweed got its name from the Jamestown settlement, where it had killed many colonists by accident and many soldiers by design. He told Sam about how certain plants could be harmless under some circumstances and poisonous under others: potatoes, rhubarb, cashews, and kidney beans. Sam had thought nothing of

Arthur's odd excitement and sudden interest in poisonous plants: Arthur had also, at varying times, been interested in keeping small sharks in an aquarium in the farmhouse living room and in building his own catapults based on medieval plans. That Arthur might have been actually growing the dangerous plants he talked about had never crossed Sam's mind, and even if the thought had occurred to him, it wouldn't have been the strangest thing to happen on the Pennywort farm. Even on the night Sam had accidentally peered into Olivia's garden and seen her there, he hadn't realized the plants around her had been so dangerous. He'd been too focused on her to notice there were plants at all.

As the fireflies circled and swirled, Olivia told the story of discovering her condition, and the way she told it—in stops and starts—suggested she'd never told it before nor ever meant to. For the first time, Sam understood why he'd been so sensitive to poison ivy that summer of his senior year; the sensitivity had never been quite as "exquisite" again, but neither had it fully left him. He remained more sensitive to poison ivy than most. It had never occurred to him that he was allergic to Olivia; that was too preposterous a leap of understanding to make. Olivia also had no idea that the cause of everyone's discomfort wasn't the garden, but was *her.*

One night, Olivia had summoned all her courage and spoke to her father about the garden, which was becoming more dangerous by the day. The Professor had been vacuuming Roger the snow leopard's fur with a Dustbuster, and Olivia had to shout over the moan of sucked-up air. *I think we should stop,* she told him as he worked on the fur between Roger's ears. She had yet to realize how connected she already was to the garden. She said, *Everyone's getting these rashes and we don't know why. I think we should just close up the walled-in garden and leave it be.* Her father turned off the vacuum, and the look in his eyes was so sad, so disappointed and forlorn that Olivia would have given anything to take her words back and would have said anything to make the sadness on his face go away. When he told her the rashes were nothing to worry about, she quickly agreed. He said that something in his detergent was irritating his skin, and she said *Yes of course,* even though she had been doing the Professor's laundry once a week and she'd been using the same detergent that her mother had used since Olivia was born. But she did not argue with him. She much preferred to see her father distracted by the plants in his greenhouse and walled-in garden than by his own thoughts, which sometimes seemed to lead him down into such remote and shadowy places that Olivia worried he might one day disappear into them altogether.

One terrible day just after the school year began and shortly before Arthur moved into the ravine, Olivia crept up behind her father and traced a distinct X with her index finger on the back of his sun-spotted neck—just to prove that her secret niggling suspicions about herself were unfounded, ridiculous, and flat wrong. But only a few hours later, she saw him mindlessly itching while he was reading his dog-eared copy of *On The Origin of the Species,* and she did not let herself draw a conclusion until she walked around behind him and saw, there on his fragile skin beneath his white hair, a red, angry X. She'd gone running into the bushes to throw up her lunch.

"It was the last time I touched my father. The last time I deliberately touched anyone," Olivia said. "Now, you understand."

She was looking out at the Night Garden, the fireflies whirling like snowflakes, the white flowers glowing, the smell of unbridled fertility hanging in the air. To think that Green Valley's odd magic had put Olivia out of reach to him—Olivia, the first woman he'd been able to feel in ages—was infuriating. And yet, as difficult as the news was for him to hear right now, she had been living with it for years.

Olivia's fingers were twisted together on her lap, her shoulders stiff. In spite of her agitation, she was lovely. Her reddish hair in the moonlight had deepened to a winelike color and had taken on a silvery sheen; her skin seemed to glow like the flowers around her. But her face was turned away from him, as if she was afraid of what she might see in his eyes now that he knew the truth about what she was.

"Olivia."

She glanced at him.

"I'm glad you explained this to me."

"I only told you because I knew you would probably figure it out."

"Still," he said. "I wouldn't have known the details. Your perspective. I'm glad you shared."

She unlaced her fingers and slid her palms down her arms. Her skin was pebbled with goose bumps that had nothing to do with the temperature, and he wanted to run his hands over the raised bumps, over the pebbling and stiffening that he knew would feel exquisite under his fingertips. Had he ever paid attention to such things before he'd lost his feeling? He wasn't certain. But he would pay attention now. The next time he made love—he stopped mid-thought. In spite of his desire, the next time would *not* be with Olivia. Maybe it never would. He didn't quite know what to do with the realization, so he put the problem aside for now. "Does anyone else know about this?"

"Only my father," she said.

"How have you kept the boarders from finding out? What about Tom?"

"It's been tricky. I've had a few close calls. But the boarders are in and out all summer long; they're never the same group twice. And even if they were gossiping about me, if someone did have a suspicion, who would believe it? It would sound too insane."

"You must be lonely," he said. She lifted a shoulder as if she didn't care. But he knew better. "Is there a way to . . . to change things?"

She shook her head. "If I don't go into the garden regularly, I'll die. I need it in some way I can't explain. It's like, you know how normal people take vitamins? I need to be exposed to all the various chemicals in my garden on a regular basis. I think maybe they can be absorbed through my skin."

"What about the winter? When your garden dies?"

"I do bring some of my poison plants with me into the silo for the winter. But I need more than that. I need a supplement."

"What?"

She gave him a sly smile. "Can you guess?"

He leaned back and crossed his arms, thinking. "Hmm. Do you dry the leaves or something? Make them into a tea?"

"No. My method is a lot sweeter."

"Sweeter . . ."

"Yes. Much sweeter."

He saw her with his mind's eye at the beehives, walking toward him, her face hidden behind her veil. "The honey," he said.

She smiled—the first smile he'd seen all evening that reached her eyes. "I knew you'd figure it out."

He thought of the apiaries, the fat, friendly, noxious Pennywort bees. "The bees pollinate the plants in the Poison Garden."

"Yes. That's why I don't let anyone buy it. It could be deadly, even in small doses, to anyone but me. A few tablespoons of honey a day seems to keep me going during the winter. It's not as good as the real thing, but it works."

"Have you tried not going into the garden? Or not taking the honey over the winter? Just to see?"

He saw her bristle. "Yes. It doesn't work."

"Are you sure?"

"I'm sure, Sam. That's a dead end," she said tightly. Maybe even defensively.

His mind was racing. He wanted to fix the problem of the Poison Garden for her, for the sake of her happiness—and also for his. He wanted, he realized, to be her hero in some way that he couldn't be anyone else's. The need to help her was an urge that was almost crushing in its intensity. "What about going to a doctor? Have you been?"

She laughed. "God, no. I'm not prepared to be anyone's exciting new lab rat. And, really, in and of myself, I'm totally healthy. I'm fine. It's everyone else that's got a problem with me, if you think about it." She stood and took a few steps away from him, the fireflies shifting and blinking around her. There was a small stone fountain in the garden, its water still for the night, and she touched her fingertips to the bowl's surface. It rippled in concentric light. "Anyway, who knows why things are the way they are. Maybe it's better this way—that no one can touch me. I've got a good life here, Sam. Quiet. The only thing I worry about except for my father is the farm. People stay away. And I'm . . . I'm used to that. I'm okay with it. It makes things easier if you think about it. People . . . people are so much more dangerous than any of my plants."

Sam pulled his legs more tightly beneath him. In a way, Olivia was not so different than the poison ivy that she grew in her garden. Arthur had told him that poison ivy was poisonous to human beings—and no other animals. Somewhere along the line, somehow, the plant developed an allergen called urushiol, which irritated the skin of most humans. But the urushiol itself wasn't harmful—it did nothing to the eerie-eyed goats that lived in Green Valley, who grazed on it as if the vines were a salad bar. Its self-defense system had evolved specifically to deter human beings from getting near it; Olivia was talking as if she thought of herself the same way.

She stirred the still fountain with her long fingers, looking for all the world as ethereal as a beam of moonlight. His heart ached with memories of her. "Olivia, what was the reason you broke things off with us?"

"Does it matter now?"

"I'd like you to tell me." She was quiet, but he resolved to wait her out. The fireflies flurried about in the bushes; in the woods, some night bird cried. "Olivia . . ."

Her words were hushed. "You must know the reason. Please don't ask."

"You were afraid you would hurt me," he said.

"Yes," she said.

And yet, she had hurt him anyway. He thought: *I should have known something was wrong.* He'd been eighteen when he decided to leave Green Valley. But leaving had never been what he'd wanted. He'd meant to stay forever, to get a job doing something suitably heroic, to build a house next to his parents' on their subdivided lot, to marry Olivia in the apple orchard on her farm. He'd figured that his future with her was as much a part of his fate as his future as a Van Winkle, Saver of Human Lives. When she'd rejected him, it hadn't just broken his heart. It had annihilated his faith in the life he'd been so certain was before him. He hadn't realized she'd sacrificed her own happiness, her own future, for his.

"I'm sorry," he said. "I didn't realize."

She shrugged. "You couldn't have known."

"Still. I wish I had."

"Don't say that," she said. "I know you and I were, oh, *close* at one point. But the best thing that you could have done was to go out there and live your life and be happy about it in every way possible. And that's exactly what you did." She turned to him, and for the first time all evening, she held his eye. Though she didn't touch him, he warmed as if she'd put a hand on his chest. "I was glad you left, Sam. I liked to think of you somewhere, living a good life. I used to picture you hunting truffles in France or golden chanterelles in Oregon. Maybe you were out there sailing, or climbing mountains, or chasing your kids around on bicycles in some city park. I don't know. I guessed I just liked the thought that you were happy in a way that—" She bit her lower lip, glanced at the fountain. Her fingers dripped.

"In a way that you aren't?"

"That's not what I meant. Just that you might have been happy in your own way."

He was quiet for a long moment. The crickets' songs filled the night air. He thought of his years away from Green Valley, years that had felt so empty and drifting to him, though he had not known why. He'd gone to college primarily to kill time; he hadn't known what else to do. He'd made the kind of friends who are lively company for a few years and who then become part of the still-life of memory. In all the time since he'd been away, he did not think he'd had a single conversation as intimate as what was passing between him and Olivia now.

"I don't think I was happy," he admitted. "Not since I left."

"And now? That you're back?"

His heartbeat was plodding and crude, his palms sweating. Olivia beside him, limned by moonlight, her fingers on the surface of the fountain, called up desires in him that were far too animal and ravenous for this delicate and dreamy garden room. If she'd asked him this morning if he was happy to be back, he would have said he was on top of the world. But in this moment, he could not touch that place where her jaw met her neck, nor could he even consider brushing his fingers over her lips or her hair. He'd been given the gift of feeling again—only to be robbed of touching the thing he most wanted to touch.

So, no—he was not especially happy. But he couldn't tell her; he didn't want to lay his misery at her feet when she had enough of her own.

"I'm doing okay," he said.

"Good," she said.

They were quiet for a long time. Occasionally, they heard the sounds of the boarders in the distance, laughing. She took a few steps toward him where he sat; he felt horribly, painfully aware of every part of her, the space she moved through. She said, "This is when you're supposed to run away."

"Why would I do that?"

"Aren't you afraid of me?"

"Afraid?"

"Do you remember what your doctor said? That constant exposure to poison ivy could make you even more sensitive than you already are?"

"Yes. So?"

"So you shouldn't be around me."

He shook his head. "I've always been a little more susceptible than most people to poison ivy. But I think that summer with you was especially bad because—well, because I couldn't keep my hands off you. As long as I don't touch you, I'm sure I'll be fine."

"Still," she said. "Even if being around me won't make you more sensitive, there are still risks. What if I accidentally brush up against you or something? It's probably better if you just stay away."

"Better for me or better for you?"

"Maybe both," she said.

He looked at her and began to understand how warped her perception of herself might have become over the years. "You know, you're not as big and scary as you think you are."

"I *am* dangerous, Sam. I might not look it, but I am."

"No. You're not. Believe me. Would you ever get behind the wheel of a car and play chicken with a bunch of teenagers just because you were annoyed at them for blasting their music?"

"No."

"Mr. Hendershot did that today," Sam said. "Would you ever get drunk and decide to use the side of an old camper for target practice and not think to check if there was somebody sleeping inside it first?"

"You know I wouldn't."

"That was Mag La Feir last week. She's lucky she didn't shoot her own kid."

"I don't understand what point you're making."

"I'm saying you're *not* dangerous. Not in a way that really matters. You would never hurt anyone on purpose. And . . ." He stood. He was only a hand's length from her, his whole body aware of the distance he couldn't close. "For the record, I'm not afraid of you."

A hint of a smile—there and gone—pulled at the corner of her lips. "So you still think we can be . . . friends?"

He nodded.

"Friends." A funny look came over her face. "I'd like to say we should shake on it, but . . ."

"Maybe not the best idea ever," he said.

"Actually—" She stopped. Looked away.

"What?"

"Nothing."

"No way. I didn't let you do that when we were kids and I won't let you now."

She took a half step back, gesturing nervously. "It's nothing. My father made some kind of serum. It's . . . it's supposed to keep people from getting hurt if they touch me. It probably doesn't work."

"Do you have it?"

"Now? I . . . no. Not right at this second."

"Do you want to go get it?"

"Get it? You want me to—? I'm sorry, but it's getting late."

"Tomorrow, then."

"Sam—"

"It's my day off. So I'll pack a picnic for us. You can meet me at the Lightning Oak in the middle of Stony Field."

"I'm not sure that's a good idea," she said. "I mean . . . you're incredibly allergic, to *everything*. For all we know, you might be exceptionally allergic to me. What if the serum doesn't work? Your reaction might be severe."

"I'm not saying we'll strip down and go head-to-toe, skin-to-skin," he said. "We'll be really conservative. Just one little touch. C'mon, Ollie. Stop thinking and say yes."

He was holding his breath; the possibility that she might try out Arthur's new serum with him was thrilling. It might be the solution to all his fears—it could fix the problem of their future together—and he wanted her to test it out *with him*. He wanted her to trust him. He loved that she'd never told anyone about her condition, but that she'd told *him*. That meant something. Her eyes scanned his forehead, his cheeks, his mouth. He stood for it; he wanted her to see that he was serious and would not back down.

She shook her head, but her mouth had curved into an odd smile. "It's not fair."

"What's not?"

"The garden doesn't give me answers. I could sit here all day thinking about this, and it still wouldn't tell me what to do."

"You don't need the garden for this," Sam said. "Decide for yourself."

He felt the air between them, warm and languid. Fireflies lit her face in passing white-green. He'd surprised himself. All day long, accompanied by the burning itch of his hand, he'd assumed that any hope of building the life he'd wanted with Olivia was over. They had no future. But now he saw the faintest glimmer of happiness in the distance—a weak and wavering flame, but a flame nonetheless. And he meant to go after it, whatever it was, finding his footing one step at a time.

"Okay," she said.

He smiled, and he did not drag his thumb across her lip, or push her hair behind her ear, or touch his palm to her cheek, though he wanted to do any or all of those things. A flash in the dark caught his attention. "Hey. Did you see that?"

"What was it?"

"I think it was lightning."

She watched the sky. A cloud lit up in silence as if a firefly had flashed from within, saturating it with interior light. Then the dark returned.

"Just heat lightning," she said. "It's lightning. But it doesn't mean *rain*."

He looked into her eyes and hoped his face could convey even half of what he was feeling. "I'm looking forward to tomorrow."

She nodded. "Do you need help finding your way out of the maze?"

"It's a good night for wandering," he said. He left her among the milky flowers, and as he wound and turned his way through the corridors he was once again beginning to recognize, he allowed his mind to churn and simmer on the question of whether it could even be possible to seduce a woman who couldn't be touched.

Pushing Daisies

The morning broke hot—hot at sunrise, hotter as the sun climbed the sky. A man from Olivia's crew told her that one of her eggplants had baked through on its stem, and he was planning to take it home to his wife so she could smother it in sauce and cheese. Olivia did not allow her boarders to work in the garden maze—the sun was simply too dangerous. Work would be limited to only the essential chores. Not one thing in the valley wanted to move in the heat. The birds hardly peeped. The plants slumped. Even the stones themselves seemed to have given up some of their stoniness, as if they'd tired in some way. Olivia resolved to spending the morning paying bills and making phone calls with Tom in his office. All through the summer, the Pennywort farm had battled mightily to remain stalwart in the heat. But it seemed the season was finally winning, and the farm was losing the fight.

All through Bethel, people talked about the heat, talked about it as incessantly as the sunbeams bore down. And after they were done talking about the heat, they inevitably talked about Gloria Zeiger's homeless shelter, which had made the papers as funds were raised leading up to the grand opening. Some of the Penny Loafers had seen the article, which showed a large picture of their neighbor and the mayor standing in front of big azaleas and holding an oversized pair of scissors together as if they might at any moment start a tug-of-war. In the humid heat of the barn, the boarders asked Olivia what she knew about it, what she'd heard. And Olivia could tell that they were fishing around to see if they would be forced to abandon their cots in the barn now that the shelter was about to open. Olivia assured them: *You don't have to do anything you don't want to do.* And yet, she knew there were laws and codes that she had been breaking for many years, and that if the town decided to give her a hard time about her boarders, it had the grounds. She could only hope that the strength of tradition and of Green Valley popular opinion would leave the workings of her farm unchanged.

She looked around at the women in the barn—her best company, her family—and felt an itch in the back of her throat. Only this morning they'd just lost Emmie, an older woman who had arrived at the maze one day wondering what to do with her retirement. Emmie had been cheerful and well liked during the three weeks she'd stayed in the barn; unlike so many of the boarders, she had not come to the maze in the grip of an especially dire problem or controversy. Instead, she simply waited, walking the maze once a day, taking her time, weighing her options, until finally she emerged from the Sundial Garden to announce that she knew what she would do with her life now that she was no longer working: She would devote herself to mentoring single mothers who came from difficult backgrounds. Olivia had liked her in the cautious and outlying way she'd liked so many of the Penny Loafers over the years, but she'd also steeled herself against liking her too much—for it was inevitable that the woman would someday go. Eventually, all of the boarders left the farm, just like all the people Olivia had loved had disappeared from it over the years. She could only hope that the Penny Loafers would not be harassed now that Gloria's shelter was open and was so glaringly obvious in its intention to move the Penny Loafers in.

Mei, the newest boarder, was no doubt a shining example of why the women on the Pennywort farm needed to be corralled and contained. Mei was a little rough around the edges: She had a mouth like a truck driver, an undercurrent of belligerence even when she was asking *Can you pass the bread?* She was nosy with the other boarders as they worked together in the garden maze, but she was especially prying with Olivia, asking pointed questions about why Olivia didn't have a boyfriend, and how long it had been since she'd let anyone touch her, so that Olivia came to wonder if perhaps Mei had known full well what she was doing the night she'd tried to open the Poison Garden's door. But then, just when Olivia was sure Mei was untrustworthy, Olivia would catch glimpses of deep vulnerability: Sometimes she seemed to drift off into thought, and the look on her face spoke of a girl who felt very, very alone.

Olivia waited for an opportunity to talk again in private with Mei. At around eleven thirty, the Penny Loafers left the garden maze and headed into the barn to make sandwiches for lunch, heaping fresh meats and cheeses on bread, filling their plates with colorful salad and their glasses with lemonade. After Mei had made her own sandwich, Olivia pulled her aside to sit in a private corner of the barn. Olivia's excuse for the conversation was that she needed to give Mei a more detailed rundown of the farm now that it was clear the girl was going to stay. But instead of talking about work, Olivia asked questions about Mei. And to her surprise, she found that Mei was pleased to answer.

Mei was originally from Newburgh, on the Hudson River, but had moved to Green Valley last year because of an ex-boyfriend that she no longer saw. Early on in the conversation, she managed to mention that the things she missed most since being pregnant were drinking and smoking pot. She'd apparently done some time in juvenile detention after she'd accidentally crashed her neighbor's car, which she'd borrowed without asking when she was sixteen. The father of her child was an on-again, off-again boyfriend in Newburgh who didn't officially have a job but who drove a Mustang and wore a diamond watch. Mei's parents wanted her to give the baby up for adoption; she wanted to keep it—maybe—even though she was supposed to be going to community college for a degree. At some point, Olivia had the sense that Mei wanted Olivia to be disgusted by her, as if she expected to be reprimanded, frowned upon, kicked out—and wouldn't be happy until it happened. When Olivia didn't react with judgment, shock, or disapproval, the details of Mei's story only became more lurid—but Olivia refused to play the game. She was as gentle as she could be: *You can tell me anything you want, Mei.*

There was, however, one small point that she needed to bring up with the girl. A couple of the other boarders had approached her earlier to complain that Mei wasn't pulling her weight, that she was lazing about all day drinking iced tea, playing with the half-feral, all-white cats that lived in the outbuildings, and hovering about the women who *were* actually working while she did nothing but talk incessantly and give the occasional opinion on what needed to be done.

"I'm wondering if you're finding the work in the garden to be too much," Olivia said to her, her hands folded on the old wooden table between them.

"Why?" Mei asked. "What have people been saying?"

"Just that you don't seem to like working in the maze. And I don't blame you. It's hot. And I can't imagine you're very comfortable right now."

"So, what? That's it? If I don't work like a slave, I'm gone?"

"Not at all," Olivia said. "But let's find something that you can do. Something you'll enjoy doing. Is there anything you'd like to work on besides the garden maze?"

Mei crossed her arms. "No. Probably not."

Olivia glanced outside; the flagpole's shadow was small, the sun high. It was time to meet Sam. "I have to go. But think about what you might be interested in working on. In the meantime, you can help me cook in the silo later instead of working in the maze."

"Where you going?" Mei asked.

"Out," Olivia said. "I'll come get you when it's time to cook dinner. For now, you just relax."

"You're going to meet that guy, aren't you?"

Olivia brushed a random piece of grass off her skirt.

"Kinda pointless, if you ask me. How is he going to be your boyfriend if he can't touch you?"

"He's not my boyfriend."

"But you want him to be. And I'm telling you, you might as well forget it. If you don't put out he'll find someone who will."

Olivia shook her head. She knew that Mei's view of men had been skewed, and yet there was something unnerving about the warning. She left the girl in the slightly cooler shadows of the old barn. Outside, the sky was a hot, burning white, the air so humid the hills were a distant blur. Everything—the powerful heat that seemed to echo her inner state, Mei's big belly that made her so secretly jealous, the persistent fruitfulness of summer raging on—made her think of Sam, as if his presence had infiltrated every nook and corner of her life, even those things that had nothing to do with him.

As she crossed the fields toward the distant oak, her belly fluttered with nerves but also with the excitement of trying Arthur's serum, of touching—however briefly—Sam's skin. This morning before the sunrise, she'd set her hair in a pretty Dutch braid around the crown of her head, put some essential oil of bergamot behind her earlobes, and added just the tiniest hint of gloss to her lips—before she undid her hair, washed behind her ears, and wiped her lips clean. She hated to remind herself: This was no date—no flirtation or mating dance. She had no need of pretty hair or pouty lips. No—she'd deliberately worn her same old clothes—a long skirt that skimmed her boots, her regulatory cotton tank, her garden key around her neck. She would accept Sam's offer of friendship, rely on the notion that he couldn't affect her any more than she let him, and try to hold him just enough away from her that she could be content with friendship and nothing more.

When she saw him standing beneath the Lightning Oak in the center of Stony Field, he waved and waited as she approached. His hair was a blue-black shadow, his face was newly shaved, his clothes were casual but nice. On a shaded gingham blanket he'd spread out a gorgeous picnic: dark red grapes, various white cheeses and caramelized nuts, fresh mozzarella and tomato sandwiches on crusty bread, wine in a galvanized bucket full of ice, and fresh green beans, her favorite food of summer. He remembered.

"You came," he said.

"Of course I did. I've been looking forward to seeing—the oak. I haven't been out here since we let this field go fallow." She touched the tree, gave it a pat for good measure.

"I assure you the oak is very happy to see you," he said. "You look wonderful."

"I'm sure I don't." She touched her hair and thought she should have left it braided. "Oh! What a beautiful picnic! Is all of this for us?"

"I wouldn't want you wasting away."

She laughed. "No likelihood of that!"

She settled herself on the blanket and wondered as he lowered himself beside her if he was having difficulty reaching the ground. The wine that she'd seen in the bucket of ice had turned out to be sparkling cider; he figured she would not want to drink alcohol in the middle of a workday. The food was delicious, fresh, simple, and filling—just exactly what she would have made for herself. She forgot about her nervousness. They talked about the police force, Gloria's forthcoming grand opening, the Penny Loafers, and—of course—the heat, the heat, the heat that would not relent.

After they'd finished eating, Sam dug into a bag and she was surprised to learn that he still had the ancient copy of his field guide to fungi after all these years. He handed it to her, and she flipped through it, exclaiming. He'd continued their tradition of labeling each specimen with the month, year, and location he'd found it. While a couple of dozen or so had been labeled "GV" for Green Valley, others were labeled Penobscot, Olympic State Park, Omaha, Salt Lake City, the Everglades.

"You've been to all of these places?"

He nodded and popped a fat green grape into his mouth.

"For work or pleasure?"

"Sometimes both. Flights can be cheap when you know people."

She looked up from the book. "How on earth did you wind up flying planes?"

He lay sideways on the blanket, propping his head on his elbow, and it did her heart good to see him so relaxed. He talked about those moments when all the little mechanisms of a person's life sync up, when he ran into a guy at an auto parts dealer who got talking to him about flying and eventually offered him a job. She had some trouble envisioning him as a pilot; he, like her, had always seemed to be so rooted to the earth. As a kid and then as a very young man, he had liked routine, to have things just so, to stay in familiar places. To think of him wheeling around the sky—the image wouldn't settle in her mind.

But . . . people changed.

Sam was no exception. Though he was cheerful and breezy on the surface, everything she might expect from a young man on a picnic on a summer day, there was something far down beneath his outward happiness that wasn't really happy at all. Occasionally, hints of pessimism would leak into the conversation—just half a phrase slipped into a sentence here or there, like *Isn't that the way of it?* or *Maybe in my dreams*—and she was shocked and concerned to hear it, for the Van Winkle men were known for their optimism, so much so that there had long been speculation that their perfect confidence was what gave them their talent for saving lives. If there was something that had upset Sam, she wanted him to know that she was not afraid to hear it. He knew the worst about her and he had not judged her. She would love to extend the same courtesy. But what was worst about him?

After a light lunch and lighter conversation, Sam told her he had a surprise for her and that she was to close her eyes. She did, and she heard him stand and move away from the blanket through the grass.

"Okay," he said. "Open."

When she looked up at him, she was so taken by the light shining on his face—a light that looked for all the world like pride—that she almost didn't notice what he was holding: a kite. One of *their* kites—a little kinked and faded, but otherwise intact.

"I found it in my parents' shed," he said. The kite was a red diamond, with a few tattered ribbons running down. "I don't think they even knew it was in there."

She got to her feet, tentatively touched a newly repaired wooden dowel.

"What do you think?" he said. "Are you up for it?"

"I don't see how we'll get this thing to fly," she said, laughing. "There's not a hint of a breeze."

Sam's smile faltered. The both looked around: The valley was stagnant with heat.

"You're right," Sam said.

But Olivia rallied: "Let's try anyway." And as soon as she said the words, a strong gust of wind riffled the tips of the grass around them, as if it had swooped in to rescue them from their plight, and Sam looked at her and grinned. Together, and with a great deal of laughing and quite a bit more sweating, they worked out the mechanics. Olivia held the cord, Sam ran, and after just two tries the kite got its teeth into the wind and made a tentative, shaky ascension.

"Woo-hoo!" Sam shouted. "I still *got* it!"

"We still got it," Olivia said.

He walked toward her, out of breath. The kite tugged on its tether in Olivia's hands, a crisp diamond of red pinned against the blue sky. Sam's fists were on his narrow hips, his shoulders bent with the work of heavy breathing.

"You okay?"

"As it turns out, I'm not a teenager anymore," he said, winded but smiling. "Sit?"

"Sure."

They walked back to the blanket in the shade, the kite trailing behind them some distance from the oak. Olivia sat and then watched Sam do the same. He definitely seemed stiff. Maybe aching. She didn't get to ask him about it. He held out his empty hand.

"Here. Let me see that." He took the kite string from Olivia. It was an old kite, cobbled together with bits of found canvas and fibrous brown garden twine. "Hold out your wrist."

She hesitated.

"Come on," he said. "I'll be careful. I promise."

Wary, she extended her arm toward him, palm up. He smiled at her, but it wasn't so much a friendly smile as a mischievous one. She was nervous and uncertain, and she didn't particularly want to feel that way. He began to talk as he tied the kite string around her wrist, setting the knot a few inches from her skin, careful not to touch her.

"One day a couple of kids had chartered a flight at the airport where I was working at the time. They were pretty young, early twenties maybe. And this guy pulls me aside and says, 'Look. I want to propose to my girlfriend. Can you fly over this one field where I'm going to have WILL YOU MARRY ME? spelled out?' So, you know, I say, 'Sure.'"

He finished tying the twine and then, with extreme care, pushed the knot so it slid down, settling not quite flush against Olivia's wrist. When he let go, she felt the strong pull of scratchy twine. It was a surprisingly tough tug, and she liked it—the bite of the brown twine that was almost but not quite painful, the nearly muscular pull of the kite as the sky tried to take it away. Sam smiled at her, then lay down on his back. He put his forearm over his eyes.

"So we go up," he said, continuing his story. "And everything's going great. And we get over the field where it's supposed to say WILL YOU MARRY ME? And you know what it says?"

"What?"

"YES."

She let her weight down onto her elbows, her ankles crossed in front of her. "Yes?"

"Yes. The girl had found out what the kid was up to from his friends, and she had *her* friends change his letters. I've never seen a guy happier or more surprised."

She looked at him, taking in her fill since he could not see her doing it from beneath the crook of his arm. In the sunlight his black hair, shorn so close to his head, had almost no luster. Around his mouth a few not unattractive lines had begun to form. He was not especially muscular—not like Tom, who was all brawn. But he was trim and pleasing to look at, so pleasing that she made herself look away.

She thought of how he seemed so tired, so uncomfortable at times. "Sam, are you . . . are you *hurt*?"

He was quiet for a long moment. Finally he sighed and mumbled something about an accident.

"A car accident?"

"A plane accident."

"Oh. God. How bad was it? Are you okay?"

He sighed. "I'm here, aren't I?"

"You can be here without being okay," she said. "Have the guys at the station heard about the crash?"

"No. And I need to keep it that way. I don't want them to—they don't need to be thinking there's anything I can't do."

"How badly were you hurt?"

He settled his face deeper into the crook of his arm. "Broken ribs. Concussion. Leg busted in three places—that's why I limp a little sometimes. And . . ."

"And what?"

"And I died."

"Died? Like . . . *died* died?"

"Yes."

"Sam . . . You died?" The reality of it was slow to sink in. He'd died. But here he was—with her, alive as far as she could tell. Her heart sped up as adrenaline coursed through her system, as if he were dying even now and needed her to save him. "They brought you back."

"Yes."

"And you're okay, now. Right? You're okay?"

He didn't answer.

A dreadful, awful, terrible feeling lumped in her throat. A horrible feeling. She watched his shallow breath. "Sam . . . were you *alone* when you crashed?"

"No," he said.

"And the other passengers?"

"Just one. He's gone."

"Oh, Sam." She cursed every god there was that she couldn't touch him, couldn't offer that small kind of comfort. For he needed comforting, to be taken into her arms, *hers,* and held there until some of the tiredness went out of his face and some of the light returned to his eyes. "I'm so sorry. I don't know what to say."

He shrugged and shifted the crook of his elbow, leaving only his mouth exposed. The wind blew slightly, bending the soft grass. In the sky beyond the red kite, a few discrete white clouds cast shadows on the valley. Sam had been slated to serve and protect in one way or another from the moment he was born. If he truly had lost someone, he would have been the first Van Winkle to do so in a hundred years. Olivia could not imagine what an incredible burden he must bear.

Finally, he began to speak. But he did not talk about the accident; he told her about how he'd found himself living in Vermont. He'd bounced around from job to job for a while before he wound up in Plattsburgh, New York, flying medical cargo in and out of a regional airport. One day, a friend asked him for a favor: He was supposed to fly a buddy down to New York City, but something had come up. Could Sam take the job?

Later, Sam said, he would think of all the ways his life would be different if only he'd turned the job down—it was the way the decision of a split second could change the trajectory of a person's entire life. But at the time, Sam figured the trip would mean a few extra dollars in his pocket and no big deal. The flight was VFR—clear skies with plenty of visibility at around 5,500 feet. The guy was a financial consultant named Patrick Kearny, though everybody called him Patty—and he was in good spirits. His oldest daughter was having a baby, his first grandkid, and he wanted to surprise her with a visit by getting in a plane and heading her way the moment he got news the baby was being born. As they made conversation, the sky began to appear spotty, but it wasn't anything worrisome.

They were over the Adirondacks when Sam felt the rhythms of the engine change. Patrick Kearny, the soon-to-be-first-time grandfather, knew it, too. He never once asked Sam what was going on, never let on that he was afraid. He was ex-military, schooled to place his trust and his life in the knowledge of people who knew more than him, and he didn't so much as break a sweat. Instead, as Sam fumbled to make things right, he gave Sam a silent look that seemed to say *I'm not worried because I know you'll take care of this.*

A few hours later, he was dead. Olivia held her breath as Sam talked about how they'd been pinned in their seats in the rumpled body of the plane for hours. Sam said he hadn't panicked. Not at all. The plane's engine had failed, but he would not. He'd put all his faith in his family legacy, talking to the man, telling him to hang on, to not sleep, to be strong—language that had been ingrained in him from countless dinners during which the Van Winkle men and women took turns telling stories of their exploits. He felt a tingling sensation at the back of his neck that he believed was the sign that his ability was rearing up; his father had described it as a sense of being stared at, not a thing you could quite place. And so even though Patrick Kearny was obviously in bad shape, bleeding from beneath his hair, Sam had no doubt the man would live to see his granddaughter. No doubt at all. And then Sam would have his own story to tell over family dinners about the life he'd saved. In a moment of quiet, when Sam could hear ice beginning to fall on the windshield, Patrick turned his face toward the window as if he needed a moment of privacy, and he passed away.

Sam said that in a way, he'd been more shocked by the man's death than by the plane dropping out of the sky. He'd had nearly three frozen days to think about all of the small things he might have done differently in those last airborne seconds, the chain of tiny adjustments that might have changed everything. He also tortured himself with the question of why he hadn't been able to save Patrick Kearny when saving him should have been as easy as breathing. Had the Van Winkle legacy skipped him because he'd left Green Valley? By the time his rescuers arrived, he'd lost the will to fight, and he succumbed.

Sam had died. Olivia had almost lost him. She let herself down off her elbows to lie beside him, and she stared at the sky. Life on the farm had its minor catastrophes of each day, but the larger shape of any given year had remained the same for much of her adulthood. How shocking it was to be reminded of the fragility of human life, the cruelty of the world, when she'd spent so many of her days trying to believe she lived in a paradise.

Sam lifted his arm from his face. When he turned his head to look at her, she turned hers as well, and his closeness went through her like a shock. "You're upset."

She tried to smile; her eyes stung. "In all the years I imagined you out there in the world, I never thought anything bad had happened."

"I'm just glad you thought of me at all," he said. "That makes it better. A little, anyway."

She looked away from him—she had to. Any illusion she'd had of trying to maintain some distance between them had been a joke: If they were in proximity, emotional distance was impossible. She cared about him too much to pretend she didn't. When she looked back at him again his expression was grave, and she knew he was thinking about the dead man.

"I'm a mess, Olivia," he said.

"No you're not."

"I am," he said, insistent now. He sat up with some difficulty and leaned down over her. His brow was furrowed. "After the accident, I stopped being able to feel anything—nothing that touched my skin."

"I don't understand."

"Not hot or cold. Not the sun, not any human touch. It felt like my skin was leather." The shadow of the kite passed over his face. "The doctors said it was all in my head."

"Oh, Sam," she said. She'd never in her life wanted to pull someone close as much as she wanted to touch Sam now. "Go easy on yourself. You went through a lot. And your feeling might come back, in time."

"That's the thing. The other day when I touched you? I felt that. I really felt it. It was like . . . I don't know . . . getting plugged back in again or something. All the circuits lighting up."

"And since then?"

"I feel everything. And it's because of you." His gaze fell to her mouth.

Since Sam had returned, the pull to be with him, to make the most of him in any way she could, was strong. But he complicated Olivia's basic idea of a good life. The question he brought into focus was weighty and fearsome: At what point was it okay to say *I could be happier than I am now* without disrespecting or diminishing her current happiness? How could she be content with the way her life was right now—the way *she* was right now—if she permitted herself to wish for something more? And how could she go back to being content with what she had now if any new joys she allowed herself were to be suddenly gone?

When he spoke again, she suspected he was having thoughts in a similar vein, about what they might mean to each other or what they might not, because he said: "When was the last time you left the farm, Olivia?"

She didn't want to tell him. But he'd just shared such a personal moment of his life with her, that she knew it would be miserly to withhold her own secrets. She told him it had been nine years since she'd made the decision to quit leaving Pennywort land. She'd gone to Lyon's Pharmacy and Sporting Goods Shop to pick up something her father needed—she could no longer remember what. She'd stepped off the curb, heading toward the old station wagon that had belonged to her father for as long as she could remember, when she heard a cry. A child—a girl no more than two—was jerkily running toward the road. And the girl's mother was doing her best to follow, but she was on crutches and lagging far behind.

Help her! the woman had screamed at Olivia. *Grab her. Please!*

Though Olivia's heart sped and her whole body seemed to break out into an instant sweat, she somehow couldn't move. The child was running for the road, and Olivia could only stand there, paralyzed and afraid.

"What happened?" Sam asked. "Was the kid hurt?"

"No, thank God," Olivia said. "At the last moment, the baby just stopped running. Just like that. Turned around and went toddling back toward her mother, laughing like it was the funniest thing in the world while the mom got on her knees right there in the parking lot and looked like she was trying not to cry."

She picked a few blades of grass and tossed them. *What is wrong with you?* the child's mother had yelled at Olivia. *What*

kind of person just stands there when a baby is running into the road?
Olivia had clutched her paper bag to her chest and said nothing.
She couldn't even apologize. In all the years since she'd discovered she was dangerous, she'd never felt more like a monster than she did that day. And she realized that it would probably be better for everyone if she stayed on the farm, where she was less in danger of hurting people, and where she wasn't constantly, unceasingly, *always* reminded that she was different than everyone else. It was easier for everyone that way.

"To tell you the truth," she told Sam now, "I don't even know if I *could* leave anymore."

"Why?"

"I think about leaving, and it's like I get this knot in my stomach from the thought of being away from the Poison Garden for any amount of time."

"But how do you get by without leaving? Don't you need things?"

"We have help," Olivia said. "Tom's been a godsend."

"You and Tom . . ."

"What?"

"Are you . . . ?"

"Oh! No. We're not anything. I'm not his type."

"Because you're sort of a redhead?"

"Because I'm a female."

"Ah."

He looked down at her steadily, seriously. Her heart began to pick up speed, a slow-building momentum she couldn't control. Her skin tingled where every blade of grass and flower petal touched her. Sam gazed down on her, his look curious and transparent, and it made her bones ache.

All this—the conspiracy of her body to work against her—was a clear warning sign that she should exit the way she came, now, while she still could. Otherwise, she and Sam were both heading at top speed toward a brick wall. The old refrain swept like blowing leaves across her mind: *If only, if only, if only.*

"Do you want to try the serum now?" Sam asked.

"I'm not sure it's a good idea."

"But why? Because you don't want me to get hurt?"

She nodded.

"I think you're afraid."

She scoffed. "What would I be afraid of?"

"That you might like it."

The wind picked up forcefully enough to lift her arm at her side. "I'm not afraid."

"Good. May I?" He reached for the bag she'd brought, which contained only the serum. He looked at it a moment—the pink plastic bottle—then unscrewed the top. "Hold out your hand."

She did. But instead of easing the serum into her palm, he dropped a pea-sized dollop on the inside of her wrist. The serum was nearly the same temperature as her body, slick and translucent gray. "What are you doing?"

"We're trying it out."

"But I thought—why didn't you put it in my hand . . . ?"

"Just rub it in. Right where I put it. Trust me."

She pulled her hand that was held by the kite, and the kite pulled back. But she prevailed and rubbed the serum into her wrist with one thumb, aware that Sam was watching. The whole thing felt intensely indulgent and impossibly intimate. So much of her fragile new friendship with Sam hinged on her ability to hide how much she desired him. If he knew, it would only make things awkward between them. Better to let him think he didn't affect her.

"Is it dry?" he asked.

"I think so."

"Good. Lay back for me."

"Sam?"

"Just trust me."

With some awkwardness, she lay back and felt the dry grasses buckling beneath the blanket. High white storm clouds were stacked in the sky, the sign of uneasy atmosphere. The kite tugged her wrist.

"You do that a lot," he said.

"What?"

"Touch things. Run your hands over things."

She stilled. She hadn't realized she'd been toying with a blade of grass near her hip, running it absentmindedly between her fingers. She let it go. "I feel everything," she whispered. "I can tell when the dew's falling even when I'm in my bed with the shades down. I know spring by the smell of the crocuses. And food—*God*. It's my weakness. Even if I never ate again the smells alone can make me feel like I just ate a ten-course meal."

"Is that a side effect of your condition?"

"Maybe. Or it's just how I am."

"Close your eyes," he said.

"I don't know about that . . ."

"Can you stand to be out of control for one second?"

"Of course I can," she said. "Just promise me you won't touch me with anything more than one fingertip. That's it. Promise?"

He put his right hand over her heart, his left pinky finger in the air. "Scout's Honor."

"I don't think that's how you do the salute," she said. But she settled back and closed her eyes. In the red dark behind her eyelids, she wondered if she might—sometimes—make a harmless exception to her rule about not leaving the farm. But she banished the thought as quickly as it had arrived. Sam had her second-guessing the structures she'd put in place that had until this point kept her life from falling apart. She needed to do a better job of appearing indifferent to him—so they would *both* believe she was.

"Breathe out, Olivia," he said.

She laughed a little, though nothing was funny. She was embarrassed by the shakiness of her breath. Then she felt the lightest press of his fingertip on the inside of her wrist, and all the sensations of the whole of the afternoon constricted into the precise and singular point of his touch, where his skin and hers connected. He kept still, the pressure firm.

"Okay?"

"Sure," she said.

He began to draw circles, then X's, then circles again. His touch felt foreign and invasive, but familiar, too. Had they really touched each other all the time at one point in their lives? She thought of evenings spent in the ecstatic torture of long, meandering hours, skin on skin, mouths on mouths, and now—this, such a small and inconsequential thing, the tip of his finger, sliding over the inside of her wrist, erotic in a way that penetrated deep, hammered every nerve, made the air feel thin.

She grasped for some shield to put up against the onslaught of sensation. "I think those clouds might mean rain."

"*Shh,* Olivia. We don't have to talk right now."

She felt him trace a spiral over the tendons of her wrist, a shape closing then opening again. Years of denial had made her tightly wound and wildly sensitive; he touched her, and she felt herself coming apart cell by cell, atom by atom—and yet, she had no will to stop it. Certainly, he'd already touched her enough for the sake of their experiment. But his touch was too delicious, too satisfying and luxurious, to tell him to move away.

"I'm going to write you a message," Sam said. "Tell me what it says."

She felt him impress three lines on her skin; goose bumps rose on her belly, her arms. *"I?"* she guessed.

"Yes," he said. "Now the next word."

She could barely focus on the letters. The breeze when it blew was like a warm kiss; the sun was indecently hot; the kite was a cuff around her wrist. Sam drew away and she felt the loss of him.

She opened her eyes. He was leaning over her, looking down. His face, so long and handsome, was marked by what was either intense concentration or a pained scowl. His eyes had darkened, the blue irises expanded to a thin, electric rim.

"Think?" she said.

He held her gaze as he traced a new pattern, and the connection was shockingly intimate. He was watching her with an intensity that spoke of midnight: muscle, sweat, secrets whispered against skin. She held her breath, waiting for the next word to take shape as his finger drew one letter, then another, on her wrist. Her voice broke. "We? I think we?"

He said nothing, and she knew she had guessed right. If she'd had any thoughts, any reservations, they drifted away like milkweed floss lifted on the summer wind. There was only the dryness of the grass, the gold heat of the sun, and beneath the pinpoint of Sam's touch, an ocean of desire for a thing she couldn't have. He stopped, lifted his fingertip, watched her.

"Guess," he said.

She'd stopped paying attention. "I'm sorry. I don't know." He chuckled knowingly. He knew what he was doing to her, what she was feeling. She began to panic. "I think we've experimented enough to know if it's going to work."

He paused. When he spoke his voice rasped. "God, Olivia. You're so responsive. So perfectly tuned in. What I could do to you if—"

"Sam. Stop." She pulled away and sat up so quickly she nearly saw stars.

"What's wrong?"

She drew away from him farther, a dozen thoughts jumbling in her brain but only one singular enough to stand apart: *What I could do to you if.* His words were as thin as a wish, no more promising than the curl of smoke from a candle blown out on a birthday cake. He *couldn't* touch her—that was the problem. They didn't know if Arthur's serum would work. And even if it did work, Arthur had said it would be best for accidental brushes, not prolonged contact like this.

This was a problem.

When Olivia had crossed the field to the oak where Sam was waiting, she'd still believed that the strength of her determination would be enough to delineate the terms of a friendship, a strict pact between two people who would not want what they could never have. But that had been a joke. In the war between restraint and desire, restraint was irresolute, unskilled, and puny; desire arrived with guns blazing, banners flying, and soldiers full of rapacious will. It always won. And yet, for Olivia, its victory could only mean loss.

Who I am kidding? she thought. Over the years, she'd mentally sifted through the possibilities of what she might or might not safely do with a lover one day, what protections or accessories they might or might not use if anyone was ever willing to get close enough to her to try. But ultimately, the thing she and Sam both wanted would elude them. She would come to feel guilty; he would grow bitter and resentful and wish for someone else. And in the meantime, the ache that seemed to transcend her physical body and hurt all the way down to her soul wasn't going to get any better. She could not have what she could not have. And no amount of wishing would change that.

She got to her feet. "I'm sorry. I just remembered."

"Remembered what?"

"I lost track of time." She tried to pull her hand out of the relatively loose loop of twine, but she was shaky and fumbling. "And anyway, you should go wash your hands right away. Just in case."

"Okay. I will. But—"

"Jeez. Where did you learn to tie knots like this?"

"I picked a few things up over the years." He stood with her, slowly and awkwardly, then held out a hand toward the kite string. "Here. Let me try."

"Don't." She moved her hand away from him. He reached out more.

"If you'll just let me—"

"I've got this, Sam. I've—*shoot!*" She'd brushed against the back of his knuckles with hers. She froze. He moved away. "I'm sorry. I'm so sorry."

"It's okay."

Their eyes met; they both knew he'd been grazed. He frowned a little, and with a flick of his wrist loosened the knot he'd made. He took the twine from her. The pull of the kite was gone.

"Thank you." She rubbed at the slight red impression on her skin.

"Are you turning chicken on me?"

"No," she said. "Of course not." But—of course—she was.

He began to wind the kite.

"I'll . . . I'll call you," she assured him, though she wasn't sure she would. She wasn't sure of anything. "I do have a phone, you know. It's been a wonderful . . . time together. Not a date. A picnic! Everything was really nice. And the cider—that was a nice touch."

"Olivia—"

"I know what this looks like, but I'm not running. I just really do have things to do. That I forgot."

He raised his eyebrows. The kite dove headfirst to the ground. Sam sighed. "Well," he said, almost to himself. "At least it stuck the landing."

Olivia walked backward. She nearly tripped when she hit her heel on a stone. And then, she turned and jogged through the field, away from the leftover grapes and sparkling juice and cool shade and fallen kite, and away from Sam, whose gaze she could feel like a weight on her shoulders, until she knew she was finally, blessedly, out of sight.

It was only later that she wished she could have waited long enough to learn what his message might have been.

Greener Pastures

n late July evenings, the sunset often hit Green Valley at just such an angle that it bent people's thoughts toward the things they wanted most but believed they could not have for fear of actually getting them. This particular psycho-meteorological summer phenomenon stood in direct contrast with a similar winter event on the year's shortest days, when the small gray sun set so quietly and slowly that people failed to notice that the change between night and day had happened at all—and this made them sleepy, and lazy, and content with everything they had.

Of course, only the oldest survivors in Green Valley, those who could recognize the telltale patterns of pink and gold in the sky, sensed that an evening of heartsickness was imminent and shuttered their minds against the coming onslaught like someone preparing a house for a storm. So when the summer evening shone its last burnt-pink light on each person's thorniest desires, most of Green Valley was defenseless against it, especially the young, the dreamy, and the newly in love.

Mei, the newest boarder to stake her claim on a cot in the Pennywort barn, told a captive audience of sleepy Penny Loafers how she had always wanted a child but never thought she would actually get one, which prompted one of the women to point out that she was about to have a baby, like it or not. In Briscoe, Tom was thinking of how he had such a terrible desire to eat the entire buttery pound cake that was displayed so seductively on a stand in the kitchen—but of course, the fat would be hell on his cholesterol levels and he couldn't decide if he wanted to deal with the various consequences from his doctor and his partner and his own uncooperative arteries.

Arthur was slumped by the feeble stream in the glen and was daydreaming about the farmhouse where he'd grown up, got married, had his daughter—where he'd had all the things life in an actual house could give a man, like razors, and hot showers, and insulation, and window fans. And yet in spite of how badly he wanted to climb out of the ravine and back into the farmhouse, in spite of how he longed, yearned, and pined for the creature comforts of a normal life, he could not allow himself to return to the place he'd been happiest. He would not be able to live with himself if he ever caught himself being happy again.

Sam, in his parents' faded blue colonial and surrounded by his parents' old furniture, was supposed to be watching television but was instead faced with the most painful wish he'd ever faced in his life—because he knew that desire for Olivia could only be desire that wasn't good for him, and he thought for a moment that the greatest failure of evolution was that human beings could not claim perfect mastery over their propensity to fall in love. Better to want something that was good for you and easy to accrue. He was certain that great numbers of humans had died indulging in desires for things that they knew were bad for them—irresistible purple berries clustered on a shrub, the latex of the opium poppy seedpod, the friendship of wild animals that could turn vicious at a moment's notice, and—even—the desire to lift wheels off the ground and own the sky. He decided that people were experts at not seeing danger when danger proved inconvenient. Although the things he wanted to do with Olivia would almost certainly kill him, that didn't stop him from wanting to do them anyway, and as the clouds changed from gold to purple to ashy gray, the weight of desire made his heart feel heavy and hollow at the same time.

Olivia too felt the ache of longing as the shadows grew. The pain of isolation stung more acutely than usual. It was so big it choked out all other feelings, growing around her heart like a tangle of murderous vines. It was unfair that desire—for a thing she'd so long told herself she didn't need or want—could shake her understanding of herself. Some part of her wished Sam hadn't come back to the farm. Hope had disarmed her—against him, against herself, against the burn of the sun going down.

The day was over, the last color draining from the pale sky, when she realized she'd forgotten something: her father. She'd promised to join him for dinner—and then she forgot. In the kitchen of her modified silo, she threw something together with panicked clumsiness: cold beet soup with cucumber, dill, and chives. Crusty bread and soft white farm cheese completed the meal. Then she hurried into the semidark, a flashlight lashed to her belt loop for the walk back.

"I'm here!" she called once she reached the gloom of the ravine. "Dad! I'm here!"

She skidded the last few feet to the floor of the gorge. She spent a long moment scanning the area before she saw her father. He was sitting at the edge of the sludgy remnants of the stream, his back hunched in a way that made her think, for a moment, that he was no more animate than the boulder beside him. Her greatest fear, which she lived with like a low hum each day but rarely allowed herself to think of, was that she might one day come down into the ravine and find that something had happened to him—that he'd fallen and cracked his head on a stone, that he'd lost a tussle with a copperhead, that he'd needed her help and she'd failed. And each day that she came into the ravine and saw him waiting for her and ready to bust out with whatever strange new observation he couldn't wait to share, she felt a thrill of relief that he was still with her and she was not yet alone.

"I'm here!" she said. "Here I am!"

"Here you are," he said, his voice like a creaking tree. "Food?"

"Cold beet soup with buttermilk. You'll love it."

She lowered herself onto a rock beside him and opened the container of soup for him. She handed him the bowl and a spoon, and she put the bread and cheese on her own lap. Arthur did not eat immediately. Around them, the night creatures were beginning to come out—bats and salamanders and owls. Olivia could sense them but could not see.

"Sorry I'm late tonight," she said. She wouldn't admit to out-right forgetting him. That would be cruel.

"I hope that there was some good reason for your having come late?"

"Good reason?"

"A *good* reason," he said. "As opposed to a problem."

"Oh," she said. But she didn't elaborate. There *was* a problem, a problem that consumed her, that made her accidentally pull up her chives in her herb garden when she should have been pulling weeds, that made her call the boarders by the wrong names. There was the problem of what she was going to do about Sam. She'd thought she could allow herself to want his companionship without wanting anything more. But that was the trouble with happiness: Once a person got a little bit of it, it was only human nature to want more, and more, and more—until the thing that might have made her quite content and sated actually made her quite wretched with longing.

But she couldn't think of Sam now. Here was her father, and though he was as pleasant as he always was, she had a sense that beneath it all he was mildly annoyed with her. She'd hated for him to be annoyed; it unsettled her in some fundamental way. Because of that, she tended to humor him when she probably shouldn't, from occasionally bringing him food that she knew wasn't good for him to letting him live for so many years down in the ravine. If she'd one day decided to stop bringing him the things he needed to survive, there was some possibility that he would emerge from the ravine and go looking for them. But the other possibility—that he would rather let himself die in the ravine than heft himself out of it—was not out of the question, either. Stubbornness ran in the Pennywort blood. And so she catered to him, allowed him to continue in his folly—just like she'd always done, just like she'd done when he'd pitched the idea of building a poison garden, and just like she did now.

"So," she said in her most ordinary voice. "How was your day?"

"Fine."

"Where's the goat?"

"Sleeping."

"Are you going to eat?"

He spooned a bite of soup. "Delicious."

"Good," she said. She'd allowed two days to pass since she'd told him about Gloria's inquiry at social services. She hadn't heard anything new since Sam's first report. But time was ticking, and she needed her father to see that he could no longer stay in the ravine without repercussions. She said, "So I'm thinking that I might clean out the old house. Just for the heck of it. It hasn't been gone through in a while—and I never feel like doing it in the winter. Is there anything you want me to bring you if I do clean it out?"

He only glanced at her.

She went on. "I also thought it would just be good to get everything ready—you know, make sure everything's clean and put together—just in case you decide to move back in."

"Olivia. I know what you're trying to do."

"What?"

He dropped his spoon into the soup. "I haven't forgotten."

Maybe it was the heat, the frustration of her afternoon with Sam, the melancholy drilling of the sunset, or a combination of all those things. But when she spoke her voice was unusually pinched with impatience. "Dad. I don't understand. I need you to explain this to me. Why won't you even *consider* moving back in?"

He stirred his soup.

"Why don't you want to?"

"I can't."

"Of course you can." She got to her feet, drew in a deep breath for fortification, and glanced around. The only thing worse than Solomon's Ravine during the day was the ravine at night. Olivia thought she saw the glint of bright eyes peering at her from the shadows, but when she blinked they were gone. She shivered. "What would it hurt to move back?"

He said nothing, but seemed to slump deeper into himself.

"Please help me. Tell me what you're afraid of and maybe I can fix it."

"I'm not afraid of anything."

"Is it that you're afraid you won't be as independent in the farmhouse as you are down here? Because I promise I won't bother you. I don't even live in the house anymore, remember? I moved into the silo. You would have the place to yourself."

He looked up at her from his seat. "And why did *you* leave the farmhouse, Olivia? Why don't you tell me?"

She was slightly startled; her father was never so direct. The question was fair, but how could she tell him the answer without hurting him? In her mid-twenties, she'd decided to use some of her extra income from the farm to rebuild the old silo into a house for herself. For many years, she'd been summering in the barn with the Penny Loafers and wintering in the farmhouse. But each winter got a little harder, a little longer, a little lonelier, and she thought it would be expedient to get away from both her old memories and from visions of a future that would never fill the house with children, with a husband, with the happy pandemonium of family.

She told her father a piece of the truth: "Part of the reason I moved out of the house was because I thought that would make it easier for you to move back into it. I didn't want you to think that you were ever imposing on me if you moved back in."

"I know you think I'm just a stubborn old man. I'm not trying to be. But I've made my decision. And I'm staying here."

"You can't mean that. It just doesn't make sense." Olivia thought that their relationship was as good as any father-daughter relationship could be, or better, even, because she and Arthur never fought and rarely disagreed. They were a good pair. Though Olivia remembered very little about her mother, and often wished she could have known Alice better, she had pieced together enough memories and stories to know that she was more like her father than her mother. Alice had been a chatter, a storyteller, a dreamer who thrived on the company of other people. Arthur was quieter, more listener than talker, and most often happy to be alone. In theory, she should perfectly understand what it meant that he did not want to move back into the farmhouse, if only because they were so alike. And yet, she didn't understand. She only said, "If you moved back up I'd see you more. I could take better care of you. And I like when you're around."

"I am around."

"You know what I mean. What is it you want me to do here, Dad? Just . . . wait? Do nothing?"

"We don't even know that Gloria is planning to do anything for sure," he said.

"We don't know she *isn't* either. I've been as patient as I can and given you some time to think. But this isn't a problem to just sweep under the rug."

"Something's bothering you, my darling," he said. "Not the farmhouse. Not me."

She stepped away from him. In the dark he was turning into a smudge of greenish black shadow. "No. I'm fine. There's nothing else."

"I am unconvinced."

"There's nothing going on. I'm just stressed-out about the neighbor. I don't want to wake up one morning and find out that they've hauled you off to some nursing home and I can't get you out. Do you understand that's what could happen?"

He crossed his arms loosely around his middle, less like he was angry and more like he was protecting himself. She hated to see him this way.

"Are you mad?" she asked.

He said nothing.

She felt a familiar, destabilizing panic and a sweeping need to keep him from being mad at her. "If it were up to me, you could stay down here forever. You know that you aren't any trouble to me—I *like* climbing down here to see you every day. I think you're doing fine. But I don't know how to stop Gloria from reporting you if she decides to do that."

"It's not your fault, Olivia," he said.

She let out the smallest of breaths. She suddenly felt tired, so tired she could fall asleep standing on her feet.

"Thanks for the soup," her father said.

She climbed the steep slope of the ravine in the darkness, knowing each stone and tree like she knew the furniture in her kitchen or living room. But instead of returning to the silo, she found herself wandering into the garden maze. In the dim light, she meandered the dusky corridors, the yew walls towering high above her, the tunnels burrowing through her thick rhododendrons. She believed her maze helped people. Alice had always said it did, that nothing could give a person a stronger sense of direction than getting lost in the garden maze. But Alice had died before Olivia had been old enough to ever need the maze's guidance for herself. Sometimes she missed her mother horribly; she wanted to be held in her mother's arms and rocked like she was still a child. She wanted to cry on Alice's shoulder because she had never been able to let her father see her weep. And most of all, she wanted to ask her mother why all the hard work she did to create a maze that helped other people would never help her.

"What do I do?" she said aloud inside the Willow Garden, where hundreds or thousands of tiny blue beetles clung to the leaves of delicate willows, turning them into iridescent chandeliers. She did not know what question she was asking—about her father, about Sam, about whether to go back to her old ways or whether it was acceptable to hope for something new. She had a sense that she was at a crossroads. But the question didn't matter because the maze didn't answer. She found no comfort in the garden, in her father, in the mother who had left her too early—and certainly no comfort in thoughts of Sam. She felt only the call of her Poison Garden, beckoning her safely inside.

Off the Rose

he Green Valley of Sam's childhood had had its share of unusual characters, and Sam was pleased that even though he and Olivia had grown up to live quite different lives than they'd expected to, some things in the valley hadn't changed. Grammercy's Pool Shack had never bothered to fix the bulb in its broken *l*. Hobo Jim—who had shown up for the Concert in 1969—had been squatting in an abandoned milk house for so many years that most people in the valley assumed he owned it. A few aging folks continued to hold peace rallies on Fridays at six in front of the Green Valley Bank, as a reminder to everyone that war hadn't actually been eradicated yet, and sometimes when the weather was just right, the streetlamp made a kind of bubble of light around them like a rainbow if you looked at it right.

By the time dawn managed to drill its way through the haze of morning clouds, Sam had stopped by the pool shack to investigate a possible shoplifting, had visited Hobo Jim just to make sure he was still alive, and had dropped by the Green Valley Bank to make a deposit and chat with the owner about his fundraising for veterans with PTSD. Sam had also done his best not to make too much of a fool of himself when he'd gone on his first call. There had been an accident—a man on a tractor had been swiped by a sports car that had attempted to speed around him. Sam and one other cop were first on the scene, finding the victim conscious but pinned in a ditch under his massive John Deere. The red car was long gone. While the other cop comforted the man, assuring him that help was on the way, Sam hung back and pretended to busy himself with the radio, with paperwork, anything so that he didn't have to look the scared kid under the tractor in the eye. Big Lou Ryerson, a dairy farmer who had come out to see if he could help, had questioned Sam with a great, deep worm of a wrinkle between his eyebrows: *What are you doing, Van Winkle? Get over there. That's Rick Glover's kid lying in that gutter, and he needs a Van Winkle right now.* But Sam had put him off, waving papers and saying *Can't you see I am trying to help if only you'd give me some space?* When they finally got the tractor out of the ditch, they discovered the victim was pretty banged up but not in mortal danger. Sam had needed to hide behind the big white wall of the ambulance to steady his shaking hands.

It was midmorning when he stopped by Olivia's. The boarders directed him to find her in the Marble Garden, which had been Alice's design and had scandalized the valley for its voluptuous and erotic nude figures. More than once as a child Sam had wandered into the Marble Garden for a curious peek; when he touched the statues—because how could he not—he swore he felt their stone bodies turn to warm human flesh under his hand. Now he found Olivia bending before a statue of some naked Greek athlete, and his brain lit up with indecent thoughts. She wore a yellow skirt with bands of yellow lace, and her thick hair had been pulled back under a purple bandanna. When she saw him, a flash of hope appeared on her face and he knew what she was thinking: that the serum had worked. Maybe even that he could touch her again. He hated to disappoint her. But all morning he'd been living with the reminder of their perfect afternoon that had turned out to be not so perfect after all.

He held up his finger with its bandaged tip.

"Oh. Shoot. I'm sorry," Olivia said. She pulled off her gloves and stood. "This is my fault. I shouldn't have let you try. I shouldn't even have mentioned the serum at all."

"It's okay," he told her in his friendliest, lightest voice—as if touching her hadn't been the most exciting thing that had happened to him since he'd lost all feeling eighteen months ago, as if he hadn't spent the night dreaming of her beneath him. "No big deal. See? I used my *left* hand. It won't get in the way."

For a couple of awkward minutes they made the lightest of small talk about the weather, about how the ladybugs in the valley had grown as large as coat buttons, about how traffic tapered off a little and they were both glad—about anything but what had passed between them yesterday. Then the only thing left for Sam to do was give her a nod and go on his way, one neighbor taking leave of another, nothing more.

In the oven-hot privacy of his squad car, he wrapped his fingers around the wheel even though it burned. He thought: *Well, that was that.*

His afternoon with Olivia yesterday had been liberating, energizing, thrilling—and not simply because Olivia was the first woman in so very long he could feel, and who made *him* feel like his old, strong, virile self again. No—what he'd glimpsed between them was more than sex, like it was his outlook that had caught the winds and climbed into the sky—as opposed to the kite they'd flown.

He wanted Olivia. The fact of it was plain, simple, and welcome in and of itself. But circumstance took his very simple desire and made a muddle of it. He was beginning to second-guess his willingness to pursue some kind of deeper relationship with her. Could he attempt a romance with a woman he could not touch? Yes. But did he want to? Could he bear it? Was he prepared for that kind of denial and responsibility? He was no longer sure.

If—*if*—he decided to try to make himself stop wanting her, there could be no more afternoons of flying kites, and eating grapes, and looking into her eyes, and confessing his most intimate secrets. He would have to keep her at arm's length—just as she'd originally tried to do to him. They would go through their lives like two friendly neighbors who waved at each other from their porches, who traded misdelivered mail, who occasionally swapped observations about the seasons and the many odd happenings of Green Valley in a convivial but passing way.

And yet, the thought of that false distance was depressing, maddening, and intensely unsatisfying. In his youth, no one had understood him the way Olivia had. No one had been more fun. Now he'd found himself telling Olivia things that not even his parents knew. To fall back into unguarded intimacy with her had been so easy. The prospect of loving her again felt not like a thing he would need to make happen so much as a thing that would happen, unchecked, on its own unless he stopped it. But under the circumstances, where could such feelings go except to a place of wonderful but miserable frustration?

The questions bothered him as he moved like an automaton through the last remaining hours of the day's shift. Like so much of Green Valley, the police department had seen very few changes since Sam used to walk through the doors holding his father's hand. The "Do you know where your children are?" posters on the wall were sun-faded and curling at the edges. The water fountain in the lobby was a foot too low, but seemed even lower now than in Sam's memory. And the current chief of police, Roddy Carlson, coming toward him down the hall, still wore his same beige plastic glasses that hadn't been all that flattering in the eighties and weren't flattering now.

Roddy's people were still considered newcomers in Green Valley, since they hadn't arrived until after the Concert. But the Carlsons had done their time appearing at community cookouts and ice hockey tournaments in the winter, and Roddy Carlson had been the first of the Carlsons to be elevated to Green Valley native status. He was the type of guy who could talk a person's ear off—and then talk the other one off, too—if you caught him on the wrong day. And so when Sam was getting ready to leave and saw Roddy coming toward him, he gave no more encouragement than a nod.

But Roddy called, "Hey! Good Sam! Where you going?"

Sam made a joke about asking himself the same question every day, and Roddy laughed in his generous way like it was the funniest thing he'd ever heard. Roddy's large head was shaved bald, his skin was peachy and shiny, and his nose, chin, and cheekbones were prominent and splotchy as cooked bratwurst.

"C'mon back with me for a sec," Roddy said.

Roddy gestured for Sam to fall into step with him, and Sam had to comply. As they walked down the hall together, he talked incessantly in his good-natured and oblivious way, about his son costing him a fortune because he was playing baseball at some fancy college, about his wife's terrible meat loaf, which gave him indigestion, about his daughter's vicious house cat named Pookie. But when they were tucked away inside the office, Roddy's cheerful tone took a forty-five-degree nosedive into formality. He said, "Why don't you have a seat there, Sam?" And Sam recognized this to be an order, not a suggestion. He lowered his sore bones into a not especially welcoming wooden chair. "Tell me. How's everything been going?"

Sam told him it was fine.

"Everybody treating you okay?"

"Perfect."

Roddy sat back in his seat and steepled his fingers. "No problems?"

"No problems."

Sam adjusted his feet beneath him, preparing himself for the inevitable: a discussion about his job performance. He reminded himself that he'd done nothing wrong. And yet, for a Van Winkle in Green Valley, not doing anything dazzlingly right was about the same thing as doing something wrong. Since he'd been back, one of his cousins—a Van Winkle in the fire department—had saved a family of six who had been living in an illegal apartment under the liquor store. A second cousin with the paramedics had been in the paper three times. But Sam had done nothing. Not one thing. Except run away when people needed him.

"Listen—" Roddy said.

"Roddy—" Sam said at the same time. He laughed. "You go ahead."

Roddy was making a face that wasn't quite a frown but could at any moment sink into one. "How long have I known you, Sam?"

"You bought my dad a cigar when I was born."

"That's right," Roddy said, a glint of pleasure in his eye. "Your father told me to keep an eye on you, and I said I would. I plan to stay true to that promise."

Sam said nothing.

Roddy looked at him over the tops of his fingers. "Word is you been spending some time at the Pennyworts'."

"They're my neighbors."

"I know, I know," Roddy said. He loosened the cuffs of his shirt around his wrists. "Your family and the Pennyworts go back together since before the Concert. But I feel it's my responsibility to your father to warn you. You'd do right to steer clear of that girl."

"And why's that, exactly?"

"Things have changed around here since you left," Roddy said, a note of wistfulness in his voice. "People just come bull-dozing into the valley like they own the place. And then money gets involved. And politics. And next thing you know, people are bending over backward to kiss other people's behinds—and, well—everything can't always stay the same."

"What exactly are you trying to warn me about?"

Roddy shook his head. "I can't say much. But I am saying, it might be a good idea to stay away from the Pennyworts. Just for a while."

"They're in trouble?"

"I can't say."

"Come on, Rod." Sam leaned forward in his chair. "Help me out here. Give me a clue."

"Look, Sammy. I got memories as fond as anybody's about the Pennyworts. First time I ever got to first base was in that garden with all the rainbow-colored stones. Hell, half the rea-son I'm a cop is because of an hour I spent in that maze. But it's you I'm trying to look out for here. There are . . . forces at work. And if a fight breaks out, you don't want to be on the wrong side."

"Is it Gloria?"

Roddy said nothing. His mouth pulled to the side as if he were considering what he could or could not say.

"It's Gloria, isn't it?"

Roddy got to his feet, but Sam remained seated. "The woman doesn't have a lot of friends. But she's got the right ones."

"Has she been at social services again?"

Roddy looked out the window into the parking lot. "Some-body, I won't say who, filed an official tip about Arthur Pennywort living back in the ravine. Now that it's on paper, a whole lot of people have to get involved. Some of them are in Gloria's pocket."

"When will they come for him?"

"Can't say. That is—I don't know. But I'm guessing soon. Nobody wants to cause any trouble for Arty. He's harmless. But Gloria's right that he can't be living down there like that anymore. It's hard to believe Olivia let it go on so long."

"It's not her fault," Sam said.

"Well, maybe this could be a good thing, then," Roddy said, sighing. "Maybe she needs some help. She's been on that farm alone for way too long."

Sam felt a knot harden in his gut. "What's Gloria got against Arthur?"

"Nothing. I think she feels like she's doing some good. Getting an old man out of a bad situation. Getting all those Penny Loafers into a shelter that doesn't leak or look like it's about to fall down. And—who knows—maybe she wants the maze shut down because, really, the road can't handle all the traffic sometimes. Don't get me wrong—I'm not saying the woman is Mother Teresa. I'm just saying—"

"She *thinks* she is," Sam said.

Roddy turned around and leaned his palms on the lip of his desk. "But this isn't about Arthur. It's about you, Sam. The Pennyworts have always had a lot of questionable things going on over there. And for all these years we've been able to look the other way. But those times are just about over. All these city types are buying their vacation homes up here and whatnot. Making over all our old farmhouses to look like pictures in magazines—as if any real farmer would decorate his own house with grain sacks and hand tools and bare bulbs hanging from a wire. Everything has to be so damn by-the-book with these people. Everything's got a paper trail—excuse me, an e-trail. It's progress, you know. *Progress.*"

Sam sat back in his chair for how intensely Roddy was looking at him. Roddy adjusted his collar.

"Anyway, when things start happening at the Pennywort farm, I just don't want to see you get caught up in it, Sam. I can't promise to protect you if it does." He picked up a framed photo of his wife and son from his desk. "I've got a kid in college, you know. I've got to keep this job. And if you do, too, it would be best to stay away from Pennyworts. Just till this all blows over."

"Is that all you can tell me?"

"Hell, Sam. It's already too much."

Sam stood. He extended his hand, and Roddy took it and held it tight. "I appreciate the heads-up."

Roddy's eyes lit ever so slightly. "So you'll stay away from the Pennyworts?"

Sam laughed. "Not a chance."

Roddy smiled as if this wasn't unexpected, as if it pleased him. "You're a good egg. Just like your old man." He clasped Sam on the back of the neck as he led him out of the office. "Now we just got to do a better job of getting you doing your Van Winkle hoodoo. This morning I thought you'da grabbed that tractor and flipped it off that kid with your bare hands."

Sam reached for the closed door. "Maybe next time," he said.

Old Chestnut

he next morning, Arthur woke to a godawful racket. He dreamed that an army of Revolutionary War soldiers was marching through Solomon's Ravine on their way back from the Battle of Saratoga, and Arthur was trying to convince them they'd wandered out of their normal time. But the soldiers wouldn't return to where they came from—they were banging and shouting and insisting it was Arthur who was in the wrong time—and when he stumbled out of the shack to see what mayhem had pulled him from his sleep, a dozen women were traipsing down the rocky hill, invading the stagnant peace of the hollow, with Olivia out in front. The goat was beside himself with agitation, bleating and stomping and being ignored.

"Oh no," he said aloud. "Oh, no no *no!*" But his protests incurred no more attention than if he were a blue jay squawking in a tree. He nearly grabbed his daughter by the arm before he realized what a mistake that would have been. "What on earth do you think you're doing, Olivia?"

She'd been hammering a loose board on the side of his shack, and she took three nails from between her lips before she spoke. "We're beating Gloria at her own game."

"But . . . I don't want all this."

"It's a compromise," she said. "We're not going to let anyone say I'm neglecting you. This is the only way."

Arthur sat down amid the mayhem—the smell of paint, the whine of hacksaws—and felt utterly helpless. Young people understood so little about what it meant to get old. In his mind, he was still young enough to jump fences and catch wayward chickens. He still had all of a young man's desires and a young man's wishes—which was cruel, because his body could no longer support the ambitions of his mind. It hadn't been the graying of his hair, or the lines deepening on his face, or the aches in his bones that had first convinced him he was beyond his prime. He'd seen the changes in his body and been able to dismiss them for many years as superficial, meaningless, in a way. Instead, he first realized he was truly getting old when people had started ignoring him, dismissing what he had to say, and writing him off as irrelevant—just like all the Penny Loafers were doing now. His opinions no longer held sway. But still, he couldn't stop himself from trying.

"Hold up there! Don't you touch that barrel. That's for the rain!"

He watched two women drag it toward the back of his house, out of sight. Boarders began to materialize relics from his old life: the afghan that Alice had crocheted when Olivia was born, a rolled-up throw rug and small houseplants in nice pots, luxury items like spaghetti tongs and tablecloths, a comfortable-looking armchair carefully slid down the ravine with a rope, pulley, and pallet. The sight of his old headboard made him want to weep, and he'd had to hide himself behind a tree to keep the others from seeing. *Oh Alice,* he said.

He was so lost in thought he almost didn't hear the boarders trying to get into the laboratory side of his shack, which he always kept locked. "I don't think so," he said, hurrying toward

the house. "I don't care if you paint the whole damn place but-
terfly pink—the lab is off-limits."

Olivia agreed with him; no one would go in his lab, provided
that he would tidy it up himself. She put her fists on her hips and
looked him up and down. "And now, as for you, Dad . . ."

One of the women was coming toward him with a towel, a
bar of soap, a change of clothes, and a pair of scissors. She
stopped a few feet away.

"I assume you can do the grooming part yourself?" Olivia
said.

"I'm perfectly groomed."

"This isn't up for argument," Olivia said. She took the bath
things from the boarder and gestured for her father to follow
her. As they walked away from the others, he wondered if she
didn't seem slightly tired. Her face would never be pale, thanks
to the summer sun and her mother's dark skin, but there was a
blue tinge around her eyes, and a softness to the set of her
shoulders, that made him wonder if she wasn't sleeping. She
stopped near a tree, leaning against it with her shoulder. When
she spoke her voice was quiet. "You're wondering why we're
doing all of this. Why *now*?"

"Naturally."

"Sam stopped by for a minute last night."

"Oh!" Arthur had almost forgotten. "Did he . . . stay?"

"No, he didn't stay."

"But you've been seeing a lot of him?"

"He came to tell me that Gloria officially reported us. They're
opening a case. I don't know how all the legalities work, but I
think somebody's going to show up here asking questions about
you. And when they do, you've got to look like you've got your
act together. We can't give them a reason to cart you away. I
mean, you have to look impeccable."

"I suppose you're right," he said.

"Thank you. I knew you could be reasonable."

"But nobody's cutting my hair."

She tipped her head and looked at him. "Not even a trim?"

"No."

"You drive a hard bargain. But . . . okay."

By afternoon, the whole thing was over. The boarders had swept into the ravine and then out again, and truth be told, the ravine did seem somewhat cheerier to Arthur than it had before. There was a bright white fence around his newly painted shack. His main living area was entirely transformed: There were actual tiles on a thing one of the women had called a "backsplash" but which he'd always just called a "wall." There were now two chairs—as opposed to one—at his kitchen table, with a candle that smelled like apples in the center. The whole place had a lived-in but homey look. It was a place for a happy family, not a curmudgeonly hermit, and all in all, it made him appear to be very respectable. Arthur couldn't help but be a little pleased.

After the boarders were gone, he and Olivia sat at his newly created outdoor seating area, eating cold pasta dressed with olives, beans, meats, vinegar, and tiny balls of cheese. Olivia rested her elbow on the table and leaned her whole weight on her arm. Her eyelids were somewhere between open and closed.

"Are you feeling all right?"

"Yes, I'm okay."

"You look tired."

"I am a little tired," she said. "Nothing to worry about."

He noticed she didn't finish her food. But when she said nothing was wrong, he had no choice but to take her at her word. His daughter's emotions were a mystery to him. He couldn't understand her. There was only one time Arthur could think of that he and his daughter had ever truly *shared* in the same emotion the way they might split a milk shake or a mince-meat pie. On the one-year anniversary of Alice's death, when Olivia had been five, they had been out walking the fields, holding hands and inspecting for invaders like purslane or quack-grass. Olivia had stopped suddenly and said *Oh!* And when Arthur looked down, first at her and then at the grass she stared at, he saw a small brown house sparrow that lay where it died. He couldn't know what had happened to the sparrow—if there was a nest nearby, if it had lost its mother, if it had been whacked with a machine. But it looked so sad, lying there on the grass, and before he knew it, Olivia was crying, and then he was crying, and then they were both standing there, crying, and not really thinking about the sparrow at all.

He turned his fork backward and used it to scratch at his face beneath his beard. "Your mother would have got a kick out of this."

"Oh?"

"The flowers. The frills and stuff. She always liked those kinds of things—even though she knew I didn't. All this—she would have thought it was hilarious. Never would have let me hear the end of it."

Olivia smiled.

"Course, she never would have let me live down here to begin with."

"But you wouldn't have wanted to, if she was still here."

"A lot of things would be different," he said. He cleared his throat. "So . . . I've been waiting to hear what happened with that serum . . . Were you able to try it?"

"Yes."

"With Sam, then?"

"Yes."

"And did it—"

"No," she said.

He felt her disappointment as if it were his own. "Ah. Well. We'll try again."

She stood up and, oddly, went to stand beside a tree, facing away from him. She wrapped one arm around it and leaned her temple against it, almost like it was more human than pine.

"Olivia?"

She drew in a deep breath.

"What is it?" he said softly. "What happened?"

"Nothing."

A choked noise came from her throat. Her shoulders were shaking. Was Olivia—his Olivia who had broken her arm falling off a wagon without shedding a single tear—*crying*?

"I think I might have blown it," she said. "With Sam."

"He was mean to you?"

"Oh no. He would never be mean. He came last night to tell me about Gloria, and he was just . . . I don't know. Normal. He was normal to me. Like . . . like I could have been anyone."

"You're not anyone. You're special."

"Unfortunately," she said.

He supposed he should have known, from the beginning, from the moment she mentioned Sam's name, that his reappearance would be a problem. During Olivia's childhood, Sam had been like the son he'd never had. Until his tenth birthday, Sam had liked to show up on the farm dressed in various costumes: a fireman, a superhero, a doctor, an Old West ranger, a lifeguard, and—once—a Swiss mountain dog. He'd been a good friend to Olivia when she'd needed one. And Arthur, he'd been horribly, sourly, bitterly afraid that Sam would one day take her away. He'd hoped that Sam's return to the farm would be a chance for Arthur to help set things right between them. But it appeared that nothing was going to change after all, that life with Olivia would go on as usual, and while Arthur was sad for her, he was also aware that Sam's disinterest meant Arthur would continue to be the most important person in her life for at least a few years more. He was prepared to give her up—absolutely. To forfeit all of his happiness, if it would help her in any way. And yet, what a relief to think he might not have to.

"Oh Olivia," Arthur said. The urge to make her feel better was like cotton caught in his throat. "Maybe it's best to just . . . let Sam go."

Her arm flexed on the tree branch. "But how can you say that?"

"My love. I hate to see you suffer."

"Is that what love is? Suffering?"

"Maybe it is for us. You must have realized by now that we Pennyworts aren't lucky. Love doesn't work out for us. Romance isn't something we do."

"You had Mom."

"For a short time, yes. But love in our family doesn't last."

"That's a superstition."

"No. It's Green Valley. The Van Winkles are heroic. The Hildebrands are teachers. The Whites are good with cows. There's something about us, Olivia. We don't get to love the way other people do. It was a miracle the Pennywort line continued as long as it did."

Olivia made a noise that was almost a sob, and immediately Arthur wished he could withdraw his words. He'd upset her again, this time because he'd managed to remind her that she was the last Pennywort and she would never have children of her own. It was a miracle that Olivia herself had shown up: While other farm families in Green Valley were having litters of children through the generations, Pennywort couples had been lucky when any child showed up at all. Olivia, because of her condition, would be the period at the end of the Pennywort line.

She turned to him; her face was streaked in dust and tears. "You can't believe that—that we fail at love. You . . . you made the serum. You wouldn't have tried that if you didn't believe someone could . . . could love a woman who's poisonous."

"Anyone could love you," he said. "And Sam's an idiot who doesn't deserve you if he thinks your condition is so completely objectionable."

Olivia had turned her back to him again, and he saw her wipe her face. "It *is* objectionable. There's got to be something I can do. I wasn't born this way. So I've just got to figure out how to get back to how I was before I—" She stopped.

"Before you spent so much time in the garden."

She turned to look at him through reddened eyes. "Dad. What happened to me wasn't your fault."

He was quiet.

"I could have stopped going into the garden at any time, if I'd wanted to. You didn't do this. There was nothing we could have done differently."

Still, he was quiet. Because of course there was always something a person could do differently, in hindsight.

She rubbed her eyes. "I've got to go lie down."

"By all means," Arthur said. But inwardly, alarms went off. Olivia never needed to nap in the middle of the day. In fact, she hated napping; it was their agreed-upon belief that naps were a waste of time.

"If there's something I can do . . ." he said.

She took in a deep, steadying breath. "I'll be fine. Sam's company—it was nice for a while. Really, really nice. But—I'll get over it."

"Olivia. Thank you. For . . . everything. The drapes and the teacups and all of that."

"It's no problem," she said. "If I'm not back tonight, there's more soup in your ice chest. Okay?"

"Yes. But I'll see you tomorrow?"

"Of course," she said.

Wild Oats

The days passed. July became August without a hint of rain. From his window Sam watched the members who belonged to the Pennywort farm show up for their weekly shares of produce and then leave frowning into their half-empty paper sacks. On television, the meteorologists continued to promise that rain was coming, and though big-bellied storm clouds paraded over Green Valley, their water droplets seemed to evaporate as they fell and did not actually reach the ground. In the mornings, people couldn't be sure if what they saw when they looked out their windows was mist or a haze of dust that rose like mist. The black bears sent midday beachgoers scattering as they waded into White Lake, emerging with waterlogged fur that made it difficult to take them seriously even when they grumbled and growled.

Sam too felt irritable under the unceasing, bludgeoning heat. He'd gone to the opening celebration of Gloria Zeiger's new shelter for the homeless, though putting on his uniform for recreation had been the last thing on earth he'd wanted to do. His boss had convinced him that it would be a good idea to make an appearance: *Just think of it as knowing your enemy,* he'd said. *Or at least, playing the game.* There had been a band with a five-piece brass section, finger foods passed on rectangular plates, champagne in delicate glasses that made Sam's hand feel as clumsy as a paw, and lots and lots of speechifying. Gloria had spoken to Sam only once during the evening, to ask him if he thought the shelter would be appealing to the Penny Loafers and if they might be encouraged to move in. Sam said he didn't know. She made an impassioned case for trying to improve the lives of people in the community—and to his surprise, Sam found her to be more earnest than theatrical. She *did* genuinely seem to be concerned about the boarders. She said she didn't like to see people suffering—not the young or the old—and she hoped Sam knew they had that in common. He wanted to call her out for trying to meddle in the Pennyworts' lives, but she was quick-thinking and unflappable, and he found it was difficult to claim the moral high ground even when he was quite sure it was under his feet. In truth, he liked the way the shelter was laid out: private bedrooms and showers, classrooms for self-improvement, even a small pool and gym. As he walked the cinder-block hall-ways that reminded him of his elementary school, he wondered if Olivia's boarders really might leave her.

The next day, he heard that the shoe had finally dropped in Gloria's scheme to "rescue" Arthur Pennywort from Solomon's Ravine. One of the guys down at social services had been sent to the Pennywort farm to ask some questions and pay Arthur a visit. Sam hadn't heard the details, but he knew the end result: As far as the social worker could tell, Arthur Pennywort had everything he needed. He was as lucid as he'd ever been. He certainly wasn't being abused. The shack wasn't pretty, but it wasn't illegal either, thanks to Green Valley's forgiving laws about structures of indeterminate age. If Arthur didn't want to voluntarily leave the ravine, no one could make him. Sam had breathed a sigh of relief for Olivia's sake. But he hadn't gone to congratulate her on the good news. He continued to stay away.

The days had come and gone, and Sam had a sense that

things should have been changing in his life but were not. He was restless. He was anxious. He wasn't happy. He had adjusted quickly to the return of sensation in his skin, and although he knew enough to be grateful that he could actually feel the irksome itching of the tag on his shirt, it was all beginning to seem very ordinary. His dissatisfaction shouldn't have been so profoundly disappointing or surprising—he had not come to Green Valley expecting to be happy. But then, for a second, he'd been infected by hope. And now he was stuck wanting something he could never have. He wanted to be the first person to greet Olivia in the morning and the last to kiss her good night; he wanted to fight with her about whatever things they would fight about and then have makeup sex; he wanted to walk through the fields with their children and teach them about millipedes and butterflies and mushrooms.

To distract himself and to divert his mind away from wanting a future he absolutely could not have, he'd taken Cindy Middleton out to dinner and a movie, and he'd even done a little old-fashioned necking with her in his car overlooking the Concert grounds. But ultimately, it had left him feeling like when he had too much of the Greek diner's premade frozen apple pie: slow and heavy and wishing he hadn't overindulged in something he didn't really like that much anyway. He attempted to flirt with grocery clerks and even with coworkers, but women seemed to smell desperation on him, and not even Sue Ellen Forman, who worked behind the bar at Boomer's, hung around to see where his innuendos might lead. By the time Cindy Middleton called him for a second date, he knew he should have been glad for whatever female company he could get. Instead, he said he was feeling under the weather and stayed home to watch a sitcom marathon.

This morning when he peered out the window toward the Pennywort farm, eight days into August and almost two weeks since the picnic under the Lightning Oak, he realized that he hadn't actually caught sight of Olivia in a few days—which was odd. He went to the farm stand across the street on the pretense of buying a bunch of fresh parsley, and when he'd asked after Olivia, he was told by one of the boarders that she was sick. He had to bite his tongue to keep from saying, *Tell her I was asking if there's anything I can do.* But that would have only been cruel. He was trying to stay away from her—for both their sakes. His longing for a future with Olivia was like a tether that wasn't actually attached to anything real. And desire was a wretched survivor: Even the smallest morsel of hope was enough to keep it alive.

He was on duty, making his rounds near the old motels in White Lake and trying not to think of what things he might be able to do with Olivia without actually touching her, when he heard a call over the radio that could not have been more surprising than if a meteor dropped through the hood of his squad car. There was an unconscious female down in the maze at the Pennywort farm.

Sam told himself: *Not Olivia. One of the Penny Loafers. Or someone who had come for a stroll.* But still, a very strong, very bad feeling came over him, the kind of premonition that a person wonders about later on, after it turns out to be true. He couldn't ignore it. He switched on the lights and sirens and sped madly toward the farm. Luckily he wasn't far away. He beat the ambulance there. A cloud of yellow dust billowed around the car as he braked into the Pennyworts' parking lot. He wedged his long body through the yellow and purple flower at the maze's entrance, then hurried deeper into the tangled, ribboning corridors. He called *hello!* and then followed the sounds of people calling back to him even as the maze seemed to be scattering the voices in every direction. Then, there in the Rainbow Garden, where pots and trellises of white flowers were colored by bright rainbows that splashed from hanging crystals, he found a few of the Penny Loafers standing over the body of a woman. Olivia. Lying on the ground. He didn't think: He only acted.

"Move!" he said.

The people around her stepped away.

She was sprawled among delicate white flowers, her head turned to the side, her hair like a rumpled flag, the toes of her tan work boots falling outward. Sam dropped to his knees. "Olivia?" She turned her head toward him, blinking up. He thought, *Thank God*. Her life did not depend on *him*. One of the women explained that she had been bending over and had simply passed out—just like that. He sent the boarders in different directions: some to get water and ice, some to fetch something sweet and sugary to help revive her, some to wait on the side of the road for the paramedics in order to lead them through the unfriendly knots of the maze. The others he told to *just go*. Olivia was very private and wouldn't want spectators. He did not ask if any of the women had touched her after she passed out: He didn't want to arouse suspicions if anyone had. He leaned his two hands on either side of her face and peered down. A faint sheen of sweat was on her forehead and cheeks; her lips were parted and pale.

"Olivia," he said. "Ollie. Are you okay?"

"Sam. What happened?"

He wanted to bundle her close. Instead, he sat back on his ankles. His heart was pounding hard. "I think you fainted."

"I did?" She started to sit up slowly. He wished he could help.

"Easy there. Did you eat today?"

"Yes."

"What?"

She told him she'd had scrambled eggs for breakfast, with ham and melon.

"Are you thirsty?"

"A little."

"Do you think you can get yourself into the shade?"

"I . . . I think so. Just . . ."

"What? What is it?"

She tucked her chin into her chest. "I need you to give me a little space."

He hadn't realized how close he was to her. He edged back. Olivia didn't stand but scooted until she was in a triangle of deep, sharp shadow that ran on the bottom edge of a white stone wall. His training had kicked in when he'd first seen her, blocking his fear and dread, but now that she was sitting up and talking he felt utterly raw and afraid. What if something had happened to her? What if she, like Patrick Kearny, had died?

"Do you have heatstroke?" he asked.

"Heatstroke. Yes. Must be."

She touched her forehead and he knew she was dizzy. He studied her carefully. It was not like Olivia to be careless in the heat. Arthur had schooled them both relentlessly on the dangers of heatstroke the year that a farmer on a neighboring property had dropped dead of it in the middle of his beans. They'd learned to know their limits, to rest as they needed, to stay hydrated and shaded. He also knew that Olivia had a streak of pride and obstinacy as a farmer that went all the way back to the first Pennyworts to stick a spade in Green Valley soil: Even if she did have heatstroke, it was unthinkable that she would admit to it so easily.

He heard sirens in the distance; she turned toward the sound. Her eyes went wide. "Oh no. Sam. You have to tell them I'm fine. Please. Get on your radio and tell them I don't need them. It was a false alarm."

He frowned.

"Please, Sam?" Sweat had broken out on her brow, and he was glad to see it. When there was a question of heatstroke, sweating was a good sign. She said, "There's nothing they can do for me. If they come, they're going to want to—to examine me. They can't touch me, Sam. They can't find out. I don't want to have to explain. Please? Hurry. Call them."

"But what *happened*?" he asked. "I'm not sending my guys the other way until I know you're fine."

"I'll tell you, okay?" Her eyes brimmed with pleading, and color came back to her cheeks. "I promise. I'll explain everything. Just—*please*. Tell them to go away. Don't let them find me like this. I don't want everyone to know."

Sam was swept up in her distress—but he was shocked by it, too. He hadn't realized how afraid she was, how afraid she *always* was, that someone might discover the truth about her. But there it was: fear. Raw and undisguised. Reluctantly, he grabbed his radio from his belt to call off the dogs. He said, *False alarm.* One of the boarders had overreacted; he was sitting with Olivia Pennywort and she was right as rain.

Together, they listened as the sirens continued their approach down the one road that snaked through the valley. Olivia was still, her chest not even moving with her breath. Then the sirens stopped. She leaned her head back against the wall and closed her eyes. Rainbows of colored light were cast about the garden room from the hanging crystals, speckling all the white flowers of the garden, alighting on white roses and white gladiolus, coloring Olivia's shoulders.

"Thank you," she said. She drew her thighs against her chest and curled around them; he could see her muscles trembling under her skin.

He had a thousand questions. But he waited quietly with her until two of the boarders arrived with a tall, sloshing glass of water, lemon candies, and a bag of ice. He wanted nothing more than to press an ice cube to Olivia's wrist and hold it there against her skin, to help her cool off, to *do* something. But all he could do was open the bag of her homemade lemon drops and watch her long throat work as she drank the water down. He had not thought about what it might mean for her to get sick or hurt. Nor had he understood the depths of her fear that people would find out about her condition. Politely but firmly, he thanked the boarders and told them to go. They ignored him, loyal only to Olivia, until she told them: *It's fine.*

She took small sips and little by little seemed to revive. He sat closer to her, as close as he dared. "Olivia . . . What's going on?"

She swallowed and rested the glass of water on her thigh.

"I want you to tell me," he said.

She looked into her lap at the bunched folds of her skirt. "I haven't seen much of you lately."

"I'm sorry," he said earnestly.

She rubbed her thumb along the column of her glass.

He asked, "Did you . . . think of me?"

"I always think of you," she said. "Even when I can't help it. Even when I would rather not."

He looked at her shoulders, the hard lines of her collarbones, the lean muscles of her arms. "I know what you mean."

She smiled, but the expression held more commiseration than joy. A sense of bone-deep understanding between them settled into his body, as if he'd spent the last two weeks suffering with her, instead of suffering apart.

"So . . . what happened? Why did you faint?"

"Oh Sam. I don't want to tell you. It's embarrassing."

"I wonder if I might be able to guess." He rested his hand on the dry earth beside her hip; small stones bit his skin. "You haven't been going into the garden."

She glanced at him, then closed her eyes, and he knew he was right.

He also knew, as certain as he knew the strength of his own bones, that she had stopped going into the garden because of him. Perhaps even *for* him. And the stark fact of her sacrifice—of her willingness to suffer so that she could be with him—made him despise himself for having stayed away from her for so long.

"You're in pain," he said. She didn't deny it. "Olivia, if you don't go back in, couldn't you die? Isn't that what you told me?"

She turned her head slightly away; it was all the answer she gave.

His heart was breaking for her, for him, and most of all for his stupidity in having thought he could stay away from her, could force himself not to love her or want her. How clear everything seemed to him all of a sudden, here, in the garden, with the fat lazy bees plodding from bloom to bloom and the large ladybugs watching them from the green tongues of the leaves. The answer to his uncertainty had been with him all along. The way to happiness wasn't nearly as convoluted as the various channels of the maze: It was simple and straight. It was unresisting acceptance of what was. He *could* love Olivia—yes—and it did not have to be about difficulty, or sacrifice, or risk, or danger, or what he might be giving up. It was only about what he could gain from loving her, about being as complete as a man could come to be by accepting his own desires and not fighting them, no matter how inconvenient. He did love her, he saw that now. There was no way around it. Nor would he want there to be. The question then was only this: Could she love him too?

"Come on," he said. He got to his feet.

She stood and leaned a shoulder against the wall. "What?" she said. "Why are you looking at me like that?"

"I'm just sorry I stayed away for so long."

"It's okay."

"I won't do it again."

"Sam—"

"I want you to feel better. I don't like to see you hurting like this." She was quiet. Her eyes were as dim as a pine forest, deep greens layered with coppery brown.

"I . . . I think I can manage to keep myself out of the garden a little longer," she said.

"But I don't want anything to happen to you. I don't want to take that risk."

She drew in a deep breath, then handed him her empty glass.

"Come on," he said. "I'll walk you there."

Slowly, they made their way out of the Rainbow Garden and toward the center of the maze. Olivia had to stop a couple of times before they arrived at the door that led to her Poison Garden, reaching out to a wisteria branch or pillar to steady herself. He thought of an art class he had taken when he'd first gone to college after he left Green Valley: In some paintings, a walled garden was a symbol of the virginity of Mary, mother of God. Olivia's garden had forced her to remain a virgin all these years, he was sure of it. But not from any kind of purity or piety. Only from Arthur Pennywort's failure to protect his daughter, and from the strange magic of Green Valley, and from the bad luck of being the wrong person in the wrong place at the wrong time. Still, Sam would rather spend his life writhing in unconsummated desire than attempt to slake his lust with a stand-in and be left equally unsatisfied.

She drew the key from around her neck but did not turn to the garden door. "I don't want you to see me go in."

"All right."

"Sam. Thanks for coming. For helping me."

"No problem." He felt his chest expand a little with the first hint of pride he'd felt since he'd returned to the valley. "I'll be back. Later."

She smiled sadly, then he turned to go.

Make Hay

y nightfall, after a few hours in the Poison Garden, Olivia was slightly revived—and far too restless to sleep. She tried not to allow her occasional bouts of insomnia to dampen her spirits; there would be plenty of time for sleeping come the winter. While the Penny Loafers settled into their cots for the night, Olivia walked out under the dome of the murky sky with the sense that there were storms in the area. She could feel them—isolated squalls that popped up fast then wrung themselves dry. They were out there, the storms. But they were not in Green Valley.

She crossed the fields, and then the shallowest end of Solomon's Ravine, and then she was walking toward the east side of the property, toward the old Pennywort stone quarry, which had been abandoned decades ago. In the still of the summer night, the swimming hole was filled with water that was always cold no matter how hot the day. At one point, the pool of still water had been called the Gates of Hell, because supposedly the very bottom of the pool contained a hidden entrance to an underground system of caves, and those caves were allegedly full of gold and silver hoards that had been mined by the gnomes who lived below the mountains. But almost everyone who wasn't a Pennywort had forgotten about the Gates of Hell a long time ago, and the only thing that kept the name alive at all had been Sam and Olivia's love of the place when they were kids. It was only when they were referring to the Gates of Hell that they'd been permitted to swear.

At the foot of the water, Olivia unbuttoned her cotton dress and hung it over a bush. The chill of the water made her naked skin pebble and tighten, but she waded up to her shins, then her knees, then her belly button—and then she was submerged to her shoulders, immersed in silky, opaque black.

And yet, the water of the old swimming hole was doing nothing to lower the temperature of her overheating body or mind. For two weeks, she had tried to keep herself out of the Poison Garden. She'd dealt with the irritability, then the shaking, then the dizziness, then the pains that lit up her nervous system like scorching fire. She thought, during moments of stillness that came between the waves of pain, *I can do this.* She had a sense that if she could only stay out of the garden long enough, she would be able to wean herself off it entirely.

Today, when she'd opened her eyes in the Rainbow Garden, she thought she'd been dreaming. Sam was leaning over her, backlit by the bright blue sky and limned by gold sun. The sight of him had reinvigorated her vow not to return to the Poison Garden—the garden cost too much, demanded too much of her. She would rather die than live without the kind of happiness that most people took for granted each day. But then, her whole body ached like someone was stretching apart her every joint, and the sun was a living nightmare, and her head was in danger of collapsing under the weight of the air, and she knew she wouldn't succeed in keeping herself out of the garden. Not now, and not ever. The only way out of her reliance on the Poison Garden was death.

She raised her arms to float them on the surface of the water. She'd been happy before Sam had returned. Or at least, she'd been happy enough not to torture herself with questions of whether or not she could be *happier.* Then Sam had come and his very presence had whispered like a devil in her ear: *Don't you want more?* And she did. Not just sex—though of course she wanted that and had spent a good number of nights during her adult life imagining it. But she wanted more than her quiet life, her tepid happiness. She wanted a relationship with another person that was as bottomless as the quarry pool.

She stepped her toes over the slick rocks and felt her inner temperature begin to drop. She did not know what Sam wanted from her. She only knew what he *didn't* want: to be with a woman he couldn't touch. She was so distraught and frustrated and bent out of shape—her every nerve threatening revolt in a way that had nothing to do with the Poison Garden—that when she saw the figure of a man on the shore in the moonlight, she thought for a moment it was her imagination. When she saw him fold his shorts and shirt and set them on a stone, she knew he was real. The moon traced the barest silhouette of silver on his shoulders and the crown of his head; his boxers were dark—blue or black, she couldn't tell. She did not raise her hand from the concealing fabric of the swimming hole to wave at him, but he seemed to know the moment he'd been seen.

"How's the water?" Sam asked.

She was acutely aware of the way the black surface obscured her from view, small ripples lapping her hair where she'd pinned it off her neck. "It's freezing."

He put his hands on his hips and his chest broadened with the movement. She was glad for the semidarkness because it let her admire him in secret, the contours and planes of his body so unlike hers. "Freezing, huh? Then why don't you come out?"

"I can't."

"Why not?"

She pointed to her dress, slung over a shrub.

"Ah. I see. Well, I could use a splash of cold water myself," he said, and he waded in. The moonlight made his skin glow unusually pale, with undertones of purple and blue so that he looked almost more water-creature than man. He dove when the surface reached his belly, and she lost sight of him. While he was underwater, she had the oddest sensation that she was alone and yet not alone, the high, dark walls of the quarry rising around her. After a time, she grew nervous. Where was he? Had he hit his head on a rock? Was he okay?

He finally surfaced ten feet behind her in the deepest part of the swimming hole. And she let out a breath she hadn't realized she was holding.

"Oh man," he said, laughing. "I'm much taller than the last time I tried this, and I still can't touch the bottom out there."

She smiled. "How did you know where to find me?"

"It's a summer night. You're either in bed, in the garden, or here. Not bad odds."

She pushed herself backward a few feet closer to the shore. In the years since he'd left Green Valley, she'd thought of what it might be like to have him back, right here, swimming with her. But in her reveries, she'd always felt very peaceful and carefree with him: They splashed and laughed and floated on their backs to look at the stars. Instead, she felt tangled, torn, and edgy. Too serious for play. She eyed him as he swam through the water, making a slow, languid circle around her, disturbing the smooth surface of the pool.

"How are you feeling?" he asked.

"Better. A thousand times better. I could jump the moon."

"Good," he said.

"I recover pretty quickly. Once I go back in."

"Olivia . . ."

She braced herself. She knew what question was coming. All day she'd thought of it, and yet she hadn't been able to settle on an answer.

"Why did you try to stay out of the garden?"

She bobbed away from him, just a few feet. Admitting the truth would put everything out in the open. She wasn't sure she could do it. She was afraid that if he felt the same way she felt, and they both spoke it aloud, she might as well condemn him. "I wanted to see if I could."

"But . . . why?"

She dropped her arms below the water. "I just thought . . ."

"What?"

Something about Sam's face made her want to tell the truth, to be brave. She said, "I want to be able to touch you again."

He exhaled, moved closer in the water. The sounds of the waves lapped at the rocks near the stony walls. She could not make out the color of his eyes in the darkness, but she could see his intentions, his longing, and—maybe—his relief. "Ollie. I want that, too."

"So . . . What do we do?"

"We figure something out. We try the serum again, tweak the formula. And in the meantime . . . we consider creative alternatives."

Her face heated. "I don't think there's . . . much. It seems like you're still pretty sensitive to poison ivy. Is that right?"

"Well . . . it's a little better."

"But not much better."

"A little better. That's all."

"So we would have to be really, really, really careful."

"We will," he said.

"I don't think I could handle the risk. I wouldn't want to hurt you. And I wouldn't want your sensitivity to get worse."

He was quiet.

"Also . . ." She ran her palms over the water. "I don't want to risk our friendship."

"You couldn't. Not even if you tried. You know that, right?"

"I do," she said. But she was not being completely honest with him. She *did* believe that she could rely on Sam's friendship for the rest of her life in one form or another. The bond between them felt strong and deep, almost fundamental. But while his friendship was certain, she did not know that she could always be *happy* with just his friendship, or if a near-but-not-near-enough relationship was destined to be more painful than rewarding. Would he tire of her someday? Would she have to watch as he slowly but surely relegated her to the "friends without benefits" category of people in his life? Would she have to witness him bringing home a real lover, a woman who could share his bed and fill his house with children—while she would be alone on the farm? How would she be able to stand it?

He seemed to sense some of her misgivings. "You don't have to have all the answers right now, Olivia. I want to be with you. Just you. Just as you are."

Two white points of moonlight shone out from the dark of his eyes. She was glad for the water around her; it held her up a little, and she needed holding. She didn't have the willpower to turn away his affection—not anymore. She wanted, more than anything she'd wanted in a long time, to wrap her arms around his neck and press her whole body against him. She knew exactly how he would feel, his skin cooled by the water, his muscles warm beneath. Her hair was damp at her neck, tendrils curling around her face. She pushed them behind her ears.

"We should head in," she said.

"Suit yourself."

She fanned her arms over the surface of the water. "My dress is hanging up."

"So?"

She laughed. "I need you to turn around."

"I'm not going to."

"Please?"

He splashed her with his fingertips. "How did you get to be so modest?"

"How did you get to be so stubborn?"

His chin dipped below the water and bobbed up again. "Oh, fine. But only because your lips are turning blue."

Olivia touched her mouth. She *was* getting chilly; her teeth were beginning to chatter. But all of it—the cool night air that smelled of wet rocks and moss, the way the water had darkened Sam's hair, and even the cold ache in her bones—she loved it all. He winked at her and turned around. On the rocky shore, she slipped on her dress, one arm at a time, then turned away from the water to work the buttons. She heard Sam making his way toward her, the whoosh of each step echoing in the quarry like a roar.

When she was done, she went to sit beside him on the grass, where he was wiping droplets of water from his chest and legs with his T-shirt. She turned to him with a smile, but his mood had changed. His cheery eyes had darkened; his mouth was a hard line.

"Olivia . . . is your hair safe?"

"Safe?"

"To touch."

"Oh." She reached up instinctively to pat the wayward strands of damp hair that had loosened from her bun. "I think so. My hair and nails don't seem to be affected. Once in a while someone will brush into my hair, if I have it down, since it's so long. But I don't think it's ever caused a problem."

"May I?"

At first, she didn't understand what he wanted. May he *what*? But then he reached out and worried a single heat-curled tendril that had fallen beside her cheek. "Oh. Yes. If you're sure you want to . . ."

"I want to."

She turned away from him to give him better access to her hair. She felt the brush of his fingers—no, the brush of the strands of her own hair, moving by his conduction—at the nape of her neck. Gently, he searched for the pins she'd used to fasten her bun. He prodded and sought and plucked until the weight of her hair landed squarely on the back of her neck. And then he was threading his fingers into the mass, twisting and untwisting it in his hands. She didn't even try to make conversation while he touched her; the sensation was too exquisite, too painful and pleasurable at the same time. He combed his fingers through her hair from top to bottom, and each time he caught a tangle it was like a little bite, a small and precise blast of desire like the spark from flint and steel.

When he was done, her hair combed through and trailing down, he asked her to lie back. He spread her hair out around her. She knew the way the thin cotton of her damp dress was clinging to her, and Sam made no secret of looking at her body. His perusal was slow and delicious, his countenance full of naked desire. With other men, her sense of her own beauty had been theoretical—a thing sketched out on paper that she didn't much care about. When Sam looked at her, she was glad he thought she was beautiful—and the sensation of being glad was entirely new.

"Do you want to know the other reason I stayed out of the garden?" she asked softly.

He ran a strand of hair through two fingers, a gentle, tugging pressure. "Tell me."

"Because nobody's ever made me feel the way you do. And I'm . . . afraid of it. I know how to solve just about any problem that can come up on any given day on this farm. My whole life is about solving problems from sunup to sundown. But with you, I have no idea what to do. There's a problem, and I don't know how to fix it. I don't know if I ever will."

"There's nothing to fix." His gaze roamed her body, greedily and intimately, and the look on his face was pained. "*God,* Olivia." His voice was tight. "Can I see you?"

She felt a breeze cool her skin, fanning the beads of water on her bare legs. The Green Valley moon was as bright and fat as it always was, magnified by the lens of the sky. "Yes. All right," she said, breathless. She reached for the top button of her dress.

"Please," he said. "Let me."

She hesitated.

"It only hurts me if I touch your skin. Trust me."

"But—"

He tugged a button and lifted the puckering fabric. "I'll be fine."

She let her hands drop to her sides.

With unbreakable focus, he worked open the top button, and then the next, and the next, leaving the two sides of her dress no more than an inch apart. She could not take her eyes off him; it was as if with each button that bared more of her skin, more of who *he* was had been exposed. She was breathing heavily by the time he got to the last button at her thighs. He looked at her face—a quick checking in to make sure she hadn't changed her mind—and then he peeled the dress open, and she was fully bared.

"You're perfect," he said. There was tension in his voice that made her skin break out in goose bumps. He looked at her for a long time; she fought the urge to move. His gaze was almost tangible, sliding over her hotly. He leaned over her to peer into her eyes. "Will—will you touch yourself?" he asked. "Will you do what I can't?"

She felt a frisson of uncertainty.

"Please?" he said.

The way his voice cracked made her bold. "Like this?" She ran her hands along her ribs, up her belly, across her breasts.

"Yes," he said.

All at once she felt immensely powerful, beautiful, and sure. She closed her eyes and heard only the sound of his breathing, and then the sound of his voice, giving instructions that were somewhere between demands and pleas. She held on to his words, his dictations and appeals, and somewhere along the line, her hands became his hands, so that it was his palms that skimmed her belly and cupped her breasts, his fingers that found her, wet and aching, until at last her body bowed, and shook, and collapsed against the grass.

She drew her dress closed, fastened a few key buttons. The wind blew. Slowly, the heat went out of her, and in spite of the warmth of the evening she began to feel cold.

"Are you okay?" Sam asked.

The water shimmered black and silver at their feet. She rolled toward him and propped her head on her palm. "I want you to be happy."

"I am happy," he said. "Are you?"

She nodded.

"Then what's the problem?"

"I just keep thinking you'll, you know, get frustrated and want to—to find someone else."

He didn't speak for a long while. "I know what I'm doing."

She bit her lips, chagrined. He was right, of course. He was willing to give up a life of normal sex. But was she willing to let him? "And what about kids?"

"What about them?"

"Do you want any?"

He cupped the side of her head over her thick hair. "I guess I always pictured myself having a family someday."

"You can't with me," she said. The words hurt.

"There's adoption."

"But I can't put a Band-Aid on somebody with a scraped knee."

He dropped his hand. "We'll just have to get a subscription service for surgical gloves," he said. "And besides, you *can* do the important things. You can read bedtime stories. And teach a kid how to plant seeds, and shuck corn, and work the farm that you love. Those things matter. A lot."

"Something tells me an adoption agency wouldn't like 'mother is deadly' when they see it listed under medical conditions."

"Mmm," Sam said.

Olivia got to her feet; her legs were shaky. "I want you in my life, Sam. Any way I can have you. But the moment you want to walk, I'll . . . I won't try to keep you in a position you don't want to be in."

He frowned and sat up. "It's almost like you're expecting me to run away."

The words caught her heart at a surprising angle, like banging an elbow in just such a spot that it radiates tremendous pain. Even as he promised to stay with her, she expected him to go. To vanish from her life as swiftly as he'd flown back into it. And why shouldn't he? He'd done it before. And he wasn't the only one. Nature took its course. People were there and gone and there again, and only the farm remained the same—the farm, and the great safe bastion of her Poison Garden, hidden in the heart of the maze.

She said, "I want you to be happy. And I just don't feel right about making any permanent claims on your heart."

He laughed and got to his feet, his T-shirt balled in his hand. "Too late for that. You had your stamp on my heart when you were eleven years old and you made me spend an afternoon chasing a frog down a creek because you were certain it belonged to a family of fairies." Carefully, he tucked a strand of her hair behind her ear. "Do you remember that night in the Promise Garden?"

She closed her eyes. She remembered. They had been fooling around together since September, and the spring before she'd turned sixteen was one of the happiest she'd ever known. The Penny Loafers had not yet arrived for the year; the garden was blooming only with the earliest of winter flowers. Even in the cold of early spring, the Promise Garden was beautiful. The walls were set with mismatched mirrors: hardy frames of plain pine, ornate and scrolling frames of brass, carved wooden frames festooned with grapes, vines, and acanthus leaves. The largest mirror was circled by a frame inscribed with the words: VIEWER BEWARE: HERE, YOUR YES SHALL MEAN YES AND YOUR NO SHALL MEAN NO.

Alice had believed that promises made in the Promise Garden would be forever binding, in part because false promises were impossible to utter there. Olivia herself had tested the theory. She'd tried saying *I promise only to eat vegetables for the rest of my life. I promise never to chase the peacock up the tree ever again.* But her promises had no blood in them. They'd dried up in her mouth and got caught in her throat and could not be spoken no matter how she tried to choke out the words.

Sam had stood in the Promise Garden that day after school had ended and he'd promised her, easy as water flowing over rocks, *l love you. I'll always love you. For the rest of my life.* And Olivia had said, *Me, too.*

"You remember," she said. "I'm glad."

"Let's just enjoy this. We'll go one day at a time."

"One day at a time," she said.

He smiled. And though she couldn't take his hand as they walked back toward the barn, and he couldn't put his arm around her, they shared the same air, and walked out under the same moon, and most important, they were together. It was enough, more than enough, for now.

A Thorn in Her Side

rom her house on the hill, Gloria Zeiger looked down at the garden maze of the Pennywort farm, a maze she had been looking down into for such a long time that she could probably walk the thing with her eyes closed and not get lost. In the last month, her retirement had become a lackluster, plodding, undignified march through the hours. Dust from the fields rose up and coated her picture windows; her husband's mother had announced her plans to move in with them next year; some person visiting the Pennywort maze had parked directly in front of her driveway yesterday and blocked her in; and all of these things increased her irritability until it was far too much to bear. She would not allow herself to consider the possibility that perhaps she'd made a mistake in constructing her dream house in Green Valley, where a woman had to drive for fifteen minutes for gasoline, where the library was a glorified collection of bookshelves salvaged from the 1950s, and where the word *nightlife* referred to things that walked on four legs. She had expected to enjoy rural life more than she actually did. There was only one thing to do: use her anger as a kind of fertilizer for her resolve to make Green Valley a better place.

Arthur Pennywort allegedly continued to live in a state of

delinquency and neglect, which saddened her, since she did not like to think of any old man being allowed to live in such a way. But the social workers had come and gone, and they'd refused to give up any details on their decision to let him be. Gloria did not plan to let the issue drop. She would go up the chain of command as far as she needed to in order to save Arthur Pennywort when no one else would.

In the meantime the homeless shelter had opened, but as far as she knew not one of the vagrant women who slept in the Pennywort barn had decided to move in. Her plastic-covered mattresses and neatly tiled showers remained unused. She'd heard a whisper that some people in town were calling the shelter the Goat Motel, since only the valley's horrid pack of goats had shown any interest, and they regularly had to be chased away to keep their disruptive little hooves off the neat green lawn. Gloria had staked her reputation on that shelter—its necessity, its good purpose, its enormous price tag. And now Green Valley talked, criticized, and grumbled about it—and by extension, about Gloria. She could only imagine what people were saying about her. Her husband, in the meantime, slept with his mouth open in his chair.

Gloria was not the only person in the valley keeping an eye on the Pennywort farm. Men and women would lean out their car windows to talk, each asking the other to confirm that Sam Van Winkle, their beloved prodigal son, had begun spending a noteworthy amount of time at the Pennywort farm. And though not one person ever saw Sam put an arm around Olivia Pennywort's shoulders, nor saw her give him a peck on the cheek, everyone remained hopeful that if any man was to crack the cipher that was Olivia Pennywort, it would be Sam.

As Sam continued to make his appearances on the farm, fixing rotten boards in the Penny Loafers' barn or patching the greenhouse sheeting, Olivia found that her popularity in Green

Valley had unexpectedly spiked. The Penny Loafers remarked among themselves that she seemed happier than usual, freer in a way they couldn't articulate. Even Tom had noticed a change; it wasn't that Olivia hadn't always been friendly, but it was as if she no longer scrutinized herself so closely, no longer measured out her words before she said them. People didn't feel quite so inclined to take a deferential distance—even when she herself tried to stay away. Members of her farm who arrived to pick up their pathetic sacks of vegetables sought her out to chat: They wanted to exchange recipe ideas for her produce, they wanted to talk about what new plans she had for the maze, and a teacher had asked Olivia if she might allow her theater kids to film their production of *A Midsummer Night's Dream* in the gardens. Her own theory as to why the valley seemed so much friendlier toward her was not that she herself had changed but that Sam's approval and companionship had made her seem more approachable. But whatever the cause for the shift, she loved it. The sticky air felt just a little lighter, people's smiles were friendlier, and even her three meanest chickens did not try to peck her when she collected their eggs but only lifted their fat feathers out of the way.

As Olivia watched the little troupe of high school thespians file into her maze, trailing ribbons behind them, she did not worry that the children might find their way into her Poison Garden. It seemed the drought had finally begun to whittle away at whatever charm had caused her garden to need constant trimming, and she found that many days had passed and she had not needed to prune it back at all. Normally, its lack of overly wild growth would have worried her, but with the brightness of Sam's company and the sense that their relationship was deepening like a plant stretching its roots into the soil, she decided she would not worry about the lack of freakish growth in her central garden.

There was only one dark spot she found in her otherwise jubilant days: The happier she felt on the sun-drenched surface of the valley, the more she dreaded climbing down into Solomon's Ravine. There, in the glowering shadows, Arthur Pennywort spent his days as he always did, and seeing him was a surprising reminder of the possibility that her dull, old life could return at any given moment, and that if it did return, she would not know how to be content with it again. For himself, Arthur was doing his best not to be annoyed with Olivia, even while the rest of Green Valley seemed to be newly discovering her. Normally, she might visit him twice a day or more in the summer, bringing news and food and a little conversation. But lately she made only one trip each day to see him—just one—and he was too annoyed with her to say anything about it. He was even more annoyed when she didn't seem to notice that he was annoyed at all. She dropped off his food or other things he'd requested without meeting his eye. And then she stood shifting from foot to foot, scraping the bottoms of her boots absentmindedly on the rocks or picking bits of bark off a tree, only half invested in conversation, until she seemed to determine that she'd stayed for a socially acceptable amount of time and made her move to go.

Arthur knew what had changed: Sam. It had to be Sam.

He wanted to be happy for her, he truly did. But how he wanted to feel wasn't exactly how he felt. He was irritated that her visits to him had become spotty. He felt slightly undermined and ignored. And yet, he'd *known* this was what would happen. It was nothing less than what he deserved.

"I hope that boy's going to be good to you," Arthur said one day when Olivia had come to visit him and seemed to be groping about for an excuse to get away.

The look that came over her face was nothing shy of dreamy.

"He is," she said. "He's . . . amazing." And Arthur's heart fell a little, because it meant his suspicions were right.

"And you're sure he'll be happy with you, the way things are? Forever?"

She laughed as if he'd said something outrageous. "I'm just trying to enjoy the moment right now, Dad. We're not talking about *forever.*"

"That's not true," Arthur said. "Maybe you're not talking about it. But you're thinking about it. I can see it in your eyes."

She looked away.

Arthur faked a smile he didn't feel. He reminded himself that he'd wanted Sam to fall for Olivia; he'd encouraged her. But now that it had happened, he didn't feel *good* about it. He felt wary and unnerved. Olivia was still a young woman. She did not yet understand the relationship between happiness and heartbreak—that all happiness was just a step in the direction of heartbreak. The rules of the universe dictated that temperature moved from hot to cold; happiness too left the body, just like heat, after a time. And there was only one true lesson that all the other minor lessons in life pointed back to: to be wary of happiness in the same way most people were wary of loss, for they were one and the same.

Arthur took a few steps toward her, and though they had long ago decided that he would not touch so much as a shoelace on her boot for fear of an allergic reaction, the thing he wanted to say to her was quite possibly the most important thing he would ever have to say to her in his life. So he reached out and put a hand on her shoulder over the sleeve of her T-shirt, and he kept it there even when her eyes went wide. "Once you've had love, Olivia, real love—the kind I felt for your mother—and then you've lost it . . . You can never come back from that. It changes you as surely as if it could move your organs around in your chest cavity. It makes you into a different person. You can't understand until you've been there. I just don't want to see that ever happen to you. And, I'm sorry, but you face a greater chance of heartbreak than most because of . . . because of how you are."

She stood for a moment looking down into his eyes, and then she pressed her lips together and took one step away. "I thought you wanted me to be happy."

"I do."

"Then will you help me?" Her eyes were full of pleading. "Will you find a way to make the serum work?"

He bowed his head.

"Dad. Please?"

"If being with Sam is what you want, I will dedicate my every talent to it. You have my promise."

"Thank you."

"But if you ever get the feeling for one second that he thinks you're not good enough *exactly as you are,* then you've got to promise me you'll break it off right there and then."

"I'll . . . take it under consideration."

He sighed. "Go on. Go back up there. Gather ye rosebuds and whatnot. There's nothing for you down here."

"Of course there is," she said, and she knocked her knuckles on the tree beside her, and he, feeling like his hand was a cannonball, did the same. Then she turned to leave, and Arthur felt the long, slow drain of helplessness as he watched her go.

Gilding the Lily

he days that had seemed to drag so heavily since Sam's accident on Moggy Knob suddenly began to soar with all the swiftness of the barn swallows that swooped about the Pennywort farm. Instead of lying in bed and trying to talk himself into a reason to get up each morning, Sam set his bare feet on the floor of his childhood bedroom with firmness and alacrity, ready to meet the day head-on. His hours with Olivia were full of infinite tiny joys. They worked side by side when they could as Sam relearned the rhythms of the farm. Olivia pointed out warblers and spittlebugs and the heads of near-microscopic flowers, and it reminded him of how to see beauty in things that were simple—he'd forgotten that in his years away. Olivia, in spite of her condition, was one of the most deeply content people he'd ever met. The dishes that they cooked together in her silo kitchen each evening spoke volumes about her. They were not elaborate or designed to impress, but they were simple, fresh, unaffected, and Sam had never eaten so well or so joyfully in his life. Arthur used to repeat his wife's advice to Sam and Olivia: *It's not a good day unless you go to sleep utterly exhausted.* Sam was half asleep before he hit the bed.

He began to amass a clearer picture of who Olivia had become in the years since he'd been away. She'd come to be a good leader of the Penny Loafers and the people who worked the farm, though he suspected that she did not have any particular love of being in charge. Her life was both simple and complicated: All summer long, she was surrounded by people she cared about who didn't know or understand her at all. In the winter, she had only Arthur. She was still the same woman he'd known so many years ago, but circumstances had changed her. It seemed to him that the whole of her life was devoted to self-preservation, protection, and—in the same vein—isolation. He wanted to show her what he saw when he looked at her, since she did not seem to look at herself in a particularly generous way. She was no monster. No menace to society. She was simply different, no more "good" or "bad" than any poison plant that had learned to adapt to survive.

In the meantime, his own Green Valley atavism continued to plague him. He was sure that with Patrick Kearny's death on the mountaintop, he'd forfeited his birthright. The guilt would rise up at random moments, and it was enough to make him stop talking in the middle of sentences, or fail to reply to questions, or forget that he was holding a sandwich near his lips to take a bite. His father called the house groping for news of Sam's exploits, and Sam didn't bother to so much as hint that he'd done something worthwhile. Since the incident with the tractor he had not seen any more life-and-death situations in the valley. But the unbidden thought arose that perhaps he might give up his position on the force, that perhaps it would be better for everyone that way. He thought, *Maybe I'm doing the wrong thing. Maybe I missed my calling.* But he did not know what his calling was if not to serve and protect. He did very much want to be an integral part of Green Valley. He had been walking around in his life as if the most fitting tribute to Patrick Kearny would be to suffer, to become—in his own way—dead, too. But now, with Olivia at his side and Green Valley around him, he saw that line of thinking had been a disservice to the man he hadn't been able to save. He wanted his life to mean something after what had happened on Moggy Knob. He wanted to *be* a Van Winkle. And yet, when calls came that hinted at real danger, he was filled with doubt and stayed away.

As far as he could tell, there was only one opportunity for him to contribute positively in someone's life. He might not be able to perform grand heroics, but he would do what he could to help Olivia. It was the middle of the day when he went to find Arthur Pennywort down in Solomon's Ravine. Sam's information about Arthur over the years had come primarily from conversations with his parents, who had given him regular Green Valley updates whether he'd wanted the news or not. As far as anyone knew, Arthur had never come out of the ravine once he'd moved down into it. Sam had been reluctant to pay Arthur a visit, but now he needed to.

He walked into the ravine the roundabout way, entering it by its less hilly eastern end, then walking down the long spine as the hills began to rise around him. When he reached Arthur's semi-cleared camp, he was surprised. Olivia and her boarders had done an enormous amount of work on it in an effort to help Arthur stay in his beloved hovel. The space actually seemed quite cozy . . . almost *too* cozy. It wasn't until Arthur moved that Sam understood the man had been standing not ten feet from him the entire time.

"Jeez, Art!"

Arthur Pennywort looked as if he himself were a part of the mountains, worn down smooth by the centuries but still stony and obdurate—still *there*. Though Arthur's clothes were clearly new—a tag hung from his short-sleeve shirt—everything else about him seemed worn down. His face was obscured by a long white beard and by frizzy white hair. And his shoulders curved forward in a way that made him seem much smaller than he was.

"Look what they did to the place," he said, shaking his head at his gingerbreadized shack. "This was supposed to make me look *less* crazy."

Sam was surprised by his own laugh. Olivia's father was not Sam's favorite person on earth. Though Olivia loved him with perfect filial deference, Sam had no such warm and fuzzy feelings toward the man. If Arthur had simply been remote because his beloved wife had died, Sam could have accepted that. But he'd outright left Olivia when she was sixteen, still a girl, and made her responsible for the Pennywort farm. Even as a young man, Sam had known this was wrong. He thought Arthur was taking advantage of Olivia. Arthur had put his entire welfare into her care and by moving into the ravine, he'd bound her to him more fully than if he'd stayed in the farmhouse and helped her grow up and then did the thing all fathers inevitably had to do: let their daughters go. As long as Arthur needed her, as long as he lived in the ravine, Olivia would never move on with her life. Her first obligation would always be to him; whether Arthur knew it or not, he'd made it that way.

"So." Arthur Pennywort crossed his arms. "I understand my daughter is in love with you."

Sam couldn't hide his surprise. "Who told you that?"

"Nobody told me."

"I don't understand."

Arthur shook his head as if to say *Why are you so stupid?* "Nobody had to tell me. It's plain as the beard on my face."

A funny sort of feeling bloomed in Sam's belly.

"And are you in love with her?" Arthur asked.

"I . . . I . . ."

"I am not asking you to perform long division in your head, young man. I'm just asking if you love her. It's a yes or no."

Sam drew himself up straighter as they reached the front door. For all the things he and Olivia had talked about, they had not said the word *love*. And yet, Sam heard himself say, "Yes, I love her." And a great rolling relief came over him, like he'd been waiting to hear himself admit it aloud.

"Would you do anything for her? What I mean is, would you change your whole life for her? Forever? Irreversibly?"

"What's on your mind?"

Arthur pushed open the door and Sam ducked to follow him into the shack. Though it looked small from the outside, the inside showed one good-sized room and a doorway to another.

"Wait here," Arthur said. He disappeared into the second room. Sam looked over the small kitchenette with its propane camp stove and two cabinets, the black woodstove, the cot that was pushed up against the far wall and decorated with throw pillows, the living room area that looked fit for human habitation—but only *just*.

There was a sound of clattering from the other room, and then Arthur returned. "I don't have any. I could have sworn I did. I could have sworn . . ."

"What don't you have?"

"Honey."

"Why do you need honey?"

"*I* don't." Arthur's eyes went to the corner of the ceiling. "Oh. Yes. I remember now."

Sam let out a breath. And for the first time, he began to wonder if perhaps Olivia was wrong about her father's grip on reality. She'd assured Sam that the man was fine; now Sam wasn't so sure. "Listen. I wanted to ask you about Olivia's situation. I want you to tell me more about it."

"I would think you're more familiar with it than most."

"I want to know how it happened. Exactly how."

Arthur leaned on the wall as if weakened. "What has she told you?"

"That she spent too much time in the garden. But there must have been something more."

Arthur sat down tiredly on a chair, but did not invite Sam to do the same. "Do you know, Samuel, that human beings share some of our DNA with the plant world? You and a potato can both trace your lineage back to a common single-celled ancestor animated in the primordial goo."

"I guess I never thought of it."

"Olivia was special from the moment she was born. She's more tuned in to the commonalities between humans and plants than most of us. You know that. You know how she was. The plants always loved her so."

Sam nodded. "She's still that way."

"If one of Olivia's cells changed, it might have set off a chain reaction. Cell after cell gaining the ability to harbor the various allergens of poisonous plants. And why not? We humans are already made up of a fair amount of plant."

"But why Olivia?"

Arthur shrugged. "Exposure. Magic. Whatever you want. Anyway, it's my only theory." He looked up at Sam with narrowed eyes. "But you're not here to ask why or how she had been affected."

"Then what am I here for?"

"You're here because you want to find a way to touch her."

Sam was quiet. Arthur was right, of course. His reason for asking questions wasn't curiosity. It was that he was searching for a loophole, an exit, a way to make things change.

"There is no cure for her. No going back. The process can't be undone. There is another matter to consider, though," Arthur said slyly.

"And what's that?"

"You."

"Okay. I'm listening."

"That's why you need the honey," Arthur said. "You know our bees are special. Olivia must have told you that she relies on their honey in the winter to keep her strong."

"What are you suggesting? That if I drink the honey, it will make me immune to her?"

"If you *drink* the honey, you'll die. But if you experience a careful and measured exposure to it, you might help your body quell the histamine response to her over time."

"I could touch her," Sam said.

"Allergy sufferers have reported that regular doses of their local honey can temper their body's allergic response. I imagine it might, possibly, be the same for you with Olivia."

"But the honey is poisonous," Sam said. "That's what Olivia told me. She said she didn't sell it anymore because it would make people sick."

"Well . . . yes."

"Won't it make me sick?"

"Probably," Arthur said.

"Is that why you haven't tried it?"

Arthur's eyes narrowed. "I'm old. Not the man I used to be. It would be a dangerous gamble." He stood up slowly, holding the back of the chair for support.

Sam barely heard him. He couldn't think of how he might get his hands on Pennywort honey. Olivia had told him that she'd hidden it so that some curious wanderer from the public could not discover it and decide to take a taste. Wherever it was, she also said she kept it locked up tight. There was no way Olivia would want Sam to try Arthur's honey solution. She would say that it was too dangerous. The only way to get away with it would be to ask for forgiveness instead of permission—preferably while he had Olivia naked in his arms.

"Where am I supposed to get this honey?" Sam asked.

"It's . . . available."

"You have some."

Arthur nodded. "I'll show you what I suspect is the right dosing and delivery system. We'll find a way to make it work together."

"Then let's get started. Tonight."

"Well, there is an additional risk I should mention."

"What?"

"A very small risk. Very slight. So small it only merits the fine print."

"What's the risk, Arthur?"

Arthur looked up at him with sad eyes. "The risk is that you could become like her."

"That *I* could become poisonous."

"You won't, of course," Arthur said. "It's completely improbable."

"Completely improbable?"

"Bah. You're afraid. I knew you would be."

"I'm not afraid of a completely improbable risk."

"Samuel," Arthur said, the word like a sigh. His eyes were weary, and it seemed he could barely keep his eyelids up. "I've had a lot of time to think about the things I did wrong."

Sam was uncertain, so he kept quiet.

"Come here."

Sam crossed into the kitchen. Arthur picked up a small wooden box that had been sitting on the table and passed it to Sam with a shaking hand. When Sam opened it, he saw a beautiful gold ring. It was old and elaborate, set with green and yellow stones in buttery gold.

"What's this?"

"It was Alice's. For when you propose."

Sam's chest grew tight.

"These are my terms," Arthur said slowly. "If you want me to help you, you've got to show me that you're serious."

"You want me to marry her."

"I want to know you'll stay with Olivia forever, and take care of her, even if the honey cure doesn't work."

Sam pulled the ring out of the box to look at it more closely. One evening, while he and Olivia had been watching the sun set over Sourdough Ridge and trying to identify the last birds in the sky by their silhouettes, the thought of marriage came to him with surprising easiness, seeming to rise up from his subconscious like an air bubble rising swiftly to the surface of a lake. For so many couples, touch was promise; sex, a conversation and covenant without words. But as the sun disappeared, he could not even put his arm around Olivia, let alone make love to her. And the desire to marry her came on so fast that if it had been a gust of wind it would have knocked him down. He'd said nothing to Olivia, though, at the time.

"I accept your conditions," Sam said. He put the ring back in the box and snapped it closed. He felt a slight euphoria and disorientation, as if he'd been transported to the future and was sent back to the present again. "And for the record, I would have married her even without your ultimatum."

"You're a good boy. And damn lucky," Arthur said.

"I know it."

"Now go on. Come back to me with a marriage license and a blood test."

"They don't do blood tests anymore."

Arthur shook his head as if to bemoan the state of the world outside the ravine. He walked toward Sam with a hand extended, and Sam felt the tremble of age in Arthur's fingers.

"Just make my daughter happy," Arthur said. "For as long as you can."

Shrinking Violet

livia had cooked a big dinner for the Penny Loafers. She'd set the long wooden banquet table with various sautéed and seasoned veggies, as well as some lightly cooked meats—and they made an impromptu little party under the high wooden beams of the old barn. Olivia could not think of many moments of her life when her heart had felt more full and satisfied: She had the company of her boarders and good food; her father had avoided Gloria's trap and would be able to stay on the farm; and Sam—Sam's affection was more than she'd ever dreamed of for herself. This was everything: food, family, good company, and love. As the boarders chatted around her, helping themselves to heaped spoonfuls of sweet corn with crushed red pepper and cilantro, she sat daydreaming, hardly eating, feeling as if she'd stepped into a dream.

She almost didn't notice when the conversation at the table changed topics. One of the boarders had apparently spent the night at Gloria's shelter, and as the others ate and chewed she was talking about what she'd found there. *Big televisions. Soft beds. Food you don't have to pick for yourself.* She made the shelter sound like a five-star hotel. Some of the women couldn't have cared less: The shelter could never have what the old barn had— the magic of Green Valley, the maze.

But others, like Mei, seemed interested.

"What are the rooms like?" she asked. "Do people share or do they have their own?"

The shelter allegedly had plenty of space for anyone who wanted to stay there to have her own room. Olivia helped herself to more salsa and ignored her worry. No one would leave the farm. Here her boarders had freedom. There they would no doubt have to follow strict schedules and rules. She kept silent as the conversation went on. *So why did you come back if it's so great?* one of the boarders asked the woman who had been away. And the woman said: *I'm not back. I'm just visiting you guys to tell you what you're missing if you stay here.* Olivia sat listening, unwilling to prejudice anyone's opinion by speaking up, believing that each woman would reach the right conclusion on her own, just as each woman came to find answers in the maze on her own. Mei was persistent.

"I might go over there," she said. "To check it out."

"How you going to get there?" a woman asked.

"I'll hitch a ride."

"No hitching," Olivia said. "It's not safe."

"How do you think I got *here*?" Mei said.

After dinner the women took up the work of cleaning, at one point teasing Olivia for the amount of time she had been spending with Sam. Olivia didn't deny their insinuations that she and Sam were sleeping together. She just enjoyed their jokes and played along. And why not? She and Sam weren't physically intimate, but they were as emotionally intimate as any two people could be. They were together, and she relished the delicious thrill that the boarders, that everyone, would know.

She had just finished cleaning up—some of the boarders settling in for the evening with books and games of cards—when Sam arrived. His hair was darkened and his skin was rosy and flushed, as if he'd just got out of the shower. He stood beside her and touched her hair in greeting, tugging a strand below her ear, igniting a familiar heat, and she smelled the strong scent of aftershave.

"Going somewhere?" she asked.

"No. Why? Does it seem like I'm going somewhere?"

She gestured to his nice pants—khakis, in the heat—and his white dress shirt, which still bore a triangular mark at the shoulder as if it had just been ironed. "You look nice. I mean—you always look nice. But, you look *really* nice."

"Let's go for a walk."

She laughed. "Do I need to change, too?"

"Only if you want to."

She looked him over, his brown leather belt and nervous, darting eyes. He was up to something. "Give me five minutes," she said.

She hurried to the silo, where she freshened up and slipped into one of her mother's long dresses. It was softly yellow, a backless halter bearing all of her shoulders and some of her chest, and it flowed like water down to her toes. She brushed her hair, put on soft perfume, and was pleased by her reflection. She looked like a woman about to go for a walk on a summer evening with her lover. She looked like what she very nearly was.

Sam was waiting for her at the door; he seemed oddly nervous. Her mind raced with possibilities, but she could think of nothing that might have made him appear so fidgety and excited. Ever since he had found her having fainted in the Rainbow Garden, it was as if all the second-guessing and negotiating about the terms of their relationship had become unnecessary. There was so much to talk about, to catch up on, and they spent hours talking or not talking as the world went by. Olivia had insisted they refrain from touching in any way because he was so exceptionally sensitive to her. And though she thought all the time of what it might be like to be his lover in more than name, she felt no loss, only gladness for his company and for the way he looked at her sometimes, as if she were a big, juicy apple hanging on a branch.

But then, something changed. Yesterday evening, Sam had brought her to the waterfall at the far end of Solomon's Ravine, and though it was not much more forceful than spray from a garden hose, he watched while she took off her clothes and stood under the water. He'd brought dark leather gloves with him that creaked when he made a fist, and they spent a long, satisfying time learning each other's bodies. She couldn't have put a stop to it if she'd wanted to.

Afterward, when they lay in the grass together, she did not see how making love the old-fashioned way could offer her all that much more than the pleasure they'd discovered in the spray of the waterfall. She could not hold him to her afterward, could not stroke his hair, but still—she saw there was pleasure for them, deep and satisfying and uniquely *theirs*. Secretly, she worried about Sam's sensitivity—that it could increase. But as she watched for signs that being with her affected him, she was relieved to see nothing noteworthy. The moment it seemed that being close to her—breathing the same air, standing in the same square of sunlight—was dangerous, she would have to let him go. But with any luck, it would never come to that.

Now Sam led her across the farm until they were in the orchard, and she wondered if he had some new erotic game in mind. They walked between rows of soft-looking trees, where hundreds of small apples were waiting to ripen into the full fertility of early fall. Because he seemed so agitated, she kept up an idle chatter about the dinner she'd made for the boarders, about how the peacock had got into the chicken yard that morning and looked pleased as a king among peasants, and about the coming orchard harvest—anything to put him at ease. But Sam seemed only half dedicated to conversation, making perfunctory noises that lifted and dropped his Adam's apple, and then gazing out to the trees.

"Sam." She stopped. He looked down into her face. How she longed to lift her arms, twine them around his neck, feel the flex of her calves as she stood on tiptoe to kiss him. She remembered yesterday, his hands smoothing over her, the water running down in droplets that he traced with his gloved fingertips, and she shivered. "What's on your mind tonight?"

"The orchard looks great."

"Yes. Thanks." She glanced into the old, gnarled branches of the trees. The apples were small this year, unable to glut themselves on rainwater, but they would be exceptionally tasty—even by Olivia's standards. Rumor had it that none of Olivia's apples ever made it as far as a tart or pie: They were all eaten fresh, straight from the hand. And the orchard itself was beautiful, too, serene and fragrant, hung with the faintly violet haze of high summer. But Olivia doubted that Sam had brought her here to point out the pretty setting. "Is there something you want to tell me?"

"I always wanted to get married in this orchard. Did you know that?"

"No."

"I thought it would be a great spot for a fall wedding."

"It would be a nice spot," Olivia said.

He turned directly toward her. His face was freshly shaven and she wondered what it might feel like under her hand.

"Olivia. I . . ."

"What?"

He pressed his lips together. Then dug into his pocket and handed her a small box. She opened it slowly, suspecting.

And there, settled in green velvet, was her mother's wedding band.

"Sam—"

"Wait. Don't say anything." He took the box back from her, pulled the ring from its emplacement, then lowered himself to one knee.

"Sam, don't—"

"I know I haven't been in Green Valley that long. That we haven't had a lot of time together. But when something's right, it's right. I love you, Ollie. I always have. I want to spend the rest of my life with you. Starting right now."

Olivia's eyes stung. Her heart was flooding with happiness. She clasped her hands together at her breastbone.

"Will you say yes?"

The word was on her tongue, sweet as a drop of candy. The stones of her mother's ring gleamed with familiar warmth, and it occurred to her that her father must have played some part in this. He'd given the wedding his blessing. In spite of his feelings about love and loss, Olivia had told him that *Sam* was what she wanted, what would make her happy. And now, here Sam was, proposing exactly the thing she was afraid to allow herself to want.

Sam's eyes were dancing. "We'll get married tomorrow. Right under this tree. What do you say?"

"Tomorrow!"

"Why not? I would marry you right this minute if I could. I would have married you thirteen years ago. Or yesterday. Olivia—you have no idea how long I've been waiting to hear you say yes."

Above them, a bird flew against the dimming sky. The night was coming alive. Olivia knew she was taking too long, and with each passing fraction of a second, the worry on Sam's face increased.

"Sam," she said softly. "I love you."

He breathed out hard.

"Everything about you makes sense to me. You being here makes sense. Please believe me—I want you by my side every day for the rest of my life."

"But . . . ?"

"But this is all so, so *fast*."

"No," he said, a pinch of annoyance in his voice. "It's not fast."

"It's fast for me."

He struggled to right himself, so he was once again standing. "Are you saying no?"

Her back teeth clenched together—if she could touch him, take his hands in hers, she was certain she could make him feel how much she loved him. "I'm not saying no. I'm just saying, not right now."

"I don't understand this. You'll marry me later, but not tomorrow?"

"We have our whole lives ahead of us together. There's no rush."

A flash of anger crossed his face. "You don't think I'm serious."

"I know you are."

"You think I'm going to change my mind and run away."

"That's not it at all," Olivia said.

"Then, what? You love me?"

"Oh yes. You know I do."

"Then what's going on?"

"I just . . . I don't know how to explain. It just feels fast. I wasn't expecting this. Not so soon."

"I know how I feel about you. I know what I want."

"But, do you understand what you're *asking*?"

He lifted his hands and dropped them in frustration. "This is what I mean. You think I'm going to get tired of you and break your heart. I won't—Olivia. I promise. Look, I know a lot of people have disappeared from your life. But I'm not going to be one of them."

"I know that," she said softly. She did not doubt his love for her, his resolve to stay. Once Sam made a decision, he stood by it—just as he would stand by her. But *she* would feel better knowing that she'd done her part in making it easy for him to release himself from her *if* he did want to—which, of course, he wouldn't. But they could not predict the future. Perhaps his sensitivity to her would increase someday. If it did—or if something else began to feel unsatisfying to him—she could promise there was an emergency exit for him, an open door he could walk through anytime without having to feel even a little guilty about it. Given her condition, she thought it would be miserly and mean to *not* give him an easy out. He had her love, all of it, everything she was. And because of that, she would protect his future with sensibility and caution, even if he would not.

"Here," he said, holding up the ring for her. "Take it."

Her stomach flipped. Was he retracting his offer? "I want you to hold on to it. For safekeeping. So you can ask me again."

"I'm asking you *now*. And the offer will always stand. I know you think I don't know what I'm getting into with this. But I do know. I know perfectly. And if I have to prove it to you—if I have to prove that I'm serious for you to marry me—then I will."

"You don't have to prove anything," she said. "I believe you."

"But you don't believe *in* me."

"Sam—"

He was walking away. She stood, bewildered, and watched him go. They'd had a fight. Their first fight. He'd asked her to marry him, and instead, they were fighting. How had it even happened? How had she gone from being so happy to so . . . confused. The sun was fading, the wind lifted Olivia's long hair off her bare back, and she felt on the breeze the first chilly kiss of the coming autumn.

"This isn't over!" Sam called without turning around, loud enough so she could hear.

"Good," she said quietly. "I don't want it to be."

Bet the Farm

I t was morning when Olivia found him.

She was walking with Mei to the beehives when something in the field caught her eye and she thought, *How odd that someone would leave a bundle of clothes on the ground like that.* Mei was going on and on about how she wasn't going to take some stupid job flipping burgers or taking movie tickets because she would rather have no job at all than get paid so little, and Olivia listened politely with half an ear. But then as they got closer, she saw that it was not just a heap of clothes on the grass in the distance, but a heap of clothes with a man inside them. She took off running with her heart in her throat, and a fearful, desperate wish: *Please oh please let it not be Sam.*

She'd spent the whole night dreaming of him. And though some of her dreams were of entwining bodies and tangled sheets, most of her dreams were . . . well . . . they were just *floating.* She dreamed she was being carried along by some current—a fast, warm current that should have scared her but didn't. She was happy in an easy, unstriving way that she'd never quite known before. She was not *trying* to be happy; she just was—a full surrendering to easy contentment. And though Sam was not technically with her in body in the dream, she knew he was all around her, that he was the current, and she no longer had to be alone.

But as she ran toward the khaki-and-white lump on the grass, all the peace of her dream was gone—instantly and fully evaporated by fear. Sam was lying with his face in the grass, his arms at his sides as if he'd made only the most modest effort to stop himself from falling. She crouched beside him, holding her hands over him, trying to decide what to do. If she touched him, would she make it worse? *Oh God,* she thought. *Please, please no.*

Mei, who had arrived at Sam's lifeless body only a moment after Olivia, was dancing from foot to foot, asking what to do.

"I need you to roll him over."

"By myself? I don't think I'm strong enough . . ."

"Just *do it,*" Olivia commanded. "Come on, Mei. Get on your knees and push!"

Mei lowered herself to the ground, then heaved Sam's shoulder. With some difficulty, she got him rolled onto his back. Olivia gasped. Mei leaned away. Sam's skin was shiny and pale, but flushed deep red across the cheeks. She could see small hives covering his neck. He was having some kind of allergic reaction. *Please be breathing,* she told him, unsure if she'd just thought the words or said them aloud. She lowered her ear to his mouth, careful not to touch him. *Was* he breathing? She couldn't tell. On any other day, she would have dialed 911 on the phone that she kept in her pocket. But all the rituals and systems of her life had been thrown off in the last few days, and her phone was sitting in her bedroom, plugged in to charge.

"Check his pulse," she told Mei.

"Me? Why me?"

"I'll talk you through it. Please, Mei. I know this is scary. But we have to help him."

"*You* do it if you know how!"

Olivia balled her hands into fists. "This isn't a question. Check his pulse. Now."

Mei looked at Sam with a hint of disgust. "But . . . what if he's dead?"

"Then you won't feel a heartbeat. Do it!"

Reluctantly Mei reached out. She moved her fingers around Sam's neck, and when Olivia began to ask "Well?" Mei shushed her. She closed her eyes. Olivia felt like she was going to throw up.

"There's a pulse," Mei said.

Olivia's relief was so great it almost knocked her knees out from under her.

"I think it's weak, though. I can barely feel it."

"You stay with him. I'm going for help. Keep your hand on his neck. And if that pulse stops, do CPR."

"But I don't know it!"

Olivia had already started to head toward the silo, but she ran back to explain.

Mei stopped her midsentence. "How about this? You stay with him and *I'll* run for help. Doesn't that make more sense?"

"I can't."

"But you *know* how to do it."

"Yes, but I can't do it."

"Why?"

Olivia threw up her hands. "Because it's true, okay? Because that rumor about how my skin is dangerous, how it's like poison ivy? That's true. And if I touch him, he'll probably die."

Mei's eyes widened.

"*Now* will you stay with him?"

She nodded.

Olivia ran.

Though she'd always believed in a Creator, she'd never actually prayed—not with real, human words because she'd always thought the sentiment of a prayer mattered more than the language. But she prayed as she ran across the field, still not quite certain that what was happening was *really* happening. Sam cheated death once; he could do it again. He couldn't die now. Not after everything he'd been through, everything that had conspired to finally bring him back to her. She ran, and prayed, and then dodged into her silo, racing for the phone.

By evening, the channels that funneled Green Valley's juiciest rumors from house to house were spilling over. The Pennyworts had been "good people" for many generations. They minded their own business, helped out when a neighbor needed helping, and mostly got along. But tides of neighborly opinion were as changeable as the wind; the right triangulation of events could turn a favorable evaluation to a tempestuous one. For everything that made the Pennyworts good, there was something difficult about them. Arthur was surly as a black bear in springtime coming out of its den; Olivia was hard to figure out and had given the runaround to many well-meaning Green Valley men. And in the drought, it seemed they *had* so much, so much more than most farmers in the area had, what with their extraordinarily fertile soil and wild gardens that caused such a stir. Usually, neighbors who felt the bite of jealousy could ignore their baser impulses with no difficulty. But when Sam Van Winkle—who had returned to do his family duty just like everybody knew he would—was found half dead not far from the garden maze, some people began to say in voices loud enough to be overheard that *somebody needs to get those Pennyworts in line.* It was one thing for the Pennyworts to irritate a newcomer like Gloria Zeiger; it was another to nearly kill Green Valley's Favorite Son.

Sam was weary when he got back to his house from the hospital two days later, but his bout with anaphylaxis had not got the better of him. Roddy had driven him home—Sam was glad that the chief hadn't decided to use the moment to reissue his warning to stay away from the Pennyworts—then he'd got Sam set up with the television, a bottle of cola, and a bag of orange cheese puffs in the living room. Outside the sun was setting. Moths had taken to randomly beating their bodies against his living room window as if they were trying to find a way in. Sam couldn't be bothered to get up and close the blinds.

Evening became night, and he fell in and out of sleep, half expecting Olivia to come by. But she did not. When he had opened his eyes in the hospital, surrounded by white sheets and white walls and white white white, he thought for a second that he was still on the mountaintop, on Moggy Knob, and that everything that had happened from the moment the plane had crashed until this moment of waking up in the hospital had all been an elaborate, wonderful, bizarre dream. He'd wept, in his medicated half sleep, for the loss of Olivia—though he hadn't quite known how exactly he'd lost her. As he got his bearings, everything came back—where he was, what he was doing there—and he waited in anticipation to see Olivia smile at him as she walked through the door into his room. But she hadn't come. He told himself he hadn't expected her to: She couldn't—wouldn't—leave the farm. Probably, she thought a hospital would be just about the *worst* place for a person as potentially harmful as she was. But still, he would have liked to have seen her just the same.

He upended his bag of puffs and dumped the last nuclear orange crumbs into his mouth. The ring that Arthur had given him sat in a box on the end table beside him, its gemstones staring at him like a cluster of unblinking eyes. Just before he'd passed out in the field, his last thought had been of Olivia, of how if he died, his death wasn't going to prove that she could believe in him, just that he'd done something stupid. Now that he was home again, he wanted to see her—if only to know that the world was just as he'd left it, and that he hadn't missed anything, and that the fragile happiness they'd found together before he'd decided to propose to her wasn't going to change.

By 2 A.M., he was as awake as if it were midday. He felt sort of hyper, like he could run a marathon or ride a wild bull. He also felt a little crazed with loneliness. He tugged on clean shorts and running shoes, then took himself outside for a brisk walk. He meant to head down the quiet road, but when his feet angled him toward the garden maze he did not stop them.

Inside, he walked the corridors that circled like eddies and the straightaways that were as stiff as flumes. Some flowers were closed tight against the night; others were open, and he felt like they were watching him. The night was dark; if there was a moon in the sky, it was obscured by clouds.

He did not know he was looking for Olivia until he found her. She was in the Moss Garden, one of the oldest rooms in the maze, and she was sleeping. The garden was a soft green pond of moss that smoothed over the stones in the ground, obscuring edges and bumps, creating a thick, soft blanket underfoot. He and Olivia used to lie on it with their storybooks spread around them. Supposedly, people who fell asleep in the Moss Garden dreamed only good dreams, but if he and Olivia had ever dozed there, Sam didn't remember.

Olivia slept on her side, her head pillowed on a mossy lump, her hands curled under chin. He sat down beside her, the thick green ground cover seeming to sigh beneath him. Her long hair flowed and puddled. Her lips were parted, her eyelids closed. She wore a dress that might have been pajamas or pajamas that might have been a dress, and the white, lacy cotton fell from one shoulder and exposed a collarbone. As he gazed on her, some of his anger toward her began to siphon away. He was disappointed in her for not being there when he'd needed her, when the hospital had illuminated his most nightmarish memories in the crisp white light of his sad little room. But he loved her, still. And when people loved each other, hurt was a given.

Though he had not made a sound, Olivia opened her eyes and inhaled as quickly as if a gun had gone off. She was startled for a second as he tried to assure her, then she cried out. "Sam!"

She sat up and almost threw her arms around him, then drew her hands into her chest in horror at what she'd nearly done. The noises she made were not quite words. She was sobbing. "Sam. Sam, you're here. Thank God you're okay."

"I'm okay," he said.

"I didn't know what to do. We rolled you over and, oh, God, I had no idea. I had no idea what to do." She was breathing hard, almost hyperventilating, as panicked as if she'd only just found him half dead in the field. "I saw you lying there, and I didn't want to touch you and make it worse, and you weren't breathing, and I thought—*Oh God, what if he dies? What if I lose him?*"

"Shh," he said. "It's okay. That's over now." He pushed her hair behind her ear, the only thing he could do. He was glad for the darkness because he knew he looked rough; he hadn't shaved in days. The hives had done a number on his skin, and what sleep he did manage was troubled. She dropped her face into her hands and outright sobbed. It was the most he'd ever seen her cry, and all he could do was watch. Any thought he'd had of giving her a piece of his mind about her unwillingness to step off the Pennywort property was gone now, replaced by a need to console.

"I thought I lost you," she said at last, her eyes full of water.

"You didn't. Apparently I'm not that easy to kill." He wanted to squeeze her as hard as he could, flatten her chest against his, bury his nose in her neck. He wanted to know she was real, alive, and vital. She seemed to understand this, and she leaned away.

"They said you got stung by a bee."

"No."

"Then what was it?"

He flexed his hand, then closed it again. There was no reason to keep the truth from her. "The honey."

"*My* honey?"

He nodded.

"How did you? I've got it hidden."

"Olivia. You hid it in the old root cellar. That was the first place I went to look. It's where we always used to put things we didn't want people to find."

"But the lock?"

"I picked it."

"Why would you do that?" she asked, her voice rising. "I told you the honey is toxic. You knew it was. You could have died!"

He rubbed the back of his neck. When she'd turned down his proposal, he'd been filled with an angry energy—not that he was angry at her, though that was part of it, but he was angry in general. If the only impediment to their marriage was her condition, then he would find a way to take that out of the equation—with or without Arthur's blessing or help. Once he set his mind on finding her honey stores by himself instead of relying on Arthur, he found the job to be surprisingly easy. In hindsight, he supposed they'd both wronged each other: he, by breaking into the root cellar; she, by not coming to see him in the hospital. They both had a right to be mad.

He told her, "I went to see your father. He said the honey might make me less allergic to you."

He couldn't quite see her face, but he heard a small intake of breath that suggested surprise. Apparently, she hadn't considered the possibility of a honey cure for their problem. "But it can't work . . . can it? Your system is too sensitive."

"We'll try again."

"No."

"At a smaller dose."

"No, Sam! No." She lifted herself a little higher where she sat. "It's too dangerous. Maybe if you weren't born so especially sensitive to things—but we can't now. Your reaction will only get *more* severe if we keep trying, not less. And I'm not going to lose you. I'm *not*." She put her hand down in the moss beside her. He heard the tears in her voice again. "Please. Don't scare me like that. I love you so much. I want you to be here with me forever."

"I love you, too," he said softly. "And that's why I want to keep trying."

She punched her hand down. "No! You shouldn't even be here right now."

"Shouldn't be here?"

"You should be home. Alone. Resting. That's what you need."

"I'm the only one who knows what I need. If I need rest, I'll rest. And if I want to try to figure this cure thing out, I'll do that, too."

"No."

"Yes! Olivia—it's the best way."

"But do you think it's necessary?"

"What do you mean, necessary?"

"Exactly that," she said. "Is it *necessary* that you figure out a cure for us to be together? Or can't you be happy with how things are?"

"Of course I'm happy."

"You don't sound happy."

"Right now, I'm ticked off," he said. "Being able to touch you isn't *necessary*. But I want to, Olivia. God do I want to. You've got to know that!"

She crossed her arms. "I don't think so."

"Sorry?"

"I won't let you try again."

"You won't *let* me?"

"I'll throw away every last damn jar of honey I have," she said. "I'll send the bees away."

"You're completely overreacting."

She started to get to her feet. "Do you see what's happening here? You see? *This* is why I couldn't agree to marry you. My father was right."

"That's a first."

"How could I make you swear to love me forever if you're never going to give up trying to change me? Or change things between us? It is what it is, Sam. The fact that you're still trying to make it something else . . ."

"What?"

Her shoulders fell forward. "I don't know."

They were both standing now; Sam had no idea why what should have been a warm reunion was turning into a fight. And though he desperately wanted to stop it he didn't know how. The momentum was bigger than both of them. "I'm not trying to change you," he said. "I'm just trying to make something happen that we both want. I want to be able to touch you."

"Well, you can't," she said. "And I'm not going to accept it if you're going to spend the rest of your life exposing yourself to all kinds of dangers just so you can. It's not worth it."

He pressed his lips together.

"What I mean is, losing you is not a risk I'm willing to take."

He was quiet. He meant to tell her about Arthur's require-ment that Sam propose—a wedding in exchange for a jar of Pennywort honey. But if he added that bit of information now, there was no telling how furious she might be.

"I don't want to fight," he said. His voice, so strident a mo-ment ago, now gave evidence of his sheer exhaustion, days of poor sleep and bad food and emotional fatigue. The freak en-ergy burst that had propelled him into the garden maze had fizzled, and he was becoming very, very tired and wanted noth-ing more than to sleep. "We shouldn't be fighting. We both want the same thing."

"Do we?" she said. She sniffed.

He was quiet.

Olivia wiped at her cheeks and he knew she was still crying. "What if this is it? What if this is where things are going be-tween us? If we've just got more and more and more fighting ahead of us? The snowball rolling down the hill."

"We probably do have more to discuss. But don't worry. We'll work it out. I know we can."

"You have to promise me you won't try the honey again," she said. "You have to promise that I'm enough for you, right now, just as I am. If I can't make you happy like this, I can't make you happy at all."

He bowed his head and thought of how much he'd wished she had been with him in the hospital, when he'd thought he was still on the top of the mountain, dying in his plane. He had told Olivia that he understood what he was getting into when he asked to marry her, but he thought now that he hadn't un-derstood it. Not really. The hard, interminable *knowing* that she might never be touchable, that she might never be willing to leave the farm, that his life would have to shift and mold to ac-commodate hers—it was like facing down a hard brick wall that, until now, he'd been telling himself he could walk straight through. But he said, "I love you, Olivia. I'm not leaving you. Not for anything."

She looked up into his face, her eyes obscured in shadow. Her voice trembled. "Will you stay with me tonight?"

"Here?"

"Why not? The mosquitoes won't bother you. Not if you're near me. It's a side effect of being inherently toxic, I guess."

She lowered herself onto the moss, her white dress making a dim circle around her, and his brain brimmed over with tormenting images, soft moss, warm air, discarded clothes, the possibility of things in the night they could not do. But he said, "Sure." He lowered himself to the moss with some stiffness, but once he was off his feet and lying down, his head pillowed by moss that covered a stone, he felt as if he were cradled in warm water, weightless and painless. He'd never been so comfortable in his life.

She looked over at him from a few feet away, her head turned sideways on the moss. "Sam. For what it's worth, I want to thank you. For trying."

He didn't think *you're welcome* was the right thing to say, so he said nothing. He slid off to sleep, and as he did, he dreamed that he and she were floating on a sea of living green water, each on lifeboats, drifting in different directions.

The Cherry

In the morning Olivia woke in the Moss Garden alone and shivering. She'd been warm and comfortable all night, with the most exquisite sense of safety she'd ever known. And she'd had wonderful dreams of the feel of Sam's body against hers, so perfectly familiar and right, so intense it felt as if he really were holding her, his hand around her waist, one knee nestled between hers. But just moments after the sun rose, a deep chill had stolen over her, the kind of chill that ices the bones, and she turned over to see that Sam was no longer beside her on the bed of moss. It was only the peacock there, jewel blue and gleaming in the morning light, blinking at her dumbly. Sam had gone home.

As the morning passed, she felt a strange sense of being outside her own body, floating through the hours. She visited her Poison Garden and was glad to see that it was once again beginning to grow as it normally did, so that she had to clip back her poison ivy with garden shears. She gathered the boarders just outside the maze entrance and gave them instructions for the day's work, not quite sure if the Penny Loafers were looking at her a little differently or if it was all in her head. As Olivia gave out assignments, Mei stood with her arms crossed over her black tank top, a bored look on her face like a child at school.

Her belly was more pronounced by the day, her face more rounded. All of the Penny Loafers had volunteered for various tasks in the maze—except for her.

"And what about you, Mei?" Olivia said in front of all of the other boarders. "Do you feel like working in the Swamp Garden today? It's a little bit more shady and cool."

Mei lifted a shoulder. "Nah. I don't feel like it."

"Are *you* doing okay?"

"Oh, fine. I just don't feel like working. I'm going to go hang out in the barn. Unless . . ." She narrowed her eyes at Olivia. "Unless you're going to tell me not to."

Olivia recognized a challenge when she heard it. She didn't know whether Mei had told the others about the truth of her condition. After the ambulance had taken Sam away, Mei had found Olivia sitting on a stump near the peacock pen, and she'd said, *So I guess now that I know your secret I'm a liability, huh? You going to kick me out of the barn?* And Olivia had told her, *Of course not!* She'd thought briefly about lying—*I only said I was poisonous because I would have said anything to get you to help him*—but she found that she was exhausted from hiding and couldn't bring herself to tell one more flimsy lie. Her poisonous condition seemed irrelevant when Sam had almost died in front of her just moments before, and she couldn't give even another ounce of her energy to worrying about protecting her secret. At least, not then.

She did, however, ask Mei if she wouldn't mind keeping the things Olivia had said to herself. Mei had looked at her and smiled: *Sure. What's it worth to you?* And Olivia had laughed, and then Mei had laughed, and that was that. But in hindsight, Olivia wasn't entirely sure that Mei was joking.

She took refuge in the idea that if Mei ever decided to tell the others about her condition—or if she'd told already—it was unlikely anyone would believe her. This was not Olivia's first brush with exposure. There was always gossip of one kind or another about her swirling around Green Valley: Anything Mei might contribute would be a drop in the proverbial bucket, just one more wild speculation to go with all the wild speculations that went around. Plus, Mei would leave the barn, eventually. All the Penny Loafers would. New people would hear about the maze and come to stay. Stories would change hands. Facts and theories would morph and bend, an idea would disappear one moment and reemerge as something unrecognizable the next, and soon Olivia's unplanned confession to Mei would become a thing that might as well have never happened at all.

Aware that the other boarders were paying close attention, she told Mei, "The rules are, if you want to stay, you've got to work. None of us care what work you do, just as long as you do something."

Mei scowled deeply. Olivia felt the tense scrutiny of all of the boarders as they wanted to see how the scene would play out. "What if I don't feel like working?"

"If you don't want to help out as best you can, then that's your choice. But you'll have to go stay somewhere else. Everyone here understands that. They prove it every single day when they head into the garden maze. Isn't that right?"

The boarders were quiet.

Mei mumbled something under her breath that Olivia didn't quite hear and chose to ignore. She didn't know how much longer she could be patient with the girl. And yet, Mei seemed to believe that it was only a matter of time before Olivia turned on her—and Olivia wanted to prove otherwise. To show her that she didn't need to be afraid of accepting help. As the boarders headed for the tool sheds and outbuildings, Olivia planned to take Mei aside to talk with her again—later, after they all had cooled down.

The hours of the day went slowly by. And as they did, Olivia found she could hardly muster any small sliver of worry about what the boarders might or might not be saying about her when she caught them looking in her direction. In the space between busy chores—the gaps in work that allowed her mind to wander—it became impossible not to feel how a person's spirit could become so heavy that it made her body heavy, too. The moment was coming when she would see Sam again. But she felt no joy at the thought of the reunion. In the course of their night in the Moss Garden, something had changed.

By early evening—after she'd given up on work, taken a long shower, and slipped into a light-as-air sundress—she'd made up her mind. And the decision had come with a kind of anesthetized, dull acceptance. No more fighting with herself. No more roller coaster of hope and despair. She would fall back on her old, dreamless life, and it would have to be fine.

When at last she saw Sam striding across the barnyard toward her in the late afternoon, she stood still and waited near the door of her silo, vowing to herself that she felt nothing, that the sight of him did not make her heart speed, that her body was not already weeping with desire for him, and that the small pains she would cause him now would spare him big pains later on. She loved Sam. She wanted his happiness more than her own. She understood, on a practical level, that Sam had taken the risk of eating Pennywort honey for *both* their sakes. But his action had reinforced her fear that he would not be happy unless she was different than what she was. And more than that— there was no telling what prolonged exposure to her might do to him. She would not let him put himself at risk again.

As Sam crossed toward her, walking quickly, then jogging, then beginning to sprint, she tried to hold on to the finality of her decision. But Sam's face as he neared her was bright, almost ecstatic, and even without knowing what had made him so happy, his obvious joy and excitement washed over her, a feeling not unlike watching the sun rise over the mountains, filling the valley with light.

"Olivia!"

In the distance, she heard a rumble that must have been thunder. And she realized the scent of lightning was in the air.

"Olivia!" He was breathless when he reached her, his eyes brighter than she'd ever seen them, and he took her by her upper arms.

"Sam—what are you—"

She couldn't finish the question; he'd kissed her. Her eyes flew open. She tried to pull away. "Sam!"

"Olivia—it's okay," he said, his lips moving against her. His arms came around her, one hand a pressure at the small of her back, pulling her against him, the other at her neck, his thumb hitting the pulse that beat hard below her jaw, angling her mouth beneath his, and then she closed her eyes and couldn't stop kissing him if she wanted to. His body was hard against hers, his shoulders wide under her hands, his kiss relentless. The thunder rumbled and she thought, *Is this a dream?* She touched his face, felt the stubble of his cheek, arched her back for the pleasure of friction against her breasts, ran her hand into his hair.

It was Sam who broke the kiss; his eyes were black and dancing. He pulled away only enough to look at her. She saw a flash of lightning, heard thunder like the snap of a whip echoing over the hills. Sam didn't turn his head. His lips were parted, his breath coming fast, his hands running over her, everywhere.

"Sam—you kissed me."

"Oh yes. I know. And I plan to do it again."

He leaned in, but she stopped him with her hands on his chest. "Wait. You have to tell me what happened."

He groaned. His thumb ran along her bottom lip even as he licked his own. "This morning. I woke up in the garden with my arms around you. I thought I was going right back to the hospital again. But I'm fine, Olivia. I'm completely fine!"

She thought of the night, of how warm she'd been, then how cold. They'd found each other in their sleep. She could have hurt him. She tried to move away. "We should go slow. You're still recovering."

"No. No more going slow."

"But we don't know that it's safe."

"I know my own body. Trust me. It's safe." He tugged her bottom lip down with the pad of his thumb, then threaded his hands in her hair. "I'm not waiting. Not another second. Please don't make me."

He kissed her again, openmouthed and hot. Her whole body flushed with heat. She felt an odd sensation on the top of her head, but she could barely register it. It took a moment to realize it was raining. *Raining!* She pulled away from him, laughing. The rain was coming down hard and fast—too much rain all at once—but she didn't care. She lifted her face to the sky, and the rain fell warm and cleansing in fat, heavy drops, and then Sam was kissing her again, her wet cheeks, her eyelids, her mouth, and touching her through her soaking clothes. His kiss shifted, an increased urgency. He drew her up against him.

"Olivia," he said. Little silver droplets clung to his eyelashes. "Ask me inside."

She looked into his face, held between her two hands. The thunder was rumbling, and through it she could hear the songs of birds. If there was a thing she meant to tell him, all thoughts of it were gone. "Yes," she said. And she took his hands tightly in hers and laughed, and then dodged through the silo door, the scent of rain dragging in behind them.

Rose-Colored Glasses

or a night and a day the rainfall continued, the initial downpour tapering off and giving way to a slow, steady, soaking rain. With preternatural quickness, Green Valley revived. The grass went from dull yellow to a bright, youthful green. The fish in Hemlock Pond did airborne backflips with quick-flashing vigor, and flowers that should have closed in bad weather opened wide. Only the valley's goats were annoyed by the change in weather; they hunkered under a plastic roof behind the salvage yard, and glared at the dance of rain.

While Olivia and Sam made the most of their newfound closeness, the rumor mill was grinding away. But this time the engine that powered the latest speculations was located smack in the center of the Pennywort farm. The source was credible: One of the Penny Loafers had said that she'd heard Olivia Pennywort say that she couldn't touch Sam Van Winkle because if she did she would hurt him. The girl, Mei, spared no detail: *She made me check his pulse because she wouldn't touch him. Would you let somebody do that to your boyfriend if you could just do it yourself?* Some women defended Olivia—everyone knew she didn't like to be touched. She'd always been that way. And Mei must have misheard.

But Mei was emphatic: *She told me flat out that she's poisonous. Seriously. She said it. There's something weird about this place and it all starts with her.* As the boarders scrutinized evidence and swapped explanations, word about Olivia's odd behavior began to spread, fanning out into the community as beans were exchanged for dollars over the counter of the Pennywort farm stand.

But Olivia had no idea. From her high silo window, she saw the whole of Green Valley, the gray clouds over her rust-red barn, the trees appearing greener as the dust dribbled off their leaves, and it was as if everything was opening up in a new way—herself included. As far as she could tell, all of Green Valley was reeling in the same high giddiness she was, as if the rain were as potent and intoxicating as wine. This, she knew, was love: the feeling of the outside world reflecting her inner joy right back at her. The feeling that happiness was a circle, with no beginning or end. She didn't know if Sam's immunity to her skin was permanent or temporary, but she was too preoccupied to spend much time worrying about it. In their haven in the silo, there was no room for the past or the future: only what was now.

She felt Sam's arms wrap around her from behind. They had not bothered with clothes since the silo door had shut behind them yesterday evening. The insides of his forearms, which curled around her midsection, were smooth and warm.

"What time do you think it is?" he asked.

"Evening," she said. He kissed her shoulder and she sighed. She felt Sam's stomach growl—felt it on her middle back where he was pressed against her—and she laughed for the joy of discovering that such a thing was possible. "You need to eat."

"I'll run out and get us something."

She turned to him, with the window at her back. She laughed and kissed his sternum, then his clavicle, then his neck. He wrapped her tighter in his arms.

"Maybe it can wait," he said. In bed, he rolled her beneath him and kissed her, and though she didn't think it was possible for her body to rally the resources to respond to him again, the now-familiar pressure was already building everywhere he touched. She let him make love to her through a haze of blissful tiredness, gave herself completely without a single thought to the approaching return of real life.

She felt his breath hitch, knew he was close, and tipped up her hips a little more. When he collapsed against her, she felt a surge of feminine triumph that she was certain went all the way back to Eve. He lifted his head from her shoulder, panting.

"Now, dinner?" he said.

She laughed again.

Olivia was not in the silo bedroom when Sam woke the next morning. He showered, dreading his return to work and whatever new failures were in store for him, then went in search of her. He found her in her kitchen. The Pennywort farm was a patchwork of things borrowed, broken, and cobbled together—tractors and harrows that had long given up the will to live were coaxed into continued use through various jury-rigged contraptions. Repairs had to be made with or without the part that was needed for the repair. But Olivia's kitchen was the exception to the Pennyworts' natural frugality: It was as big and beautiful as a kitchen could be. Olivia would not spring for new clothes or order designer bedsheets, but her kitchen was modern and high-tech. *Why have a farm if you're not going to enjoy your food?* she said.

But now, as Sam stood in the doorway of the kitchen, the work she did seemed more anxious than relaxing. She was shuttling glass jars from one counter to another, lifting silver lids to check boiling vats on her stove, banging and clanging and thumping as she went. The air was as muggy as if a tropical storm had passed through the valley and left a thick, soupy humidity in its wake. Heaps of fruits and vegetables were piled on the counters or lumped in bowls. She wore a yellow tank top that was nearly threadbare, her hair piled high on her head and her face ruddy with heat and hard work.

Sam wanted to go to her. But he only stood and watched her strange and obsessive work that put him in mind of a lunatic scientist hell-bent on bending the laws of nature to his whim. When she finally did notice him standing there, she barely offered a nod. She continued on with her work—hyper and almost klutzy—as if he weren't there.

"So . . . what is it you're doing, exactly?" he asked.

"Canning," she said. Then, after a moment. "Getting ready."

"For what?"

"For winter."

She continued to work in silence.

"Is there anything I can do to help?" She didn't answer immediately; she was slicing a carrot with such focused rage it appeared the tuber had personally offended her. He spoke softly. "I'm not great in the kitchen, but I know for a fact that I've got an exceptional talent for stirring things."

"I've got it," she said.

He sat down on one of the stools at the granite counter. He watched her fevered work as she removed one set of glass jars from a boiling pot, then carefully lowered other jars in.

"Do you do this every year?" he asked.

"Yep."

"How many . . . jars do you make?"

"Enough," she said.

He understood what she was doing—why she was sealing up the summer's tomatoes and cucumbers beneath glass and tin.

The past few weeks had been the best of Sam's life. If he could take them and stretch them out to fill all the years of his life, he knew he would never be in danger of unhappiness again. He too wanted to bottle up the moment, preserve it under wax or metal. He knew something that Olivia did not: It was coming to an end.

A rash had appeared on his belly this morning. It was just a nothing little hint of red, a faint wisp like a distant cloud. He told himself, *It could be anything,* and he tried to make himself believe it. But deep down, he knew.

The effects of his allergic reaction to the honey had only been temporary.

Olivia lifted another bunch of mason jars out of a boiling pot, then set them down on tea towels. She was sweating, and her skin glistened as if she'd spent a day at the beach. Sam knew they had a lot to discuss—not only the short-term effects of his reaction and his interest in trying to replicate the response again, but also they needed to talk about marriage. His feelings had not changed. Marrying her, sealing up their future together, seemed even more imperative than it had five days ago. But he would not be able to bring it up now—not when there was a more troubling problem at hand.

"Olivia."

She didn't slow down. She was frantic with the drive to work, spooning bright red preserves into glass jars.

"Olivia—*stop.*"

She glanced up, her eyebrows lifted. Her hair was curling and darkening in the humidity. She ran the back of her wrist across her forehead. *"What?"*

"Can you stop doing that?"

She looked around the kitchen as if her pots and jars could offer him the reason she could not stop.

"Please?"

She put down her spoon and gave him her full attention. But to his surprise, her lower lip started to tremble.

"Olivia—"

She held up a hand, her shoulders curling, her face crumpling in sorrow. "I don't want you to tell me."

He was quiet.

"Once you say it out loud, it's real."

"You already know."

She gestured vaguely to his midsection, her face reddening like her jam. "I saw the rash this morning. While you were asleep."

"You're angry."

"Of *course* I'm angry. I'm angry! I'm so angry! But . . ." She wiped a tear. "Not at you. Don't think I'm angry at you. I'm just—I'm sad. And I haven't been in the Poison Garden for almost two days. It takes a toll."

He went to her but did not take her hand. He felt a wall had been erected between them once again, and he reminded himself: He hadn't *lost* anything. Not really. Being able to touch Olivia, for however brief the interlude, was a windfall, not a loss.

"The last two nights with you were an incredible gift," he said.

She sniffed.

"I wouldn't trade them for anything. Would you?"

"No. I just . . . For one second I was so happy. The way you looked at me—and touched me—I mean, I thought it would be good with us. But I didn't know it would be like *that.* How am I supposed to come back from that, Sam? How are you?"

He touched her cheek; he didn't care about rashes. "This doesn't have to change anything between us."

"How can you say that? I don't think there's any way around the fact that it *does.*"

He stepped closer, needing to hold her.

"No, Sam."

"It's okay. It's not that bad yet. Come here." He gathered her close, felt the stiff resistance of her body softening as the fight went out of her. His immunity was vanishing, but his desire for her was not. He thought, *Just one more time.* He kissed her, then. And kissed her again, and again. But when he reached for the hem of her shirt, she pulled away from him abruptly, her hand over her mouth, a look of horror in her eyes.

"Don't," he said. But she was already panicking.

On the stove one of her pots had started to boil over; she ran to it and flipped the flame off, but the mess had already been made.

"Son of a—" She grabbed for a towel.

"Here. Let me help you—"

"Don't you have to go?"

He pulled himself up straight.

When she spoke again, her tone had softened. "I'm sorry. I don't want you to go."

"I know."

"I want you to stay here forever."

He smiled.

She touched her own mouth. "You know you should probably—"

"I'll take care of it," he said. "I know what to do."

She turned and bent her head over the spilled water, and he knew she was crying again.

"I'm coming back tomorrow morning, after my shift."

"That's okay."

"I love you," he said. He was glad to hear her say it back. His heart cracked like ice in a glass. "We'll continue this later," he said.

* * *

As Sam crossed the barnyard and trailed wet footprints behind him in the mud, he was so lost in thought that his sixth sense failed to make him turn his head and notice that he was being watched. With no orders from Olivia and no visitors to occupy them, the Penny Loafers took up the pastime that all people in Green Valley engage in when summer afternoons get long: gossiping. And Sam Van Winkle's morning trek across the barnyard was excellent lubrication for wagging tongues. The boarders speculated: *What was he doing up there that whole time?*

Before the rain, Mei had the Penny Loafers quite convinced that Olivia Pennywort was as poisonous as poison ivy—impossible though it did sound. She'd had nearly all of the Penny Loafers comparing notes and swapping stories until they finally seemed to believe that—yes—Olivia Pennywort was toxic. Possibly.

But then Sam and Olivia had gone and spent a day and a half holed up together in the silo. And what could they have been doing in there for so long except having sex? Mei made the point that long hours in private did not automatically mean skin-on-skin contact, but the women of the barn remained unconvinced. Mei repeated old arguments, swore that Olivia *said* she was poisonous, and tried to convince the Penny Loafers that it wasn't safe for them on the farm, that they needed to go somewhere else—until finally one of the other women offered the suggestion Mei was angling for all along: The only way to know if Olivia was poisonous was to ask her to prove that she *wasn't*. If she wasn't poisonous, she would surely relax her "no touching" rule for a moment just to put everyone at ease. The boarders, those who were convinced of Olivia's ability as well as those who thought Mei was nuts, agreed that it was time to get all of the speculation out in the open—if only so they could put it behind them and go on with their lives.

It was noon when Olivia emerged from the silo, squinting

into the sun. She had whiled away a good part of the morning feeling sorry for herself, and when she walked out into the cooler air of afternoon, she felt as if she'd stepped into a different world. Everything was sparkling and cheery, the air clean and fresh. There would be a lot of work to do now that the rains had come. The plants that had been such sad little things would start growing fast even though it was nearly the end of the summer season, and she would have to be vigilant about harvesting just before the quick-swelling flesh of her fruits and vegetables caused their skins to split.

As she approached the garden maze, she saw that it too had gone wild with the joy of the rains. The smell of flowers was so thick it crossed the line from pleasant into nearly repulsive. Inside, Olivia wound through the turns and twists, admiring how rambunctious and joyful her maze seemed, as if it were spring instead of late summer. Morning glories the size of dinner plates stayed open all day long, and thickened beds of coreopsis gave off a mustardy glow. There was a slight breeze that carried the faintest scent of autumn, and far beneath that sweetness, the mineral scent of winter. Her Poison Garden was calling her; she felt its deep pull and promise. But for once, she felt no joy in having to visit her favorite plants and flowers. She hated the garden—hated it for everything it was. She wound her way toward it, ducking under garlands of wisteria and pushing aside sprigs of bright forsythia that had bloomed overnight. Each step and turn brought her closer and closer to the Poison Garden, her sanctuary and hell.

When she reached it, she saw she was not alone. The boarders had gathered in the alcove and they seemed to be waiting for her. A dozen pairs of eyes were turned to her, some women smiling sheepishly, some with gazes like steel. They blocked the way into her Poison Garden. Mei stood in front with her arms crossed above her belly and her black hair pulled up high on her head.

"We want to know what's in there," she said.

Olivia was momentarily stunned. "In where?"

"You know where," Mei said. "Behind those walls."

"Oh, it's just . . . it's nothing." Olivia giggled falsely. "It's a garden. A private space."

"But what *is* it?"

One of the women beside Mei nudged her. "Ask her the real thing."

"What's the real thing?" Olivia asked.

"We want to know if you're poisonous," the woman said.

Olivia was too shocked to speak. Mei had told. She'd told. But—Olivia could see herself through this. It would be okay. "I don't even know what you mean by *poisonous*," she said. But her voice was trembling and she worried it gave her away.

"We mean, *poisonous*. Like, to touch," Mei said. "I told them what happened. That you wouldn't touch Sam. They know."

Another woman spoke up. "So either you really are poisonous, or you wouldn't save your own boyfriend when he needed you to. Which is it?"

"Neither," Olivia said. And she was surprised to discover that she hated lying about herself. She'd always been able to get by with omissions and artful dodging. But she'd never had to outright lie before because she'd never been outright accused. She didn't like the feeling of lying; it felt disrespectful toward herself. But there was no choice. "I don't know what Mei here told you, but I'm not poisonous."

One of the other women stepped forward. "We know it's a ridiculous rumor. We just want you to set it straight."

"She means, prove it," another woman said.

"Yes, just prove it!"

"Let us in the garden."

"Prove you're not dangerous."

"Let us in!"

Olivia took three steps backward as the voices increased. The sound, so brash and hostile, nearly made her want to hold up her hands against it, as if she could block it that way. "Stop," she said. "Please. Just stop. Everyone."

The boarders grew quiet.

"I'm not poisonous. That's not even possible."

Mei stepped forward. "So then you won't mind proving the theory wrong." She held out her hand, palm down. "Just one little touch. You can draw an *O* for Olivia. And if nothing happens within a day, then we'll know what people are saying isn't true."

Olivia looked at Mei's outstretched hand. In her mind, she could imagine the raised red *O* that would eventually form there if she did as she was asked. How damning it would be. Everyone would look at Mei's skin, and they would know the truth. Would they leave if they found out what she was? Would they leave if they *didn't*? And what would she do without them?

She gazed at Mei. "Why are you doing this?"

Mei said nothing.

"Are you angry that you didn't get your answer yet?"

Mei shrugged.

"Someone's making you do this. It's not a choice. Who?"

"Enough talking," Mei said. "Are you going to touch me or not?"

"Look, I don't have to prove *anything* to you or to anyone."

"We say you do."

"And what if I don't?"

Mei tipped her head. "Your leaky old barn isn't the only place for us in town."

Another woman, Libbie, stepped forward. "This is getting out of hand. Olivia, you don't have to touch her if you don't want to."

"Thank you, Libbie."

"Just let us peek in the garden at least, so we can set the record straight about the things people are saying you've got in there."

"No!" Olivia nearly shouted, surprising herself. "No one's touching me and no one's going in the garden. And if you all don't like it then you don't have to stay here. You can—you can just—"

"What?" Mei said. "We can what?"

"You can go!" Olivia's breath came fast. And then the words were spilling out of her, angry and hurt and defensive, all her pain over Sam, her sense that she'd failed him, failed her father, failed everyone. "Just go! Right now." She saw the boarders look at one another in confusion and disbelief. "I mean it. All of you—out! No more questions. Don't just stand there looking at me. Go!"

One of the boarders stepped forward. "Wait—Olivia, we just—"

"No. No more. Everyone out. Now. I don't want to see any of you again."

"No skin off my back," Mei said. "Come on, ladies."

It was a moment before they began to move—some of them glaring at Olivia, some looking at her with a kind of pity that Olivia wished she hadn't seen. Olivia was struck dumb by the sense that she'd just done something horribly and irreversibly wrong. But what else could she do? They'd forced her to it. They'd brought it on themselves. Whether she revealed her secret to them or not, they were going to leave. And the only choices she had were either to see them leave in horror of her, with the full knowledge of her monstrous nature, or see them leave like this—annoyed, suspicious, but still uncertain of anything that could damn her.

She watched the boarders file out of the little alcove at the foot of the Poison Garden, Mei sauntering behind. "Mei," Olivia said.

Mei turned around and looked at her.

Olivia spoke through clenched teeth. "I know you think you're here looking for an answer about whether or not to keep your baby. But what you don't realize is that the real question you're trying to figure out is who you want to be. That's what everyone here's trying to figure out. It's the *only* question."

Mei frowned.

Olivia pulled herself up. "Who do you want to be, Mei? Yourself? Or the person that other people want you to be?"

"You figured it out."

Olivia nodded. "I don't know what Gloria promised you. But I hope it was worth it. Now go. I don't want to see you here again."

When they were gone, Olivia stood at the door of the Poison Garden, key in hand and Mei's words ringing in her ears. Though every cell of her body wanted her to open the door, she did not. Instead, she ran as fast as her exhausted legs could carry her, down and down until she was at the bottom of Solomon's Ravine. She had lost the safety and pleasure of touching Sam and had become once again dangerous to him. She had lost the Penny Loafers. Winter was going to come whether she liked it or not, the smell of it lurking under the changing breezes. She at least wanted to know that nothing with her father had changed.

But instead of finding Arthur bent over his grill in Solomon's Ravine, she found only a notepad on his kitchen table. It was full of crossed-out words and did not look like a finished draft, but there was her name on the top of a paragraph, clear as day, in her father's handwriting. She began to read, and as she did, she sat down.

About the Bush

olomon's Ravine was haunted—that's what people said. It was haunted, alternatively, by a virgin in a prom dress, an Indian shaman, a murdered slave, and a turncoat soldier from revolutionary days. Arthur Pennywort was intimately familiar with the ghosts who lived in the bottom of the ravine, but the ghosts that haunted him were far more terrifying than any ghosts in stories. He saw himself again and again, his young self on repeat, making the mistakes he wished he could go back and unmake, while his old self tried fruitlessly to make sense of it—what he'd done, why he'd done it, and how it all seemed to have gotten away from him so fast.

One day shortly after Sam Van Winkle had reappeared in Green Valley, Arthur had sat down and started writing. He had resolved to put his last confession on paper, with the intention of either giving it to Olivia on his deathbed or of burning it someday on the coals of a simmering fire and taking his secrets to his grave. The decision of what to do with his confession could wait, but the urge to write it—which sat so heavily on his chest he sometimes could not breathe for the weight of it— could not be put off. And so each night he sat scratching at his notebook and trying to find a way to explain.

Very early on, he and Alice had known their daughter was unusual, just like so many things on the farm were unusual in their varying ways. One day when she was three, Arthur had found Olivia wrapping her chubby hands around a stray sprig of poison ivy that had climbed up a post around the chicken yard, and he'd panicked and scooped her up and away. She'd had no adverse reaction—not to that ivy, not to the pokeweed berries he'd caught her eating, not to the stinging nettles that she'd tried to give her mother as a bouquet. When the three of them were together, it seemed that nothing could harm them, that happiness was effortless and would go on forever and ever and never change.

After Alice died, Arthur's mind became like a pit of black tar under a black sky and a black moon. He raged and groveled and moped before a God that he didn't even believe existed—as if he could haggle and bargain for things to be other than how they were. The Pennywort fields produced a barely adequate yield, which everyone said was miraculous given how little effort Arthur made to help things along. Olivia had assumed responsibility for her father's basic needs, keeping him fed and functioning, and attempting to bolster his mood with agreeable behavior and good food, to point out beautiful things he might not have otherwise noticed, to encourage him to find tiny reasons to be happy if he had no big reasons. Though Arthur sometimes felt guilty about Olivia fussing over him, he made only the most feeble attempts to tell her that she shouldn't bother so much with him, that she should be going out with her friends and doing the things kids do. But Olivia insisted on staying close, and since she was the only thing that made him happy, he didn't really have the strength to shoo her away. As she grew older, the maze and even the farm began to thrive under her care.

For all those years the only thing that made Arthur happy was his daughter. Hers was the only company he could stand. When he wasn't with her, he sometimes felt he didn't exist—or at least, that he had no point in existing. But then, when Olivia was not quite thirteen, something changed.

It started with a dog. A neighbor had come with it in the back of his pickup, saying he'd found it by the side of the road and asking if Arthur wanted it. It was a furious, red-brown mutt named Sagebrush that growled, barked, and lunged toward anyone who got near it. It drooled and snarled and looked at Arthur with blood rage in its eyes. Arthur took one look at the animal and felt violently energized. *I'll straighten him out,* he said.

For six months Arthur had been dedicated to bringing the beast into submission, promising Olivia that the dog she was so desperately afraid of would soon be her most loyal protector and friend. But then Sagebrush had decided to pick a fight with a black-clawed sow in the late spring, and that was the end of that.

When the snarling dog was gone, Arthur took up collecting snarling taxidermies, which were less intimidating to his sweet daughter but equally as thrilling to him. Anyone could get a mean dog, but not anyone could get a snow leopard. He invited the other farmers in the area to the farmhouse to show off his magnificent hunting owl and snappish wolverine, and for a time, the joy of it sustained him. But soon the thrill of stuffed animals eventually stopped being so thrilling. And so next he turned to antique firearms, the older the better. Unfortunately, the farm barely broke even that year and he'd already spent too much money on his taxidermies, so he could afford only one-half of a set of eighteenth-century dueling pistols. But inevitably, even that partnerless gun failed to please him. On and on it went, one not exactly dangerous hobby leading to another, each leaving him emptier than the one before.

In Solomon's Ravine, where he'd had a lot of time to think, he understood what his young self could not: that after Alice died, he'd wanted to thumb his nose at death, to dominate it in his small way. He'd wanted to take charge of a world he had no control over, to be master of dangerous things. He was— looking back—more than a little unhinged.

One day when the early spring clouds were splotchy in the sky, he found his beautiful daughter behind the barn admiring a delicate young lattice of bittersweet nightshade, and though he'd seen the plant before, each sweetly drooping dart of petals now struck him like an arrow to the heart. He suggested, in that moment, that he and Olivia start their own garden of poisonous plants and flowers. If Olivia had reservations, she didn't voice them; she just said yes.

A space in the center of the garden maze was cleared— because where better to hide questionable judgment than in plain sight? Walls were put up, and the first flower they transferred was the nightshade behind the barn. Olivia seemed proud of their work; she made decisions about which plants should go where and how they should be cared for. Arthur enjoyed seeing his daughter take charge of the garden; she was an accomplished gardener, fearless and creative. She'd taken Arthur's idea of a garden of poison plants and she'd made it her own.

But as he and Olivia watched the new flowers and shrubs flourishing in the Poison Garden, Arthur also began to notice Olivia spending more time with Sam. As far as he could tell, they were as innocent as they'd ever been. But then, one late summer day when Olivia had not known he was inside the chicken coop swapping out old bedding for new, he caught a glimpse of the two with their arms around each other beneath the old hickory in a way that was definitely not innocent.

He looked away, finished with the chickens, and resolved that he would not bring up what he'd seen. He wanted to be happy for his daughter. He truly did. But in those days, his pessimism about his own life lent a pessimistic lens to what he predicted for her. He worried about her. Sam was a good boy—but would he always be? He was older than Olivia; Arthur knew his daughter had a good head on her shoulders, but nature was nature, fate was fate, and youth was a garden of bad choices. He became suspicious of Olivia—and paranoid. He worried that one day he would wake up and discover that she and Sam had decided to elope, that she'd left the farm and left him alone there forever. And why wouldn't she want to leave? It was a miserable place, with only her miserable father for company. Probably she'd been making secret arrangements to abandon him and thought him too old and doddering to know.

When he wasn't fretting about her secret plot to forsake him, he began to worry that something would happen to her—an accident with a tractor, a slip on concrete, lightning and falling trees. There was nothing in the universe that could guarantee he wouldn't lose Olivia, too. When she complained about a headache or a tickle in her throat, he felt as if his world was about to go into a tailspin, as if she were dying. There was no small voice in his mind to point out that he was being excessively nervous and paranoid—there was only fear, fear like he'd never known before. A mistakenly identified mushroom had killed Alice so fast that when he'd learned she was gone it took days and days before he really understood it. He couldn't lose Olivia so suddenly and unexpectedly. He *wouldn't*.

And so, as Sam's interest in his daughter continued to increase, so too did Arthur's worries. Until one day, the worst thing—the very worst thing that could have happened apart from Olivia's death—came to be: Sam sought him out among rows of acorn squash the summer Olivia was sixteen and said:

Sir, I'm in love with your daughter. And I want to ask your permission to marry her.

If the rows of his fields had turned black in that moment Arthur could not have been more distressed. But he hid his anger away under the guise of fatherly concern, even while he was already making secret plans. He *was* perfectly prepared to part with Olivia—all fathers must part with their daughters someday. But not *yet*. Not *then*. He would die before he let Sam take her away from him, Sam who walked around Green Valley like he held the key to the town, but who was definitely hiding something dark and sinister within him that Olivia needed to be protected from.

He'd wiped the dirt off his hands and stood upright, not quite believing what he'd heard. Sam told him Olivia had no idea that a proposal was coming, and that while he planned to propose now, they wouldn't actually marry until next year. Then she would be of legal age to get married—but only if Arthur would give parental consent.

Arthur had looked Sam in the eye and clasped his hand and said that he was doing the right thing by asking permission. But in the meantime, a wicked thought had formed, an incredible thought, a thought that jolted him like the old thrill of holding a new stuffed predator or a sharp antique blade. Olivia was becoming poisonous: Arthur knew it. He had realized just that morning, and he'd planned to tell Olivia she should never go into the garden again.

But now, with a black fear growing in his heart like a cancer, he made a new decision. Sam was foolish—excessively young, excessively amped up on teenage hormones. If only Sam could no longer touch Olivia for a while, his ardor would cool and he would not feel so intent on plunging into marriage. There was a way Arthur could make that happen: He would simply guard the secret of the Poison Garden inside his own poison heart.

It was the most terrible thing Arthur had ever done in his entire life—in eighty-three years of living, he could pinpoint the moment that had doomed him to hell. In his old age, with his head clearer and memories of Alice becoming more distant by the day, he knew that he would never have taken such a risk if he'd been in a more generous state of mind. But it all happened almost exactly as Arthur thought it might. Olivia realized her condition, the school year started, and Sam stopped coming around. The threat of marriage was over. Arthur was momentarily pleased.

But then, Olivia grew sullen. Autumn came. The Penny Loafers left—just as they always did—and the gardens died. To Arthur's dismay, Olivia's condition did not reverse with the death of her Poison Garden. He'd never once thought the effects of the Poison Garden would be permanent. He watched her grow sickly, thin, and pale—and he was certain that he was facing the punishment of an angry God for what he'd done. It was sheer accident that had taught them the Pennywort honey could help revive her; they spread it on their toast one October morning, and while Arthur had gotten sick eating it, Olivia had been slightly revived.

But she had not recovered. The light of childhood went out of her eyes. Her optimism and warmth vanished, a new kind of coldness and aloofness settled into her bones. As the autumn progressed, Arthur's guilt rubbed him raw. The Olivia he'd known faded away, even with daily doses of honey. He could not bear to see it. Nor could he stand the sight of himself. In trying to keep Olivia by his side for just a few summers more, he'd accidentally bound her to the farm forever. In a way, he'd got what he wanted: Olivia would never be able to leave him. And he would spend the rest of his life in penance at the bottom of Solomon's Ravine, suffering in the green gloom and murk like an animal. If he lived to be a hundred, it wouldn't be enough time to atone for what he'd done.

Olivia finished reading her father's messy and disjointed confession. And when she was finished, she went up to the Poison Garden and shut the door.

Late Bloomer

hat happened next went down in the lore of Green Valley for generations to come, although the way it all went down was up for debate, and even those who were there the day it happened argued about what was honest fact and what was just the natural human tendency to exaggerate. Mrs. Lee McAlester said she knew something was about to happen because while she was doing her crossword on the back deck, she turned around to see an owl sitting on the eaves, and everybody knew an owl over your shoulder was bad luck. Jesse Marshall said he knew because all the starlings that liked to gather on his lawn on August mornings just up and vanished, and didn't return for three days.

Gloria Zeiger had remarked to the cashier at the nail salon that the thunderstorms had kept her up all night—only to be told that no one else heard so much as a raindrop on the window. But Gloria had been sure she'd heard storms, and she'd argued the point: Every few hours she woke up to feel that the metal coils of her mattress were buzzing as if being vibrated from below, and she heard a sound like distant, groaning thunder. The girls in the nail salon found it was better to agree than argue, or else the conversation would never move on.

But Gloria was not the only one to hear the groaning, grumbling creaking: A mile away, a middle-aged dairy farmer named Johannes Larsen had pushed open his screen door in the wee hours expecting rain, but the sky was crystal clear and starry, the great swath of the Milky Way stretching from one end of the night to the other in a glittery band.

Sam too had not slept well, but he had not expected to sleep well given the events of the day. He believed the low, sporadic sawing-groaning-creaking kind of noise that kept waking him up was nothing more than the sawing of his own teeth in his head. His shift had kept him busy well into the night, and so he had not seen Olivia since he'd left her in the silo kitchen yesterday. His dreams of her were choppy and disturbed. When he woke in the morning to the sound of banging, he realized that someone was at the door and he hurried to answer it.

The little pregnant girl from the barn was there in a black shirt and glittery blue shorts. Her features were small and solemn. "What is it? What's wrong?"

"I think I made a mistake," she said.

He pushed open the door.

She followed him, then sat down on his couch as if she'd made herself at home in his house a thousand times before. He listened as the girl—*Mei,* he remembered—told him what had happened on the farm: that the boarders had turned on Olivia, that Mei had instigated them to do it, that Olivia had booted them out. Sam listened with increasing panic. Mei said Gloria had promised her a hundred dollars for every Penny Loafer that she could get to move out of the barn and into the homeless shelter. Mei knew she wouldn't get anywhere trying to convince the women to leave—they were too in love with the barn, too set on staying there until the maze gave them their answers. If Mei wanted the women to leave, she would need to work on Olivia, to create a reason strong enough that Olivia would need to kick them out.

Mei looked up at Sam from beneath short, dark lashes. "I shouldn't feel bad about this. I shouldn't. I mean, I got the money—I should have just skipped town already."

"So why are you still here?"

Mei played with a thread that hung from her shorts. "Olivia said something to me. It just . . . it made me think."

"You got your answer," Sam said. "In the maze."

Mei nodded and touched her belly. "I guess . . . I just have a better idea of who I want to be."

"So, what can I do?"

"I want you to help me fix it. Get Olivia to invite the boarders back to the barn."

"Did you start by apologizing to her?"

"That's why I came back. But . . . she wouldn't talk to me."

"Did you *ask* her if she'll take the boarders back? I'm sure she will. She's never been stubborn like that."

"Sam, I think something's wrong. Like, really wrong."

"What?"

"I think it would be better for you to see for yourself," she said.

"See what for myself?"

She stood with effort, one hand on her lower back. "Go to the garden. You'll find her there."

He didn't wait; every instinct in his body that had failed him on the night Patrick Kearny died suddenly filled him with the certainty that Olivia needed him. He didn't pause even to escort Mei out of his house; he walked quickly toward the maze thinking of the last time he'd seen Olivia, with her skin glistening in the kitchen of her steamy silo, jars of preserved fruits all around. When he crossed the street into the old barnyard, the farm appeared to have been abandoned. No boarders in their odd collections of mismatched clothes were crossing in and out of the garden maze. He could not hear any of the usual sounds of

Tom and the farm crew calling to one another over the puttering drone of a tractor in the fields. Even the wandering peacock was relatively somber, dragging its train of feathers and blinking at him with beady eyes. There was nothing: just an eerie silence. But suddenly, through the quiet, he felt the ground tremble beneath his toes, heard a low creaking groan like the earth itself was sighing.

He began to run, across the farm, into the maze, toward the Poison Garden. The maze unraveled, corners kinking before him, spirals winding him one way and then the other, and he had a sense that it was leading him, but also that it was changing around him like water, so familiar paths seemed strange. He was certain the next right would bring him toward the center of the maze, but instead he found himself in the Sundial Garden and had to double back. The lines of sunflowers that stood along the corridor had all fallen over, crisscrossing the pathway like rows of ceremonial swords, and Sam did his best to stand them upright as he passed them.

Finally, he reached the alcove at the foot of Olivia's Poison Garden. What he saw stopped him.

A great wave of poison ivy had swelled over the top of the walled garden like the hand of some enormous green god. Finger-thick tendrils had wound around the barbed wire at the tops of the walls, then cascaded in a green waterfall down toward the ground. Olivia had planted the outside of her garden with touch-me-not, which was actually a cheery and benign plant used in folk medicine to treat poison ivy. But now the leaves-of-three had formed such a thick mat on top of the touch-me-not that it cast a shadow so dense it was nearly blue. He circled the garden, looking for a break in the vines, but there were angry, lush, matted, zealous, wild, perilous green snares covering every inch of the walls.

"Olivia!" Sam called. "Olivia? Are you in there?" He took a

few steps closer toward the plants, his toes just an inch away from the edge of the ragged green tide. "Olivia! Are you there?" He was standing before what he thought was the door to the garden, but he could barely make it out. He worried: Was she in there? Was she stuck? Was she hurt? "Olivia—if you're in there you've got to tell me. Otherwise I've got to find a way to get in."

"Don't come in." He heard her voice over the wall.

"Are you okay?"

"Just go away."

He looked down at his shoe: a tendril of poison ivy had curled on top of the leather toe. He kicked it off. "We've got to get you out of there, Ollie. You wouldn't believe what's happening out here. It's like poison ivy Armageddon."

"I told you to go away."

"I know about the boarders. Mei told me."

She was quiet.

"We'll work it out, Olivia. We'll just ask them to come back. It won't be a big deal."

"I don't want them back."

"You don't?" She didn't answer. "What's going on then? What's got you upset like this? Is it because I can't touch you anymore?"

"I want you to go away, Sam. Just leave me alone."

An awful feeling constricted like a vine cutting into his heart. This—the dangerous flood of poison ivy—this was no freak co-incidence. Olivia was doing this in some way. He took a small step backward. His throat itched. Was she mad at him? He knew she'd been hurt by the boarders, but her anger as he stood out-side the walls seemed to be directed *at him*. Was she mad at him, too?

"If this is about your father, it wasn't a secret or anything. I was going to tell you."

She didn't speak.

"Olivia, please. You know I want to marry you. I was going to propose even if your father hadn't tried to make me."

The vines were not moving, not that he could see. And yet, they seemed closer. The air had grown thicker with the smell of green.

Her response came after a long pause. "He *made* you propose to me?"

Sam took a step back. His throat was definitely itchy. He wasn't sure how much longer he would be able to stand so close to the vines. And yet, apparently Olivia hadn't known about Arthur's scheming, so Sam had no choice but to explain. "Listen," he said. "Your dad told me he would help me with the honey, but not until we were married. I was going to ask you anyway. And he was just trying to look out for you."

"Look out for me! Ha!" she said, and he couldn't tell if the sound was a laugh or a sob.

Sam's throat was getting tighter. "Olivia I can't stay here. And the vines—you have to stop this. It's dangerous. You have to come out."

"I don't have to do anything."

"What happened? Talk to me, Ollie. You can tell me. I love you. Just . . . just come out of there and we'll sort this all out."

She didn't answer. He was talking to a wall. And his throat was tightening. "I can't stay here," he said.

"I don't want you to stay," she said. "I wish you'd never come back in the first place. Before you showed up, everything was fine."

He tried to hold back a swell of anger. "Everything was not fine. You were just pretending it was fine. You can't hide forever, Ollie. You have to come out."

"Did you not hear me? I don't want to talk to you. I don't want to see you. And I certainly don't ever want to marry you."

He drew himself up straighter. "What the hell? What's gotten into you? Why are you acting like a child?"

She replied with words that shocked him, two words he'd never thought he would have heard her say—and certainly not to him. He threw his hands up and turned his back. He started to walk away from the center garden, but the urge to finally get his frustrations off his chest was too strong. "You know what, Olivia? I've been bending over backward for you, trying to make this work, and you're not even trying to meet me in the middle. You didn't even come see me in the hospital when I was on my damn deathbed because you couldn't leave your precious farm. And I'm tired of it! I'm tired of pulling all the weight for both of us. I'm tired of having to give so much and not getting anything back."

She didn't answer; he didn't expect her to. He balled his hands into fists.

"I want to love you. Just as you are. But I can't do it if you won't let me. What kind of future is there for us if you're always thinking I'll leave you and you're literally hiding behind a wall?" He took another step back; in another minute, he would be in real danger—if he wasn't already. He needed an antihistamine, fast. "Ollie. Do you hear what I'm saying here? You have to decide what you want. And if you want me, then you've got to come out of there. Right now."

He told himself: If she said one word, any word at all, to make him think she was willing to work for them, to put in some effort, then he would resolve not to give up. But a man could only handle so much failure, so much of a sense that he could not make the woman he loved happy. And when she remained quiet, he knew he could not succeed with her, and he quietly slunk away. Behind him, the vines crawled.

* * *

Inside the Poison Garden, Olivia sat with her back curved against one of the stone walls that she and her father had built. Overnight, she'd slept deeply, as if at the dark bottom of a great, heavy lake, but she woke in the morning with no sense of having been restored. Her body ached and her heart was as low as if she had not gone looking for the rejuvenating breath of her Poison Garden at all. Around her where she sat, scowling at the earth, vines of poison ivy had formed a kind of pod or shell, all woven together in a spindly and tangled mess. The sun shone through the toothed leaves and cast a yellow green on her skin in between clusters of shadows. Olivia had not panicked to have woken up caught in a living green cage; instead, she'd felt only a kind of sour acceptance, as if it was the most natural thing in life that she should be entombed by poison vines.

She gathered her knees in closer to herself. Soon, the news of how she had evicted the boarders because of their suspicions—and the news of how her Poison Garden had gone haywire with her inside—would be all over the valley. Her secret would be out. People, neighbors that she'd always liked to think of as friends, would be afraid, hateful, maybe even malicious. Perhaps they would accuse her of trying to harm others, or of being negligent with their safety, since it was about to be known that she'd purposely cultivated the valley's most toxic plants in the valley's most visited garden. How her father ever could have thought that making her this way would protect her was beyond comprehension. The fact that he had betrayed her so horrifically meant anyone could.

Only her plants seemed to promise any kind of real and permanent safety to her—perverse though it was. In her Poison Garden, many of the toxic alkaloids of her leaves and berries were bitter—nature's weapons of self-protection. She too felt a kind of deep bitterness growing in herself, a bitterness she'd never quite felt before, and she did not hate it. This was what happened to a person when happiness proved just how fickle it could be: She found ways to guard herself, protect herself. She became as bitter as her plants.

And what was so bad about that? Olivia thought in her cave of vines. Wasn't that natural? Happiness filled a person up, filled and filled and filled. And when it was gone, and only a vulgar empty sac was left behind like a deflated balloon, *something* had to ease in and take its place. Bitterness was the urge toward survival in the face of danger—functional as any alkaloid. Plus, there was something nasty and gratifying about giving in to mean-spiritedness. Happiness would *not* disappoint her again. Soon, Olivia thought, the vines would grow too thick to get through without serious equipment; Olivia did not feel as worried about this as she probably should have been.

Her sin was in focus: She'd wanted too much for herself. Before, she'd been happy with her quiet, calm, even *dull* kind of life. She'd been safe, and when a person was safe, she could be happy—or at least content, which was as much as a woman could dare hope to be. It was wrong to have thought she could take her satisfactory life and add more happiness to it without skewing the precise balance of everything and ruining what she'd had. The farm had taken care of her in its way. But when she'd started questioning herself—asking, Am I happy *enough?*—everything started breaking down.

She looked up into the vines, where the leaves had turned translucent around her in the sun, and then she lowered her shoulder to the earth and curled up in a ball to sleep, not caring if the vines were thickening behind the walls, even if they engulfed all of Green Valley before they were done.

In the midafternoon, Gloria happened to glance out of her window and down into the valley while she was vacuuming her living room carpet. What she saw was enough to make her turn off the machine: The Pennywort garden maze was overgrown—not with bright flowers but with some kind of climbing green vines. The passageways had all been obscured as if a child had taken a green crayon and covered the middle parts of maze with circles and spirals and tangles and slashes that paid no attention to staying in the lines. Gloria paced in front of the window; the whole valley seemed to give off a terrible groaning breath that made the floor of her living room vibrate for a moment, barely perceptible, under her feet. A single antique white dinner plate fell off her wall.

She reached for the phone. Reached for it—then stopped. For once she decided that she would *not* call the police to alert them. If a giant alien man-eating vine was swallowing the garden maze whole—hell, if the thing got up and started tap-dancing—well then, more power to it. The important thing was that the poor, defenseless Penny Loafers were no longer in danger on the farm. Yesterday, her girl Mei had finally found some way to convince them all to move to the shelter, where it was safe, and comfortable, and halfway across town. Gloria wasn't quite sure how the girl had managed to move the homeless women off the farm: Mei got a funny look in her eye and refused to go into detail when asked. But at any rate it was done, and that was the important thing. The shelter was at full capacity and her unwanted neighbors were safe behind its walls. Feeling a sudden urge for a strawberry daiquiri, Gloria closed the shades.

Halfway across town in Gloria's shelter, the Penny Loafers were feeling itchy—not the kind of itch that attacks the surface of the skin, but more deeply itchy. Restless. Shortly after the grouped had arrived at the shelter and filled out their paperwork and signed all the forms, Mei had taken off—saying that she was finally feeling ready to go home. She'd barely bothered to say goodbye, leaving the boarders quite perplexed and feeling abandoned without their unofficial new leader. It was as if when Mei left, she took all her anger and irritation at Olivia Penny-wort with her: The bluster went out of the little group as they sat in the common room watching commercials play on the television, and as their hands itched for the tasks of weeding or watering in the garden maze, they began to wonder what exactly they were doing at the shelter anyway and wishing they could go back.

But they could not leave: Olivia Pennywort would not welcome them back, not after how they'd betrayed and embarrassed her by believing the preposterous rumor that had been going around. They sat on couches with wooden arms and overly firm cushions, and they did not speak about it but inwardly wondered if they had ruined their shot at getting clear answers to their individual questions now that they were no longer welcome in the garden maze.

In Solomon's Ravine, Arthur too was having his own kind of crisis. Yesterday he had taken himself for a little stroll to Hemlock Pond, just for a bit of exercise. He'd been working on his Great Confession, and he'd needed a break from the difficult memories of the past. He'd left his notepad on his spiffy new kitchen table because he had not expected Olivia until later. And now, he knew she'd seen it. She'd pulled out the pages and left them crumpled so that he would know she'd been there. If he'd felt guilty before about what he'd done, he felt a thousand times guiltier now. He'd spent all of his years since he'd realized Olivia's condition was irreversible punishing himself by remaining in the gloom of Solomon's Ravine, by not shaving off his damn beard even though he hated it, by taking himself away from the farm he and Alice had loved. He had no idea how he could fix the horrible thing he'd done—and he was beginning to think there was no way to fix it. No apology would ever be enough. He sat in the bottom of the ravine and watched the newly swollen river dragging debris downstream. Sometimes he thought it would be more convenient for him, and for everyone, if he would just die.

The night passed. Not a single bird made so much as a peep. The Green Valley goats were missing from their usual haunts—but wherever they'd gone, they were certainly up to no good. When morning came, Sam excused himself from work with a phone call, saying that he suspected an ear infection—and yet, he knew that there had never been a day when it was more important to show his face at the station than this one. After he'd left Olivia, he'd gone straight to the bar, hoping to drink his blues away as he'd sometimes done in the years before he'd returned to the valley. A couple of guys had got drunk and started posturing like roosters and flapping their knives at one another near the doorway. But instead of throwing himself between the potential fighters, as everyone seemed to expect him to do, Sam had gone bottom's up on his beer, slapped his money on the counter, and said to the men as he was leaving, *Good luck.*

The good news was that the idiots had been so startled to see a Van Winkle abandon a very serious, very life-and-death fight that they'd lost interest in it and walked away with their pocket-knives sheathed. But the bad news was that all of Sam's buddies were on to him now, if they hadn't been before. They knew he was a coward, a crappy, careless cop. They did *not* know that the Van Winkle talent had skipped him, that Sam was as likely to kill people as save them.

It was 11 A.M. when Sam walked into Roddy's office, knocking as he entered instead of before. Roddy glanced up but then went back to his work. "Sam. I see you're feeling better. That ear infection cleared up already?"

"I'm quitting," Sam said.

Roddy looked up from his computer, then took off his glasses and folded his hands. "Sit down."

Sam shook his head. "Not staying long."

"I assume you're at least giving me the courtesy of two weeks' notice?"

Sam frowned; he hadn't thought about that. "I guess."

"Then I'm still your boss and you still work for me. Sit down."

Sam sighed and obeyed.

"You think I don't know why you're quitting. But I do."

Sam was pretty sure Roddy had no idea, so he kept his mouth shut.

"This is because the guys give you a hard time. You've got to get a thicker skin, Sam. You know it's always been that way."

"I don't give a crap what they say to me. Or about me. I'm quitting because I have to."

"Far as I can tell, nobody here is making you quit."

"But I can't do this," Sam said. "You don't want a Van Winkle on the force who can't even save a damn kitten from a tree. Really."

Roddy spoke slowly. "Nobody in this whole town thinks that but you."

Sam slammed his hand on the edge of the desk. "Then *I'm* the only one who has his head on straight."

Roddy stood up, his old chair creaking beneath him. Then he came around to the front of his desk. The bright window behind him made him look formidable and wide. "Sam. Is this because of Olivia? Did something happen?"

"A thousand things happened," Sam said, and he tried not to remember the way she'd arched her neck to him when he leaned down to kiss it. He gripped the arms of the chair.

"Oh well now. Don't take it too personally, Sam. You're not the first guy to get chewed up and spit out by that girl, and I guarantee you won't be the last."

You have no idea what you're talking about, Sam thought. There wasn't a man in Green Valley who could compare his broken heart to Sam's. Olivia had opened up to him; he knew her in a way no one else ever did and—he was certain—no one else ever would. She loved him, he was sure of it. But her love wasn't strong enough to make her willing to take a risk. The pain of her unwillingness to meet him halfway was surpassed only by the pain he'd felt sitting alone in a plane with a dead man. Sam curled his hands into fists on his thighs. "I asked her to marry me," he said.

"Let me guess. She turned you down."

"Yes. But it wasn't like that. We were serious. At least, I thought we were."

"Oh I know it," Roddy said. "That girl was ass over teakettle for you. Hell, everyone in the whole damn valley knew it the day she parked her tractor at the hospital and went inside. First time anybody'd seen her off that farm in God-knows-how-many years. I was there myself, Sam. I saw the look on her face. If you'd died . . ." Roddy shook his head. "It would have taken a lot more than the Van Winkle magic to save her."

"Wait. Wait. She *was* at the hospital?"

"Stayed by your bed for an hour before they kicked her out," Roddy said. "You didn't know?"

"We . . . we didn't really do a lot of talking since I came home," Sam said. They'd only lain in bed, and made love, and talked about everything in the world except for the things that actually might matter. It had been some kind of unspoken agreement, a measure of protection: They did not talk about the past—not about cures or serums—or the future—not about marriage or children or the possibility that their pleasure was temporary. Only when Sam saw the red spots freckling his belly did reality intrude back in.

"So why do you think she won't marry you?" Roddy asked.

Sam looked out the window at the parking lot. "I don't know. Afraid?"

"What's she afraid of?"

He bounced his fists on his knees. "What isn't she afraid of?"

"You're missing my point here, Sam."

"What your point?"

"My point is that girl did something for you she's never done for anybody. Maybe she's saying she won't marry you, but she does love you—that's clear as day. And to my eye, something doesn't add up. There's an element you and I aren't seeing. I don't know what it is. But if I were you, I'd want to find out."

Sam stood, anxious. He'd lain in the hospital and wondered how he was going to live the rest of his life with a woman he'd nearly died for but who hadn't been willing to drive across town to see him. But he'd been wrong—Olivia was willing to fight. Or at least, she had been. She'd kept herself out of the garden for him at one point, and he'd been the one to escort her back in. He should have guessed she'd gone to the hospital as well.

Now Olivia was hurting in some way that put her beyond his reach. He wanted to show her that he was willing to fight for her—for as long and as hard as he had to—because he could not give up on the dream that they would be happy together if only they could get through this first treacherous leg of their path. He didn't know how he was going to coax her to come out of the Poison Garden, but at least he could find a way to be there with her. He told Roddy, "I have to go."

Roddy nodded as if he'd expected as much.

"But," Sam said, "this doesn't mean I'm not quitting."

"We'll just see what happens. Now get out of here before somebody sees you. You're supposed to be sick today," Roddy said.

What You Sow

Gloria was furious: A dozen of the Pennyworts' creepy white barn cats had showed up on her porch, apparently looking for food in the absence of the Penny Loafers. And no matter how Gloria stamped her feet, or squirted them with water bottles, or chased them with a broom, they simply hopped up a tree or into the yard and then sat blinking at her with mildly curious aplomb. To make matters worse, the weather had turned beastly hot again; it was heat that collected in a person's lungs, heat that smothered and saturated, heat for which air-conditioning was little match, heat without a hint of wind.

As she swatted at white cats with her broom, she noticed what appeared to be a man in a silver suit crossing from the boarded-up Pennywort farmhouse toward the maze. Since yesterday, the vines had exploded out of the central garden and swamped all but the outermost ring of the maze, so that the whole thing looked like a bulbous, wrinkly blister of green. Gloria was half worried that the growth might climb the hill and bury her house in the night. But her husband had told her she was being ridiculous; as far as he knew the maze always looked that way.

Olivia, in the meantime, had no idea that her poison ivy was thriving beyond the walls of her garden; nor did she know that Sam was even now struggling to fight his way through the thickening mass. She only knew that when she awoke this morning inside her walled garden, poison ivy had claimed every available surface—scaling walls, coating the ground, toppling poppies, and wrapping around her rhododendrons like a thousand green boa constrictors. And now, with no new territory to conquer, the vines were bulking up and thickening into muscular ropes and braids.

Yesterday, all interest in living had drained away from her; her very soul had wilted as dramatically as the fields before the rain. She'd discovered—and then lost—an incredible pleasure with Sam; it was a glimpse of happiness from which she would never recover. Their relationship was doomed to be forever complicated, burdened, and always on the brink of collapse, and Sam deserved better.

Plus, now that the Penny Loafers had what they probably believed was confirmation of her secret, one of two things would happen: She would be burned at the stake for being an abomination of nature, or she would be forever ostracized as a monster—and she wasn't sure which fate was worse. She wanted her secret back again.

She also wanted, perhaps more than anything, to believe that her father could not have played God with her future, that he hadn't been so cruel. But she'd read the words right in his own handwriting: He'd known what was happening to her in the Poison Garden, and he'd allowed it to happen. When she thought of him, with the poison vines creaking around her, she only felt anger—anger so pure it was not diluted by any other emotion. For many years, he'd been her only friend, the only person she'd dared to trust, the only person who knew her secret. If he could betray her, anyone could. She'd gone to sleep not caring if she ever opened her eyes again.

But then, from behind her eyelids in the morning, she thought, *Something about the light seems odd.* And when she opened her eyes, she saw that the vines had thickened into a dense cocoon around her, with only enough room to stretch out one arm in any direction. The stems were thick as her wrists; the leaves, as big as her hands. She had come because she'd believed her garden would protect her—and that it would keep others away. But this—this was too much. This would kill her.

She tested the strength of the vines around her by shaking them; they held firm. She tried to pry the vines apart, she pushed at them with her shoulder, she squatted and heaved her spine against the low, rounded ceiling—but the vines wouldn't even bend. She worked for five full minutes, until sweat formed on her skin and her head began to ache, before admitting she was stuck—completely and hopelessly stuck.

Yesterday, the poison vines had seemed to be her protectors; today they were her captors. She was trapped. She was dehydrated already and the sun was getting hotter by the moment. She hadn't had water in nearly twenty-four hours; she could die in the heat, in not too many hours, if no one came for her. And the threat of *real* death, as opposed to the fantasy of it, was not at all comforting: Fear made bile rise at the back of her throat. She wished she'd listened to that small voice that had said, *Get out while you still can.*

She was sweating now, pulling frantically at the unmoving vines, tearing off the poison ivy leaves in her fists just for spite. Who would save her? Not her father, who didn't come out of his gloomy mountain glen. Not Sam—she'd been so mean to him. And he was more allergic to poison ivy than anyone she knew. Not the Penny Loafers; she had sent them away. She'd repelled the people she cared about as surely as if she herself were reaching out into the world with arms like poison vines.

No one could help: She would need to find her way out on her own. People were known to cut off their own limbs pinned under boulders—the urge to survive could be *that* powerful. And Olivia felt it powerfully now—a desire that trumped all others, a need that eclipsed all questions of happiness, of what makes a good life or a full life, of what reason could be found behind sadness and loss. It was the desire to survive. Primal, fundamental, innate. And in the heat that became more dangerous by the second, she could not survive in her Poison Garden for many more hours—happiness aside.

She worked at the vines until crescents of blood formed under her fingernails. She was sweating, hungry, weak from having not eaten. The enormous vines around her and the prolonged exposure to her Poison Garden should have filled her with superhuman strength. Instead, she was fading. An hour passed, then two. The sun burned. She worked at the vines with decreasing energy; her hands felt no more useful than lumps of clay. And when it crossed her mind to wonder how long a human being could live without water, she shoved the thought away.

She *would* get out; she had to believe that. She would. She panted against the wooden bars of her cage. Her arms were shaking, her hands were cut, heat and fatigue were beginning to wear down her strength. Her brain was bleary and she thought, *I'm going to have a lot of apologizing to do if I die in here.* She leaned back against the warm stone of the wall and closed her eyes. She needed to rest. Just rest. Just for a while. Then she would try again.

The day grew hotter as the sun rose higher in the sky. A gray catbird landed on a strand of poison ivy, flicked its tail feathers a few times, then lifted freely away. Occasionally a slim tendril of green would corkscrew from the hunched ceiling of her little cave, fingering her shoulder or cheek as if to see how close it could get to her, but she'd snap it off and toss it away. She was sweating even when she wasn't moving at all, the water going out of her. She drifted in and out of something that she wouldn't exactly call sleep: It was light, disturbed, and shallow, and sometimes she could not drag herself out of it even though she felt her heart accelerating with panic and her breath coming fast. When she did dream, the vines came and curled around her wrists, her ankles, her throat.

She heard Sam calling her, and she went looking for him in her dream. But even after she found him—he was waiting for her in the sun-drenched afternoon of three days ago, when she'd crawled into bed with him between cool white sheets—he still continued to call her, and call her, and she realized she was not dreaming the sound of his voice; he was actually there.

She opened her eyes and sat up slightly; the sun was behind a cloud and the vines that had intersected and knotted all around her were a dull green. But otherwise, she was alone. Sam wasn't with her—why would he be? She'd driven him away. She leaned back against the wall, begging herself not to cry because she couldn't waste water on tears.

"Olivia?"

"Sam?" She got to her knees. "Sam? Is that you?"

"I'm here," he said. His voice came from over the wall, and the sound of it gave her an instant jolt of adrenaline. "I'm coming in there," he said. Or at least, that was what she thought he said. His voice was muffled.

"Sam! I'm stuck!"

"Just hold on."

"No—no, you can't come in here! It's too dangerous! Get . . . get someone else!"

She pushed herself against the small pod of vines and peered with one eye through the leaves. Something that looked weirdly reflective and off-putting was climbing down the thick brambles that had enveloped the stone walls. It was Sam—holding a small ax and wearing Arthur's ancient bio-protector suit. He must have gone into the farmhouse and found it. Her heart lifted— she would not die in her walled garden after all. And, equally as important, *Sam* had come for her. *Sam.*

"Where are you?" he asked, looking around.

She shoved a hand through the vines to catch his attention. "Here. I'm right here. Oh, Sam. I didn't mean for this to happen. I went to sleep and the next thing I knew it was morning, and— hey, are you all right?"

He had worked to get himself over the bristling carpet of vines until he was as close to her as the poison ivy would allow. Behind the clear plastic of his mask, his face was a bright, deep red and his skin was shiny.

"Sam. Oh my God. You're overheating in there!"

"I'm fine," he said.

"No, you're not. Sam—that suit is practically an oven. You've got to get out of here and take it off!"

"I'm not leaving without you," he said. But he leaned heavily against the tangled vines for a moment, breathing hard. She knew he was in danger, as much danger now as when he'd decided to try a mouthful of Pennywort honey. The heat was more deadly than standing in an open field during a thunderstorm; Sam was in real, mortal peril—from the sun, the suit, and the poison plants around him.

She wrapped her fists tighter around the vines. "You came for me."

"Of course I did," he said. "I knew something was wrong."

He didn't ask what had driven her away from him and inside the garden—and she was glad. There would be time to talk about what her father had done later. In the meantime, she looked at his face, obscured in part by leaves and by the scratched-up plastic of his visor, and she knew she would never doubt him—would never doubt *them* together—again. How could she have ever thought it was a *good* idea not to marry him? She'd never felt so clear or so sure of anything in her life—that when a person could find happiness, she should seize it without question, without a single thought for the future, and with a steady resolve never to become bitter once it was lost. For all her years of having not found a single hint of clarity in the garden maze, it now seemed ready to teach her what she had never before understood about herself.

If only it wouldn't kill her in the process.

"Sam. I'm stuck in here. The vines—I can't get out."

"Don't worry. Just get back—as close to the wall as you can. We'll cut through these vines like a knife through hot butter." She did as he asked, pressing herself against the stones. She couldn't help but admire him as he lifted the ax over his head, a look of firm resolve crossing over his face, her hero, after all.

The ax came down in a brilliant silver flash.

And stuck there, embedded in the vine.

"Oh. That was kind of unsatisfying," Sam said. He tugged on the ax, wiggled it around. It finally popped out of the vine. "Let's try that again."

He swung the ax again; and again it stuck. But this time he pulled it out more easily. Soon he was hacking at the vines with focused energy, and the visor of Arthur's bio-protector suit was fogging with his breath, and his face had grown as red as Olivia's beets. He'd chopped through only one vine.

"You have to stop," she said. "You have to take a break."

But he wouldn't.

"Sam! Please! If you pass out, I can't climb out of here and help you. And then they'll find us both dead. I need you to take it easy!"

He lowered the ax; his face was weary and apologetic. "It's hot."

"I know," she said mournfully, wishing she could relieve him.

"I've been at this for hours," he said.

"Hours? You only just got here."

"*Hours,*" he said. He sat down and leaned a shoulder against the hard vines. "The poison ivy is covering everything from here to the edge of the maze. It took me three hours to get here."

Olivia shuddered. "But . . ." She started to say that wasn't possible. But she supposed in Green Valley, anything was. "How did you get through it?"

"One step at a time," he said.

She moved closer to him. Her Poison Garden had become dangerous to others. And she had a deep, real sense that it was her fault. She'd always thought her plants had a life of their own, and that *she* was dependent upon them. But she wondered now if she'd been wrong the whole time: that she was not *responsive* to her plants, that in fact they were a by-product of something inside her and were actually responsive to her.

In the back of her mind she wondered: If that was the case, that she controlled her relationship to the Poison Garden and not the other way around, then perhaps there was hope that someday, maybe, she might simply no longer need it?

Sam put his gloved hand on a fat vine, holding her gaze through fogged plastic. "Did Arthur ever tell you that I wanted to marry you?"

"*You* told me," she said, worrying that he was cooking his brain in that damned suit. "Remember? You proposed."

"No—I don't mean last week. I mean, when we were kids. I took that job at the lumber yard, rode my bike there every day, and saved up to buy you a ring." He laughed under his breath. "It think it would have turned your finger green. But I was so set on marrying you."

She adjusted herself a little on her knees to better look into his eyes through the crosshatch of vines. She reached to squeeze his shoulder through his suit; she could barely feel his flesh beneath the layers of plastic and padding. His skin was beginning to look clammy. Of the two of them, he was in much more immediate danger. "I would have said yes," she told him. She touched the plastic above his lips with her fingertips. "I am saying yes, now."

His smile was weak.

"But first we've got to get ourselves out of this mess," she said.

He rested another moment, then lifted himself back to his feet. The sound of the falling ax echoed all through the valley, and when he had cut a hole big enough, he handed it through to her so she could go at the vines with the blade on her own. When she finally managed to squeeze herself out of her cage of poison ivy, her skin was scraped and her muscles were sore. But she was out, and she vowed that no matter the perceived pain of it, she would never go back in again. She pulled Sam's arm around her shoulders to bear up some of his weight, and together they retraced his steps out of the tangled vines.

Coming Up Roses

t was said that Olivia Pennywort came out of the great terrible maw of poison ivy without an itch on her, that she walked across the vines as gracefully as if she were walking on water that her feet barely touched. While Sam Van Winkle was by her side, entombed in a heavy suit of plastic and trudging as if gravity had spontaneously increased, Olivia emerged from the entrance of the maze with bare arms and bare legs—and not so much as a hive on her glowing skin.

There was in fact quite an audience for their escape from the maze. A dozen people had heard about the tsunami of poison ivy that had grown so monstrously overnight at the Pennyworts', and they'd come to see the explosion in the same way that they would have stood on their porches and watched if a car accident had happened outside of their homes. The Penny Loafers too walked the long roads from the homeless shelter back to the farm, slowing traffic as efficiently as if they were a herd of cows or sheep, ignoring beeping horns and swearing drivers. *Everything's true,* they said, passing the rumors about Olivia along to the police as they arrived, and to men on the fire trucks as they arrived, and even to the fire department's whiny, spotted dog. *She's poisonous. She must be.*

But Olivia didn't care if fifty people, or five hundred people, were staring at her and Sam as they stripped the last clinging vines off their legs and arms and broke out of the maze. She waved to the paramedics, called them over when they hesitated, told them Sam needed help. They took him into the shade and quickly peeled him out of the awful bio-protector suit, then gave him water and held ice to his pressure points. Some of the men clasped him on the back, offering brash congratulations and boasts about close calls. Sam turned his head weakly and smiled.

Olivia, who had accepted a glass of water of her own, approached the Penny Loafers. They were clumped together like clustered flowers, looking at her with wary gladness and perhaps a bit of mistrust. Tom was with them, his hand on one woman's shoulder even as he looked at Olivia with eyes that were frightened and wide. Olivia stopped before them, threw her long braid behind one shoulder, and said: *Just so there isn't any confusion, all of this means I really am poisonous—just like everyone's been saying.*

The Penny Loafers looked at one another with concern, but Olivia told them not to worry. She was quite healthy and not a danger to anyone as long as people stayed away. And as for the walled-in garden—which she admitted was full of poisonous plants—she wasn't sure how they were going to clean up all the poison ivy, but she would figure something out even if it meant cutting every last vine from its root by herself. The maze would come back bigger and better—next year, or the year after—and that would be okay.

"Does this mean you're not mad at us?" one of the women asked.

"Mad?" Olivia tipped her head, considering. "What would I be mad about? You guys are welcome to come and go however you please."

She saw some of the women glance at her, and they appeared to be relieved. Olivia couldn't say what had happened to them at the shelter, but she knew for certain that there was no better place to be in Green Valley than the wide, enchanted acres of her farm.

"And what about our answers?" one of the women asked. "Now that the maze is, um, inaccessible."

Olivia glanced at Sam in the distance. "You don't need a twisted and tangled old maze to give you clarity about what you want. The only thing that stands in the way of your inner wisdom is your fear of it. You can stay here as long as you need. And when you're ready, you can just let your fear go. Maze or no."

Some of the women glanced at one another; Olivia wasn't sure if they thought she was crazy or prophetic. But at any rate, the group seemed to want to stay. Tom took a few steps away from the crowd. Olivia wasn't sure, but he seemed to be . . . hurt.

"So that was it all along," he said. "You were just poisonous? That's why you always stayed away?"

She nodded.

Then, to her surprise, Tom began laughing. "Oh for God's sake. Come here." He went to her and wrapped his arms around her, quick and strong, and picked her feet off the ground.

"Tom! What the heck? Did you not hear me say I'm a danger to society?"

He put her down. "I've never had so much as an itch from poison ivy in my whole life. Olivia, I've cleared it off this farm for years with my bare hands."

She smiled, but she found herself looking toward Sam, whom the paramedics were plying with water and ice. Some people had no allergies to poison ivy—or barely any at all. Others were exquisitely sensitive. It was the luck of the draw.

Tom touched her shoulder and squeezed it. "Go on. Go to him. He needs you."

She smiled. And for the first time, she truly understood the depth of her relationship with Tom. While she had been telling herself that he was an acquaintance only, that they spent time together only because they had to, she saw that in truth he had a lot of affection for her, the same affection that she felt for him. He'd been a friend even when she'd believed she hadn't had any. And she'd been his friend, too, even when she'd believed she was holding herself away.

She nodded at him, then crossed the yard to sit by Sam while he recovered, and then a long time more.

The day passed, then the night. A storm blew through with gentle thunder and quiet rain. The people of Green Valley began to speculate: What on earth was Olivia Pennywort going to do about the hazardous mess that was her garden maze? How would she clean up all that poison ivy? Not even she could do the task herself. In the newspapers, the tremendous growth was attributed to the particular juxtaposition of drought, rain, and the return of a tropical heat that made everything grow with bloodthirsty fecundity. The city transplants who lived in Green Valley believed the explanation; the old-timers did not.

Sam slept in the silo, slept and slept, and while he was sleeping, he began to look better. Olivia smoothed his skin with calamine lotion and gloved hands, she kissed the pillow beside his head, she watched him sleep with such a strong sense of wanting to take good care of him that it brought tears to her eyes. How could she have been so lucky? She had resolved, in the quiet of the night, to try one last time to see if she might be able to keep herself away from the walled-in garden, which was now neither walled in nor a garden at all. She knew it would hurt;

her body had become dependent on it in some way, like any brain can become inclined to addiction. But she believed deep down that the garden had not claimed her so much as she had claimed it—and she could, if she tried hard enough, wean herself off it with patience, determination, and lots of mind over matter. If she lost motivation, she would simply remember the afternoon she'd spent with Sam in her silo, when the sun had seemed so bright and friendly, and pleasure came as easily as water running downhill, and the hours were soft as down. It would not be easy to quit the garden, but Sam would be there to help her through.

And in the meantime, her father was on her mind. For the duration of the long night she'd spent in her Poison Garden, she had been insensible with grief, with anger, with bitterness. And she'd had no idea what was happening, what was *really* happening. Yes, she'd gone to sleep knowing that the vines were growing dangerously, that they were reaching toward her and around her. Yes, she'd been aware of a lurking danger. But she hadn't been able to process it in a *real* way; her anger was too great, her sadness too deep, and any hope of clearheadedness was obscured by insecurity. The result had almost got her—and Sam—killed.

She'd been irresponsible because of her anger. She could see what she'd done, and in a way, it was not so different from the situation her father had put himself in when he'd allowed his pain over Alice to shape his decisions. She could no longer be angry at him; she only felt sad. He'd hidden himself away from the world; he'd grown bitter with the injustices of life—just like she'd almost done. But she'd found her way out of cynicism and bitterness. He hadn't. And though she would do everything she could to show him the way back to happiness, she had to accept that she could never heal him from the loss of Alice if he didn't want to be healed.

She decided to go see him. She whispered to Sam that she was going, ran her hand over the shape of his calf where it was safe beneath a blanket. Outside, the rain was falling lightly beneath gray skies, but she did not bother with an umbrella. She liked the rain; it was so cool and gentle that she was soon wet without having felt a single drop fall. She walked past the barn, where the boarders were inside amusing themselves with card games, then across the spongy-wet earth of the field toward Solomon's Ravine.

In the bottomland, she saw that the creek had swollen with the rain. The birds were singing cheerfully; a white-tailed deer had bent its head for a drink and it did not bolt when it saw her. But neither her father nor his goat was around.

She did not dwell on his disappearance; he was probably fishing at the pond. She would find him soon enough. As the rain fluttered and tapped lightly on the leaves above her, she made her way up and out of the ravine.

She was nearly back to the silo when she saw that there was a man standing on the farmhouse porch. *A reporter,* she thought. *Asking about the garden maze. Again.*

She made her way toward him. He was of middling height with good pants and a shirt that had seen better days but at one point was "nice." His white-gray hair was neatly trimmed and slicked back with gel or with rainwater. His face was shaved clean.

She started to say, *Can I help you?* But when the shape of a little goat appeared beside him, a strange feeling of recognition kicked in, followed by a jolt of understanding. *This,* this stranger, was her father. She hadn't recognized him.

He wore no hat—that was the first reason she hadn't known him at a distance. But also, he looked like a bigger, stronger man than her father, who was imprinted in her mind as being somewhat feeble, stooped, and decrepit. The most shocking change, though, was the loss of his fat gray beard. Now that it was gone, she could see that his face was startlingly young. He was an old man, yes, but not *as* old as he'd made himself out to be. His cheekbones and chin were still strong, his eyes were sad but full of alertness, and life itself seemed to flow strongly through him—which was a shock, since there had been some days when Olivia had thought him to be a hair's breadth from death. He was a little more of what she'd remembered him to be before he'd moved down into the ravine.

"Dad?"

He went to the top of the porch stairs while she looked up at him. The goat stood beside him, nervous to be out of the ravine. She could tell her father was fighting to hold her gaze; he wanted to look down. "I don't know how to apologize to you, Olivia. I don't even know how to begin. I've never known."

She was quiet; she dropped her hand on the post at the foot of the stairs.

"I had this idea," he said, "that if I stayed down in the ravine, it would be punishment for what I did. That if I stayed down there long enough, someday I might get the stain of it off my soul. But that was only part of it. Really—Olivia—I was afraid. I've always been afraid."

"You don't have to do this," she said. "It's okay."

His gaze flickered up to meet hers, just for a second. "I don't want to stay down there anymore if it doesn't make you happy."

"You being happy would make me happy," she said. She climbed the stairs to stand beside him. And standing so close, she saw that he was crying. Though he did not sob or sniffle, his eyes were brimming over not with raindrops but with tears. "I don't think I'll ever understand why you did what you did. Some things just never make sense. But I love you. Nothing can change that."

His shoulders shook. "I want to see the house again. If it's okay with you."

The doors had been locked up, the windows boarded. The paint was peeling, weeds had grown into trees around the foundation, and fishtail shingles had been caught in the cockeyed gutters. She said, "It might not look exactly as you remember it."

"Still. It's a sight for sore eyes," he said.

He knocked on the porch rail. She did the same.

The rain was letting up and the dark purple clouds were breaking apart above them, revealing ribbons of glowing, brilliant blue.

"I'll get a crowbar," she said.

Epilogue

utumn came; the air in the Catskills cooled, the asters bloomed, the Canada geese flew in great, noisy V's overhead. To everyone's amazement, the motley band of skin-and-bones goats that had been terrorizing the valley for the better part of a hundred years began to grow fat, their dull coats shining, their eyes brightening, and their general temperament improving overall. At first, no one could quite understand what change had come over them to make them so lazy and portly and disinclined to antagonize. But on the last day that the Pennywort farm stand was open, someone saw the entire family of goats going into the garden maze that had been obliterated by poison ivy. Though the garden remained closed to people, the goats went in and out as they pleased, munching poison ivy with happy contentment. They would eat until it was gone.

And in the meantime, the people of Green Valley found endless fascination regarding *what had happened on the Pennywort farm*. Sam was toasted and feted and fawned over in all the hamlets of Bethel, and when the snow began to fall he was asked to ride on a float in the annual holiday parade. He declined, saying he was busy. But apparently his wife decided she would talk him into doing it, and she was said to have stood on the sidewalk and waved to him as bits of red and green confetti were tossed in the air as the float passed by.

As the years passed, the stories people told about Olivia Pennywort–Van Winkle began to change. The people who claimed to be at her wedding said that her bouquet of flowers seemed to shimmer, almost glitter, under the light of an early September dusk as she walked barefoot through the grass, and that so many unseasonal fireflies attended the wedding that a person could tell who had attended by the green lights that danced in their eyes for a week afterward. Decades after the wedding, neighbors continued to have the same old *not-this-again* argument about whether the bride and groom had actually kissed that day, with some factions saying that *of course* they didn't kiss, because everyone knew Olivia Pennywort was as beautiful and toxic as a poison berry. But others would swear to their graves that Olivia and Sam *did* kiss, that they *specifically remembered* the kiss as clear as they remembered the kiss at their own wedding, or at least, they remembered a look of such love passing between the handsome couple that they might as well have kissed, and it was practically the same thing.

The summer's Penny Loafers had stood in attendance as Olivia's bridesmaids, garbed in various dresses that ranged from sparkly pants to gowns fit for proms, and they were said to have made a heterogeneous, if not oddly beautiful troupe in their way. Mei too had come with her newborn, the child she had decided to keep, and motherhood appeared to have agreed with her, softening her roughest edges, though not her inclination to say what was on her mind. Shortly after the wedding and after the asters in the maze started blooming up through the poison ivy vines, the women went their separate ways, back to wherever it was they came from, like Persephone returning to Hades at the sign of the first frost. By the following spring, a few women returned to Green Valley looking for the answers they'd failed to receive the previous year, but most never came back at all—leading Olivia to believe they'd found their answers in their own ways—and a new troupe of women came to the farm to take their place. The goats ate back the poison vines, the months passed, and the maze grew in room by room, until it had reclaimed not only its previous grandeur, but a fair bit of *extra* grandeur besides—which was annoying to Gloria Zeiger because it attracted increasingly large crowds.

As for the women's shelter, the organizers found themselves in an unexpected situation when women who actually needed shelter began to arrive, some with dogs and children in tow. Gloria came out of retirement to run the shelter, which became one of the most celebrated models of a community coming together in all the western Catskills, and she was given a fancy award from the governor for her selfless and tireless commitment to the less fortunate, and she seemed less preoccupied with the goings-on of the Pennywort farm.

As for Arthur Pennywort, he moved back into the old farmhouse and relearned the workings of his fields, though some said his skin never did lose its pale greenish tint from too many years spent in the bottom of Solomon's Ravine. After a time, on a February day when the first crocuses were coming up in the garden maze, he passed away quietly in his sleep—which was not especially surprising to him, since everyone, eventually, had to die and he was no exception. But before he died, he'd found a happiness that he hadn't thought he had the strength or worthiness to claim ever again, and he did not let himself dwell overlong on what he might have done differently and how much time he'd wasted in the ravine, because he refused to allow the past to mar the future again. They buried him by Alice on a hillside not far from Solomon's Ravine. And people said a ghost—which was possibly his, or possibly Alice's, or possibly both of their ghosts—liked to dance through the maze on nights when the Green Valley moon was bright enough to read by.

Olivia and Sam lived very happily and quietly together in her silo, though Sam did occasionally come home telling stories of daring rescues that made Olivia's heart skip for fear that she might one day lose him as he was saving someone else. People wondered how the young couple withstood it—to be as in love as the two of them so obviously were and not be able to express that love in touch. But then, one spring morning after the Pennywort–Van Winkle family had stayed secluded in their farmhouse for a long, especially cold, dark, and cozy winter, a farmer driving past on his tractor swore that he heard the sound of a baby crying from somewhere on the Pennywort homestead. The weather broke and the child was rumored to be the most beautiful, healthy boy born in the valley in quite some time—and he was barely old enough to talk when he was said to have saved an old woman from a very scary spider that had made a home in her carton of strawberries. When anyone asked, Olivia said that the child had been left on her doorstep by the fairies who lived in Chickadee Wood.

Inside the maze, which was said now to be as haunted as Solomon's Ravine, Arthur Pennywort's spirit watched over his grandson splashing the massive goldfish in the Rock Garden, and he thought of how it was said that stories that seemed to end happily were merely stories that had not been told through to their bitter ends. But this, he had learned, was the line between cynics and optimists. Green Valley would change. Some days would be cloudy and some days the sun would shine, people would be born and then die, but as long as the great sweeping spirit of optimism that had come into the valley in 1969 still found fuel to thrive, there would be more happiness than sadness, more vegetables than weeds, and the maze would grow, and the rumors would grow around it, and plants and people would evolve new ways of managing disappointment, and life for life's sake would go on.

Acknowledgments
and Author's Note

So many incredible people have worked on or helped with this book. I'm grateful to my editor Kara Cesare, who encouraged me as I stumbled my way into this story only during my second, almost fully rewritten draft. Kara—I can't be thankful enough for your grace, patience, and guidance. Thanks also to Hannah Elnan—Hannah, I'll miss you terribly!—and to Nina Arazoza, who jumped in and kept everything moving forward so seamlessly (not an easy thing to do!). Thanks to Belinda Huey and Virginia Norey for their artistic talents, and to Jane von Mehren, Jennifer Hershey, Kim Hovey, Maggie Oberrender, and Lindsey Kennedy for their continued support for both *The Wishing Thread* and this story. My agents Andrea Cirillo and Christina Hogrebe continue to be my real-life heroines—thank you for your voices of both passion and reason. I also want to thank my husband, who continues to encourage my writing even to the point of his own sacrifice: Matt, I'd marry you a thousand times over again. Thanks to Alphia for sitting down to talk with me about what life was like growing up on a farm, and to the writers listed in the RHRC pages that follow for their books and stories that helped inspire mine. Finally, thanks, as always, to people who read, love, and talk about books: You make my publications possible. And I'm truly grateful for that every day.

If you, reader, want to connect with me, please send me a note via my website (www.WriterLisaVanAllen.com) or visit me on Facebook. Thanks in advance for reaching out; I look forward to hearing from you!

The
Night Garden

A Novel

Lisa Van Allen

A Reader's Guide

Recommended Reads from
Lisa Van Allen

I've always had a fascination with poisonous plants. I think it started when I was a little kid and my siblings and I used to play in the woods, swinging from vines and carving forts out of thick brambles. A bush of small red berries grew "down back"; they were bright, tempting little things, but we were told under no circumstances were we allowed to eat them. We didn't, of course. But sometimes we liked to *pretend* they were food, tossing them into fake salads as we provisioned ourselves for grand journeys into imaginary lands. I'm not sure that I ever stopped wondering what those berries would taste like—everything about them said, *Eat me!*, as if they might make a person grow very tall or very small.

As an adult, of course, a person encounters other kinds of temptations, the allure of things that we know are bad for us but that we cling to or desire anyway. The allure of poisonous plants never stopped calling to me. And so when my wonderful editor asked for my next proposal, I decided it was time to indulge in my fascination—from the safe distance of the written word!

Alas, only about half a percent of the research I did actually ended up in the story (the characters demanded most of the book's "real estate," and rightly so). But there's a great, fascinating world of folklore and science surrounding poisonous plants out there, and if you're curious, or if you're just looking for your next read based on something that sparked your curiosity in *The Night Garden*, here are a few books I'd recommend.

Rappaccini's Daughter by Nathaniel Hawthorne—This was the tale that started it all, twenty years ago when I first read it in high school. The story is about a beautiful and mysterious woman who flits about an enchanted Italian garden and can kill insects with her breath. "This lovely woman . . . had been nourished with poisons from her birth upward, until her whole nature was so imbued with them, that she herself had become the deadliest poison in existence. Poison was her element of life. With that rich perfume of her breath, she blasted the very air. Her love would have been poison!—her embrace death! Is not this a marvellous tale?" I loved the concept, and wanted desperately to love the story, but for various reasons, I just couldn't. The ending got me. (You should read it, seriously. It's short, and worth discussion). For a very long time, the story haunted me, even *bothered* me—I thought about it again and again over the years. *The Night Garden* was, I suppose, an effort to reconcile my feelings about the story as well as a chance to indulge my curiosity about poisonous plants.

The North American Guide To Common Poisonous Plants and Mushrooms by Nancy J. Turner and Patrick von Aderkas— I bought this book when I first started getting serious about *The Night Garden,* and I left it sitting on the dining room table one day when my husband got home. He picked it up, looked at me, and asked, "Is there something I should be worried about?" For many years he's been incredibly patient on walks through the woods with me as I'm constantly stopping to either consult my various guidebooks or take pictures for future identifications. This book is a bit too big to cart into the woods, but it's a great read for a serious-minded student of poisonous and dangerous plants.

Wicked Plants by Amy Stewart—If you're looking for a wild, fun, fascinating, thrilling, unbelievable read about all the incredible factoids in the world of dangerous and obnoxious plants, *this* is your book. I adored it, front to back. It's a brief, highly readable look at the science and stories that emerge when humans and plants collide. Oh, and apparently the author *has* a garden of poison plants, which just proves the adage that life is stranger than fiction.

Turn Here Sweet Corn by Atina Diffley—I read this book as one of many that I hoped would give me a glimpse into farm life. Some of my own family members were farmers, and I have childhood memories of running through the fallow fields of an old family farm that has since been sold to a developer. Atina's book is intimate, emotionally generous, authentic, and engaging. The story of how she lost a farm to urban expansion is heartbreaking, but her family's perseverance is an inspiration. I think of her often when I'm in the grocery store and looking at the produce section, wondering (at her prompting) why it's the organic vegetables that get labeled, instead of the other way around. This book was a huge eye-opener and if you're interested in farm life, the organic food movement, and environmentalism, give this a read.

The Red Garden by Alice Hoffman—One of my favorite books in recent years, this short story collection traces the life of a Massachusetts town from its frontier settlement days to the present. It's chocked full of folklore with hints of magic—and to me, these stories feel quintessentially American. I swear, reading it fills your nose with the smells of forest soil and freshly sawn wood. This is on my keeper shelf to read again and again.

Thanks for reading *The Night Garden*. I would love to hear from you by email on my website (www.WriterLisaVanAllen .com) or on my Facebook page. And if your book group reads this story, please be in touch! I may be able to Skype or call in.

Good things,
Lisa Van Allen

Questions and Topics
for Discussion

1. Olivia Pennywort has a unique condition that causes anyone she touches to develop a rash. What would you do if you had Olivia's condition? How would you cope if you knew there was no way to get rid of it?

2. Olivia keeps her condition a secret at the risk of being perceived as a monster and driving everyone she knows away. What do you think would happen if Olivia was more open about her condition? Is she right to fear the public's reaction?

3. Because of her condition, Olivia believes she "would be wrong to expect more of her life than what she had" (page 27). Even though she has everything she needs to survive, do you think this is an acceptable attitude? In what ways can expectations shape how you live your life?

4. At the start, Sam's condition has stripped him of the ability to feel. If you had this condition, which sensations do you think would be the most jarring to lose?

5. When she was younger, Olivia chose not to be with Sam because she was hurting him, even though she still loved him. Did she make the right decision to break up with him? Should she have told him the truth? What would you have done?

6. Sam comes from a family of rescuers and feels pressure to be a rescuer as well. In what ways can a positive family legacy be both a blessing and a curse? To what extent should a person attempt to live up to a family legacy? What happens if this legacy comes at the expense of carving an individual path?

7. A central theme in the novel is temptation, or the idea of desperately wanting what we know may be bad for us or for others. Is there a right way to deal with temptation? In what scenarios would it be okay to give in?

8. Another core theme is the importance of touch. How important is touch and feeling for a happy life? Is it possible to find happiness without it? Do you think you could?

9. Olivia is appalled that her father knew she was becoming poisonous and did not try to stop it. What makes Arthur's act so reprehensible? Do you think it's possible to atone for such a destructive act? How would you go about making things right?

10. When Sam comes to rescue her out of the poisonous garden maze, Olivia realizes that "when a person could find happiness, she should seize it without question, without a single thought for the future, and with a steady resolve never

to become bitter once it was lost" (page 307). Does her reasoning make sense? Is this the best way to live your life?

11.   When the boarders ask Olivia what they will do without the maze, Olivia replies, "The only thing that stands in the way of your inner wisdom is your fear of it" (page 312). Do you agree with Olivia? Why do you think it's so hard to figure out what we really want?

12.   If you had a magical maze that could help you figure out what to do, what would you want it to help you with?

13.   Why do you think Gloria continually tries to change the Pennywort farm? What do you think her actions suggest about how we respond to what we don't understand?

About the Author

Lisa Van Allen's writing has been published in many literary journals and has been nominated for the Pushcart Prize. She currently lives in northern New Jersey with her husband.

About the Type

This book was set in Dante, a typeface designed by Giovanni Mardersteig (1892–1977). Conceived as a private type for the Officina Bodoni in Verona, Italy, Dante was originally cut only for hand composition by Charles Malin, the famous Parisian punch cutter, between 1946 and 1952. Its first use was in an edition of Boccaccio's *Trattatello in laude di Dante* that appeared in 1954. The Monotype Corporation's version of Dante followed in 1957. Though modeled on the Aldine type used for Pietro Cardinal Bembo's treatise *De Aetna* in 1495, Dante is a thoroughly modern interpretation of that venerable face.